MISHAPS IN MILLRISE

Also by Tilly Tennant

Hopelessly Devoted to Holden Finn
The Man Who Can't Be Moved
Mishaps and Mistletoe (the inspiration for
the Mishaps from Millrise series)

Once Upon a Winter (a new four-novella-part series):
The Accidental Guest
I'm Not in Love
Ways to Say Goodbye
One Starry Night

And writing as Sharon Sant

The Memory Game
Dead Girl Walking

The Sky Song Trilogy:
Sky Song
The Young Moon
Not of Our Sky

Runners

Mishaps in Millrise

The Omnibus Edition

All four parts rolled into one –
with an extra surprise at the end…

Tilly Tennant

Mishaps in Millrise © Tilly Tennant 2015

ISBN-13: 9781517455798

Part One
Little Acts of Love

The bunny ears slipped forward again. Maria puffed out her cheeks and reached up to straighten them. 'They're too big,' she said, wrinkling her nose.

'They are a little on the big side but that was the only size we had left. And your hair is so silky that everything slides around. What if I put some hairspray in to help make them a bit more secure?'

'Hairspray?'

Phoebe rifled through her handbag and produced a small canister. 'Turn around and cover your eyes.'

Maria clapped her hands over her face and hunched her shoulders up.

'There's no need to look so terrified,' Phoebe laughed. 'It won't hurt!'

Maria's shoulders shook as she let out a giggle from behind her hands. 'I love you, Phoebe.'

'And I love you too. Now stand still and let's get these ears sorted or those Easter eggs will have melted by the time we find them.'

'Or Daddy will eat them.'

'I wouldn't be surprised. He's probably eaten most of them while he was hiding them.'

Maria giggled again. 'You should have hidden them.'

'But who would have put your ears on then?'

'Daddy.'

'Hmmmm.' Phoebe spritzed a light coating of lacquer over Maria's head. 'I'd like to see your daddy handle a can of hairspray like this. He'd probably have stapled the ears to your head or something.'

'I heard that.' Jack's voice came from the back door. A gust of fresh, crisp air followed in his wake as he closed it behind him. 'You'd better get your coats on, girls; it's bright but it's still cold out there.'

'You're such a big wuss,' Phoebe laughed as she put away the hairspray and straightened her denim jacket. 'It's April.' The smoothing down of her clothing was instinctive. Phoebe and Jack had been together for four months now, but they were still in that relationship phase where everything was new and shiny and Phoebe was always conscious of how she looked when he was around.

'I've been crawling through the undergrowth,' he replied cheerfully, 'I'm bound to be cold.'

'We've got bunny ears to keep us warm, haven't we?' Phoebe made a final adjustment to Maria's headband and smiled down at her.

'And bunny fur,' Maria added, pulling at her pink fleece.

Jack stepped over and zipped it up for her. 'Right up tight,' he said.

'Snug as a bug in a rug,' Maria laughed. Phoebe smiled. She had discovered over the last few months that it was an oft-repeated mantra but one that Maria never got tired of. It was the little things that were so endearing, that made Jack and Maria so special to be around. It was like they were sprinkled in fairy dust, and everyone who came into contact with them caught a little of it too.

'Ready to rock?' Jack jumped up, his hand hovering over the back-door handle.

'Ready!' Maria cried, bouncing up and down and giggling.

'Never been readier!' Phoebe joined in.

'Let's go hunt some chocolate!' Jack yanked open the door and they trouped out, Maria's chat turning into a stream of words that tumbled over one another in her excitement. Phoebe could only catch the odd syllable and half-word, but she didn't really need to follow the meaning at all. There was no sound lovelier on earth than the sound of that little girl's excitement and she was happy just to let it wash over her.

It was funny, Phoebe mused as she watched Maria race across the lawn to the shelter of the trees at the bottom of the garden, that only a few months ago she really hadn't cared for children at all. They were like an alien race, to be treated with suspicion and avoided unless absolutely necessary.

3

Her stint working as an assistant to Hendry's store janitor-cum-Santa-cum-resident alcoholic hadn't done much to dispel those beliefs. After a day of trying to communicate with the strange little hordes that streamed through and laid waste to the grotto on an hourly basis in the manner of a Viking invasion, she had decided that in future she would do all she could to avoid them. Maria had wiped all those beliefs clean in one afternoon. But then, she was an exceptional little girl. The cure had been so profound that Phoebe had actually been excited when Steve, her boss, had asked her to stay on at Hendry's after the Christmas job ended. Phoebe Clements working in a toy shop – the centre of the kiddie universe? It was a strange turn of events indeed.

Almost as strange as how quickly she had found herself falling for Jack. After Vik's death, she had locked her heart away and it had withered. She had believed that nothing or no one could bring her back from that point. But that was before Jack's blue eyes had smiled at her, before those dimples that played at the corner of his mouth worked their peculiar magic, before his soft voice and attentive nature had taken her by surprise with their power to charm and heal what she thought was forever broken. Some days she was frightened by it all. Sometimes, in her darker moments, the old pangs of guilt returned, and she clung onto the memory of Vik, forcing herself to remember his face and his voice for fear they would disappear for good. And in those darker moments were the conflicting emotions, the fear that by con-juring up Vik, she was somehow being unfaithful to Jack, and that karma or fate, or whatever strange and invisible power ruled the universe, would take him and Maria from her as punishment for her ingrati-tude. The only thing she ever knew for certain was that when she was with Jack, everything felt right and good. She held onto those feelings and tried to cher-ish them while she could.

'Come on!' Jack called, shaking Phoebe from her musings. 'Maria's got two already!'

She realised with some surprise that she was standing in the middle of the still frosted lawn. She must look like a brain-addled loon staring into space with the absent smile she could feel on her lips.

'Three now!' Maria shouted from the depths of the Leylandi hedge.

Phoebe adjusted her own rabbit headband, waggled her bum to shake the bunny tail she had attached, and twitched her nose, sticking her teeth out and sniffing the air. 'Bunny powers – activate!' she cried as Maria, watching her, dissolved into a fit of new giggles. 'All the chocolate will be mine!'

Racing over to the trees, she pretended to barge Maria aside and proceeded to snuffle around in the bedding plants like a deranged pig on a crack-fuelled truffle hunt. Maria's giggles became shrieks of delight, all thoughts of her own search forgotten as she watched Phoebe's larking about become more and more absurd. She glanced up to see that Jack was watching too, a huge grin spread across his face. Phoebe sent a radiant smile back, and then pulled Maria's arm to join her.

'We're bunnies, not pigs!' Maria protested in between gales of laughter.

'We're bunny-pig mutants,' Phoebe replied. 'Go with it girl!'

'Found another one!' Maria suddenly squeaked, pulling a bright pink egg from the undergrowth and holding it aloft with a look of triumph.

'You're good…' Phoebe held up her hand for a high five. 'I need to get a move on or there'll be nothing left.'

And that was when she saw it. Glinting from within the thorny branches of a wild raspberry bush, a sliver of gold. 'Aha!' she cried, carefully reaching inside to retrieve it. She winked at Maria. 'I do believe that's now four: *one*. Never underestimate the Man United of Easter egg hunting; comebacks are always possible.' As she dropped it into her basket, she noticed this particular egg gave a dull clunk, as if it was made of something harder than chocolate. Then she saw the label.

To Phoebe. A special egg.

With a glance at Maria, who was now scouring a patch of primula as if her life depended on it, Phoebe turned her attention back to the egg with a puzzled frown.

'Aren't you going to open it?' Jack asked from behind her.

'You made me jump!' Phoebe laughed, blushing without knowing why.

'Well?'

'It's against the rules of the game, isn't it?'

'I don't think anyone's looking,' he whispered.

Her hand was trembling a little now, but she did as she was asked, and carefully removed the gold wrapping. Beneath, was an enamel egg, decorated with intricate gold swirls and interlocking spring flowers. She held it up and gave him a brief kiss. 'It's lovely. Thank you.'

'Open it.'

Now, her heart was beating like a steam train on an antique line. Fear of what she might find inside crept in. This was too soon, wasn't it? How could she say no without ruining everything they had? But how could she say yes? They'd been together barely four months. She was happy now; why did he have to go and complicate things?

'I haven't put a bomb in there, if that's what you're worried about,' he said with a playful nudge.

A bomb might feel less dangerous right now, Phoebe thought. Locating the seam, she took a deep breath, cracked it open and peered inside.

'A key?' she said, holding it up. Relief flooded through her making her feel weak at the knees. 'What's this for?' she asked with a shaky laugh.

'For this place,' Jack smiled. 'I know you think it's too soon to move in and I respect your decision, but

I want you to feel as if you belong and that you can come and go as you please.'

'Wouldn't that be a bit weird and awkward?'

'I don't walk around the house in a gimp suit, you know. You won't find me doing anything kinky if you call around unannounced.'

Phoebe giggled. 'Now, there's an idea…'

'So, you'll take it in the spirit in which it was intended?'

She reached to kiss him, that warm glow spreading through her again. 'Thank you.' As she pulled away and nuzzled into his embrace, a slow smile spread across her face. 'I'll call around tomorrow with the whips and chains,' she whispered.

⚜ ⚜ ⚜

Midnight revved up the tiny car and watched it flirt across the shop floor as she let go. She turned to Phoebe with a grin.

'You really couldn't work anywhere else, could you?' Phoebe asked with a wry smile.

'Where else would I get paid for playing with toys all day long?'

'You're not actually supposed to play with them. Your job is to sell them so that other people – mainly the small people they were intended for – can play with them.'

'Those funny little people who aren't quite the right size and are always covered in sticky substances?' Midnight asked.

'Yes... commonly referred to as *children*.' Phoebe made little speech marks in the air.

'I'm testing. To make sure everything is play-worthy.'

'Hmmm, I wonder if Steve would buy that.'

Midnight waved a dismissive hand. 'What Steve doesn't know won't hurt him.'

Phoebe glanced up as a figure approached. 'You'd better look sharp; otherwise he will know in the next few seconds!'

Midnight leapt to her feet. 'That brain donor will have to get up early in the morning to catch me. In fact, he'd have to get up the night before and camp out.'

Phoebe stifled a giggle as he made his way over.

'What are you two looking so cheerful about?' Steve's nostrils were flared in a way that suggested a permanent state of near-fatal high blood pressure. At first, Phoebe had been alarmed by this sight whenever she had the misfortune to witness it. But as the months progressed, she realised that this was actually her boss in a good mood. Steve in a bad mood looked like an atomic bomb ready to go off. That, or the scarily angry man from the Frankie Goes to Hollywood *Two Tribes* video she had once seen on YouTube at the height of Vik's eighties music obsession.

'We love being here,' Midnight replied with a cheeriness that Phoebe knew would set the Steve-bomb ticking. 'We're delirious as soon as we set foot in the door. In fact, when I say my prayers at night, I ask for an extra special favour from God. I ask him to please make sure nobody shoves a box of lit fireworks through the letterbox of Hendry's toy store so that I can just have one more glorious day of working there.'

Steve's jaw tightened. He seemed to be labouring for an appropriate reply but then abandoned the cause. 'Is that doll display finished, as I asked you half an hour ago?'

'Yup. I left Barbie and Ken doing a sixty-nine over the bonnet of a beach buggy.'

Steve snorted, his face transforming from crimson to a dangerous shade of puce. 'You'd better not –'

'The display looks great,' Phoebe cut in, trying not to laugh. 'Midnight has a real creative flair. You should give her the window dresser's job.'

'Her!' Steve jabbed a finger in Midnight's direction. 'God only knows what gothic monstrosities we'd have in there. She'd have Frankenstein complete with bolts scaring the children half to death.'

'The monster didn't have bolts and he wasn't called Frankenstein,' Midnight fired back. 'And I'm not a goth...' she glared at him. 'Ignoramus,' she added under her breath.

'What do you call that then?' He flapped a dismissive hand at her purple hair. 'Left to me we'd have a policy against that sort of weirdness in my shop.'

'You'd be the first one to get sacked then,' Midnight pouted. 'And it's not actually *your* shop. It's owned by people who aren't narrow-minded bigots with no concept of creativity or artistic expression.'

Steve opened his mouth to argue, hesitated for a moment, gaping like a basking shark waiting for a fishy feast, and then shut it again, clearly deciding that, once again, he had no reply for Midnight's assertions. Phoebe wondered whether he had even understood most of it. 'Just get the place ready before the doors open.'

'Chill… it's a Wednesday in April. It's not like we're going to get mobbed, is it?'

'Ten minutes!' Steve called behind him as he marched away.

Phoebe glanced around the pristine shop floor and shrugged at Midnight. 'You can't help yourself can you?' she asked. 'It's like catnip to Mr Tiddles… throw a Steve in your path and you have to wind him up.'

'The man is a prize dick,' Midnight replied as she watched his retreating figure.

'Prize dick or not, I've got to keep on his good side for the next week. At least until this interview is done.'

'Ah, I wouldn't worry about that. Steve likes you.'

'How do you figure that out? He's vile to me.'

'He hasn't actively tried to get you sacked yet, though. Always a good sign.'

'It won't last if you keep riling him. I'll be targeted by association.'

Midnight gave her a sideways look. 'You don't have to hang out with me.'

'That's true. But you're about the only person working here who doesn't have hair on their palms so I'll take my chances.'

'I won't tell the others you said that.'

'You don't talk to the others.'

'I do!' Midnight said in a hurt voice. 'I talk to Jeff.'

'Only to see if he has a spare drop of whisky in his hip flask.'

'And I talk to Sally in Pre-School.'

'Only because she always has fags.'

'You make me sound horrible.'

'You are,' Phoebe laughed, 'that's why I like you so much.'

'I wonder if you'll still like me when you land this new job in promotions. I'm counting on you to get me another elf stint at Christmas.'

'You want to do that again?' Phoebe said with a faint look of disbelief. Apart from the fact that she had met Jack and Maria whilst working as an elf, which was undoubtedly the best thing that had ever happened to her, Phoebe shuddered at the memory of the days she'd had to endure in the claustrophobic and pungent room that served as Santa's grotto. She was much happier working out on the shop floor *sans* rosy cheeks and green tights.

'Are you kidding?' Midnight raised her eyebrows. 'That was the most fun I've had in ages. Do you remember reading all the kids' letters? They were hilarious! And Janitor Jeff as Santa… that choice of personnel was so mental it was genius!'

'You wouldn't get me in those curly-toed shoes again for anything.'

'Well, my little friend, if you get this job next week you get to hand out the curly-toed shoes instead of wearing them.' Midnight swung herself up to sit on the sales counter and grinned. 'What does Mr Stalker think about you going for this new job?'

'Jack?' Phoebe asked. She'd never been able to convince Midnight that it was Maria who had insti-gated most of the stalking. And then Phoebe herself. If anyone was actually innocent of that moniker it was Jack. 'He's all for it; thinks it's a good move for me.'

'It's funny…' Midnight swung her legs as she sat atop the counter, 'you say that I don't talk to anyone at Hendry's but you're not exactly Mrs Sociable your-self, are you?'

'I don't need to be.'

'Surely in promotions you have to be a bit jolly and friendly?'

'I don't think it's all that important,' Phoebe replied amiably. 'I think the job is more about organising silly costumes and events for the rest of you minions. As promotions coordinator I have to dream up new and excruciating ways for you all to humiliate yourselves.'

'See… you haven't even got the job yet and all that power has gone to your head.'

'I'll go easy on my friends though. So you make sure you stay in my good books.'

'Roger that!' Midnight gave a neat salute. 'Bagel and coffee for lunch, ma'am?'

'Followed by a nice foot massage... maybe you can do something about my bunions while you're at it.'

'Don't push it, blondie!'

Phoebe chuckled. From the corner of her eye she could see the car that Midnight had sent racing across the shop floor peeking out from beneath a shelving unit. She bent to pick it up and handed it over. 'You'd better hide the evidence before Hitler comes back.'

Midnight leapt down from the counter and pocketed the car. On the way past a giant pink Barbie display she stopped and looked at the dolls thoughtfully. After doing an elaborate impersonation of an artist measuring up his subject, she began to rearrange two of them.

As she walked away from the stand, Phoebe looked over to see that Barbie and Ken were top-to-tail, lying on top of each other across the bonnet of a beach buggy.

'You know Steve will kill you if he sees that,' she laughed.

'He won't have any idea what they're doing,' Midnight replied carelessly. 'Only people who've actually had sex would know, so that clearly exempts him.'

Phoebe shook her head with a smile as she watched her friend head to the stand where the toy cars belonged.

❧   ❧   ❧

Scratching her head through a mop of bed-tousled hair, Phoebe yawned widely. Although... the word *tousled* implied something sexy, a little bit of effortless glamour. As she caught sight of herself in the mirror, she decided that this was more like the coconut matting she had out by the door of her flat. The inside of her mouth felt similar too. Inwardly, she cursed herself for getting so worked up about her impending interview. No matter how many times she had told herself that it didn't matter whether she got this promotion or not as she tossed and turned the previous night, running over every possible interview scenario in her head, she realised that it did. The fact was, she had the overwhelming feeling that it was somehow a tipping point in her life. It felt huge, like the break she had been waiting for, the final end to the run of depressing, dead-end jobs she'd had since school. This was the chance to get a proper career off the ground. She had never been much for studying, although all her teachers had told her she was bright enough to go onto higher education, but there were days, as she had stood behind a crowded bar, or shoved a toilet brush down yet another urine streaked bowl, that she seriously regretted her decision not to. And then, after a few years, it had all felt too difficult to unpick. When Vik came along, she'd been so happy that it really didn't matter what job she did as long as she came home to him at night. It was just another way in which Vik's death had undone her life completely that first year. She'd been left without the man, without the education, without the career… without anything that made life worth living.

But Jack had ignited her spark again and now she wanted to get back on track. She was tired of feeling like a failure, of the pitying looks from people she bumped into from school, friends she had lost touch with who had gone on to bigger and better things. Even her own parents had that look when they asked her how work was going, on visits that were becoming increasingly rare: that ever-so-slightly disappointed smile when she replied. They told her they loved her and didn't care if she worked in a sewer as long as she was happy. But Phoebe heard only their bitter disappointment in her life choices. They loved her, of course, but that was biological conditioning. It didn't mean that they approved.

This year, she had resolved to change all that. Baby steps, she had told herself back in January and she had begun slowly. She had moved from the damp flat she had endured for three winters, where the walls crawled with mould that set off her asthma during every cold snap, and had taken a better one, closer to work. It was smaller than her old one, but that had kept the rent within her budget and what it lacked in space it more than made up for in cosiness. She had taken the opportunity to part with trinkets that meant too much: reminders of days gone by. It had been hard, but she began to see that if she held onto Vik's

CDs, his books, even his things in the bathroom cabinet, she would never be able to move on. She owed that much to Jack at least. It seemed strange to her at first that she never saw anything in his house that looked as though it had once belonged to Rebecca, Maria's mother, but perhaps, she reasoned after a few visits, he had come to the same realisation much sooner than her. After all, Rebecca had been dead for five years. Phoebe wondered what her thoughts and feelings about Vik would be after five years.

Despite her resolutions to stay focused, however, there were times, like now, when she wavered. She was beginning to wish she had accepted Jack's offer the night before to stay over with him, but she'd known that if she did she would drink too much and stay up too late and wouldn't have felt ready for the interview. As it turned out, the same thing had happened at her place, only she'd spent the evening alone when she could have been with Jack having a lot more fun being unable to sleep.

With a deep sigh, she wandered into the kitchen to retrieve her coffee and took a swig. She grimaced as she found she'd let it go cold while she stared into space and felt sorry for herself. At least she'd had the foresight to pack a decent outfit the night before to take with her today. Replies to her enquiries about the dress code for an internal interview had been vague at best, but somehow she felt that her usual Hendry's uniform – a red polo shirt and black skinny jeans – weren't going to give the right impression.

❧ ❧ ❧

'Morning, gorgeous! You're just in time and I think it's my turn to buy.' Midnight handed Phoebe a coffee she had just lifted from the vending machine. Phoebe tried not to make her distaste too obvious as she peered into the cup. Midnight insisted on subjecting them to this ritual at least once a week, despite the fact that they had a kitchen equipped with a kettle and perfectly acceptable instant coffee from the corner shop. It was as though Midnight, in some bizarre act of masochism, actively enjoyed subjecting herself to a caffeine-based form of torture. If indeed, caffeine was an ingredient in the substance that spewed from the offending machine.

'It was either coffee or death by cyanide,' Midnight said as she turned and punched in the code for her own drink. 'I thought coffee would be kindest.'

'I think I prefer the cyanide. Hand it over and stop hogging it all for yourself.'

Midnight laughed. 'Are you nervous about today?'

'About the interview? Of course not,' Phoebe lied. 'How hard can it be?'

'What's your presentation on?' The machine whirred into life as it prepared Midnight's drink, and she was distracted for a moment as she watched the milk squirt in with a hiss.

'Presentation?' Phoebe asked in a dazed voice. She felt as if her legs had been replaced by jelly replicas.

'You did know they'd want one, didn't you?'

'Yes, of course…' Midnight turned to Phoebe and raised her eyebrows. Phoebe's lie crumbled instantly. 'Well of course I bloody didn't! What am I going to do?'

Midnight shrugged carelessly. 'You'll have to write one.'

'This morning?' Phoebe squeaked. 'I can't believe you didn't think to tell me about this until now!'

'Hang on a minute, how is this my fault? I thought you'd checked the application pack about a million times. At least, every time I've seen you this week you've had your nose buried in it.'

Phoebe took a scalding gulp of her coffee and winced. 'I'm sorry… you're right, of course. So why don't I know?' She mentally went through the interview paperwork now sitting on her dresser at home. She was as certain as she could be that there was no mention of a presentation. Had she somehow, despite her best efforts, managed to miss that bit? Had there had been a page missing? Whatever the answer, nothing was going to help her now.

'Deep breath… Ok… So I have to write one this morning.' She looked up at Midnight, who nodded acknowledgment to a male colleague who was hanging his coat on a peg. 'What can I write about?'

'Write about toys.'

'Brilliant! Write about toys…' Phoebe tried to rally her muddled thoughts into some sort of order. Toys was a rather vague and obvious subject area. What could she write about toys that would really fire them up? She supposed, anyway, that they would more likely want something incorporating promotions and PR *and* toys. She had no visual aids, no notes, no plan of any kind and her interview was straight after lunch. She would have to work for the whole morning too, down on the main shop floor at ground level, Steve's favourite hunting ground, so no opportunity to sneak off and write something.

'What if I do something about enthusiasm and how that's like fifty... no, seventy-five percent of the battle when it comes to promotions?' Phoebe said, brightening as the thought occurred to her. 'Hearts and minds, you know?'

'Sounds amazing. What are you going to do? A little song and dance number for them?'

Phoebe opened her mouth and then closed it again. Midnight took a sip of her coffee and continued to eyeball Phoebe as she waited for a reply.

'I'll do a rap!'

Midnight grinned. 'Oh. My. God! I so wish I was in on that interview panel! Please, please, do the rap for me now!'

Phoebe gave her a sheepish smile. 'You're going to have to help me write it first.'

❖ ❖ ❖

Throughout the morning, Phoebe and Midnight threw lines across the shop floor at each other and Phoebe wrote down the most promising ones, trying to get them into some form of rhythm and rhyme. What had started out as a stupid and desperate idea began to look less so. It was even becoming fun. Phoebe wondered whether the humiliation she had envisaged might actually give way to triumph. Nobody else's presentation would be quite as original as hers, she was sure, and even though the thought of the performance had her running for the toilet every time it popped into her head, perhaps thinking outside the box (oh, yeah, she watched *The Apprentice*, she knew the buzzwords of success) could win her that job after all.

At lunch, Phoebe watched with some regret as Midnight finished off her chicken and sweet chilli rap from the Bounty. Usually, the days when she got to fetch one of Stav's legendary lunches from the local deli instead of her own paltry attempts at making sandwiches were a highlight of her week. Today, she had hoped that it would encourage at least some appetite in her, but she had picked at the edges and given up after two mouthfuls. She was often plagued by migraines if she skipped meals. Today, there was no way she could eat and she just hoped the adrenaline she was running on would be enough to see her through the next hour or so.

'I think it's more or less finished,' Phoebe said, turning her attention back to her notepad as she chewed on the end of a pen.

'I think you've got bigger balls than Steve going in with that,' Midnight mumbled through a mouthful of chicken and rocket.

'I don't have much choice, do I? I really need to know how you knew about the presentation, and I didn't.'

'You have to wonder if someone in HR did it on purpose.'

Phoebe threw her a questioning look.

'You know, maybe one of the other candidates is a mate or something, so they sabotaged everyone else's pack…'

'Great. I feel so much more confident now you've planted that little seed of doubt.'

'Could happen.' Midnight shrugged.

'So how did *you* find out it was part of the interview if no-one else knew?'

'I'm not saying *no*-one else knew. It's just a hypothesis, you know? Anyway I heard Valerie Cox mention it to Steve the other day.'

'Valerie Cox is going for it? She never said… bloody hell, she's good and Steve actually likes her.'

'Luckily for you, the decision isn't Steve's to make. You'll be ok.'

Phoebe chewed her pen and read over the page again. 'Perhaps it's a blessing in disguise,' she said thoughtfully. 'My mum always says things happen for a reason.'

'So long as the reason isn't someone else getting the job…' Midnight crammed the last of the wrap into her mouth and chewed with a thoroughly contented look that reminded Phoebe of an Alpaca she had once seen at the zoo as a kid. 'Anyway,' Midnight continued as she swallowed the last of it, 'you'd better get your interview kit on, hadn't you?'

Phoebe glanced up at the clock. 'Yep. I'll be back in a tick.'

She reached for the carrier bag stowed under her seat and left Midnight to stand guard over her *magnum opus* while she went off to get ready. She had finally decided to go with a suit regardless of what anyone else was doing and then at least she would look the part, even if she didn't exactly feel it. She couldn't remember the last time she had been so nervous... hang on, yes she could. It was her first date with Jack at Christmas. She had been like a puppy on bonfire night and that had turned out alright in the end, hadn't it? More than alright. She was happier now than she'd been in a long time. Besides, she told herself, nerves were good, they would make her alert, focused, hungry for success...

By this point, she found herself standing in front of the large mirrors that lined the walls of the ladies toilets, having no recollection of arriving there. She was obviously more nervous than she thought, and that was bad enough. She stared at herself and let out a deep breath. Another one in... another one out... Just like the stress counsellor had taught her. *Get it together, Clements.* She focused her mind on positive thoughts: how pleased and proud Jack would be. She tried to picture his face if she could take home the news that she had got this promotion. The key he had given her last week had meant a lot more than he was letting on. He played it cool for her sake; they had discussed her moving in before and she had insisted that it was too soon. But, in truth, that was only part of it. She wanted it almost as much as he did. She felt so comfortable in his world that she had no doubt their bond would only strengthen. The truth was that Phoebe was financially embarrassed. Her debts were so big and her pay-cheque so small that she felt she would be a burden to him. He already had a five-year-old daughter to support; she wasn't about to add to his worries. If she ever moved in she would pay her way and right now, she wasn't in a position to do that.

Reaching into her bag she pulled out a bundle of clothes. But as she unfolded them, she went cold. *Her gym kit? What the hell?*

She threw the leggings and t-shirt to one side and dug deeper into the bag. All that came out were her manky old trainers. In a ridiculous and futile gesture she tipped the bag upside-down and shook it. A forlorn flake of mud floated out into the sink below. Surely she hadn't been that half-asleep this morning that she'd grabbed the wrong bag on the way out? If only she'd invested in a proper suit cover, with a zip and hanger and everything, as her mum had suggested, this would never have happened. What had she been thinking, packing a suit in a carrier bag? She needed a slap. The irony was that although her gym kit often came into work with her in this bag, it wasn't often that she actually made it there in the end, usually succumbing to offers of food or alcohol (usually both) from Jack instead. Her mother had commented only the previous week that she thought Phoebe was 'filling out a little' which was her not-so-subtle way of telling Phoebe she was getting fat. She had replied, in a rather outraged tone, that she weighed barely more than one of Stav's meat and potato pies and that her mother really ought to keep her damaging opinions to herself. Did she want her only daughter to develop an eating disorder? Her mum had looked suitably horrified and spent the rest of her visit mumbling about how she was only trying to be helpful and had Phoebe's best interests at heart. On a different day, Phoebe might have agreed. There had been a flurry of activity in January, part of her decision to shake up her life, which had gradually dwindled in frequency; a combination, she supposed, of settling down, of contentment, of lack of time and sheer laziness.

Phoebe took another rescue breath and felt her chest tighten. Damn it, her inhalers were in her locker in the staffroom. She tried to concentrate on regulating her breathing; none of these other distracting thoughts were going to help her now. Pulling at the hem of her polo shirt, she squinted down at it. Not as clean as it would have been had she been planning to wear it for the interview, but maybe, if she positioned her arms just right, nobody would notice the stain where she had spilled coffee on it at break time. Or the remains of the bogey that some three-year-old had wiped on her trousers. Letting her top fall back over her midriff, she looked into the mirror and did her best to tidy her hair. It had always been that strange gravity-defying state between curly and straight, where the merest whisper of damp transformed her into a frizzy blonde version of Albert Einstein. Today was just such a day.

Tucking it behind her ears, she gave up and took one last look in the mirror. It wasn't the first impression she had wanted to create. But at least she still had her presentation. She gave a groan. The more she thought about the hurriedly-written rap she and Midnight had thrown together, the more it seemed like a car crash waiting to happen. Perhaps, after the humiliation of today she would be forced to leave Hendry's for good. Perhaps she should leave right now? But she wanted more than anything to give Jack good news. She thought about how excited Maria would be without really understanding why, just being happy because Jack was. Holding onto those thoughts, she steeled herself. She was going to get through this and she was going to come out of that room the new promotions coordinator for Hendry's Toy Store.

❧ ❧ ❧

The office lady showed Phoebe to a seat. Everyone at Hendry's called her *the office lady*, partly because she was the only member of staff solely dedicated to admin and seemed to pick up anything that the managers and supervisors didn't, and partly because nobody knew what she *actually* did, other than sit in the office on the top floor, rather like Norman Bates' stuffed mother in *Psycho*. Just like her movie counterpart, she was strangely inanimate and never seemed to leave her desk. There was another rumour that she was simply Steve in a wig, but this had been disproved when Phoebe witnessed them in the same room at the same time as she signed her new employment contract after Christmas.

Phoebe sat down, mesmerised by a close up of the woman's face. She did look like a creature that hadn't seen daylight for thirty years and Phoebe was quite surprised that she didn't see any signs of rickets in her American tan stocking-clad legs. Midnight referred to her as *The Mythical Warden of the Personnel Files*, but then Midnight did have a dramatic streak as wide as the shopping-trolley-filled river that ran through the heart of Millrise.

Phoebe barely had time to bite a nail clean from her finger before the door to the interview room opened and a man she recognised as the store PR manager waved her in.

'Phoebe? Are you ready?'

She wanted to say: no, I'm not in the slightest bit ready; would you mind giving me thirty years or so? But she nodded and followed him in.

'Take a seat, won't you?' He indicated a chair facing a long table, behind which sat two of his colleagues. She glanced at them, suddenly feeling very isolated in her solitary seat and deeply disconcerted. Perhaps that was the intention? The manager sat down in the last vacant seat; he seemed nice enough: a jolly looking man who obviously enjoyed a pie or two judging by his size. So far so good. Next was a man she recognised as the MD of Hendry's. His presence caught her off-guard. She hadn't imagined that a man in his position would take an interest in such mundane affairs as the appointment of a promotions coordinator. His steel-grey eyes weighed her up from behind designer-framed glasses, inscrutable and slightly terrifying. He made no attempt at a greeting but watched her intently like a snake watching prey. The PR manager introduced him.

'This is Mr Hendry... The third Mr Hendry to take control of the store, actually,' the PR boss said, a note of obvious pride in his voice. Mr Hendry gave a short, silent nod.

Lastly was a woman Phoebe recognised. She had seen her around the store from time to time, had even exchanged the odd pleasantry, but had no idea what she did. When she was introduced as Sue Bunce, personnel manager, all became clear. Steve had always taken personnel matters upon himself, choosing to avoid contact with the official channels wherever possible. He had become such a successful middle man that many of his staff, including Phoebe, had been given no reason to have any dealings with Sue at all. Phoebe had never understood Steve's motives for this behaviour, but she suspected that it was really the sign of an underlying insecurity in his own abilities to perform his job. Midnight always said it was because he was a monumental twat.

'I'm Dixon...' the PR boss continued. 'I don't live in Dock Green, luckily though...' he began to snigger. Phoebe gave a weak smile, having no clue what he was talking about. Nobody else seemed to find the joke amusing. For a man whose job relied on large amounts of charm and humour Dixon didn't seem to have much of either. 'Dixon is my Christian name...' he added. 'Just to clarify. It's Dixon Montague. A mouthful, I know. My friends call me Monty.' Phoebe tried not to frown at him. Did that mean he wanted her to call him Monty? Or was he simply letting her know that he had friends?

Silence descended, broken only by the rustling of papers as Dixon and Sue turned to what Phoebe assumed were their interview questions. Mr Hendry continued stare at her. It was making her sweat – she could feel the trickles down her back as she sat there and the harder she concentrated on making it stop, the more she seemed to perspire. Under his fierce scrutiny, she began to quail, acutely aware of how messy her hair was and how grubby and crumpled her uniform was. Things weren't about to get any better. She glanced at the clock. Five minutes of her allotted forty-five had already gone. She only hoped that the rest would be over quickly.

'Phoebe...' Dixon began, looking up from his notes. 'I wonder if you'd tell us what you know about the role. What is your understanding of what's expected of the person who is successful at interview today?'

'As I understand it, if I got the job I would be answerable to you in the first instance, but I would also have to liaise and report to various other managers as and when required. I would help to coordinate promotional campaigns in-store and around the local area, utilising local radio, newspaper and TV as well as keeping up a social media presence on all the main websites. I would be expected to attend events, chat to customers and members of the public at such times, and be generally as nice and helpful as I can to continue the good reputation of Hendry's within the Millrise community.' Phoebe had read the job specification so many times she could almost recite it word for word.

Dixon nodded sagely and Sue smiled. Mr Hendry was as stony-faced as he had been since the beginning. Phoebe was beginning to wonder if he had some sort of brain disorder that they had neglected to mention.

'Very good. And how do you feel about those duties?' Dixon asked. 'You'd be expected to do unsociable hours at times and you wouldn't always get away from events on time. How would that impact on your life outside work?'

Mr Hendry's expression changed for the first time: he sent a look of utter disdain in Dixon's direction, as if the question he'd asked was the most ludicrous thing he had ever heard. *A life outside work? How dare you!*

'I don't have much in the way of family commitments so I don't think it would be a problem,' Phoebe replied. 'If it's all part and parcel of the job then I would accept that.'

Sue glanced at Dixon and Mr Hendry in turn, who both nodded. 'Perhaps you'd like to show us your presentation now?' she asked Phoebe. 'Do you need anything... the projector, perhaps?' She gestured to the back of the room where a laptop stood idle next to a wall-mounted screen.

'That's alright,' Phoebe replied, wondering whether her legs would support her when she stood. 'It's a bit more performance based than techie.'

'Sounds intriguing...' Sue smiled. 'Whenever you're ready, please...'

Phoebe stood uncertainly and moved away from her chair. She cleared her throat, wishing desperately, as she psyched herself up to begin, that she had decided on something else – anything, rather than this rap. But she was committed now, like a cyclist tearing down a hill with no brakes towards certain disaster and, other than running from the room and never setting foot in Hendry's again, there was no escape. And she had to commit fully – no half measures, no mumbling, glued to the floor in a motionless, mortified trance – if she was going to perform it, she had to *perform* it, heart and soul. There was no other way to deliver something like this, no matter how stupid she felt.

Striking what she thought was a typical rapper pose – arms folded high across her chest, chin in the air, legs apart – she began in her best (more like Newcastle than New York) rapper accent.

Listen up y'all
I'm gonna put out the call
To my homies at Hendry's
You know it ain't no ball
When your toy sales fall
No one shops in your store
They're dissing up and down the town
Hendry's ain't fly no more

She began to leap around, jabbing her fingers in the air. Her captive audience stared from across the table. Phoebe couldn't decide if it was awe, confusion or just plain terror on their faces. Either way, if she had offered them a severed head on a plate she couldn't have received a worse reaction than this. But, as her mother had always said: in for a penny...

But what's that, in the distance?
It's your new promotions assistant!
She's cool, she's fly, she's gonna make the sales spry
It ain't no mystery
She'll make Hendry's history

Phoebe dared to glance up at her audience. It looked as though they were now searching for exits.

She'll look like a fool
Break the fashion rules
Coz she's crazy 'bout Hendry's
Like a good employee should be

She didn't dare look at them again, but geared up for the finale and thanked whatever god was looking down on her that it was almost over.

She's dancin', she's singin'
Gonna get your tills ringin'
It's her mission and duty
To bring love from your city
She knows how it's done
That fifty to seventy-five percent of promotions is
all about enthusiasm and belief...

'Sorry, that last line is a little out...' Phoebe panted as she came to a standstill. 'I just needed to get that point across... you know, that if your promotions person looks as if they're having a good time everyone else will buy it. A bit like believing your own hype... you know?'

'Yes... erm... thank you Phoebe. That was certainly... original...' Sue said in a dazed voice.

'The interview pack did specify a ten-minute presentation, Phoebe,' Dixon added. 'And that was only about two by my watch.'

'Oh...' Phoebe said. 'I could talk you through it, if you'd like?'

Mr Hendry spoke for the first time. 'I really don't think that's necessary... I've heard quite enough. I'm content to progress with the rest of the interview. Personally, I don't think I could have endured another minute of that. I'm sure it's considered very creative amongst young people but it's certainly not for me.'

Phoebe forced a smile.

After a brief moment of uncertainty, where nobody asked her to retake her seat but simply stared at her as if she ought to know what to do next, Phoebe sat down, hands clasped together on her lap. It wasn't the positive body language she'd read so much about, but it was difficult to know where else to put them. In a conscious bid to look more confident, she pulled back her shoulders and sat up straighter. Then she wondered if, perhaps, the resultant pushing out of her chest might give the impression that she was trying to employ her cleavage (as paltry as it was) as a tactic to win some sort of favour with the men. Immediately, she slumped back to her original posture.

'So...' Sue began, 'you've been with us for four months?'

'I started as a temp, three weeks before Christmas and was then offered a permanent contract in January. So I suppose it's really about five months now.'

'It's still not that long, though, is it? Not long to learn the business of Hendry's. Don't you think it's a little premature to be thinking about promotion?'

'Maybe,' Phoebe replied carefully, wondering if there was a trick to this particular question, some obvious answer she was expected to give. 'When I began I had no preconceptions about the store. I mean, I came here all the time as a kid... it's the shop every adult in Millrise has fond memories of. But that was all I knew and having no children of my own I hadn't really needed to come in for a long time. But once I started to work here I realised what a special place it is and how dear it is to the town. I don't mean dear as in expensive...' she added quickly. 'I mean people care about it. Now that I work here I love it too and I think that my future lies here. That's why I'm taking steps to secure that future by applying for this job.'

Sue gave her an encouraging smile. So far so good; her answer must have been the right one, or at least, not a terrible one. Phoebe glanced across at Mr Hendry but his face had regained its marble-like stillness. Even so, she began to relax a little.

'Would you consider yourself reliable?' Sue asked.

'Steve – my line manager – has no complaints about my work or my timekeeping. I've never had a day off sick since I've been here.' Phoebe reflected for a moment on what a miracle that was considering the hangovers she'd turned in with, but she kept the wry smile to herself.

'May I ask something?' Dixon cut in. Sue nodded. 'Phoebe, what do you think you can bring to my department that the other candidates can't? What would make you better for this role than anyone else?'

This was it: the crunch question and one that Phoebe had expected to be asked at some point. It was the question she would ask, after all. She had thought long and hard about it since she had found out she'd been short-listed. Some of the other candidates had been open about being picked for interview, others had been more cagey; Phoebe couldn't be sure who she was up against and what they had to offer. Yet she had to find something that no one else would have, she had to make these people sit up and take notice, tell them something that nobody else would tell them and it had to be compelling enough to convince them to choose her over people who had worked for Hendry's half their adult lives. She had to take a risk and she already knew what that would be. She had made such a hash of things today that perhaps it didn't really matter anymore, but going for broke was her only option now.

'My life depends on this job,' she said.

The stares were back. Dixon was unashamedly open-mouthed, whilst Mr Hendry widened his eyes by a nano-millimetre. Phoebe decided this must be his incredibly shocked face.

'Five months ago I had no job, no money and no prospects,' she continued. 'I lived in a crappy flat, still grieving for a man I'd watched die the Christmas before and I couldn't move – it was like I was a photo standing in the middle of a crowded shopping centre. The rest of the world was hurrying around me and I was stuck. When I came to Hendry's all that changed.

Working here saved my life and I want to make a success of this job. I can't comment on what the other candidates can offer, but I guarantee that they won't want it more than me.' She paused, looked along the row to see every eye was still trained on her, listening intently, and then went for the biggest gamble of all. 'I'll be straight with you. My presentation was crap. That's because, for some reason the instruction that I should prepare one was missing from my application pack, so I didn't know I had to do one until this morning. I screwed up, but would any of the other candidates still have come to the interview and humiliated themselves by performing that pile of excrement for you? That's how much I want this job. If someone wants it that much then you have to believe that they will work their backsides off to be great in it.'

Even as the words tumbled out of her, Phoebe knew they were true. Hendry's was the most annoying place to be and yet the best. There were mornings when she stood at the counter as the first shoppers wandered in and longed to be back in her bed. There were days when she watched the clock hands crawl round the dial, willing them on. There were weeks when she wished her life away waiting for that golden day off. The people she worked with were silly, often socially challenged, irritating and juvenile. The customers were rude and demanding and the managers even more so.

But she loved it. Suddenly, she couldn't imagine working anywhere else. Along with Jack and Maria, the strange, archaic toy store that had stood on the High Street of Millrise for almost a hundred years had dragged her back from a void that had opened up with Vik's death and had very nearly swallowed her whole. It was an unexpected and emotional epiphany of such force that she had to try very hard not to cement the lunatic reputation she was in the process of carefully constructing by bursting into tears.

'Well…' Mr Hendry said, 'At least we're agreed on one thing… that presentation was a pile of crap.'

Phoebe tried to get a fix on what he was thinking, but he remained stubbornly expressionless. Dixon looked across at him.

'I don't have anything else to ask.'

'Me neither,' Sue added.

Had they cut it short? Where were the questions about demographics and sales trends? Where were the questions about bestselling toys and peak shopping times? Had she really performed so badly that they were kicking her out early? She looked at Mr Hendry.

'I think I've heard enough,' he agreed. 'Thank you for coming, Phoebe.'

He turned his attention to a sheaf of paperwork in front of him and started to shuffle through it, so Phoebe got up.

'I'll wait to hear, then?' she asked, hovering at the door.

'Yes, we should be able to tell you tomorrow one way or the other,' Dixon said. At least he was smiling again, even if he wasn't very forthcoming with anything else.

'Right... erm, thank you.'

The Office Lady looked up from her computer as Phoebe made her way out into the corridor. She gave a brief smile, about as friendly as Phoebe had ever seen her, and then bent her head back to her work again.

So that was it. Back to work and try to forget about the whole embarrassing episode.

❧ ❧ ❧

The door swung open and Jack greeted her with a faint look of surprise. 'Don't you have your key?'

'Yeah, right here,' Phoebe replied, showing him the key clutched in her hand.

'So why have you knocked?' Jack moved aside to let her in and kissed her lightly as she passed.

'You were in.'

'So why not just come in?'

'I don't know... it felt kind of weird, just walking in, like I'm sneaking up on you or something.'

'But we've invited you, you're part of the family now,' he laughed. 'You can be so strange sometimes.'

'Thanks,' Phoebe said, cocking an eyebrow at him. 'I'll try to turn it off when it becomes a problem though.'

'Hmmm, sounds like someone needs a drink,' he said, following her into the kitchen where she took a seat at the table. It had become a habit to head straight there in the anticipation that there would be food prepared and waiting for her and this evening was no different. He had promised homemade Hawaiian pizza with all the extras, and the salad and breadsticks already sat on the table.

There was a squeal of delight from the doorway and Maria raced through waving a sheet of paper in the air.

'Phoebe!' She threw herself at Phoebe, who pulled her up onto her lap and gave her a hug.

'How's it going little girlfriend?'

'Good!' Maria squeaked. She shoved the piece of paper in her hand up to Phoebe's face again.

'What's this?' Phoebe asked, taking it from her.

'It's my drawing from school. I had to draw a special memory so I did you and me playing Twister.'

'Wow, it's fab,' Phoebe replied, holding it up to inspect. 'Who's that?' She pointed to a third figure. 'Is that your dad?'

'Yes. He's laughing at us.'

'He's always laughing at us. One of these days we'll get our own back. Are you having a good time at school?'

Maria nodded enthusiastically. 'Mrs Poxon says I'm a good drawer.'

'She's right about that. When you're a famous artist I don't want you to forget my invitation to all the posh art parties.'

Maria took the sketch back and placed it with great care on the table. She studied it for a moment, before moving it again so that the edge of the page ran parallel to the table edge. She looked thoughtfully at it again, and then finally seemed satisfied. Phoebe smiled as she watched. For such an exuberant and energetic little girl Maria could be impossibly neat and meticulous at times, almost beyond her years. Sometimes she reminded Phoebe of herself as a child. Phoebe had always been the one who worried about the other kids at school, the first to offer comfort at the scene of a scraped knee or banged head, always afraid that a spat between her parents over an open milk carton or other such nonsense would snowball into divorce, and most likely to win 'caring friend' awards at school. It wasn't a bad thing, she reflected, but it made her soft and she felt it had held her back in life. And then, the one moment she had stopped caring had ended in tragedy. If she had pushed Vik under that bus herself she couldn't have felt any more responsible for his death. They had been drunk, he was messing about on the edge of the pavement and she should have stopped him, not stood there laughing like an idiot. If she had cared more in that one second, she would have seen the dangers, but she hadn't.

'Hungry?' Jack asked as he brought two glasses over to the table. 'I've made far too much, as usual.'

'I put the pineapple on!' Maria said. 'I made a face on yours!'

'What about yours?' Phoebe asked.

Maria shook her head. 'Not so much on mine. Daddy's looks like a car.'

'A pineapple car? This I have to see.'

'You're about to,' Jack said, wafting scorching air away as he opened the oven door. The aromas of sweet bread and tomato and rich herbs that had subtly hung in the air on Phoebe's arrival now burst upon the kitchen with force. She realised just how hungry she was as her mouth began to water.

'That smells amazing!' Phoebe gave an exaggerated sniff of the air, suddenly aware that she looked like the Bisto kid and probably a bit silly.

Jack smiled. He loved to cook for anyone who would let him and the obvious pride he showed when anyone complimented his food was second only to the pride he showed in Maria. Phoebe had asked him once why he hadn't become a chef and he said that doing it for a living would suck all the joy out of it. He loved the ritual of cooking, being able to take his time and absorbing himself in the scents and flavours of culinary invention. Tonight's meal was only a quick tea by his standards, but would have taken Phoebe three times as long to prepare and produced a lot more stress. At the end of all that it still wouldn't have been anywhere near as good.

'Want me to help with anything?' Phoebe asked as she watched him pull three perfect pizzas from the oven, one after the other.

'Only to eat them.'

'Oh, you know I can do that, and make a pretty fine job of it too.'

Jack placed the smallest pizza in front of an empty chair and Maria obediently hopped from Phoebe's lap and took her place at the table.

'Want me to cut it?' Phoebe asked as Jack went to fetch the other two. Maria nodded and Phoebe quickly scored it and separated into manageable slices.

'So...' Jack began as he slid their pizzas onto plates and sat down. 'Tell me what happened at the interview.' He poured a glass of white wine and pushed it towards her.

'It was awful.'

Jack stared at her for a moment. 'It can't have been that bad, surely?'

'It was, trust me. I don't think I want to talk about it and I certainly don't want tomorrow to come. I'll have to go through the humiliation all over again when they tell me exactly why I didn't get the job.'

Jack gave an encouraging smile. 'People always assume they've performed worse than they have. It's natural to have doubts when it's something that important.'

'It's not about doubts or anxiety on my part; it's a cold hard fact. First of all I messed up on the presentation...'

'I didn't know you had a presentation.'

'Neither did I until I got to work.'

'So what did you do?'

'I wrote a quick one with Midnight.'

'It didn't go well?'

'It was a rap.'

Jack bit back a grin. 'Sorry… It's just that I can't imagine you rapping somehow.'

'That's a good thing. I think the interview panel are signing up for hypnotherapy as we speak so that they can forget they've seen me rapping too. It wasn't pretty.'

'But it wasn't just a presentation. How did you get on with the interview questions?' He spread some rocket on his slice of pizza and bit into it. Maria watched him before examining her own slice and then copying him. She screwed up her nose and fished the sprig of rocket from her mouth again.

'I suppose I answered some of the questions ok. I was just such a mess after the rapping fiasco,' Phoebe continued. 'I think I overdid some too but it was all a bit of a blur to be honest.'

Jack swallowed his mouthful. 'They'd be crazy not to give you the job. I would.'

'Unfortunately, you don't own Hendry's.' Her mind went back to the granite-featured Mr Hendry. 'There'll be jobs coming up all the time, I suppose,' she mused as she sipped her drink. As always, Jack had managed to chill it to precisely the right temperature.

'That's a good way of looking at it. Stay positive. And the next one will be easier because you'll have more of an idea what to expect.' He found some more rocket in his side-salad and laid it over another slice of pizza. 'Honestly, you're braver than me. I go to pieces in situations like that. It's lucky I don't have to do things like job interviews because I'm sure we'd be poverty stricken if I did.'

Phoebe sighed. 'It would be great to be self-employed. I just wouldn't know what to do.'

'You could always look at web design like me. There's a huge market for it.'

'I couldn't even upload some photos onto Facebook the other day. I don't think anything remotely IT-related is for me. As it is I would have had to rely on a crash course in social media to do the promotions job, which I was kind of hoping you'd help me with. Besides, I quite like working at Hendry's. And yes, I know that sounds weird as I'm always moaning about it.'

'I'd like to work at Hendry's,' Maria chipped in. They both turned to her and she beamed across the table at them.

'It's a lot of fun,' Phoebe replied, 'but it's still work and not playing. You can't always do what you want. Although…' she paused and nibbled at a carrot baton, 'Midnight seems to get away with doing what she wants…'

'Is she behaving?' Jack asked with a chuckle.

'For the moment. And she was great today, really helped me out with the rap. It's just sometimes I wish she'd be a little less…'

'I know,' Jack said, glancing at Maria who had turned her attention back to her meal. 'So, they're going to tell you about the job tomorrow?'

'Yes. But I won't hold my breath.'

'No, don't do that. I'm terrible at CPR.' Jack smiled. He looked at Maria. 'You want some more?' he asked. Phoebe looked across to see that while they had been talking Maria had cleared her plate.

'I'm full now.' Maria rubbed her tummy with a grin.

'Too full for cake?'

Maria's grin spread. 'Not *that* full, Daddy!'

'Me neither,' Phoebe added. 'If I leave any pizza do I still get some? I'm worried about running out of room for your amazing cake.'

'What kind of example is that?' Jack laughed. 'Of course you have to eat all your pizza before you get any pudding.'

Phoebe gave him an exaggerated pout and Maria giggled.

'Granny came today,' she squeaked suddenly.

'She did?' Phoebe asked, wondering at the speed with which Maria's thoughts seemed to lurch from one subject to another. 'Did you have fun?'

'Granny doesn't play,' Maria returned sagely. 'She only drinks tea and talks.'

'A lot,' Jack added.

'Which granny?' Phoebe asked.

'Granny Carol,' Maria said.

'My mum,' Jack clarified as Phoebe looked to him.

Phoebe still hadn't met Jack's parents. Neither had he met hers. She had her own reasons for avoiding that event for as long as possible and she suspected that Jack was doing the same. He always seemed to arrange visits for times when she wouldn't be there, or to make certain that there was no chance of over-lap. She didn't really mind; it would be another awk-ward hurdle that she could do without and she liked things just as they were right now – no approval to seek, no stilted conversations with prospective in-laws who were really hoping you wouldn't make it that far – just an easy time with Jack and Maria that got more comfortable and familiar every day. She was just beginning to feel that she knew them and every-thing else could wait, at least for now. Vik's mother had always been the epitome of courteous tolerance, but Phoebe could tell that she was disappointed that Vik hadn't brought home a nice Sikh girl instead of this non-denomination disaster. The first time he had met Phoebe's parents hadn't been much better. They weren't racist, they said, they just hadn't expected her to date anyone but English men. Phoebe had patiently explained that Vik was probably more English than they were and although they had smiled and nodded in the right places she knew that they were going to be shell-shocked for some time to come by the culture clash. She and Vik had put off getting both sets of parents together for as long as possible, but had eventually decided that Christmas would be as good a time as any. At least there would be plenty of booze around to soften the ordeal. But it had never happened.

As she looked at Jack now, smiling over at Maria, she thought there was no way her parents could fail to love him. She just hoped that when the time came, his parents would feel the same way about her.

'She wanted to stay for tea but Daddy said we were going out,' Maria said.

Phoebe looked sharply at Jack. He gave an awkward shrug.

'I thought we were going to Pizza Hut,' Maria added, 'but I didn't mind when Daddy changed his mind after Granny left because I liked putting the pineapple on.'

'It's… just not a great time…' Jack began a hasty explanation. 'You know… there's stuff going on and she's not in the best of moods… but it's totally not about you… before you start thinking that.'

'You don't have to explain. I know that it's early days for us.' Phoebe thought back to the times during the past few months when she had wondered whether to introduce Jack to her own parents. But she had decided it was too soon, just like he seemed to have done. In fact, she hadn't even told her parents she was seeing someone, although she suspected they had worked it out. But how long should she and Jack wait before too soon became too late? Might it seem as though they had something to hide, something to be ashamed of? At what point would one or both of them feel that the other was withholding the meeting because they were embarrassed or because they felt their parents wouldn't approve?

'We'll do it soon, I promise,' Jack said, as if reading her thoughts. 'I mean, I really want them to meet you. Maria's talked about you non-stop this afternoon. I just want the timing to be better... you know?'

What Phoebe felt he wasn't adding, was *so I can prepare them, make sure they don't have any reason to disapprove of you.* But she said nothing. Instead, she turned her attention to her salad and began to dig around in it with her fork.

'Phoebe...?'

She looked up at Jack.

'It's ok, isn't it?'

'Yes.' She pushed the corners of her mouth up in a bright smile. 'Of course it is. The same goes for me too.'

'Granny says she can't wait to see what Granny May has to say about it all,' Maria said into the ensuing silence. If Jack had looked awkward before he now looked as though he wanted the foundations of the house to swallow him up.

Phoebe looked at Jack. 'Granny May? As in...'

'Rebecca's mother,' Jack confirmed.

Of course Phoebe had always known that Rebecca's mother would have more than a vested interest in the girls that Jack was bringing into her granddaughter's life.

'They're very good friends,' Jack continued, 'they see each other every week.'

'I imagine that's lovely for you and Maria,' Phoebe said, wondering why a sudden spike of jealousy had lodged in her heart. Rebecca was dead and it was only natural that those left behind would want to stay close, if only for Maria's sake.

'Sometimes they take me to the park together,' Maria said, nodding her little head. 'And they take me for cake at the coffee shop too.'

'That's wonderful.' Phoebe forced another smile. She seemed to be doing a lot of that this evening. 'What a lucky spud you are.'

'Uh huh…' Maria crammed a carrot baton into her mouth and chewed solemnly.

'Maybe we should do it,' Jack said suddenly. Phoebe shot him a questioning glance. 'Do the parent thing,' he elaborated. 'Get it over and done with. What do you think?'

'Maybe,' Phoebe replied slowly. 'But how about we hang on for just a little while longer though?'

Jack looked relieved at this suggestion. 'Ok,' he nodded. 'Let's give it a bit longer.'

✤ ✤ ✤

'Steve's been after you.' Midnight handed Phoebe a mug.

Phoebe's night had been disturbed and restless. When she had managed to sleep her dreams had been full of Vik and photos of a dead woman she'd never met. And in her periods of wakefulness her thoughts had been preoccupied by worries about what the morning at work would bring. When the alarm had gone off, Phoebe had only been asleep for about half an hour and now, two hours later, she still felt groggy.

'Did he say why?'

'No. Just wanted to know what time you'd be in.'

'And did you tell him if he hung on I'd be here any minute?' Phoebe asked, panicking that he'd assume she was late. Today was definitely not the day to sow that little seed...

'I told the lazy sod to go and check his rota. I don't get paid enough to do his bloody job for him.'

Phoebe groaned inwardly. She handed the mug back. 'I'd better go and find him.'

'Chill... he'll come looking again if it's important.'

'That's just it...' Phoebe called as she left the staffroom, 'it might be really important and I don't think my nerves can take it this morning.'

She met The Office Lady on the stairs. Out of context and away from her natural habitat she looked paler than ever and rather like a vampire from a fifties horror film.

'I was just coming to get you,' Office Lady said. 'Sue asked Steve if you were in yet and he was supposed to be checking but he hasn't come back.'

'Oh,' Phoebe said.

'Could you come up to the office with me now?'

'Yeah, no worries.' Phoebe followed as Office Lady turned back up the stairs, her stomach doing back flips, front flips, triple pikes with half turns – any manoeuvre that could make her feel sick. This was the hour. Part of her didn't want to hear what they had to say so that, just for a short while, she could carry on pretending there might be the tiniest chance of success. But she also wanted to get the ordeal out of the way so she could put it behind her and move on.

The unique smell of damp, of old lunches, dusty stationery and an overheating printer assailed her as she followed Office Lady in.

'Dixon will be up in a minute,' Office Lady said before taking a seat at her cluttered desk and then promptly ignoring Phoebe as she returned to her computer monitor. Phoebe stood for a moment before deciding she'd feel less conspicuous sitting down. Her gaze travelled the room. There were placards and posters taped everywhere bearing slogans like 'You don't have to be mad to work here but it helps' and 'Too bad the people who know it all can't do it all', along with photos of kittens falling off washing lines and penguins with photoshopped umbrellas and briefcases. There was a wad of newspaper stuffed under one leg of the desk, and the PC Office Lady worked on looked like an old Commodore 64.

Still, she mused, Office Lady looked as though she was right at home amongst the mayhem and decay. Her range of mugs bearing more humorous legends took pride of place on a shelf where she had also stacked boxes of cornflakes, tins of biscuits, over-ripe fruit and a twelve-pack of cheap cola. If there was ever a three minute warning whilst she was at work, Phoebe knew where she was heading. While the rest of the staff were busy eating each other downstairs, she'd be dining out on peach slices and Garibaldi biscuits.

Her musings were interrupted by Dixon's entrance.

'Phoebe...' he smiled broadly at her. 'How are you this morning?

'Apprehensive,' Phoebe replied automatically, cursing herself even as she said it for not processing her thoughts before she expressed them. It was something she never seemed to master no matter how much trouble it got her into.

Dixon gave a low chuckle. 'Well, well... I hope to be able to put you out of your misery. Would you like to follow me?' He gestured to a doorway and Phoebe tramped back into the scene of her lunacy the day before.

'Take a seat,' Dixon said.

Phoebe obeyed and he closed the door behind them before pulling up a chair alongside her instead of behind the desk where she would have expected him to. It was a nice gesture, and one that immediately calmed her nerves. She was already beginning to regret not getting this job, because Dixon seemed like a decent guy.

'How do you think yesterday went?' he asked.

'Not very well,' Phoebe replied, giving him a rueful grin. She hoped her humiliation would be short and sweet.

He nodded. 'You could say that. Mr Hendry said he didn't have a clue for most of it what you were talking about and Sue said…' he cleared his throat. 'The point is, you're right in thinking that it didn't go well. But…' he paused, 'we do want to give you the job.'

Phoebe blinked. She stared at him. What had he just said? 'I'm sorry, I must have misunderstood.'

'We all agreed on one thing about yesterday. Mr Hendry summed it up best, I believe, when he said that the fact he couldn't understand anything you were talking about, together with your very expressive hand flapping, probably means that you're more in tune with the younger generation than any of us are. And that's what we need. Hendry's have been selling toys and games to the children of Millrise for almost a hundred years but in that time we've never really moved with the times, relying on local loyalty rather than competitiveness and progress. All the while multinational toy companies and internet traders have opened up and moved in on our business, cutting it smaller and smaller. We need someone to pull our image into the twenty-first century. I have all the experience in PR and the connections but the point of my assistant is to give me the edge, someone to bounce things off and come up with new and fresh ideas. I need a right hand man… sorry, woman… with their finger on the pulse and youth on their side, who knows what's current and what's trending. After yesterday, we decided that while you weren't the best performing candidate you could be worth taking a risk on. So we'd like to offer you a six-month trial. How does that sound?'

'I don't know what to say.'

'Sue will go through the contract we're willing to offer you this afternoon if you're in agreement. Feel free to give it some thought until then if you're not sure. I will speak to Steve about relieving you of your shop floor duties so that you can start with me as quickly as possible once you give us your answer.'

'I don't need to think about it,' Phoebe replied breathlessly, 'I'd love to work with you!'

Dixon smiled. 'I was hoping you'd say that. I think we'll get along well. And please don't lose the enthusiasm and commitment to the company that you showed at the interview yesterday because that's exactly what we need. I won't kid you, Phoebe, we may have some stressful times ahead, but I'm sure together we can pull this business around and get those tills ringing again.' He stuck his hand out to shake hers. 'Welcome aboard.'

'Thank you,' Phoebe said. 'I won't let you down.'

Dixon nodded and then stood up. 'Come and see me anytime you have questions today. You know where I'm based?'

'Along the corridor from here?'

'The attic room. It gets a bit nippy in the winter so bring some arctic grade thermals and soup when you come to visit.'

Phoebe grinned up at him. She was vaguely aware that it might be making her look like the village idiot but she couldn't help it.

'Right then,' Dixon said, 'I'll see you later when I've had time to get things sorted.'

'Thank you!' Phoebe called after as he left. Once alone, she did a little jig in her chair, squealing and stamping her feet in excitement. She'd done it! God only knew how, but she had.

※ ※ ※

Midnight nudged Phoebe as she looked down the menu board and frowned. 'Seriously, Clements, if I'd known how long it would take you to choose I'd never have suggested a celebration lunch.'

'I'm sorry, it's just that everything always looks so nice. That's why I never come in.'

'I think that might be a compliment,' said Stavros, owner of The Bountiful Isle delicatessen and something of a larger-than-life local celebrity. 'But I hope my menu does not frighten all my trade away.'

'Don't worry, she sends me instead.' Midnight shot her a sideways glance. 'While she's pratting about I'll have chicken and mango salsa on white bloomer.'

'Coming right up!' Stavros yelled a rapid stream of Greek through the beaded curtain hanging over a doorway behind him and then turned back to Midnight with a broad smile. It was a transformation that never failed to amaze and unsettle the observer.

'Oh, I just don't know!' Phoebe said for the third time. She was aware of a queue building up behind her, although Stavros didn't seem concerned.

'Just pick something already!' Midnight sighed.

'Ok… I'll have the houmous platter.'

As Stavros fired another instruction through the beaded curtain, Midnight cocked an eyebrow at Phoebe. 'All that calorific goodness on offer and you go for the veggie option? The concept of celebration seems to have escaped you. You're supposed to throw caution to the wind and let your hair down.'

'I happen to like houmous and salad,' Phoebe replied, her tone a little defensive.

'Well, if that's letting your hair down I'd hate to see you being sensible.'

Phoebe grinned and they moved to one side as the customer behind them was greeted warmly by Stavros.

'Linda!' he boomed. 'Beautiful Linda! How is the business of selling greens these days?'

'Same as it was yesterday,' Linda replied in a bored voice. 'Same as it is every day. I'll have corned beef and pickle on white bloomer please, Stav.'

'Anything for you!' He turned and yelled into the back room again.

Linda eyeballed Phoebe and Midnight. 'You two work at Hendry's?'

Both girls were wearing t-shirts bearing the Hendry's logo under open jackets. Midnight glanced quickly at Phoebe before she opened her mouth to reply. Phoebe held her breath, hoping that she'd keep her sarcasm in check, then let it go again in relief as Midnight seemed to behave herself.

'We do, for our sins.'

'Right…' the woman nodded and then turned an intense eye on Phoebe. 'Either of you know a girl named Phoebe who works there?'

Phoebe stared at her.

'She's Phoebe,' Midnight replied, hooking a thumb at her friend. Linda took an even greater interest now as she measured Phoebe with a penetrating gaze. Phoebe could feel the heat travelling to her face. This was the point at which she could do with Midnight's irreverent and fearless personality coming into play. She recognised Linda from the odd time she had popped into Applejack's, the greengrocer's further down the high street, but she was hardly a regular and certainly not on first name terms. Besides, Linda obviously didn't recognise her, as she'd had to ask. But the situation seemed rather odd and strained, and she wondered why Linda hadn't followed up her enquiry. Phoebe was about to say something herself as Midnight clearly wasn't going to do it for her, when Stavros called them to take their orders. The hunched figure of a little old lady slapped two parcels onto the counter with a grunt at Stavros before disappearing back behind the beaded curtain. Stavros pushed the parcels towards Midnight, who collected them.

'Enjoy!' he called after them as they thanked him.

With one last puzzled look at Linda, who simply nodded to them, they left the shop.

'That was a bit weird,' Phoebe said as they made their way down the street, the fresh spring breeze whipping the hair from their faces.

'What, that woman from Applejack's?'

Phoebe nodded.

'She's a nosey cow. She knows everything that goes on in the shops around here. I wouldn't worry about it.'

'Why would she want to know about me?'

'She's probably heard about your rap. It's already a thing of legend in Hendry's.'

Phoebe blanched. 'Oh my God! Seriously, you don't think...?'

Midnight burst out laughing. 'Your face! That was priceless! Of course not, you dolt. How should I know? Why didn't you ask her?'

'I was sort of hoping you would.'

'Well then you'll have to keep guessing, won't you?'

Phoebe was quiet for a moment. 'I don't like it, that's all. Someone I don't know knowing something I don't know about me.'

Midnight looked across at her with a baffled frown. 'You know that made absolutely no sense, don't you?'

'You know what I mean.'

'Forget about it. All you have to focus on now is how awesome your new job is going to be. No Steve breathing down your neck all day, no brats wiping snot on you… don't forget your mates when it comes to prime assignments, will you?'

'I won't. I'll kind of miss working with you every day though.'

'Me too. But we can still hook up at lunch and I can sneak up to your office when Dixon is out. You'll probably be down on the shop floor a lot anyway.'

'Maybe,' Phoebe agreed. 'Although I'm not entirely sure what they're expecting me to do yet.'

'It's easy street for you now.'

'I'm not so sure about that,' Phoebe said, her mind going back to the conversation that morning with her new boss. She felt like there was something she was missing; something he wasn't telling her, or rather, was trying to tell her without being obvious. She hadn't really given it much consideration throughout the morning, but now it nagged at the back of her mind, taking the shine from her ecstatic mood. 'I think it's going to be harder than I imagined.'

'They must think you're up to the job.'

'They think I'm cool and hip with my finger on the nub of youth or something.'

'Oh. My. God!' Midnight laughed. 'They've definitely got you confused with someone else. You're the most granny-fied twenty-seven-year-old I've ever met!'

'Thanks,' Phoebe said with a rueful smile. 'I'm not that bad, surely?'

'The other day you told me to do my coat up because I might get a chill.'

'It was raining. And the temperature at this time of year is very changeable.'

'We're hardly on Everest, though, are we? You know you can come to me and I'll help with any ideas you're not sure about.'

'You don't mind?' I'm sure I'll be taking you up on that so many times you'll wish you'd never offered.'

'Probably. Just promise me one thing.'

What's that?'

'Make sure you give Steve something really shaming to do for your first promotion.'

Phoebe grinned. 'It's the least I can do.'

✤   ✤   ✤

Phoebe made her way down King's Road at a half jog. She had been dying to phone Jack to tell him her good news. The whole day had passed in a blur. Once she'd been given the news herself, there were conversations with various managers about when she could begin her new duties, and then breaking the news to her colleagues. She had phoned her mum, who sounded almost as excited as Phoebe and would doubtless be making short work of informing the rest of Phoebe's relatives, saving her the job. Which just left Jack. But she wanted that one to be special. She wanted to see his face when she told him. He would be so proud and impressed, perhaps even convinced that he was dating a girl who was a worthy equal. Jack always wanted to pay for things when they went out and it wasn't done to patronise, but out of a genuine concern for her lack of funds. Just for once, she wanted to be able to treat him. It wasn't a huge pay rise, not yet anyway, but it would improve. And for now, even a little more helped.

At their front door, Phoebe pulled the key from her bag. Her hand hovered over the lock. He had told her so many times just to come in whenever she arrived. He had given her the key to show how much they considered her a part of their family now. But it still felt strange.

Twisting the key in the lock, Phoebe pushed the door open. 'Hey... it's only me!' she called.

Maria instantly came thundering down the stairs at a rate that had Phoebe's heart in her mouth.

'YAY! PHOEBE!' she cried.

Phoebe bent to give her a hug. 'How's it going?'

She stood, expecting Jack to emerge from the kitchen, the dimples in his cheeks showing as his face crinkled in a delighted smile. But he didn't. 'Where's your dad?' she asked Maria.

'He's with Archie.'

Jack appeared in the living room doorway. 'I thought I heard your voice.' But he didn't look his usual self. Where his blue eyes were usually full of mischief and barely disguised sex appeal, today they were dull and shadowed; his features were taut and pinched. The smile he gave her was so fleeting as to be almost non-existent.

'I didn't realise you had visitors,' Phoebe said.

'It's ok, it's just my brother. But he's going now.'

Phoebe held back a frown. Maria, who loved people and visitors more than anything, had been upstairs.
And the visitor in question was her nineteen-year-old
uncle who had almost enough energy to keep up with
her; at least more than anyone else Maria viewed as a
playmate. And Jack didn't look happy at all. Had he
sent Maria upstairs to get her out of the way, and if
so, out of the way of what? Hard on the heels of that
thought, another one crashed in. Phoebe was finally
about to meet another member of Jack's family. He had
mentioned his brother, of course, but he had seemed
even less keen for Phoebe to meet him than he had his
parents. Now there was no escape – for either of them.
Her heart began to beat just a little faster.

Another face appeared behind Jack and his
brother nudged him aside.

'So, you're the mystery woman we keep hearing
about? We were beginning to think you were Maria's
imaginary friend.'

Phoebe stared at him. He was undoubtedly Jack's
brother. He looked a lot younger, of course, a little
fuller in the face, something more arrogant in his
eyes, but he shared the thick black hair and dimples
when he smiled.

'I suppose I must be,' Phoebe said. 'And you must
be Archie.'

'That's me.'

'Archie's just going,' Jack turned to him, 'aren't
you?'

'I'm in no hurry. I could stay. Mum's only got left-overs for tea tonight so she won't care if I'm late.'

'It was a rhetorical question.' Jack gave him a pointed stare. 'But don't think that we won't be talking again later.'

'Nothing to say later, bro,' Archie replied with a cocky grin. He dug his hands in his pockets. 'I'm off then,' he added as he sauntered down the hall. He gave Maria's hair a ruffle. 'See you later, gorgeous.'

Maria giggled. 'Bye, Archie.'

'See you around, maybe.' Archie turned to Phoebe and gave her a wink. She returned it with a weak smile, unable to shake the knowledge that something in this picture was very wrong. Why did Jack seem so tense around his own brother? She had never seen him like this before.

The door swung shut and Archie's footsteps sounded faintly down the path.

'So… that's your brother,' Phoebe asked, unable to think of any other remark to make.

'Archie's funny,' Maria said.

Jack's jaw was still clenched; Phoebe could see the muscles working clearly beneath his skin. She smiled brightly, hoping to somehow diffuse the tension that still lingered. She was beginning to wish that she hadn't come straight from work with no warning and she was definitely regretting using her new front door key. Of all the times she could have picked to finally let herself in. From now on it was back to knocking – much safer that way.

'I um... I called in for a menu at that new Chinese takeaway that's opened up around the corner... thought we might have something from there if you hadn't already planned a meal...' Phoebe said uncertainly. 'You know... because we might want to celebrate.'

Jack seemed to shake himself from whatever dark place his thoughts had taken him to, and smiled. He wasn't quite back to his usual self but Phoebe was hopeful that with a bit of gentle coaxing he'd be laughing and joking in no time. 'Celebrate? Does that mean...?'

'I got the job!'

Jack rushed to hug her and swung her around in his arms. 'That's brilliant! You're so clever! I knew you couldn't have been as bad as you said you were.'

'Oh, I was,' Phoebe replied as he put her down and kissed her briefly. 'They completely agreed with me on that. But apparently I have 'street cred' and that's what they're looking for.'

'Fantastic. You're going to be amazing, isn't she, Maria?'

Maria nodded enthusiastically. Phoebe bent down to her.

'I'm definitely going to need a little helper to try out some ideas. How do you feel about being my guinea pig?'

Maria frowned. 'In a cage? Like the one at school?'

'No,' Jack laughed. 'This sort of guinea pig is someone who tests things out.'

At this Maria looked even more confused. But then she seemed to get over it and smiled at Phoebe. 'I can help. Do you need me to try out toys?'

'Maybe sometimes. But mostly I need you to tell me whether ideas sound fun or not. And as you're about the most fun girl I know I'm sure you'll be brilliant at it.'

'Yes.' Maria nodded again.

'Right…' Jack clapped his hands. 'We need to get some wine chilling if we're having takeaway.'

Phoebe and Maria followed him into the kitchen. 'It feels very indulgent having takeaway on a Wednesday night,' Phoebe said, shrugging her jacket off and hanging it over the back of a wooden chair.

'It's not every day my girlfriend gets a new job, though, is it?'

Phoebe watched as he fussed over which wine to put in the fridge from the stocks in the rack, and then set about perusing the menu, chatting to Maria all the time about what she was going to have. He was playing at being cheerful, and she supposed he was genuinely pleased for her, but something still wasn't right with him. Whatever Archie had brought to Jack's door, it wasn't good. He had never mentioned a problem with his brother before, but now she thought about it, other than informing her he had a brother, he didn't talk about Archie very much at all. Phoebe wondered whether she should come straight out and ask him why that was. But Maria was there and he obviously didn't want to discuss it in front of her, no matter how coded they managed to make the conversation.

'Do you think it's too early to eat?' Jack interrupted her thoughts. 'I mean, we could wait a while if you want to order later.'

'I'm happy to eat now. Maria has to go to bed early, doesn't she, so maybe we should.'

'Good point,' Jack replied, pulling his mobile from his jeans pocket. He placed it on the table and then slid the menu over to Phoebe. 'Come on then clever girl, choose something nice and don't worry about the cost.'

'No way,' Phoebe said. 'Tonight is my treat and I don't want any arguments.'

'But –'

'I said no arguments. Just once, let me get it.'

Jack leaned over and kissed her. 'Just this once then.'

※ ※ ※

Maria made as much fuss about going to bed as a five-year-old girl can make. Eventually, after bribery, cajoling and reverse psychology, Jack threatened that if she didn't get her backside up the stairs Phoebe wouldn't be coming to tea again. Phoebe made a pretend shocked face, and Maria moved faster than Phoebe had ever seen her move before.

'Little madam…' Jack said as he came back down after tucking her in. Phoebe gave him an indulgent smile.

'I remember wanting to be downstairs whenever my mum and dad had company at that age. You always think you're missing something spectacular when actually all they're doing is discussing the price of paint in B&Q.'

Jack laughed as he flopped onto the sofa and slipped an arm around her. 'What do you fancy doing? I'm not up-to-date on the current stock prices at B&Q but I could do some research.'

'That's ok,' Phoebe giggled. 'I can live without it for the moment.' She paused. He seemed in a pretty good mood. Perhaps he would be a little more open to probing now that Maria was out of the way. 'Jack… about what happened with your brother earlier.'

'Leave it, Phoebe. There's nothing to talk about.'

'But –'

'He's always getting into some scrape or another, it's nothing for you to worry about.'

'But I do worry…'

Jack pulled his arm from Phoebe's shoulder. His whole body tensed.

'I can see it's upsetting you.'

'Please… leave it.'

'But I can help –'

'Phoebe!' Jack snapped. He lowered his voice. 'Sorry. I just don't want to talk about it and I don't want you to ask me again.' He reached for the TV remote and switched it on, flicking through the channels with an intense expression of concentration that suggested his mind wasn't on what he was watching at all.

Phoebe wasn't about to give up, but she knew when to throw a battle for the sake of the war. Tonight, it was best to leave things alone.

⚜ ⚜ ⚜

Phoebe trudged across the muddy field, wishing she'd worn more practical shoes for the occasion. She was also beginning to wish that she'd arranged to meet her mum and dad in a café or pub like normal people did on a Sunday. But she'd promised to show her face and she hadn't actually been to one of her dad's events for a while now so she didn't really feel that she could back out. She spotted her mum sitting on a bench nursing a thermos flask with a rug over her legs. It was nippy, but not that cold, although Phoebe supposed that it might be if she'd had to sit there for the usual length of time. Her mum looked around and waved at Phoebe as she drew nearer. Phoebe glanced around at the other benches. There weren't many people here. Others obviously had more sense than Phoebe and her mother and better things to do at the weekend.

'He's not finished yet?' Phoebe asked as she took a seat and kissed her mum on the cheek.

She looked at her watch. 'Shouldn't be long now. I heard cannon fire five minutes ago so I think that will finish off most of the survivors. Once that happens the rest will probably surrender.'

'That's good. He's not going with them to the pub afterwards?'

'Yes…' her mum threw Phoebe a sideways look. 'I thought we were all going?'

'With the society? Why would we do that?'

'They haven't seen you for ages and I thought you might want to tell people about your new job.'

'I don't think anyone would be remotely interested. 'They'll be too busy tallying up the dead and dissecting the battle. That's all they usually talk about.'

Phoebe's mum shrugged. She produced a plastic container from a tartan bag at her side and prised the lid from it. An overwhelming stench of processed fish wafted out. 'Salmon paste sandwich?'

Phoebe shook her head and tried not to gag. She had been feeling delicate enough already after a late night with Jack.

'Suit yourself.' Her mum replaced the lid and dropped the container back into the bag. The roar of frenzied, testosterone-fuelled men reached them from across the distant fields, a soundtrack embellished by the clash of steel upon steel and the occasional explosion.

'Sounds like a good one,' Phoebe observed.

'They had to cancel the last one so they've probably got a lot of pent up rage and frustration to get rid of by now,' her mother replied serenely. 'Biscuit?' she asked, shaking a custard cream pack.

Phoebe shook her head again. 'No thanks. You didn't fancy watching this one?'

'I've sat on the sidelines of enough battles to last me a lifetime. When you've seen your husband

70

killed by musket for the tenth time it loses its impact. Besides…' she picked up a book she'd been reading and waggled it at Phoebe, 'this is brilliant. It's kept me good and entertained.'

Phoebe nodded sagely. 'The rain held off for them too.'

'Thank goodness. You know what havoc it plays with the armour when it rains. The amount of money your dad has to spend on WD40…'

The earth-shattering boom of a cannon blast made them both look sharply across the fields where a dark plume of smoke was rising into the air. The sound of a horn followed.

'Looks like they're finished.' Phoebe's mum stood and rolled up the blanket before stuffing it into the tartan bag along with the thermos. 'We'd better go and meet your dad.'

'I wonder if he survived,' Phoebe said as they started to march across the fields, every few steps having to yank a foot from the sticky mud.

'I doubt it. The infantry rarely do.'

'I thought he was going for officer.'

'He couldn't afford the new uniform this time.'

'Right…'

'So, any more news about your new job?'

'As a matter of fact, I'm starting tomorrow.' Phoebe smiled.

'Really? That quickly?'

'Well, they wanted someone in the post as soon as possible and as I didn't have to work notice anywhere else there didn't seem much point in hanging around. I'm glad; I just want to get stuck in now.' As she said this, the little butterflies that had plagued her every time she thought about her new job started their pesky circuits of her tummy again. The nerves would settle, of course, and she was sure that in no time at all it would all be humdrum, but that thought wasn't helping much now.

As they chatted, the first casualties of war began to file past. Most were drenched in sweat, some in a fair amount of fake blood, all dragging swords or muskets along. For dead and injured soldiers they were remarkably cheerful. Phoebe's mother smiled and nodded at one or two. As the crowds swelled, steel helmets and feathered hats filling Phoebe's view, a familiar face appeared. It was hard to tell where his beard ended and the mud began, his face was so covered in grime, but through the mess he gave them a huge grin.

'Alright, love?'

Phoebe leapt out of the way of a muddy hug. 'Don't you dare, I haven't got time to wash this jacket before tomorrow.'

Her dad chuckled. 'Sorry, love, I forget about normal behaviour when I'm in costume. How are you? Not been waiting too long, have you?'

'Not really. I've been telling mum about the new job anyway.'

'Oh yes…' he began to walk back across the fields with them. 'Are you excited?'

'Moderately,' Phoebe replied.

'That's the spirit; play it cool.'

'So…' Phoebe continued, 'how was today?'

'Fantastic! I died three times.' He brushed a hand down his breastplate and beamed at her.

'Aren't you only supposed to die once?'

'Depends if anyone sees you get up. I was like the *Highlander.*'

Phoebe burst out laughing. 'You're such a naughty cheat! You'd have made a brilliant, ruthless, Roundhead soldier for real.'

'Tell that to my commanding officer.'

'Phoebe wanted to know if we're going to the pub now,' her mum chipped in.

'I think it was *you* who wanted to go to the pub,' Phoebe said to her.

'I did say I'd go for an hour,' her dad said. 'I'd love it if you came too – the lads were saying they don't see much of you these days.'

Phoebe groaned. 'They'll only spend ages telling me how much I've grown and how they can still remember when I had braces and spots. It's so embarrassing.'

'I'll shut them up the minute anyone mentions braces, I promise.'

Phoebe let out a sigh of resignation. 'Ok. Just a couple of halves but you'll need to run me home afterwards.'

'Your mum's driving today, aren't you, love?'

'I didn't have much choice.'

Phoebe's dad pulled her mum into a hug. 'Ta, love.'

'Ugh, get off you filthy man!'

'Awwww, I'll buy you a new jacket. Come here and give us a kiss…'

'Dad…' Phoebe laughed, 'not in front of the children!'

'Not in front of the other soldiers either,' a Cavalier sporting a dirty bandage across one eye shouted behind as he marched past, laughing.

'Alright, Ed,' Phoebe's dad called back. 'You're just jealous.'

'Of course I am! That Martha Clements is one fine looking woman!'

'Oh, do shut up!' Phoebe's mum replied, blushing and running a self-conscious hand over her hair. Despite her protestations, she was clearly delighted.

'Come back and say that to my face!' Phoebe's dad shouted. Ed strode off, chuckling loudly.

'See you in the Badger.'

Phoebe smiled at her mum. 'I think it's going to be a lively one today.'

'You're not wrong there.'

⚜ ⚜ ⚜

Phoebe nudged her way through the heaving crowd of Cavaliers and Roundheads, swords prodding her and protruding bits of armour catching her hair as she tried to squeeze past. It was bad enough trying to hold three drinks steady under normal circumstances, but this was proving a particular challenge. The stench of sweat wasn't helping either and so many bodies were making a lot of heat. The Bald Badger was alive with animated chat and booming laughter as men teased each other about their performances on the battlefield that day.

Finally, Phoebe managed to reach the relative sanctuary of the table where her mum and dad were deep in conversation. She felt as though she had been through a battle herself just to get their drinks back without spilling any. She dumped all three on the table. 'Pint of mild,' she said, pushing one towards her dad. 'And a Britvic orange,' she added, sliding a second one towards her mum before sitting with her own glass.

'What on earth is that?' her dad asked, nodding at her drink.

'Raspberry cider.'

He shook his head wonderingly. 'What's wrong with a decent pint of ale?'

'Nothing... if you're a big hairy Yorkshireman,' Phoebe shot back with an impish smile. 'I happen to be a small, slightly less hairy girl from Staffordshire.'

'You've Yorkshire blood in your veins so be proud of it.'

'I am. I just don't want my veins to be full of ale as well.'

Her dad let out a roar of laughter. 'You've genuine Yorkshire honesty and humour so I suppose I can let you off a girly drink from time to time.'

Phoebe glanced at her mum, who simply rolled her eyes with a quick grin.

Her dad leaned towards Phoebe and lowered his voice. 'Geraint's been asking about you again.'

'Geraint's the size of a combine harvester and with about as much subtlety,' her mum cut in.

'He's a nice bloke,' her dad replied defensively.

'He's a lovely bloke,' Phoebe said. 'He's not for me, though.'

'You're only trying to fix her up with Geraint because you think it will persuade Phoebe to join the society.'

'I'm not. Although we do need more women.'

'And I'm not joining either before we go down that tired road again,' Phoebe's mum said.

Her dad shrugged and sipped his pint. 'I was just saying, that's all.'

Martha glanced around and lowered her voice. 'Geraint isn't right in the head. He can't really expect Phoebe to find him attractive.'

'Excuse me, but how do you know who I'd find attractive?' Phoebe asked giving her mum an indignant sideways glance.

'I'm just saying that I'm sure you'd want someone more your own age who shares your interests.'

Phoebe looked from her mum to her dad and then back again. The conversation seemed to turn to potential suitors with a frightening inevitability these days. She had often wished they'd leave her to get on with that whole business herself, when and, indeed, if, she ever felt like it again. But now that Jack was on the scene it was getting beyond awkward. She took a deep breath. Maybe it was easier to get everything out in the open at last.

'I'm um… actually seeing someone anyway.'

Martha broke into a wide smile. 'You are? Since when?'

'A little while. Maybe a couple of months.'

'Why on earth didn't you say so? I'd have laid off the matchmaking,' her dad laughed.

Phoebe ran her finger around the lip of her glass and shrugged. 'It was early days. I didn't know whether we'd last long enough to make it worth me telling you.'

'It's quite serious now then?' Martha exchanged a significant glance with her husband.

Phoebe looked up. Was it serious between her and Jack? Now that she thought about it, she supposed it was. Things had been so easy and relaxed between them and neither had really questioned where they were heading. Maybe that fact alone made it serious. Until the key incident, of course. She nodded slowly. 'I really like him.'

Martha clapped her hands. 'When are we going to meet him?'

'I don't know. I'll talk to him, see if we can fix something up. It's not always easy for him, he has to make plans for his daughter, Maria and –'

'Daughter? He has children?'

'One child.'

'He's married?'

'No, of course not, Maria's mother is –'

'So, how old is she?'

Phoebe suppressed an irritated frown. Why did it suddenly feel as if her mum was interrogating her? 'Five. And absolutely adorable. And she's lost –'

'A big responsibility. Is he expecting you to take her on?

'Nobody is expecting anybody to *take her on*. Jack is a great dad and he's looked after Maria since she was a baby just fine all by himself.'

'Where's her mum? Off having babies with other men all over the place?'

'Dead.' Phoebe took a gulp of her cider.

'Oh…'

'That's a shame for the little tyke,' Phoebe's dad cut in. He picked a lump of dried mud from his beard, examined it, and then flicked it onto the floor before taking another swig of his beer.

Martha wasn't to be put off. 'Are you sure this man isn't just after a new mummy for his little girl?'

'So what if he is? Wouldn't that be between me and him and nothing to do with anyone else? What if I did want to be Maria's new mum?'

'Do you?'

'That's not the point! Even if I did it's up to me. She's a great kid. She doesn't need a new mum because nobody is going to replace Rebecca. I like Jack and it's not about Maria or her mum. Can we please drop it now?'

'I'm just trying to look out for you.'

'Because I'm not capable of looking out for myself?'

'You have to be careful. People's motives aren't always what they seem. And I don't think you want to get tied down with a child at your age, especially one who isn't yours.'

'I'm twenty-seven, Mum! And I think I'm old enough to decide what I want.'

Phoebe's dad cleared his throat. 'Perhaps we should just butt out, Martha.' He turned to Phoebe. 'I think it's great that you're courting again.'

'Thank you, Dad,' Phoebe replied. She knew her mum meant well and in the end her only concern was for Phoebe's happiness, but her comments rankled all the same. It was the deep-seated distrust of anyone who was not just like Martha Clements that bothered her no matter how much she tried not to let it.

'He must be a decent fella if he's raised a bairn like that,' her dad continued. 'Not many would.'

'What does he do?' Always Martha's second question about any new man in Phoebe's life, roughly translated as *how much does he earn?*

'He's a web designer.'

'One of those made-up jobs, then,' Martha replied tartly.

'It pays him a good salary and there's a lot of demand for it these days.'

'Are we going to meet him?'

'Of course. We'll just need to find the time. He's very busy and with my new job I will be too. But I do want you to meet him; I honestly think you'll like him.'

'I'm sure we will,' her dad said.

'Hugh!'

Phoebe looked around to see a bear of a man grinning down at her dad. As if the newcomer wasn't tall enough, a lavish spray of feathers sprouting from a huge Cavalier hat added superhuman inches.

'Geraint!' Phoebe's dad returned a warm greeting. 'Cooled down a bit, lad?'

Geraint smacked his lips as he held a half empty pint glass aloft. 'I have now. Cracking fight today, eh?'

'It was indeed.'

Geraint turned to Phoebe and her mum. 'Martha… Phoebe…' he gave them both a courteous nod of recognition. 'Haven't seen you in a while, Phoebe. You're looking well.'

Phoebe returned the compliment with a polite but neutral smile and took a sip of her cider in order to avoid having to give any sort of response. She dearly hoped he wasn't going to do anything daft today like ask her out. It would be mortifying to have to refuse him and he was such a nice man that she really couldn't bear to do it. This wasn't the first time it had been a possibility either. She suspected that his interest in her had more to do with her dad's involvement in the Millrise Historical Battle Re-enactment Society than with actual physical attraction. A girlfriend that (sort of) understood the society would be a bonus to someone as obsessed with it as Geraint was. Not only that, but Phoebe also suspected that he didn't often go to the sorts of places men usually went to in the hope of meeting prospective partners.

Geraint simply smiled down at her in a rather vague way and tipped his hat. 'Lovely to see you ladies again.'

'And you,' Phoebe replied. She felt desperately sorry for him. He was a sweet man. Even his odd little hat-flourish was rather sweet, if somewhat eccentric. But she could never fancy him in a million years. She watched as he shuffled off again, his great bulk cleaving a path through the crowded bar like a human snowplough. 'You'll have to say something, Dad, put the poor bloke out of his misery.'

'I will, love. I didn't know about this Jack bloke before, did I?'

Phoebe frowned. 'To be perfectly honest, Dad, it wouldn't have made any difference if I hadn't been seeing Jack. I was lonely, but I wasn't desperate and Geraint just isn't my type.'

He gave her a sheepish smile. 'I'll have a word later, I promise.'

'Thanks. You really don't need to worry about me, you know.'

'But we do,' Martha cut in. 'We're parents and that's our job.'

'Never mind all that now,' Hugh smiled. 'Who's up for a bowl of chips? I'm famished.'

⚜ ⚜ ⚜

The early night was a big mistake. Phoebe had suspected it would be but had convinced herself that she needed the extra sleep to be at her absolute best and brightest for her first day as Hendry's new promotions assistant. The reality was that she couldn't get to sleep because she wasn't really tired by nine o'clock. And the longer she lay awake the more agitated she became and the less able to relax and close her eyes. By the time she had finally dozed off the clock was showing four-thirty. Two hours later it buzzed her awake and she was so tired she could barely see straight.

By the time she had walked into Hendry's she was running on a potent mix of coffee and adrenaline and little else. Dixon had welcomed her, hastily cleared off a dust coated desk that looked like a hostel for down-and-out woodworm and told her to start creating.

Phoebe was still *creating* when morning break came at around ten. Creating in this case could be loosely translated as staring into space, chewing on the end of a pen and rearranging the small collection of office equipment on her desk while Dixon frantically made phone calls and frowned at his computer screen. She had cleaned her desk, customised her computer desktop with a large picture of Angel from *Buffy the Vampire Slayer* and had sent a text to Jack to tell him everything was going really well. It wasn't, of course. Everything was going really badly. As she found herself staring at the opposite wall again, Phoebe reassured herself that first days were always a little disjointed. Once she got into a routine and made the job her own she'd be fine. Although, that was one of the problems. There hadn't been a job to make her own. No handover from a previous employee, no existing duties to continue, no routine in place, no shoes to fill – she had been given a blank sheet to bring the job into existence and was starting from scratch. Where did she even begin?

Every so often Dixon lifted his head from whatever he was doing and smiled at her. 'Everything ok? Anything you're not sure about or want to run past me?'

Phoebe rather thought that she would like to run past him… down the stairs and back to her old job. At least she knew what she was doing on the shop floor. She didn't want to run actual thoughts past him for fear of looking stupid. Not that she had any of consequence anyway. There were vague, half-formed ideas floating around her head but nothing that would blow anyone's socks off.

So when break came Phoebe was only too happy to clatter downstairs and search for Midnight. Their breaks no longer coincided and Phoebe found her trying to squeeze her mass of hair beneath a Captain America helmet and facemask in the stockroom.

'Hey, look at you in your suit. Sexy!' she called as she spotted Phoebe, who dearly wished she could return the compliment. But as she had never seen anything quite as odd as a fully-grown, purple-haired (not forgetting rather buxom; as if anyone could forget) woman in a Captain America balaclava/helmet combo, it would clearly be a lie that even Midnight would see through.

'Thanks,' she replied instead.

'How's the first day?'

'Ok,' Phoebe said carefully. 'Actually, pretty shit.'

'That sucks. Anything that won't get better once the first day nerves wear off?'

'Probably not.'

Old Hendry been in to bother you yet?'

'Mr Hendry?' Phoebe frowned. 'I haven't seen him today.'

'He's stalking the corridors, surveying his empire somewhere with Hendry junior, or so I've heard. I thought they might be coming to see what you're up to.'

'I hardly think I'm that important. It's my first day too so I wouldn't have anything to show him really.'

'You never know with old Hendry. He's a bit weird if you ask me.'

Phoebe tried not to laugh. Midnight still hadn't removed her headgear and seemed to have no concept of the irony of her comment in light of this fact. But then the thought that Mr Hendry might turn up unannounced in her office at some point and demand to see what he was paying her for pushed all other thoughts from her head and ramped up her already hyper anxiety levels. She tried not to dwell on it. 'I didn't know there was a Hendry junior.'

'He's next in line to take over the family business when Hendry senior retires. He's pretty hot too.'

'Really?' Phoebe recalled the cold, expressionless features of Hendry senior and couldn't imagine him spawning the sort of son Midnight might find attractive.

'Everyone fancies him,' Midnight said, as if she somehow needed to clarify the matter further.

'Everyone?'

Midnight nodded. 'Even the straight blokes have man crushes on him.'

'I don't care how good looking he is, I don't want him in our office today.'

Midnight pushed herself up to take a seat on a shelving unit and swung her legs in a roguish manner. 'Is it really that bad?'

'It's just...' Phoebe let out a sigh. 'I don't even know where to start. I don't know what Dixon is expecting from me... not really. He's given me these vague and cryptic instructions that I have to get Hendry's modern and popular again but I don't really know what that means.'

'Why don't you ask him?'

'I don't think he knows what it means either.'

'Tricky...' Midnight agreed.

Phoebe opened her mouth to speak again but then her forehead creased as she tried to hold off her frown. 'Can you just take that mask off? I'm struggling to concentrate on anything today as it is and I feel like I'm hallucinating at the moment talking to you like this.'

Midnight patted her head. 'No way. Cap stays.'

'Aren't you supposed to be on the shop floor any-way?' Phoebe asked in an increasingly exasperated tone.

'I'm thinking about it, yeah. The Cap still stays though.'

'I suppose the kids would find it funny…' Phoebe said, finally admitting defeat. But then her frown turned into a smile as enlightenment lit her features. 'The kids would find it brilliant…'

'Show me the kid that wouldn't.'

'Have you got the rest of that costume?'

Midnight pointed to a box on the floor. 'In there somewhere. You fancy joining in?'

'What do you think about a superhero day? All the staff on the shop floor could dress up.'

'Cosplay?' Midnight high-fived Phoebe. 'Now you're talking my language. Our costumes won't fit most of the fat bastards up there, though; we only have kids' sizes.'

Phoebe was silent for a moment as she mulled it over. 'We could order adult sizes in.'

'You think they'd give you a budget for that?'

'Maybe not… I don't suppose you have your own at home?'

Midnight flashed her a saucy grin. 'Yeah, I've got loads. They might be a bit on the kinky side for here, though.'

'I don't suppose everyone will have stuff like that at home. I bet we'll have to order some in. I'll ask Dixon what he thinks about a budget for something like that. We can reuse them too, make it a regular thing.'

'Better still, you could even sell them in adult sizes in the store. Comic cons are big business and Hendry's are missing out on it.'

'Comic cons?'

'Conventions…. For sci-fi and fantasy nuts. They love dressing up and they spend loads on their outfits. You could advertise on comic con websites that we sell the cosplay stuff here.'

Phoebe gazed at Midnight thoughtfully. 'I suppose we could do a small trial run first to see what sort of reaction we get. What costumes have you got at home?'

'I thought you'd never ask! Want me to bring some in? Or you could come over and I'll talk you through them.'

'And we're going to need help with the website and leaflets designing… I think I know just the man for that. How do you feel about doing a bit of cosplay around town? I mean, you can say no if you don't want to.'

'Are you kidding? Get paid to walk around town dressed as Black Widow? I'm so there I was there last week!'

Phoebe giggled. 'You are amazing. I wish I had half your confidence.'

'My friend, you are mistaking confidence for giving a shit, which I don't. I can't wait to see Steve's face when you tell him you have to borrow me. Even better when you hand him a Spiderman costume and tell him he's got to wear it.'

'Spiderman? That's far too cool for Steve. Aren't there any really naff superheroes that nobody likes I can save for him.'

'I can take care of that – leave it to me.'

'I suppose I'd better run it all past Dixon before we get too carried away. I'll let you know what he says.'

'You know what else I've just thought of for even more days under Steve's radar?'

Phoebe raised her eyebrows in a silent question.

'A little bit of industrial espionage…'

'Huh?'

'We could go out mystery shopping to the other toy stores – see what they're doing.'

'I think Dixon already does that,' Phoebe returned doubtfully.

'But I bet he doesn't see it like we would… *comprendez*?'

'Sort of. I suppose I can ask. I think that might be pushing Steve just a little too far though.'

'I'm sure a woman of your persuasive talents can talk him round.'

'This is Steve we're talking about?' Phoebe checked her watch. 'I'd better get back to my desk.' She threw her arms around Midnight. 'Thanks for being amazing.'

'I haven't done anything yet,' Midnight called back as Phoebe hurried away. 'But I bloody well will be when I do!'

❀   ❀   ❀

Phoebe hurried up to the attic office. At last she had something, the germ of an idea to give to Dixon. It only took a spark like this to set her creativity on fire; one little spark would be the catalyst for many more.

But when she burst into the office, Dixon wasn't alone. She froze as Mr Hendry and a man she'd never seen before turned at her entrance.

'Here she is,' Dixon said with an amiable smile, 'my new assistant.'

'I just… I was just on a break,' Phoebe stuttered.

'Of course… you are allowed to have breaks, even in the cutthroat world of PR,' Dixon laughed. 'We don't want to work you into an early grave just yet.'

'Settling in?' Mr Hendry asked. Despite the solicitous nature of his words he wasn't smiling. He didn't seem to care less whether Phoebe was settling in or not. However, it was the warmest he'd been to Phoebe since she'd met him. That had to be progress, didn't it? 'Yes, thank you,' she replied. Her gaze travelled to the man she assumed was his son.

He was tall, imposing, something regal about the way he held himself. She guessed he was in his mid-twenties and he was undoubtedly handsome, but not in a way that would make a woman feel safe and loved. He silently appraised her with steel grey eyes in a way that felt dangerous, formidable. Phoebe had hoped not to run into him on her first day but, as always, that stubborn, irritating bitch fate had other ideas.

Dixon turned to Mr Hendry's son. 'Have you had the opportunity to go down onto the shop floor yet, Adam?'

Adam Hendry nodded. 'First thing. It was only a brief visit and there wasn't much going on that early.'

'It certainly livens up later in the day,' Dixon agreed. 'Would you like me to talk you through what we do here in the meantime?'

Adam glanced at Phoebe who was just about managing to hold in a groan of distress. She silently prayed that he wouldn't be keen to discover more about the world of promotions. The two men's presence was making her decidedly on edge and she wanted them to leave. Her first day was stressful enough without this.

But, of course, Adam gave Dixon a curt nod. 'That would be very helpful.'

Dixon pulled up a spare chair and positioned it at his desk alongside his own. His gaze flicked up at Phoebe. 'May we borrow your chair?'

'Be my guest.' Phoebe wheeled it across as he unlocked his computer and the three men sat down. She hovered uncertainly behind them. She couldn't slink back to her own desk and pretend to work now that she didn't have a seat and she wasn't sure if she was expected to contribute to Dixon's impromptu presentation. 'Um...' she flailed around for ideas to remove herself. 'How about I make coffee?' she asked brightly. 'Or tea? Mr Hendry... I mean, both of you...' she felt the heat rise to her cheeks as she blushed.

Old Mr Hendry looked up from the screen. 'We've already had one this morning.'

'I'll have one,' Adam said with a look that Phoebe found hard to interpret. Was that mocking humour in his expression? Or was he just mocking her?

'Dixon?' Phoebe asked.

Dixon looked up from his keyboard with a slight look of surprise, as if he had forgotten she was there.

'Oh, yes... coffee... lovely. If it's no bother.'

'None at all,' Phoebe replied, thankful to be out of the frame for ten minutes. Once Dixon had got his talk underway without her perhaps he wouldn't need her to chip in at all. Even better, if she could slope in at that point and watch, she might actually learn something about what Dixon did for Hendry's. 'Sugar?' she asked.

'None for me,' Adam said.

'Two,' Dixon called after her, already out of the door.

She rushed out onto the landing. There was a jar of coffee in the staffroom, a floor below, that she shared with Midnight. She often found their coffee jars depleted as people sneaked in and raided them, regardless of the fact they were labelled clearly with her name. She hoped this time there would be enough left to make two drinks, otherwise she'd have to do some thieving of her own. Hers was a cheap make too – did Hendry Junior drink only the best?

She couldn't help a half smile – it would be an introduction to the world of the working class for him. Perhaps he'd be so appalled by the quality of the coffee they were forced to suffer that he'd insist on giving out hefty pay rises for all his staff. Or at the very least Starbucks allowances.

Finding there was still plenty left in the cupboard, she set about washing two very old and chipped mugs and hastily prepared the drinks.

Back in the office, as she had hoped, Dixon was in full swing. With as little fuss as possible she placed a mug in front of him and the other beside Adam Hendry.

Dixon thanked her but Adam merely gave his cup a cursory glance before returning his attention to a graph that Dixon was explaining to him. Phoebe hovered behind them as Dixon began to speak again. She watched as he toggled from that screen, through spreadsheets on the results of marketing campaigns and information on local demographics. None of it really meant a great deal to her but she did her best to make some sense of it. She had never been a number cruncher – more of a people person, connected to the world emotionally rather than by logic and facts. Was that, perhaps, what Dixon was hoping she'd bring to his new team? It was certainly all she had to offer at the moment.

Her thoughts were interrupted by Hendry Senior. 'Phoebe... do you have any ideas for the coming weeks? Plans to capitalise on the summer months?'

Phoebe fought to suppress the blush that spread across her cheeks again. She knew it made her look like a silly schoolgirl rather than a confident career woman with something relevant to say. 'Um... I will... I mean.... Today I'm concentrating on finding my feet...'

'But you must have given it some thought already. You have been preparing to take on the job for a week and were aware of the interview long before that. You must have known that you would be required to make a meaningful contribution early on. After all, that is what I'm paying you for.'

She gave a weak smile. She had, of course, thought of little else. But faced with his demands here and now, everything she'd talked about earlier with Midnight, seemed stupid and pointless. 'I'd rather finalise the details and submit my ideas properly when I do.'

'I'd like to hear about your cosplay idea,' Adam said.

Phoebe stared at him, the blood now draining from her face. Had he been hiding somewhere in the stockroom? If so why, and how much of her conversation had he heard? Had old Mr Hendry been somewhere in the vicinity too? More to the point, how had Adam got to the attic room so bloody fast? He had been there before Phoebe who had gone straight up after leaving Midnight and had pretty much run. She forced herself to calm down. If he'd been up here when she arrived back then he couldn't have been in the stockroom long enough to hear the conversation between her and Midnight in its entirety. But she would have to remember that seemingly empty stockrooms had dark and dusty corners where people could lurk undetected. In future, conversations of a possibly compromising nature must be held safely away from Hendry's toy store.

She tried to read Adam's expression again. And was still confused by his intentions. She was sure she could see that mocking humour, but no anger or malice.

'I haven't had time to think that through yet.'

'Share what you have,' Adam insisted.

Phoebe took a deep breath, wishing she could slap him. 'I was thinking we could tap into the current craze for adults to dress up –'

'Silly student types,' Mr Hendry cut in, barely disguised disdain in his voice. Clearly his values were still of the type where respectable people who would make something of themselves in the world stopped having fun the moment they stopped wearing nappies.

'Money from a student loan is just as good as anyone else's to us,' Adam replied. 'All that matters is that it ends up in our tills, wherever it comes from.'

'Erm… right…' Phoebe agreed uncertainly. She glanced at Mr Hendry who didn't argue but didn't look as though his son had changed his opinions of students one bit. 'It's actually much bigger than that, though,' she continued. 'If you think about comic conventions, fundraising events, Halloween, parties… there's a lot of demand nowadays. We could even think about a fancy dress hire department.'

Dixon nodded enthusiastically. 'Brilliant.'

'Surely,' Mr Hendry interrupted, 'these plans are more to do with our buying team than promotions.'

'But we could liaise with our buying team to make sure we're stocked for events and special promotions that we run,' Phoebe continued, getting into her stride now that she could see the merest sniff of interest. He was doing his best not to show it but she could see it just the same. 'So if, for instance, we ran a superhero-themed day where the staff dressed up and we ran special prices on say, Marvel merchandise, we could get the buying team to ensure we have the stock in to capitalise on that…'

Old Hendry nodded slowly. 'Good… anything else?'

'We could link up with local comic cons… comic conventions… to perhaps give sponsorship or get our name on their websites and advertising as their preferred costume supplier. And the dressing-up possibilities are endless. It's not just about comics but about gaming, big movie franchises and cult TV. People like to dress as anything they've seen online or on film as well as books and comics so not only could we make money on ready-made costumes but on props for people making their own – things like fake swords and magic wands.'

The two Hendry men looked at Dixon. Neither of their expressions gave anything away. 'What are your thoughts?' old Hendry asked.

Dixon paled slightly. Phoebe felt guilty and wished she'd had more time to give him a fuller picture of her plans before he'd been put on the spot. But then, she'd been put on the spot too. He would have to make a snap decision and if one or both Hendrys didn't agree he'd look bad. It was a tough break for someone in his position.

'I'll need time to look at it all properly. And I'll need marketing information. In principle I have no objections to a small-scale trial.'

Old Hendry nodded. He turned to Phoebe. 'Any other brainwaves you'd like to share?'

'Um...' Phoebe began. Far from being relieved that she had been able to offer something not instantly dismissed as rubbish, she now felt even greater pressure to follow it up. 'I had some ideas for younger children... perhaps a featured story of the day, with linked props and toys available to buy at strategic points in the store and close to the story area throughout the session. We could even charge a small fee for admission to the story area... something nominal that appeals to the customer but still makes us a little on the side. So if we got twenty children at a time, three sessions a day, for instance, at one pound per child, that would net us sixty pounds for that day plus additional toy or book purchases.'

'One pound?' Mr Hendry's shocked glare was almost comical. Phoebe felt the blush rise to her cheeks again.

'It's just an example, off the top of my head.'

'We could charge two pounds per child and it's still low as far as the customer is concerned,' Adam cut in, 'but then the figures start to look good for us.'

Instead of a reply, Old Hendry stood up. 'Work out your proposals – anything you've told us about and anything else you've got. Let me see them on paper with proper figures. Then we'll see what we agree on.'

'No problem,' Dixon jumped in and replied for Phoebe. 'Leave it with us.'

With that, Mr Hendry nodded to his son who took the signal that it was time to leave. Adam gave Phoebe a look that lasted just a little too long and was just a little too intense. Once again, she felt the colour rise to her cheeks. She didn't even know why.

As the two men closed the door to the attic office behind them, their footsteps receding, Dixon turned to Phoebe.

'Ruddy hell! Welcome to the world of PR!'

Phoebe gave him a bemused smile.

'When did you dream that little lot up? You've sat there, as quiet as a gagged mouse all morning, and not mentioned a thing. I thought you needed time to settle in but you were way ahead of me.'

Phoebe almost laughed out loud. She had been thinking that she was expected to hit the ground running and been panicking about it, where Dixon hadn't hassled her because he thought she needed time to settle in.

'Perhaps a bit of communication might be an idea in future,' Phoebe smiled. 'Sorry about that.'

'Good idea,' Dixon agreed. 'So... let's get the low down on these ideas of yours, now that we don't have our lords and masters breathing down our necks. At least we can think and discuss things without any pressure.' He gave a broad smile, like a proud parent who'd just been handed a particularly pleasing school report. 'I've got a feeling we're going to make a good little team once we're up and running.'

Phoebe sincerely hoped so. She had more riding on it than he could possibly know.

❧   ❧   ❧

'Oh my God, I am so sorry I made you sit through that film!' Jack groaned as the movie credits rolled. 'Archie says it's brilliant. Just goes to show that we have very different ideas about what makes a good film.'

Phoebe laughed. 'I've seen worse.'

'Like what?'

'Attack of the Killer Vampire Sex Bees from Outer Space...'

'Sounds like a classic. Are you quite sure that film actually exists?'

'Sure. On some dodgy cable channel I bet.' Phoebe stretched out. She was lying across the sofa, her bare feet resting on his lap. With a wicked grin he grabbed them and started to tickle her.

'OI!' she squealed. 'STOP IT!'

'Shhhh!' he laughed, 'you'll wake Maria!'

'You're the one making me scream,' Phoebe giggled as she yanked her feet away and held a cushion over them.

'His eyes sparkled as he gave her a sly glance. 'I could make you scream…'

Phoebe threw the cushion at him. 'Filthy boy.'

'Alright,' he continued with an impish grin, 'any other ideas? What do we do now?'

'We have to dissect the film, obviously,' she replied, trying to look stern.

'Crap. That's it… film dissected and conclusion reached and it's only nine-thirty. So what else can we do?'

'Dishes?'

'Naked dishes?'

Phoebe let out a snort of laughter. 'That's the weirdest image. I won't be able to get it out of my head now.'

'I'm sure I could find ways to make you forget.' Jack leant in to kiss her. Then his hands were tugging her close, in her hair, his lips taking no prisoners as her senses exploded. She was molten as he worked his mouth over her neck, his fingertips along her arms in gentle relays making her shiver with desire. His touch was so gentle and yet so potent. She didn't know what it was he did to turn her into a puddle of lust but he did it so well she could never get enough of it.

'Bed?' he whispered as she took a minute to catch her breath.

'Bed sounds good,' she replied, her voice barely a sigh.

He leapt off the sofa and swept her into his arms as though she weighed little more than a feather. At the foot of the stairs he kissed her again. She gazed at him as he pulled away, drinking in every inch of his eyes – so close she could make out the amethyst flecks in the dazzling blue, shining with intelligence and sensitivity – the thick hair so dark it was almost black, the fine shadow of stubble that dusted his chin and accentuated the dimples of his smile. She could lie in his arms and stare at him all day every day for the rest of her life and it still wouldn't be enough. Did she love him? It was a question she was asking more and more these days. She was beginning to think that she did, truly and completely.

His foot rested on the bottom step.

'You can't carry me up there; you'll break your neck,' Phoebe giggled.

'Strong man, mighty man, mighty horny! Can do anything!' he replied in his best caveman voice.

'Put me down, you mentalist! There'll be no rumpy pumpy if you do your back in.'

'I have to impress you with my strength as well as my chocolate cake.'

Phoebe burst into laughter again as he wobbled up the first three steps.

And then a knock at the front door sounded through the house. Phoebe watched his grin turn to a frown.

'Who the hell is that now?'

'Perhaps it's Doreen from next door?' Phoebe said. 'Maybe she needs something.'

'I doubt it's Doreen at this time of night.' Jack lowered Phoebe to the step. The letterbox opened and a voice called through.

Jack's frown turned into something far darker. The muscles in his jaw twitched and tensed. He turned and thundered down the stairs, yanking the front door open.

'Archie! Don't you think you should have called first?'

Jack's brother glanced up at Phoebe, still standing on the stairs in a state of semi-undress, her hair tousled. He threw Jack a wide grin.

'Was I interrupting something?'

'What do you think?' Jack growled.

'I won't be long; I just need a favour. Aren't you going to let me in?'

Jack looked up at Phoebe, who shrugged slightly. He opened the door wider to allow Archie in. 'Ten minutes,' he said as he led him through to the kitchen.

'I'll go and tidy the living room,' Phoebe called after them. Something about Jack's manner told her that any conversation he was about to have with Archie was private. She took herself down to pick up the bits and pieces they had left lying around during their film evening. She could hear them, in the kitchen, their voices low – Archie's tone jaunty and mocking, Jack's deeper and more solemn. As she tidied up, Jack's voice got louder and more agitated, though still not loud enough for her to make out what they were saying. Every so often she caught the odd word, like 'mum' and 'idiot' and 'money' but the meaning of all this remained frustratingly absent.

When every cushion had been plumped, every throw folded into a neat square, every DVD case on the shelf positioned so that they were all perfectly aligned, Phoebe could stand it no longer. She was going to confront the two of them and get to the bottom of whatever was troubling them, whether Jack liked it or not. She and Jack shouldn't have secrets anyway, she reasoned; it wasn't healthy and it wasn't a good basis for a long term relationship. Besides, perhaps she could help if she knew what it was.

But Jack and Archie emerged from the kitchen and met her in the hall. For once, Archie's cocky and carefree demeanour had faded, replaced with an expression almost as thunderous as the one Jack wore.

'Everything ok?' Phoebe asked, looking from one to the other.

'I'm off,' Archie snapped back. 'Enjoy the rest of your evening,' he added in a savage tone.

Phoebe threw Jack a questioning look but he shook his head to indicate that she shouldn't ask. She wouldn't ask – not until Archie had gone, anyway. She winced as Archie slammed the front door behind him before stalking off into the night. There was no way the racket could fail to have roused Maria. Jack must have had the same idea, because they turned as one to look towards the stairs and listened. But all seemed quiet. Phoebe released a breath she hadn't even realised she was holding.

'Archie didn't seem very happy,' she said in a low voice.

'He wasn't. Neither was I.'

'Want to tell me what's happening?'

Jack didn't reply. Instead, he went back into the kitchen and pulled a bottle of beer from the fridge. 'Want one?' he asked as Phoebe joined him.

She shook her head. 'I have to be up early and a hangover won't help.'

He shrugged, opened the bottle and took a long swig, almost slamming it back onto the worktop afterwards. Leaning against the marble surface, he exhaled loudly and ran a hand through his hair, his gaze turned heavenwards. Phoebe had never seen him look this troubled before, not even when she had walked in on him and Archie arguing the week before. Something was going on between them and it wasn't good. It concerned her and upset her in equal measure. Her own brother, Josh, had moved to Australia three years ago. She missed him terribly and she couldn't imagine hating him like Jack seemed to hate Archie right now. If there was something she could do to help make things right between them then she wanted to be allowed to try.

'You have to talk to me, Jack.'

He turned his gaze to her. 'About what?'

'Whatever is going on with you and Archie.'

'What makes you think anything is going on? He annoyed me, that's all, turning up unannounced at this time of night.'

Phoebe frowned. 'You still feel like going to bed?'

'Not really.'

'That's what makes me think something is going on. Are you going to tell me?'

'It'll blow over. There's no need for you to worry about it.'

'But I do worry. It's clearly affecting you and that means it affects me. It affects Maria too, if it comes to it.'

'How?'

'It just does.'

'I don't want to talk about it.'

'Please, Jack –'

'I said I don't want to talk about it!'

Phoebe glared at him. 'There's no need to shout.'

'Then shut up about things that don't concern you.'

As he took another long gulp of his beer Phoebe held him in a silent gaze. He was angry and he was being unreasonable and as much as she wanted to she fought the impulse to retaliate. This wasn't *her* Jack talking right now.

'Shall I go?' she asked in a measured tone.

Jack lowered the bottle. Despite his neutral expression, she could see he was distressed by the fact that he'd obviously hurt her. She could also see anger still burning him up.

'Perhaps it's best if you do.'

'I'll call a taxi then.' Even now, Phoebe hoped he would argue against this, but he simply nodded and sat down at the table, studying his bottle. After a heartbeat's pause, she went to fetch her phone, trying very hard not to cry.

⚜ ⚜ ⚜

Midnight twirled.

'You do look amazing,' Phoebe smiled.

'Want me to try any of the others on?'

Phoebe glanced at a huge pile of multicoloured clothes lying on the chair of the staffroom. One or two others getting ready for the morning shift looked on with barely disguised amusement, whilst Gareth Parker, long-time admirer of Midnight's ample curves (an admiration sadly not returned) visibly drooled at the sight of her poured into her faux leather Catwoman suit. Phoebe wondered whether she ought to go and close his mouth for him; there was no telling what might fly in.

'Maybe it's a bit too sexy,' Phoebe acknowledged.

'But sexy is what the male sci-fi geek loves,' Midnight returned.

'True. But we have to be careful not to cross the line. Remember we're a kids' store first and foremost.'

'I've got my Wonder Woman outfit.' She held up a red and gold basque and blue satin pants. Gareth Parker choked on his coffee.

'I think you'd lose small children in that cleavage,' Phoebe laughed. 'How about we do a photo shoot outside the building? That way we can get shots of you wearing everything and run it past Dixon. We'd have lots of promo shots for websites and social media doing that too.'

Gareth Parker might have been wishing he was Dixon, or the photographer, or even the gusset of Wonder Woman's pants; no one could tell. But there was an audible squeak from his direction, before he dashed from the room, his expression somewhere between distress and outright lust. Midnight and Phoebe watched him go.

'What's his problem?' Midnight asked with a bored shrug. Phoebe grinned.

'I'm not sure whether you made his day or ruined it. Let's have a look at what else is in that pile of stuff...'

Phoebe had thrown herself into the morning's duties and hadn't said a word to Midnight or anyone else about what had happened between her and Jack the night before. She had tried desperately not to dwell on it herself, let alone discuss it with anyone. This new job was too important and she couldn't get distracted. But as they pondered this outfit and that scenario, it seemed that Midnight knew something was amiss. Every so often she threw Phoebe a puzzled glance, as if trying to fathom what was out of place.

'What?' Phoebe asked finally.

'Nothing...'

'Then what's the matter?'

'I could ask you the same thing.'

'There's nothing the matter with me... I've just got a lot to do this morning.'

She was saved further interrogation by Steve bursting into the staffroom.

'Shop opened fifteen minutes ago and I seem to be down one checkout operator.'

'Have you checked under the desk?' Midnight said.

'Very bloody funny. Are you going to stay up here all day parading around in that ridiculous get-up?'

'Not all day, no. Perhaps all morning...'

Steve's mouth worked but no sound came out. Either that, or in his rage his voice had gone so high that only dogs could hear it.

'She's helping me...' Phoebe cut in. 'I hope you don't mind... I did clear it with Mr Hendry.'

She had done nothing of the sort, not officially anyway, but she hoped the conversation she'd had with him the day before would be a kind of permission. The fact was that Midnight had got so excited by the idea of being able to dress up at work that she had turned up with her entire wardrobe before Phoebe had even had a chance to get the proposals on paper and approved by Dixon or Mr Hendry. But Steve didn't need to know that and she didn't want to get Midnight in trouble.

Steve stared at her. She could almost see the cogs working. It must have pained him immensely to utter his eventual reply.

'I see… In that case can I have my checkout operator back ASAP?'

'As soon as we're finished. I'll be as quick as I can.'

As soon as the door to the staffroom swung closed and Steve was gone, Midnight snorted. 'Did you see his face?'

'You'd better be careful,' Phoebe warned. 'You're not bullet proof, you know.'

'I don't need to be. Steve's gun isn't even loaded.'

'Just watch it, that's all I'm saying. You can only push him so far before he goes higher with his complaints and then you'll be on disciplinary.'

'That's where you're wrong.' Midnight flashed a grin. 'He'll never go higher because that would mean him admitting he can't control his staff which would mean he has failed.' She grabbed the basque and pants from Phoebe's arms. 'So let's have some fun and get these photos done.'

Out of sheer habit, Phoebe reached into her pocket and checked her phone as Midnight reapplied her lipstick. Usually, there would be a message by now from Jack – something silly and unimportant to do with the weather or a new cake recipe he'd found online – his way of letting her know he was thinking about her. But today, there was nothing. Was he really angry about last night? She knew she hadn't done anything wrong, unless you could consider trying to help wrong. She had thought about calling him first thing and apologising, but kept coming up with reasons why she shouldn't: he would be taking Maria to school, he would be working, he might be on the landline to a client. What she found hard to admit to herself was that she was plain afraid to call him. She was afraid that she would be rejected again, as she had been the night before.

'Ready?' Midnight asked. 'Shall we do Cat Woman first and then try out some of the others?'

Phoebe shook herself. 'Yeah, sounds good.'

⚜   ⚜   ⚜

On the pavement outside the store, Midnight's unabashed performance was drawing a small crowd and they'd hardly begun. It seemed that Millrise on a Tuesday morning was bored and ready for action, which Midnight was only too happy to provide. As the morning sun shone kindly down on them, Phoebe snapped away as her friend twisted her body into a series of increasingly theatrical poses. She was clearly loving every minute of it.

'Right…' Phoebe said, 'I think we've got enough of that outfit. You want to go and change?'

'You wait here; I'll be back in a minute.'

Phoebe nodded. One or two women with children watched and she wandered over to them as Midnight disappeared into the store. 'Do you like superheroes?' she asked one of the boys. He looked about Maria's age, maybe younger, and he smiled shyly at her.

'He loves The Hulk,' the woman with him said. 'Don't you, Nathan?'

'That's cool,' Phoebe replied. 'We should get him in to do a visit. Would you come to see him if we did?'

The boy nodded, a small smile appearing on his face.

'Brilliant,' Phoebe said. She turned to the woman. 'It's good to get ideas from our customers.' She glanced up at Hendry's majestic store frontage and then back again. 'Do you shop here?'

'Sometimes,' the woman said. 'We mostly go where there are offers.'

'Right... but if we had events on... say, story times, superhero events... would you come to those with your children?'

'I'm all for anything to entertain them,' she said. 'There're only so many times you can watch children's television and look at the ducks in the park before it starts to melt your brain.'

'I was hoping you'd say that.' She looked at the little boy. 'So maybe we'll see you in the store soon?'

'Absolutely,' the woman replied. 'Will you be advertising when you do these events?'

'I expect so. Do you use social media?'

She nodded.

'We're just putting a new Facebook page together. If you like us on there you'll get the details of anything coming up in plenty of time.'

'I'll do that,' the woman said. She tugged on her little boy's hand and led him, still staring at Phoebe, up the high street.

Phoebe suddenly felt a hand on her shoulder. She spun around to see Adam Hendry behind her.

'Oh!' she cried, the exclamation more violent than she would have liked.

'Nice to see you charming the population of Millrise,' he said.

'I was just… you know… getting a feel for what people want.'

'I heard. Very well handled.'

Phoebe blushed. She really wished she could stop doing that in front of him all the time. Jack would have laughed and kissed her, but she didn't imagine it had quite the same effect on the future boss of Hendry's. She glanced behind him.

'I'm on my own today,' he said, seeming to read her thoughts. 'My father has important business to attend to in Edinburgh.'

Phoebe was relieved. One Hendry was quite enough to contend with. 'Have you come to see someone in particular?'

'Perhaps,' he replied.

Phoebe blinked. Terrifying and cryptic. She gave a silent prayer that Midnight would come back soon and save her from any more of this excruciating conversation. Now that would be a superhero deed.

'What are you doing out here?' he asked, nodding his head at the camera in Phoebe's hand. 'I take it you're not just hobnobbing with the public.'

'Photos.'

'Of the store?'

'For the cosplay ideas we talked about. To illustrate our proposals for Mr Hendry.'

'Which Mr Hendry?'

Ok… terrifying, cryptic and facetious. Where the hell was Midnight? Phoebe forced a smile. 'Dixon is just putting some marketing figures together if you wanted to go up and take a look.'

'I think I'll stay down here and watch what you're up to, if it's all the same to you.'

'It's just silly messing about really…' As soon as she said it she blushed again. He raised his eyebrows. 'I mean… I didn't mean I was messing about… I am working of course… I meant that Dixon is taking care of the cold, hard business facts and I'm doing the creative stuff…'

'I'm interested in the creative stuff. Four years doing an advanced business degree means I already know the rest. Show me something I don't know… impress me.'

What she wanted to do right now was shove his head in a bin and see how much that impressed him; he was making her morning very difficult and it had been bad enough to start with. She glanced at the shop entrance again. She had never been so desperate to see Midnight.

'I think my model might have got waylaid. You won't want to be waiting out here for her all morning.'

'I don't mind.'

'But she might be quite a while. Especially if she's been grabbed by her line manager to do something on the shop floor for him.'

'Who is her line manager?'

'Steve Thomas.'

'Hmmm,' he was thoughtful for a moment. 'Ah, yes. Why don't you go and have a word with him while I wait here?'

'I doubt he'd do me any favours,' Phoebe said, instantly regretting her reply. It sounded as though she was slagging him off and she hadn't meant to.

Adam's gaze was now fixed on her in that same way it had been up in Dixon's office the day before – just a little too intense for her liking. 'You mean there is someone in this company who can say no to you?'

'Apparently,' Phoebe laughed self-consciously, unsure of the true meaning behind his comment.

'I find that hard to believe…' He gave her that look again. She had never understood the phrase *undressing with his eyes* until now. It was deeply unnerving… and weirdly a little bit sexy… if you lumped dangerous and sexy together… which Phoebe did not of course…

'Perhaps we can show you the photos later when we get Dixon's approval.' Phoebe stumbled over her words. He was having a strange effect on her and she had to get rid of him before she said something really stupid. And something more stupid than all the stupid things she'd already said would be very stupid indeed.

'You really don't want me to hang around, do you?'

'It's not that... it's...'

Phoebe's awkward reply was saved by the appearance of Midnight, her breasts barely contained by her red-and-gold satin basque, teamed with the blue satin pants, huge shiny platform boots and a long black wig. She had ramped up the make-up and now had massive red lips that looked like two mutant strawberries having a fight.

'Wonder Woman...' she sang (if wailing like a castrated cat could be categorised as singing in any way) as she leapt from the entrance of the store and whizzed around. 'What do you think?' She stopped dead in her tracks as she saw who was standing next to Phoebe. If even Midnight was thrown by his presence, then Phoebe reasoned that he must provoke a strange sort of reaction in everyone and she was thankful that it wasn't just her.

'Very creative...' he said smoothly. 'And which demographic, exactly, is this campaign aimed at?'

'The cosplay market...' Phoebe said uncertainly.

'I think teenaged boys might rather enjoy it too. Although I suspect they'd have very different reasons for that.'

'I… erm…'

'Well, I think I've seen enough creativity for one day.' He checked his watch and then looked at Phoebe. 'I look forward to catching up later for those photos.' Without waiting for her reply, he strode off in the direction of the shop entrance and disappeared through the doors.

'What the hell?' Midnight whispered as they watched him go.

'I know… where were you? I was on my arse out here!'

'On your arse? The way he was looking at you I think he would have liked to have been on your arse.'

Phoebe glared at her. 'Shut up!'

'What? I'm just saying. *I look forward to catching up later for those photos…*' Midnight mimicked. '*And I might just get my cock out and rub it on your face…*' she added.

'MIDNIGHT!' Phoebe cried. 'That's so disgusting!'

'But true.'

'Not true one bit. Are we going to get these photos done or what?'

'Yes… Mrs Hendry…'

'Shut up!'

'Adam and Phoebe sitting in a tree, K-I-S-S-I-N-G…'

'That's it! Either you stop making idiotic comments or I go and hand you back to Steve.'

Midnight grinned. 'You wouldn't.'

'Behave then,' Phoebe replied, her face burning.

'Right...' Midnight placed one booted foot on the base of one of the Corinthian style pillars that marked the entrance to the store, pouting and thrusting her chest out as she did. 'You must be a bit flattered though... I mean, he's really hot.'

Phoebe put her camera to her face and started to click. 'There's nothing to be flattered about. Besides, I have a boyfriend.' Phoebe's mind went back to her phone. More than anything right now, she needed a text from Jack. But she couldn't look, because she didn't know what it would do to her mood if she found there was still nothing. She lowered the camera. 'Maybe you should get changed into something slightly more *action girl* and less *seen too much action girl?*'

'Lara Croft?'

'Too dated for our younger audience.'

'Black Widow?'

'Could work.'

Midnight raced off towards the entrance. Phoebe perched on one of the bases of the pillars and pulled her phone out yet again.

Nothing. What was wrong with Jack? Of all days, why had he picked today to be silent and unforgiving? Were they having their first row? She hadn't done anything wrong. Had she? If she could have done, she would have raced over and thrown herself into his arms; she just wanted to know that they were still alright. But right now, it felt like there was an invisible barrier between them. Something had shifted in their relationship – silently, imperceptibly, but definitely, nonetheless. And Phoebe was afraid that they might never go back to what they'd had.

❧ ❧ ❧

PART TWO
JUST LIKE REBECCA

'Who, here, has ever been eaten by a troll?'

Every kid sitting on the carpet giggled. Some shuddered, their laughter slightly more nervous. The space in which they sat was decorated specially for the event and there was separate seating for the parents, most of whom were absently flicking through magazines, grinning at phones or hugging take-out coffee cups – all clearly relieved to have an hour more or less to themselves. Brightly-coloured pictures depicting various stories drawn by the groups that had gone before decorated one wall. Another wall had a giant fairy-tale frieze populated by the best-known characters. Lanterns and piñatas hung from the ceiling along with paper butterflies, aeroplanes and pterodactyls. It was an eclectic space that she was sure most people would hate in their homes, but Phoebe was proud of what she and her little team of helpers had achieved. She was also immensely proud of the business she had pulled in to Hendry's toy store over just a few short weeks.

She stood at the back of the room now, leaning against a post, watching the story unfold with almost as much enthusiasm as the children. It had taken some persuasion for nineteen-year-old Melissa Brassington, a shy but obviously creative girl, to finally have a go at the story hour, but now that she'd done them for a week, Phoebe could see she was a natural and was pleased she'd agreed in the end. Midnight had begged to do it, of course, but Phoebe was afraid that left to her own devices, she would terrorise the children with an ad lib version of Little Red Riding Hood that involved chainsaws, bondage gear and cannibalism. Melissa, however – sweet, lovely and barely older than most of the children she was reading to – was a much safer bet. The kids loved her and she seemed to enjoy interacting with them now that she had got used to it.

'If you've ever been eaten by a troll,' Melissa continued in a spooky voice, 'you'll know that it's awful slimy in there…'

One boy's hand shot up. 'How can you stay alive if you've been eaten?'

'Ah… that's a good question…' Melissa smiled. 'And I'm about to tell you the answer…'

A low voice sounded in Phoebe's ear. 'Going well, isn't it?'

Phoebe spun round to see Adam Hendry standing close. Far too close. He seemed to be everywhere she turned these days. If he wasn't some day destined to be her boss she'd be having some serious conversations with him about personal space.

'Melissa's great,' Phoebe agreed.

'I don't know why you're not reading the stories.'

'Oh no...' Phoebe shook her head vigorously. 'I'm no good at that sort of stuff.'

He raised an eyebrow. 'Surely it's just like giving a presentation?'

'Have you seen any of my presentations?'

'Yes. I do believe I've seen something you presented with Dixon last week.'

'Then you'll understand why I don't do story time.'

He gave a low chuckle.

'Was there something you wanted me for?' Phoebe asked.

'I just came to watch the entertainment.'

'Right...' From across the room, Phoebe saw a familiar figure waving at her. She straightened up and gave a tiny wave back, before holding her hand up in a gesture that told her visitor to wait where he was. 'Would you excuse me? It's time for my lunch break and I'm meeting someone.'

Adam nodded shortly. Phoebe hurried off without waiting for a reply. Jack greeted her with a quick kiss on the cheek. He smelt of shower gel and fresh air, his blue eyes smiling.

'This is good,' he said.

'Isn't it?' Phoebe smiled. 'But I think I might get used to you taking me out to lunch on a work day. It will certainly break the week up a little.'

'I know. I'm sorry I'm always so busy.'

'Don't be. If you'd been working out of town you wouldn't have been able to anyway. I'm happy to get you when I can.'

Aren't you sick of the sight of me by now?'

'Never!' Phoebe laughed. 'Aren't you?'

'Never!' He gave her a dazzling grin. 'Where do you want to go?'

'I… erm…'Phoebe was momentarily distracted by the sight of Adam, still leaning against the post at the back of story area, glowering in their direction. Jack followed her gaze.

'What's his problem?'

'That's Adam Hendry.'

'Old man Hendry's son?'

She nodded.

'No wonder he looks so miserable. Uncle Fred says they're a right pair of tossers.'

'Uncle Fred?'

'He owns Applejack's… I must have told you.'

'Nope…' she paused. 'Although it does explain something… a few weeks ago someone from Applejack's came up to me in the Bounty and I had no idea who she was until Midnight told me where she worked. I guess your uncle Fred must have told her about me?'

Jack suddenly looked troubled. 'Right…' he said as they began to walk to the exit. He reached for her hand. 'Perhaps my mum mentioned you to him… I don't really see him a lot.'

'He's your mum's brother?'

'Yes.'

Phoebe took a moment to process everything she knew about the proprietor of the local greengrocer's. He had a reputation for being boorish and it was hard to believe, from what she had heard, that he was related to her boyfriend at all. As Jack had still skilfully avoided any mention of her meeting his parents, she had to assume that his mum might be similar to her brother. This all felt like rather a sore point. A couple of weeks ago, Jack's brother Archie had turned up at the house and there had been a huge row. When Phoebe tried to get to the bottom of it, Jack had turned his anger on her too. Things had been smoothed over between them since, but he still seemed to be at great pains to keep his family away from her. Or was that *her* away from *them*? Phoebe still hadn't decided who he was ashamed of and it troubled her that the answer might be the wrong one. She wasn't exactly a catch, she was well aware of that.

And she still hadn't got to the bottom of the problem with Archie. Although things had quietened down, she wanted to know what was going on and resented the secrets that Jack seemed determined to keep. Thinking about it now made her feel suddenly belligerent.

'We should do the parent thing soon,' she said. 'Get it out of the way, you know?'

'Really?'

'Don't you think it's time?'

'I don't know…' he sighed. 'Maybe. What did you have in mind?'

'You mean you agree?'

'You're right; we do have to do it sooner or later. It may as well be sooner.'

'Great!' Phoebe said in a voice that suggested it was anything but. She had brought it up, of course, but in a fit of pique that now seemed reactive and foolish, and she was already wishing she hadn't. What on earth would Jack make of her unconventional parents? 'Maybe we should do one set at a time first… no need to make everything too stressful to start with.'

'God no! We don't want everyone meeting each other for the first time together. Yours first then?' he suggested.

'Um…'

'It was your idea.'

'I suppose so.'

They emerged into the gentle sunshine of a late spring afternoon. Jack gave her hand a squeeze. 'It'll be alright, won't it?'

'Yeah…' Phoebe said in a small voice. 'Of course it will. I mean, they're only our parents, right?'

❧ ❧ ❧

The more Phoebe thought about it, the more she was beginning to wish that she hadn't suggested the parent meeting at all. Was it too soon? Was their relationship strong enough to cope with the fall-out should things not go well?

As she tossed all the foods into her shopping trolley that her mum told her not to eat, Phoebe's pessimism felt big enough to crush her. Chest tightening, she stopped and rifled in her handbag for her asthma inhaler and took a desperate pull. Why did it seem like such a big deal?

As she dropped her inhaler back into her bag and stood for a moment, getting her panic under control, her phone rang.

'Hey Mum.'

'I'm glad I've caught you...' Martha's voice came from the other end of the line. 'Have you eaten yet?'

Phoebe's gaze ran over the sorry assortment of goods in her trolley: a value pack of fish fingers, four-pack of own-brand beans, three Pot Noodles, shampoo and cat food for a cat she didn't even own but which had decided that Phoebe was a good bet (even animals could see the word *sucker* invisibly tattooed across her forehead). Her pay rise, in the end, hadn't amounted to much and things, although better, were still not great. Money wasn't everything, right? It sure did buy you a better class of fish finger, though.

'Not yet,' she replied. 'I'm just getting some odds and ends now at Tesco.'

'Good. Your dad has brought in a load of steak someone at the society got off the back of a lorry. We've plenty if you want to come over and don't give us the excuse about buses because your dad will come and pick you up.'

Phoebe hesitated. She had wanted a night to herself but steak did sound good, back of a lorry or not (what did that even mean nowadays?). And perhaps this was the ideal time to bring up the subject of meeting Jack.

'Sounds lovely, Mum. Let me finish up here and I'll call you back.'

'You're struggling with a load of shopping on the bus?' There was a faint sigh from the other end. 'Why on earth you don't you let us lend you the money for a car… Hang on there when you're finished and your dad will come and get you from the supermarket.'

Phoebe gave a grateful smile down the phone. It didn't matter that her mum couldn't see it, only that she felt it.

'Thanks Mum. Tell him to give me another twenty minutes and I'll wait for him at the entrance.'

⚜ ⚜ ⚜

'I don't see what's wrong with the Bald Badger.' Hugh pouted.

'There's nothing wrong with it. It's just a little… rough…' Phoebe said, wincing as she caught his hurt expression. Her dad loved that pub almost like a second home. Martha always said that the amount of time he spent in there it might has well be his first home. 'I didn't mean rough, I meant… down to

125

earth,' she added, wishing it was possible to swallow words back in once you'd spoken them.

He threw another burger onto the barbeque. Steak had become burgers (someone had been exaggerating about the quality of the meat on offer, apparently) but Phoebe didn't mind. It was still better than what she had planned to eat. She watched as a flame licked around it and made a mental note to check the middle of the burger, just the same. The griddle was a bit too close to the gnarled old lilac tree that clung to the frame of the back door too, and she wondered vaguely if her phone was to hand so she could call the emergency services if he set fire to it. As a sudden, brisk breeze rattled through the garden she tried to put such thoughts from her head and pulled her cardigan tighter around her.

'I told him it was too cold to start a barbeque,' Martha said as she noticed Phoebe shiver.

'It's summer!' Hugh retorted over the hissing of meat juices on hot coals.

'Not yet it isn't. We don't all have a beard like an alpaca's coat to keep us warm.'

'You're nothing but a couple of wimps,' Hugh muttered. 'It's not cold at all.'

'Anyway,' Martha said, ignoring his sullen jibe, 'Phoebe's perfectly right. She can't bring her boyfriend to the Bald Badger on a first meeting. What would he think of us?'

'He'd think we were honest types who liked a proper drop of ale in a proper pub,' Hugh said.

'He'd think we were rough,' she said, repeating Phoebe's earlier insult.

'I don't...' Phoebe began but her mother cut her short.

'You do realise that his uncle owns Applejack's? He's a businessman so they're obviously a good family.'

'Oh aye! Fred! I know him.'

'How do you know him?'

'Well... I don't know him, exactly... but Les, you know, infantry Les... he knows him... tried to get him to join us but Fred said he were too busy.'

'He's obviously got more important things to be getting on with than rolling about in a muddy field playing soldiers.' She turned to Phoebe. 'How about Sunday lunch? That place next to the canal? It's lovely there.'

Phoebe frowned. 'Do I know it?'

'The Bargeman? Oh, they do a nice drop of ale in there. Suits me,' Hugh put in.

'I don't think I've ever been there,' Phoebe said.

'Of course you have,' Martha replied. 'Cousin Barbara's sixtieth... you got locked in the toilet cubicle and had to slide out underneath.' She chuckled. 'It's a good job you were so thin back then.'

'I'm thin now, thank you!' Phoebe squeaked.

Martha ran a critical eye over her. 'Filling out a little, I think. Contentment... it happens to us all when we settle down. Next thing you'll be wearing jeggings and convincing yourself that it's a fashion statement and nothing to do with the fact that your clothes won't do up.'

'Mum!'

'I bet Jack's getting a nice little paunch too.'

'Seriously! There is nothing wrong with Jack! And there is nothing wrong with me either… I'm exactly the same size I've always been.'

'That's right, Phoebe, you are…' Martha said in the careless tone she used when she wanted to have the last word without an argument. Phoebe decided it wasn't worth pursuing. But she did make another mental note to get on the bathroom scales later.

'If we're going for Sunday lunch, can he bring Maria?' Phoebe asked.

'I don't see why not,' Hugh remarked. It earned him a glare from his wife.

'It's our first meeting,' Martha said.

'And she's his daughter. If you're meeting him you might as well meet her too. It makes sense.'

'I suppose she could. The restaurant's not terribly child friendly, though.'

'She's a good girl. I'm sure it'll be no bother. And it will make it much easier for Jack as he won't have to find a babysitter.'

'Doesn't he have his parents? And *her* mother…'

By *her*, Phoebe knew that she was referring to Rebecca, Maria's mother. For some reason best not questioned, Martha had always referred to her that way, even though the poor woman had died when Maria was born.

'He does. But he doesn't like to keep asking them. He doesn't want to be the sort of dad who is always dumping his child on others; he's very hands-on.'

Hugh waggled a spatula at his wife. 'You can't argue with that.' He bent back to his range, prising a burger up to examine the underside. Phoebe let out a silent gasp as his beard came perilously close to going up in flames too. He moved away again and her heart regained its proper rhythm. She hoped that he would hurry up and finish cooking; she didn't think her nerves could take much more. 'He sounds like a decent fella to me.'

'He is,' Phoebe said. 'I know you'll like him when you meet him.'

Martha didn't look convinced but she said nothing. Then she leapt up and looked at her watch. 'Josh!' she squeaked and ran to the house. A moment later she returned with her iPad. 'He said he would Skype us at eight,' she said by way of explanation, propping the iPad up on its case and placing it on the table in front of her. She folded her arms and stared at the blank screen, as if waiting for it to perform some miracle.

'He didn't mean eight on the dot.' Phoebe sent an exasperated glance in the direction of her dad, who grinned.

'I don't want to miss him.'

'Turn the sound up and you'll definitely hear it ring…' Phoebe reached across to do the honours, but her mother wrenched it back again.

'I'll miss him if you start fiddling!'

Phoebe blew out an impatient breath and just as she did, the screen flashed up a FaceTime message. Phoebe shifted her chair to get a better view and Hugh peered over from his station tending the mountain of burgers and sausages he was incinerating.

Josh's face appeared on the screen, the picture blocky and delayed, but Phoebe's heart leapt at the sight. No matter how used she was to his absence she still got excited when she saw him. People had often remarked on their similarity – with a wig and make-up, he could almost be Phoebe's double. Sometimes she wondered how her dad, a huge hairy ale-supping Yorkshireman could have sired such a petite and feminine looking man, but Phoebe knew that he was hugely proud and loved his son fiercely, their physical differences never having been an issue. Hugh's grin was as wide as everyone else's as Josh gave them a cheery wave.

'G'day!' he quipped.

Phoebe rolled her eyes. 'You've never said that before.'

'How's it going?' Josh asked.

'We're all good,' Martha squeaked, beaming at her son. 'What's the weather like there?'

'You've never said that before either,' Phoebe cut in. Martha frowned at her in a good natured way. Nothing could detract from the pleasure of seeing her firstborn, even if it wasn't in the flesh.

'Your sister has a new boyfriend,' Hugh boomed from behind them. He always did this, as if somehow he might be heard in Australia without the aid of modern technology.

'Dad!!!!' Phoebe groaned. 'I'm sure he doesn't need to know about that!'

'Course I do,' Josh said amiably. 'I hope he's a saint though, coz he'll need to be to take you on.'

'Shut up, weed,' Phoebe fired back. Josh stuck his tongue out and grinned. Phoebe's heart did a little dance, all the old feelings of sisterly love and affection rushing back. She just wished she could throw her arms around him in a huge hug.

The conversation turned to people Josh had met recently, how the weather was (hot, as always) and what animals had been spotted roaming his garden (a cassowary, snakes of various descriptions and a very curious koala) and then Phoebe, Hugh and Martha shared their own version of the same events, where the people were rather less interesting and the wild-life rather more tame (wagtails, squirrels, and next door's *bloody shit-filled cat*). Before they knew it, an hour had gone and the connection began to break up. Phoebe promised to try to visit this year as they said their goodbyes, as she did every time she spoke to him. But the day when she'd have enough money to get there seemed a very long way off indeed.

⚜   ⚜   ⚜

The Bargeman was a cosy place – dark wood panelling and sumptuous wallpaper, large windows looking out over a pretty canal populated by colourful, renovated barges with romantic names like *The Rosie Lee* and *Gypsy Elena*. The pub itself was very traditional, some might say a little old-fashioned, but there was no doubting the warm, welcoming atmosphere of the place.

Maria diligently chased a roast potato around her plate, tongue poking out of the side of her mouth as she concentrated on the task. Jack watched with a smile.

'Are you sure you don't need help with that?' he asked.

Maria looked up and shook her head. Then she bent to her plate again. It was easy to see why she was having so much trouble – apart from a miniscule slice of turkey and a lone chunk of carrot there was little else around to hold it in place. Martha had raised her eyebrows when Phoebe returned from the hotplates with Maria and her almost empty plate. She knew her mother hated the idea that someone had paid perfectly good money for what amounted to nothing, but was thankful that this time Martha had kept her opinions to herself.

'She's a bright spark,' Hugh said to Jack as he watched Maria. It was the fourth time he had made exactly the same remark.

'She is,' agreed Jack, as he had done three times before. He threw his daughter a fond glance. 'And she absolutely loves Phoebe. I'm so lucky that they get along like a house on fire.'

'It was a house on fire that brought us together,' Phoebe laughed.

Jack grinned. 'Not quite but almost. Lucky for me you got a defective Christmas gift for my little girl; we'd never have met again otherwise.'

'I think Maria had ideas of her own on that score,' Phoebe replied. 'I'm sure she'd have found a way to arrange it.'

If Maria heard her name being mentioned, she didn't show it. She seemed thoroughly engrossed in attempting to cut her turkey with the wrong side of the knife.

'So... Jack,' Martha turned to him. 'Phoebe tells us you work for yourself.'

Jack nodded as he swallowed a mouth full of green beans. 'Web design. I'm not overrun with work but I do ok. As long as things tick over I don't mind that. While Maria is young I want to be around for her as much as I can.'

Hugh nodded his approval. 'I wish I'd been around a bit more for the kids when they were young. Always something to do, though: overtime at the plant, DIY in the house, that sort of thing. You always think it's so important but the next thing they're all grown up and you realise it didn't matter at all.'

'You worked long hours?' Jack asked.

Hugh nodded. 'Things calmed down when I got promoted off the assembly line but by the time that happened it was too late and my babies had flown the nest.'

'It does rush by,' Martha agreed.

'HUGH!' A voice thundered across the restaurant, making them all snap their heads round in surprise.

Phoebe's dad broke into a broad grin. 'Geraint! You big lump, what are you doing here?'

Geraint ambled over. Looking at his plate, groaning with a tottering pile of meat and potatoes and not the ghost of a vegetable to be seen, it was pretty obvious what he was doing. A plan to single-handedly exacerbate third world hunger, break the world record for most gravy sucked up in one go, embarrass Phoebe by making some inappropriate comment that would reveal how much he fancied her, possibly introduce Maria to some choice new swearwords... any of the above would probably fit the bill. As Jack stared wonderingly at the human mountain before him, Phoebe wanted to slide under the table and hide until he was gone. She prayed that her dad wouldn't do anything stupid like invite Geraint to–

'Come on, lad,' Hugh said, 'pull up a chair and join us!'

Phoebe swallowed the groan in her throat. She wanted to throw the salt cellar at her dad's head.

Geraint's gaze ran over the party. He seemed to do a little mental calculation as it rested on Phoebe for a moment, and then on Jack, and then back again.

'I wouldn't want to intrude,' he said. For once, Phoebe was impressed by his gallantry and perception of the situation. Maybe he wasn't such a big Muppet after all. Geraint continued, 'I just wanted to say hello. Didn't think it would be right not to.'

'Quite right, lad. After all, you'll be shooting me next time I see you.' Hugh let out a huge roar of a laugh and Geraint joined in.

'I thought I might disembowel you or something this time. I'm a bit bored of gunning folks down.'

Just as Hugh was about to throw a witty remark back, there was a splutter from across the table and Jack started to choke. Phoebe looked around in alarm as Maria leapt up on her chair and hammered on his back. Phoebe poured a glass of water and shoved it into his hand as he became redder. It was all Jack could do to get any of the water to stay in his mouth with the force of Maria's blows, and he couldn't speak to communicate that she should stop.

The next moments were a blur. Geraint dropped his enormous plate to the table and hauled Jack from his chair. Martha let out a squeal of horror as Geraint flung Jack around, wrapped two gargantuan arms around his midriff and began to squeeze the life from him in violent bursts. It was possible that he was performing the Heimlich manoeuvre but it was a pretty safe bet that nobody present in the restaurant that day had ever seen it done with such misguided zeal. Jack's arms flailed madly as Geraint pummelled him. Maria wailed as she watched; Hugh was open-mouthed and dumbstruck, while Phoebe and her mother bellowed instructions to put Jack down that Geraint completely ignored. Other diners were now staring at the commotion and wondering what to do as Jack gasped and Geraint squeezed. Some dialled for ambulances while others took surreptitious photos. At some point during the next twenty-four hours, it was likely that a video featuring violent man-love would be going viral. A chef from the carvery hotplate came hurrying over, at which point, a particularly gristly chunk of beef flew from Jack's mouth and hit the unfortunate chef square in the eye.

'That's got it!' Geraint said, releasing his grip on Jack and wiping sweat from his brow. 'Better?'

Jack nodded mutely, a hand to his throat. The chef stared at each of Phoebe's party in turn, shook his head in wonderment, and made his escape. Geraint, meanwhile, tipped an imaginary hat to Phoebe and Martha, retrieved his plate and sauntered through the crowd to his own table as if nothing had happened. 'See you next month for a bit of blood and gore!' he called as he went.

Hugh gave a tiny nod while Jack took his seat with a slight whimper.

'One of your re-enactors?' he asked in a hoarse voice.

'He is,' Hugh replied, taking a huge glug of ale.

'I don't think he needs weapons. He could tear a man limb from limb.'

By this point Maria had thrown her arms around Jack, her face buried in his shoulder and sobbing noisily.

'Daddy's alright,' Jack said, stroking her hair and pulling her into his arms. 'There's no need to get upset.'

'Oh my God, Jack! Are you alright?' Phoebe squeaked. 'What on earth happened?'

'Went down the wrong hole. It would have come up, I'm sure.'

'It came up alright,' Hugh said, taking another massive swig of his drink.

'I really thought you were going to get carted off in an ambulance,' Phoebe said.

'That was all a bit embarrassing really, wasn't it? Talk about an introduction we won't forget in a hurry.' Jack gave a rueful smile.

Hugh suddenly erupted into hearty laughter. 'Aye lad, this is one Sunday lunch we won't forget for a long time to come!'

⚜ ⚜ ⚜

Maria seemed back to her normal self as Jack closed the front door and she raced upstairs to stow away the new pink pony Martha had given her to add to her collection. Phoebe thought it a lovely gesture on her mum's part. Martha Clements seemed to disapprove of many things and voiced her opinions rather too vociferously at times, but underneath it all, she was kind and sweet. That she had been out and bought Maria a gift for their first meeting (and had even chosen a moment when Phoebe was not in work so that the question of the staff discount would not arise) had touched her and made her very proud of her mum. The fact that Martha had behaved herself too and not aired any embarrassing views was an added bonus. One thing was certain as far as Maria was concerned, the new toy and the half gallon of ice-cream she had consumed in place of any actual food meant that Jack's choking drama was well and truly forgotten.

Jack draped an arm around Phoebe's shoulder as they stood in the hallway and watched her go. 'It wasn't too bad in the end, was it?'

'Apart from the fact that you nearly choked to death? I suppose it wasn't. All those weeks of worrying for nothing, eh?'

'Do you think they approve of me?'

'I do...' Phoebe smiled. 'I knew they would.'

'I thought... you know... with me having a child... well... some people can be funny about it, can't they?'

'In your circumstances I don't know how anyone could hold that against you.' Phoebe put her mother's initial reservations firmly out of her mind and resolved never to mention them to Jack.

'So, they like us?'

'Definitely. Although I'm sure the thing with Geraint helped.'

'Really?'

'You'd have to love a man who endured an assault like that and didn't press charges.'

'A man that size?' Jack rubbed absently at his throat as if reliving the event. 'I wouldn't dare press charges in case I met him afterwards in a dark alley. I'd have to go into a witness protection programme just for sneezing in his direction...'

'Ah, he's just a big, cuddly grizzly bear really. Dad's known him for years. Besides... I have a lot to thank him for right now. I don't know what I would have done if you'd properly choked.'

In a swift movement, Jack pressed her up against the wall, his nose touching hers as he gazed into her eyes. 'Are you saying you'd miss me?'

'Maybe... only a little bit... for getting rid of spiders and stuff...' she giggled.

'Is that all?' He gave her a kiss that took her breath away.

'You make good cakes too.'

He smiled and kissed her again. 'I feel as though we've reached a milestone today... y'know?'

'Kiss me again while I think about that,' Phoebe whispered.

He obliged, the delicate skill of his touch setting her nerve ends alight. It was all she could do to stop herself dragging him through to the sofa and ripping his clothes off. 'You're going to save me some of that for when we're alone later?' she asked.

'What the lady wants the lady gets.' He kissed her lightly on the nose.

'What the lady wants right now she can't have. But I'll settle for a cup of coffee until later.'

'Come on, bossy.' Jack laughed and took her hand to lead her to the kitchen. She flopped into a chair at the table while he filled the kettle.

'Seriously, though, I'm glad that's over.' Phoebe leaned on the table as she watched him spoon instant coffee into two mugs, chin resting on her fist. 'We just need to do your parents now and then we can relax.'

'Yeah…' Jack's reply trailed to nothing.

'So…' Phoebe continued, 'when shall we do it?'

'Do you want something with this? I mean, I have syrup if you want it flavouring or anything.'

'No, I'm good. Plain coffee is fine.' She waited for him to reply.

'When shall we do your parents?' she asked again.

'Soon…' he hesitated, 'there's stuff going on at the moment…'

'But they know about me. Even your uncle does. Don't they want to meet me? Aren't they a bit interested?' Phoebe frowned. 'My parents wanted to meet you right away. It was the first thing they asked when I told them I was seeing someone.'

'The difference is that you didn't mention me to them at all for months. I hardly think you can have a go at me.'

'I'm not… of course I'm not. Jack… I didn't mean…'

'I know.' He let out a heavy sigh. 'We'll do it. I want them to meet you and love you just like I do, it's just…'

'What?'

'Mum's kinda protective.'

'Of Maria?'

'Partly. And of Rebecca too.'

'Oh, I see.'

'It's hard to understand, I know. My mum adored her. She was devastated when Rebecca died. It was like she'd lost her own daughter, and she's still very close to Rebecca's mum too. I think she has this weird idea that she'd be betraying her or something, if she let someone else into her heart.'

Phoebe wondered about a woman who didn't want her son to move on and be happy rather than spend his whole life mourning. 'But Rebecca died five years ago...'

'I know. I'm sure it feels odd to you that I've learned how to deal with it and my mother hasn't. I just don't know if she's ready to accept a replacement.'

'I'm not trying to replace her.'

'I'm sorry, that didn't come out right. I know you're not. Listen... I'm being an idiot. I'm sure it'll be fine.'

'Archie will have told them bits about me, won't he?' Phoebe mused. 'So I won't be a complete shock?'

Jack's expression darkened. Phoebe felt the ground shift uncomfortably beneath her. If the conversation about his mum was difficult enough, further discussion of his brother promised to be a minefield. Perhaps it was best avoided at this point.

But fate had other ideas. Jack's phone buzzed in his pocket. He pulled it out and glowered at the screen.

'Alright?' he asked as he swiped the screen and took the call. It didn't sound as if he cared much about the welfare of the caller.

Phoebe could hear the distant murmur of another voice at the other end of the line but couldn't make out the words. Jack's were clear enough though.

'No, absolutely not! If mum finds out... this is not funny anymore...' Jack glanced at Phoebe. 'Hang on...' He made his way to the kitchen door. 'Sorry,' he said to Phoebe, 'I'll be back in a minute.'

She heard the living room door slam and then his voice instantly muffled.

With a feeling somewhere between anxiety and irritation, Phoebe made a snap decision. She hurried through to the hallway and pressed her ear to the living room door.

Jack's voice was low and tense. 'This can't keep happening. You're going to break mum's heart when she finds out.' Phoebe listened, her brow contracted into an involuntary frown. 'No!' Jack continued. 'That's absolutely not going to happen...'

She was distracted by a noise from the stairs. Maria stood on the third step looking down at her.

'Shhh,' Phoebe raced up with a finger to her lips, embarrassed that she'd been caught, even though Maria probably didn't understand that anything untoward was going on. 'What do you need, sweetie?'

'Where's Daddy?'

'He's on the phone... do you want a drink? I can make you a hot chocolate.'

Maria shook her head.

'Want to play a game?'

'Tag?'

'I'm a bit too full to play tag. How about I spy?'

Maria nodded and followed Phoebe to the kitchen.

'Right then...' Phoebe said as they sat down, 'I spy with my little eye, something beginning with... T.'

Whilst Maria went through a list of everything in the kitchen, regardless of what letter it began with, Phoebe's thoughts whirled. She only half listened, more concerned with the drama unfolding in the living room and frustrated that she still couldn't get to the bottom of it.

'Table!' Maria yelled, interrupting her thoughts.

'Sorry?'

'Table!' Maria repeated with a sigh. 'I said it three times.'

'I'm sorry; I was in my own little dream world.' Phoebe smiled. 'Table is right. You're too good for me at this game.'

'My turn now... I spy with my little eye, something beginning with... um... light!'

'Hmmmm, is it light?' Phoebe laughed.

Maria giggled. Then Jack appeared at the kitchen door.

'Sorry about that. Everything ok?'

Phoebe nodded silently, trying to gauge his mood. He looked about as far from relaxed and happy as it was possible to look. Phoebe had never seen a man

143

cry but she was afraid she was about to. She glanced at Maria, who seemed to sense the tension too as her giggles evaporated.

'Are you feeling poorly, daddy?'

'I'm fine, spud.'

Phoebe couldn't agree less, but knew that now wasn't the time. In fact, she wondered whether she ought to get Maria out of the way for a while and let him pull himself together. She didn't have children of her own, but she had learned pretty quickly over the last few months that they sensed with unsettling ease when something was really wrong and could be affected by it too.

'Hey, Maria...' she said. 'How do you fancy a go on the swings in the park?'

Maria's troubled expression brightened. 'Yes! Now?'

'Sure, why not now? Get your coat and shoes on and we'll go.'

Maria raced out to get ready.

'There's no need...' Jack began, but Phoebe held a hand up.

'I think there is. Besides, I could do with some air.'

He looked as though he might argue for a moment, and then gave her a strained smile. 'Thanks. Don't be out too long; Maria needs a bath ready for school tomorrow.'

'An hour, tops. If you need me I have my phone.'

'I don't deserve you,' Jack said.

'Damn right,' Phoebe smiled. 'There is one thing though...'

'Yeah?'

'When you've pulled yourself together I want to know what's going on.'

'There's no point in dragging you into it.'

'I'm already in it. We're together now; you shouldn't have to muddle through everything alone.'

He let out a long sigh. 'You're right. I've been single for so long that I've forgotten how to share my life with someone else.'

'So I get to hear it?'

'Yes. Although you might wish you hadn't asked when you do.'

❧   ❧   ❧

Like a whippet on race day, Maria tore across the playground. Apart from the two of them, there were only three other families making use of the facilities and a small gang of sullen looking teens showing off to each other on skateboards across the far end. Phoebe was a little surprised to see it so empty on a Sunday afternoon, but there was a newer, bigger playground across the other side of town and perhaps people who had transport preferred to take their children there. She watched Maria clamber up the steps to the slide as she jogged to catch up. 'Be careful!' she shouted. 'Your dad won't let me bring you again if you end up like Humpty Dumpty!'

'I'm ok,' Maria replied. In her haste to get to the top of the steps her arms and legs flailed madly; she looked like a stranded octopus trying to get back to the sea. 'Look at me!' she cried at the top before throwing herself down the slide at terrifying speed. She arrived safely at the bottom, but Phoebe didn't think her heart would take another round of that. Maria simply grinned with manic glee and ran for the steps again.

'How about I push you on the swings?' Phoebe called, stopping Maria in her tracks.

'Ok!' Maria raced off again, this time her head narrowly missed by the feet of a kid on the big swings, his legs outstretched as he swooped back and forth.

'Jesus!' Phoebe muttered with her heart in her mouth. It was the first time Jack had given her sole charge of his daughter and Phoebe wasn't sure she ever wanted the responsibility again. It was a lot scarier than she'd thought it would be. In fact, she'd seen less scary brawls in the pub she used to work in as barmaid.

At the smaller swings, Maria grasped a chain and tried to haul herself up into the seat as Phoebe made a panicked dash to assist her. 'If you'd waited I could have helped,' she said as she eased Maria into the safety seat.

'I was ok,' Maria squeaked. 'High, Phoebe; I want to go high!'

'I bet you do. Not too high or you'll fly up into the clouds and get carried off by a bird.'

Maria giggled. 'Silly!'

'No I'm not. It's a true thing that can happen.'

Maria's eyes widened for a moment as she looked back at Phoebe. But then she grinned as she saw that Phoebe was unable to keep her face straight.

'Higher, Phoebe!'

'You are demanding, aren't you? I bet you wear your daddy out every day.'

'Mostly I'm at school.'

'True. But when you're at home.'

'The grannies help him.'

'True too.'

'You help too.'

'Not so much,' Phoebe laughed. She paused. There was another question she wanted to ask and she had a feeling that Maria would give her a more honest answer than Jack would do later. But she knew it wasn't fair to ask. It wouldn't be right to pry and manipulate, to put a little girl in that position. But then again, if the little girl in question didn't know she was being put in a position...

'Does Archie come to your house a lot?'

'Sometimes,' Maria said.

'Does he talk to Daddy when you're not allowed to listen?'

'Sometimes,' she repeated. 'If I'm just watching telly they talk. Then I can't hear the telly very well but Daddy doesn't hear when I tell him so I just watch the pictures until Archie has gone.'

Phoebe nodded, deep in thought as she slowed the swing.

'High again!' Maria cried.

Phoebe yanked it to a halt. 'Let's see the ducks first. Then we'll come back to the swing afterwards.' She wouldn't get Maria's full concentration whilst she was whooshing up and down.

Maria looked uncertain for a moment but then relented. 'Ok.'

'So... what do Daddy and Archie talk about when you can't hear the telly?' Phoebe lifted Maria clear of the bars on the swing seat and they began to stroll towards a rubble-strewn ditch that passed as a pond in these parts. Council funds were being splashed around in Millrise in an attempt to make it a place that tourists and day-trippers might like to stop off at, but it obviously hadn't reached as far as here. There wouldn't be a team from *Spring Watch* stopping by any time soon, but the ducks were entertaining enough for someone young enough to use their imagination.

Maria shrugged in answer to Phoebe's question and reached for her hand. Phoebe was at once touched and surprised by the gesture. She'd never be Maria's mum, but when she reflected on their blossoming relationship it gave her a warm feeling to imagine that she might become something close one day. Who knew what the future held, or how things would work out, but for the first time since meeting Jack and Maria, Phoebe felt that she might like to embrace motherhood in all its terrifying glory. She wondered what it would be like to hold a new, tiny world of possibilities in her arms, a brand new life.

Maria's voice interrupted her thoughts. 'They talk about money and they talk about Archie's college and they talk about bookies.'

'Do you mean books?'

'I don't know. Daddy just tells Archie to stop going in them. He says all Archie's friends in there are bad.'

'What else does he say?'

'That I can't tell granny.'

'About Archie?'

'Yes. About the bookies.'

Was this all about gambling? It sounded the most likely explanation. But it still didn't explain why Jack had to get so involved and why he was so stressed about it. He cared, of course, but this was more than brotherly concern.

'There's two ducks having a fight!' Maria shouted, pointing at the pond. Phoebe looked in the direction of her outstretched arm. She didn't know much about ducks but it looked like a male and a female to her and what they were doing certainly didn't look like fighting.

'They'll stop in a minute,' Phoebe said, hoping sincerely that they would. There was something deeply unsettling about animals getting it on in full view of Sunday afternoon families. 'Is Daddy cross with Archie?' she asked in an attempt to refocus the conversation.

'Hmmm... I don't think so. He doesn't tell him off that much or say that he can't have TV time.'

'It must be alright then,' Phoebe said in a sooth-ing voice. She was suddenly struck by the worry that she might be planting anxieties in Maria's head that hadn't been there before and wouldn't be healthy for a five-year-old. Jack had considered it necessary to keep her out of things but Phoebe might be undo-ing all of his good work. 'Race you back to the play-ground!' she cried.

Maria immediately hared off, back in the direc-tion they had just come from. Phoebe gave her a good head start before she took off after, theatrically feign-ing exhaustion as she almost, but not quite, caught up. Although, by the time she had she was beginning to wish she had brought her asthma inhaler with her. Much more running and she wouldn't need to fake breathlessness.

'Oh, you're just too fast for me!' Phoebe said with a grin.

'I am fast!' Maria giggled.

Phoebe glanced at her watch. 'One more go on everything and then we'd better get back.'

'Awwww, not yet…'

'I promised your dad we wouldn't be out late. You want him to let us come out again together, don't you?' Maria gave a reluctant nod. 'We'd better not keep him waiting then,' Phoebe continued. 'You need a bath too. Personally I think you smell like pep-permints and rainbows and he's the stink bomb who needs a bath, but that's just my opinion.'

Maria clapped a hand to her mouth and giggled raucously from behind it. 'Does Daddy need a bath?'

'I think he might.'

'Will you bath me tonight, Phoebe?'

Phoebe froze, taken by surprise. 'Me?'

Maria nodded vigorously.

'I'd like that.' Phoebe smiled, that maternal warmth spreading through her again. 'I'll try to do it properly.'

'All you have to do is make bubbles on me.'

'That sounds easy enough; making bubbles is one of my favourite things.'

'YAY!' Maria raced back towards the slide. Nobody would ever be a replacement for Rebecca, and Phoebe didn't want to be, but it might be nice to be a close second.

❧ ❧ ❧

Jack was still sitting at the kitchen table, staring at his phone, when Phoebe and Maria arrived back. This time Phoebe had used her key to let them in, knowing that Jack was expecting them. He looked up with an absent smile.

'Had a nice time, spud?' he asked Maria.

'Yes! Phoebe raced me and we saw some ducks fighting and she swung me really high!'

'It wasn't nearly as eventful as it sounds,' Phoebe added.

'Can Phoebe do my bath?' Maria asked.

Jack gave her a bemused smile.

'I don't mind if you don't,' Phoebe said.

'If you're sure…'

'Of course. It'll be fine.'

'Maria…' Jack began, 'why don't you go and find your pyjamas and your hairbrush ready for Phoebe to bath you and she'll be up to run it in just a minute, ok?'

'Ok.' Maria skipped from the room. Phoebe and Jack listened to the patter of her footsteps on the stairs, before Jack spoke.

'About before…'

'Don't worry about it.'

'I was wrong not to let you in. You had every right to ask me for an explanation and I owe you that much at least. It's just that… I suppose I was ashamed.'

'Of what?'

'Of my family. I thought if I told you about Archie then we'd all look bad.'

'He can't have committed that much of a terrible crime, surely?' Phoebe asked, thinking back to what Maria had told her in the park and hoping not to slip up now. 'Besides, you're not his keeper. His actions aren't your actions. Why would anything he does affect the way I feel about you?' She forced a laugh, more to put him at ease than because she found anything remotely funny. 'Seriously, my dad pretends to kill people at the weekends so I can hardly point the finger at anyone else for their family.'

Jack gave her a weak smile. Phoebe's attempt at reassurance seemed to be working. 'What did I ever do to deserve you?'

'You were obviously very wicked in a former life.'

'Obviously.'

There was a heartbeat's pause. 'Archie has a gambling problem,' Jack said into the silence.

'It changes nothing. I want to support you if I can. Are you trying to help him? Is that what the phone calls and visits are about?'

Jack's jaw muscles twitched. 'I wish it was that simple. He doesn't want help, just money. Helping him would be a lot easier to do.'

'He asks you for money?'

'Me and anyone else. He's convinced that he's actually doing people a favour, borrowing money from them, like he's cutting them in. He thinks the next big win is just round the corner and that he'll be able to pay everyone back with handsome interest. I know he really means this, and would do it if it happened, but of course, we all know why gambling is big business. Punters hardly ever win everything back.' Jack gave a hollow laugh. 'He's so deluded it's almost funny. At least, it would be if it wasn't ripping the family apart.'

Phoebe frowned slightly. 'Do you give him money to gamble?'

'No, of course not! At least, I try not to. But he comes to me saying he's skint for this and that and I help him out with a few quid; in the end, though,

I don't know what he's doing with it when he leaves here. I suppose I'm just as guilty of feeding his addiction as he is in that respect. But I can't see him go without. I hate it, but I always cave in when he asks.' Phoebe went to him and ran her fingers gently over his hair. His eyes closed at her touch and he gave a deep sigh. 'I'm sorry…'

'Hey, stupid… you want to talk about it, I'm all ears.'

He looked up to hold her in a sorrowful gaze. 'Not tonight. I don't want to waste another precious moment thinking about it when I should be thinking about you.'

Phoebe bent down to kiss him. 'You can think about me any old time. Family is important.'

'You're important. Tonight I want to enjoy you being here and worry about everything else tomorrow. Ok?'

'If that's what you want then ok.'

❧ ❧ ❧

'Are you alright?' Phoebe glanced across at Dixon again. For the past ten minutes he had been massaging his temples and staring at his computer screen in a way that suggested he wasn't seeing what was there. He'd been distracted all morning, and Phoebe had put it down to tiredness or Monday morning blues – God knows she felt the same – but now she was quite worried.

'Hmmm?' He looked up with an absent expression.

'I was asking if you're ok. You look sort of… troubled.'

He smiled, fleetingly. 'I'm always troubled. It's working in this place.'

'Ok then, more than usual. Nothing wrong, is there? Something I can help with?'

'You're already doing a great job of helping me.' The earnest sincerity of his tone caught Phoebe by surprise. It wasn't like she'd saved him from a burning building or anything.

'Oh, I just sit here and clutter the place up,' she laughed awkwardly. 'And occasionally give you logistical headaches trying to work out how to persuade all the shop floor staff to paint their faces and wear dog ears.'

Phoebe expected Dixon's customary belly laugh, but he gave her a quiet smile and turned back to his work. She watched for a moment, uncertain whether to push for more information. But then she decided that perhaps it was something in his personal life that he needed to tackle alone, and she didn't want to pry.

Framed by the high window that slanted down the attic roof, there was a square of cornflower sky and Phoebe stared at it. Outside, the pavements would be glittering from the morning's rain, as the early summer sun bounced off them. This had always been her favourite time of year – too early to be plagued by wasps or suffocating heat, but warm enough for the gardens to start bursting with lush flowers and blossoms. Later, perhaps, she, Jack and Maria might take a picnic tea out somewhere to make the most of the warmer, longer days.

'Phoebe, I haven't been completely honest with you...' Dixon's voice put all thoughts of summer out of her head.

'What do you mean?'

'Our jobs – yours and mine – they're not safe.'

Phoebe sat back in her seat and stared at him. 'Not safe how?'

'We have to prove that there is a need for us at Hendry's. Old Mr Hendry is not convinced – never has been really – that we need PR. He thinks it's part of the *modern malady.*'

'But I thought... I mean, you've been here for years, haven't you?'

Dixon nodded. 'And PR used to be as easy as the occasional ad in the local paper and sponsoring the annual Millrise carnival. The customers came because we were here – it was as simple as that. But things have changed and life is so much tougher now. The market share is shrinking for us.'

'You told me that at the interview,' Phoebe smiled. 'I knew what I was getting into. I know you took me on to help.'

'And you're doing a fantastic job.'

Phoebe felt a little kick of pride and excitement deep inside. She had certainly hoped to prove herself and to hear that she was doing that was a real boost.

'I'm just afraid that it might be too little too late,' Dixon added.

In a cartoon, Phoebe would have seen her fluffy dream balloon pop in the air above her. She eyed him silently, not sure what she should ask next and even less sure that she wanted to hear the answer.

'Hendry's is in trouble,' Dixon continued. 'They have been for a while now. Only a few people know. Adam is here to help his father try and pull things round and part of his plan is to step up on the PR and see what that can do for us. There are other things in place... things that haven't yet been implemented because they would be a last resort and nobody wants to see them happen. Mr Hendry may seem reserved and aloof, but he cares deeply about his staff and this store. Not only that, but making redundancies sends out very bad signals, and rats are first off a sinking ship.'

Phoebe shook her head slowly, trying to digest all that he was telling her.

'Shareholders,' Dixon clarified. 'Nobody wants to be stuck with a load of worthless shares.'

The conversation was taking Phoebe into unfamiliar territory. She had always been somewhere around the bottom rung where jobs were concerned – in fact, she was often holding the ladder up – and had never needed to think about decisions at the top end. But she could see the logic in what Dixon was saying. She certainly understood the new pressure of responsibility it transferred to her.

'So we have to get results here?' Phoebe asked, although the answer was obvious.

'You're doing so well already. Adam is delighted with what you've done so far, and so am I.'

Phoebe wondered when Adam and Dixon had been having their cosy chats because she certainly hadn't seen them. Had they deliberately waited for times when she wasn't in the office? What else had they said about her and her role in all of this? What, exactly, were they expecting of her. She wanted to ask but for some reason the question wouldn't come out.

'Not well enough, though,' she said. 'We have to get more people in. Lots more?'

'And it has to be a sustainable market, not just one-offs.'

Phoebe leaned her elbows on the table and fiddled with a lock of hair tugged free from her ponytail. 'What do you think? Where do you think our best chances lie?'

'If I had to, I'd put money on your costume department. But you'd need to bring people in from further afield than Millrise to make it work and that's the problem. Our town simply isn't big enough for a strand of the business as specialised as that in the long-term, but I do believe there is money in it... according to my research, anyway.'

Phoebe nodded. 'I know there is. People spend hundreds on outfits for conventions and it's not only one every now again – they go back two or three times a year to different ones, year in, year out. We just have to get those people coming here. How about a big internet push? That's a really good way of getting the message wide.'

'Yes, but it's also full of competition from established suppliers, people with lower overheads who can undercut accordingly; likewise sellers from countries like China who can cut out the middle man and sell directly at little more than cost price straight from the factory. We have to give people a reason to come to us, a unique selling point, some edge that makes customers seek us out – either online or in person. If we can give them that we'll have them.'

Phoebe was thoughtful for a moment. Dixon really had done his research – he already knew the cosplay market far better than she did. 'I was planning to go out to some conventions and mingle – talk to stallholders and attendees, hand out leaflets, that sort of thing. But if I do that we'll need have to have the stock in when they come to look and it would have to be a good enough selection to impress them enough to come back and bring their friends too. And I think it needs to be a fun experience, shopping here, so that they can't wait to get back for their next purchase,' Phoebe replied, airing the thoughts as they ran through her head.

'I'll speak to Adam about the stock if you finalise some ideas. I was thinking I could use my contacts at the *Echo* to drum up some local interest too, which means we'll need to come up with a story angle good enough to make it worth their while.'

'What if I could get some big stunt going on, something that would pull big crowds? Maybe we'd even get media interest bigger than the *Echo*?'

Dixon smiled, looking like his old self for the first time that morning. 'We should brainstorm this; see what we can come up with.'

'I know just the person. One of the girls on the shop floor is as crazy and fun as they come and she's really into this scene. It might help us to bounce ideas off her.'

'Your friend with the purple hair?'

Phoebe nodded.

'I don't see why not. If she can bring in some valuable ideas then I'm in. To be honest, right now, if your budgie had some good ideas I'd be in.'

'Sadly I don't have a budgie. Although there is a particularly bright looking pigeon I sometimes talk to on the roof...'

Dixon laughed. 'I feel better already. I'm so glad I have you working with me now.'

She knew it was meant to reassure her, but that made Phoebe feel even more anxious. He had put a lot of faith in her – everyone had – and now it seemed that there was more riding on her success than she had ever imagined. How was it that they had tasked a young, uneducated, inexperienced shop girl with this terrifying responsibility? Of course there were others working hard to save Hendry's, but knowing that her part in it was so much bigger than she had been aware of was enough to make her stomach turn.

Dixon, Old Mr Hendry, Adam, every member of staff down to Jeff the drunken janitor – they were all relying on her. She was terrified she would let them all down.

❧ ❧ ❧

Phoebe found Midnight sucking on a Mr Frosty in the stockroom. As her gaze fell on the open box, the various slushy making components strewn across a shelving unit, she let out a little gasp.

'It was a return, before you start lecturing me,' Midnight said. 'Want one? Won't take me a minute to whip it up.'

Phoebe frowned. 'No thanks. Aren't you supposed to box up returns and send them back to the suppliers for a refund rather than use them yourself?'

'I will,' Midnight grinned. 'Just as soon as I've had a nice refreshing frosty drink. They'll only throw it out at the factory anyway… think of it as quality control if it makes you feel better. I'm actually doing everyone a favour by trying to ascertain the nature of the fault.'

'And what is that?'

'No idea. It tastes pretty yummy to me. I may have to make another couple to get to the bottom of the mystery.'

'You're impossible, you know that? If Steve catches you you'll be in the shit.'

'Yeah, but he's got to catch me first.'

At that moment, Jeff the sometimes-Santa-janitor came past, leaning on his broom as he shoved it idly along the stockroom floor. He'd have shifted more dust if he'd gently squeezed the breath from an asthmatic ant at it. He was also sucking at a slushy that looked remarkably similar to the one Midnight was drinking. He gave Midnight a conspiratorial wink as he went past.

'What the hell…' Phoebe cried as he went on his way.

'I couldn't leave Jeff out, could I? Granted, he does look way too happy about it. I've a feeling he's given it a special kick with the contents of that bottle he keeps in his locker.'

'Bloody hell! You'll get shot if that comes out!' Phoebe was beginning to have serious doubts about involving Midnight in her plans. Whilst her friend was creative and lively, she could also be unreliable and unpredictable and there was way too much at stake. On the other hand, this was exactly the sort of task Midnight needed, to distract her from her more subversive pursuits. Either way, Phoebe was committed now, and she needed Midnight's knowledge and left-field thinking to make it work.

'How are you fixed for helping me and Dixon out?'

'With what?'

'Some ideas for the new cosplay department.'

'Cool! So they're going for it? I never thought I'd see the day when old Hendry embraced the twenty-first century. He'll be coming to work in a cap next and calling everyone dude.'

'It's only approved in principle and we have to make it look good enough for them to finance it… there's not a lot to spare in the budget…' Phoebe trailed off. How much could she tell Midnight about what she knew of Hendry's financial problems? It was probably better to say as little as possible.

'That much is obvious,' Midnight said nonchalantly.

'It is?'

'Everyone's talking about it. They say we're going under.'

'Where has that rumour come from?'

Midnight shrugged. 'Where does any rumour come from? They're rumours – nobody knows whether they're true or not.'

'Well, I haven't heard it and I work upstairs in the offices.'

'Yeah, you'd generally be the last to know.'

Phoebe reflected on the irony of that for a moment. Did everyone else really know what Dixon had told her in confidence? It was just like her to miss something that big going on right under her nose.

Midnight slurped at her drink. 'Ok, so what do you need from me?'

Phoebe shook herself. 'Your nerdy sci-fi brain.'

'Most people want my body but hey, it's your party. Want me to dress up again?'

'More… much more. How about we and go find Steve and tell him your services are required upstairs? I'll treat you to a working lunch; we might be a couple of hours, though.'

'We can be as long as you want; it's all the same to me.'

'Brilliant! Finish that drink and destroy the evidence, please, you're going to give me a heart attack!'

⚜   ⚜   ⚜

'Don't ask me to be your Batman.' Jack clasped Phoebe's hand as they watched Maria run ahead down the path. The park was buzzing with people enjoying the evening sun. There was a slight chill in the air but with her cardigan pulled tight and Jack by her side Phoebe felt cosy enough. The sun was slipping down the sky at the far side of the manmade lake that was the crowning glory of the park. Jack led Phoebe to a seat on the newly-built viewing platform that overlooked the water while Maria raced to the railings to look at a crowd of ducks that had gathered below with their fluffy ducklings.

'Don't lean over too far,' Jack called.

'Have you seen all these baby ducks?' Maria squeaked.

'We'll come and look in a minute,' Jack smiled.

Phoebe leaned over and kissed him. 'I wouldn't subject you to that humiliation. That's what Midnight is best at.'

'The inimitable Midnight... one of these days you'll have to bring her over.'

'I would, but I'm not sure you'd ever get over the trauma.'

'So, you're planning a street party? Is that what it is?'

'Not a party exactly. It's more of a launch event. But we don't have enough security to keep track of everyone if we hold it in the store so we're doing it outside on the street.'

'Won't they want to go in to buy the clothes?'

Phoebe nodded. 'We've got that covered with a special stall we're setting up outside where the fun is.'

'Right...You're going to dress up?'

Phoebe laughed. 'Not if I can help it. We've got a load of cosplayers to help out and mingle with the crowds and we're going to encourage as many guests as possible to come along in costume. The more people get into the spirit of things the more fun it will be and the bigger splash we'll make.'

'You really think people will go for this? Don't these cosplay types only go along to conventions where they can meet celebrities?'

'Midnight seems to think it will be ok. It's not really a convention as such, anyway, more of a fancy dress party. If they're all like Midnight they won't be able to resist the opportunity to wander around town in costume, especially if the television cameras come as we're hoping they will. I just hope the weather holds. And I thought we could give away some prizes and have special offers for extra encouragement, things that won't be on offer afterwards. We'll have food and drink too.'

'Are you worried about what will happen if people don't come?'

Phoebe shot him a sideways look and raised her eyebrows. 'Proper little ray of sunshine today, aren't you?' Jack grinned. 'Of course I'm terrified but I was trying not to think about how dead my career will be if I spend huge chunks of Hendry's money on a complete flop.'

'Sorry… it's just that I know how stressed you get about things.'

'Jack…' Phoebe paused. There was no harm in sharing what she knew with Jack, was there? 'Hendry's is in trouble. I have to do what I can to save it. If that means taking some risks, well… I suppose I don't have a choice.'

'Hendry's is in trouble? Like financial?'

Phoebe nodded.

'Mum always said she wondered how they stayed open. But they've always been there and I can't imagine Millrise without them.' He wrapped an arm around her shoulder and pulled her close. 'If you need any help with the internet or social media, I'm all yours.'

'Thank you. I might just take you up on that. I don't suppose you know anyone famous while you're at it, do you?'

'Sorry. Not unless you count the goalie for Millrise United.'

'Maybe not. And you're quite sure you don't want to come along and dress up for me?'

He pulled her closer. 'I can dress up for you but it would have to be in the privacy of a locked bedroom.' Phoebe giggled. 'I bet Maria would love a huge dressing up party, though. I assume it's going to be family friendly?'

'Definitely. I'll probably have to have a word with Midnight about covering up her cleavage…'

Jack chuckled as Maria came racing over.

'Come and see the ducks now!' She grabbed Jack's hand and tugged at him to get up from his seat.

'Alright, alright… I'm coming.'

'You too, Phoebe!' Maria squeaked. 'Come and see.'

'Ok, Miss Bossy. I don't know how you still have so much energy after a full day at school.'

'I'm not tired at all.'

'I can see that.'

Jack and Phoebe followed Maria to the railings, and all three gazed across the sun-dappled water as the little duck families that had got Maria so excited traversed the lake leaving gleaming trails in their wake.

'So you're coming then?' Phoebe asked Jack as they peered over.

'Where?'

'To the launch, silly!'

'Oh, yeah,' Jack laughed. 'Of course. I'd be crazy to miss a night like that, especially if my clever girlfriend is organising it.'

'You'll have VIP tickets, of course.'

He lowered his voice and leaned into her. 'Does that mean I get to kiss and fondle the organiser?'

'I don't think Dixon is into blokes.'

Jack erupted into laughter and planted a kiss on Phoebe's lips.

'That one's lost!' Maria cried, cutting short their banter.

Jack looked over. 'I don't think so, spud. See... there he goes after his mummy.'

'Are Granny and Granddad coming over? I heard you on the phone.'

'Not tonight. But maybe for dinner at the weekend,' Jack glanced at Phoebe as he spoke. He hesitated, seeming to weigh up the outcome of his next sentence. Or maybe Phoebe was imagining the reticence in his voice when he did finally speak again. 'Maybe you'd like to join us? Unless you have plans at the weekend... seeing your own parents or something... which I would totally understand...'

'No...' Now that the moment had presented itself she suddenly wasn't sure she wanted it after all. His parents obviously had a great deal of influence on Jack's life and their opinions could make or break his and Phoebe's relationship. Jack had already said how devoted his mother was to Rebecca. How could Phoebe live up to such irredeemable perfection?

Rebecca could never again lose her temper, utter an ill-advised word, accidentally snub, irritate or incite anger. The longer she was gone the more saintly her memory became. It was crazy to be this jealous of a dead woman but Phoebe was finding it very hard not to be. She felt she was insulting Rebecca's memory simply by existing. And she knew the feelings Jack's mother had were only natural. Phoebe was fiercely protective of her memories of Vik in much the same way.

All these thoughts ran through her head in a matter of seconds. But another, overriding thought took their place. If she was to have any future with Jack they had to get this hurdle out of the way. Whether they did it sooner or later would make no difference. She forced a bright smile.

'Sounds great. I'd love to come.'

He leaned across and kissed her. 'They'll love you, I know they will.'

Phoebe could see the lie in his beautiful eyes. He was less certain than she was of the outcome but she had to be grateful for the encouragement all the same.

⚜   ⚜   ⚜

The dress joined the others on the bed – a rapidly growing pile. Phoebe glanced at the clock again. She had allowed herself an hour to get ready but had already wasted half that precious time trying to decide what to wear. Every time she thought she was happy, she scrutinised her look in the mirror and decided that her choice of outfit was dreadful after all.

In only her most demure bra and knickers (somehow, having even slightly sexy undies on felt wrong, as though Jack's parents would know) Phoebe stood at the open wardrobe doors and worked down the rail one more time. Her style was nowhere near as wild as Midnight's, but conventional was not exactly her thing. Most of the dresses she owned were a little on the short side, not that she owned many, and the ones that did look halfway respectable made her feel frumpy and not herself at all. She couldn't remember why she had bought them but assumed it would have been for a family christening or birthday bash to escape the disapproving stares of her mother. Work suits were pretty much the only other option, and there was no way she was rocking up to Jack's house in a pinstripe skirt that had already had its backside worn smooth by hours spent on an office chair, visiting parents or not.

She quickly checked the clock again. The shopping centre would be keeping Sunday opening hours. Was it a crazy idea to go and buy something on the way to Jack's? She could get a taxi, dash into Next and pick up a dress, couldn't she?

Without another thought, she dialled the number of her favourite taxi firm and ordered a cab. Then she pulled on her jeans, pinned her hair into a topknot and rushed outside just as the taxi arrived.

❧ ❧ ❧

'Wow!' Jack gave a low wolf-whistle at the door. 'You look amazing.'

Phoebe was far from happy with her choice of strapless floral maxi dress and coordinating shrug, but in the circumstances felt she had made the best of a rush job. At least she looked respectable enough for Jack's parents (as long as the dress stayed up and didn't reveal she'd had to ditch her bra) and still pretty and flirty enough for Jack. His approval made her feel a little easier – at least that was one hurdle out of the way. Never again, though, would she cut a situation like this so fine; she had arrived in a second hastily-procured taxi (another small fortune) with literally moments to spare.

She handed Jack a carrier bag containing her jeans, top, and abandoned bra. 'Can you stash this somewhere for me?'

He peered inside and looked up at her with a silent question.

'Long story,' she replied, tucking a stray hair back into a bobby pin. 'Are they here?' she added in a whisper.

Jack stuffed the bag in the under-stairs cupboard – the 'glory hole' as her mother called it. 'They're in the garden with Maria,' he said. 'I thought we might do chicken and salad outside as it's such a lovely day, rather than a stuffy old roast dinner inside.'

'Is Archie here too?' Phoebe asked, wondering whether he might be at least one ally in the extended Andrews camp, even if a rather flighty one.

Jack shook his head. 'Archie doesn't do civilised family get-togethers. It's just Mum and Dad.'

'Ok… I didn't know whether I ought to bring something… I mean, I don't know what your mum likes and –'

Jack held up a hand to stop her. 'No need; it's not expected.' He took her by the shoulders and smiled down at her. 'Try not to be nervous. Just be your wonderful self and everything will be fine.' He kissed her tenderly on the forehead. 'Shall we go through and get the introductions out of the way before you explode?'

'Yes please. Exploding wouldn't make a very good first impression, would it?'

'Come on then,' Jack laughed.

Phoebe followed him through to the kitchen. The smell of roast chicken and delicate seasonings intensified as they went in. Normally, she would have been asking him questions about what he was cooking and trying to stop her stomach rumbling. It was the one talent of Jack's that everyone she knew, especially Midnight, was insanely jealous of. Midnight should have been a queen with hundreds of male slaves feeding her dates and wafting her with huge feathers all day, and acting out all her sexual fantasies at night. And she definitely should have had her own private chef, at least, according to her.

But Jack's food was the last thing on Phoebe's mind today. Her stomach flipped like a circus trapeze artist on his tenth tube of Smarties as she walked through the kitchen and towards the back door. She longed for this awkward first meeting to be over so they could all get used to one another and move to a place where, if not comfortable or particularly fond, they were at least familiar with each other.

'Ready?' Jack rested his hand on the doorknob.

'What would happen if I said no?'

'I'd shove you out there anyway,' Jack said with a smile. 'It'll be fine.' He opened the door that led out onto a slate-paved patio where there was a wooden table surrounded by chairs. The table was already laid with bright striped crockery; a wine cooler, trays of stuffed olives, artichokes, dips and breadsticks sat in the centre where they were being steadfastly ignored by the two people seated around it. Instead they were watching Maria race around the garden on a manically grinning orange space-hopper. Jack cleared his throat and they turned as one.

'Mum... Dad... this is Phoebe.'

Phoebe forced a smile. 'Hi...'

There was an immediate and swift appraisal from Jack's mother as her gaze swept Phoebe up and down. There was no mistaking the iciness of the look, or the fact that Phoebe knew from that moment she was in for a trying afternoon. She took a moment of her own to assess them both – albeit in a rather less obvious and aggressive way.

Jack's dad shared the same gentle look as his son in the same bright blue eyes, same black hair (though his dad's was thinning now), same warm smile. He looked thinner than Jack, less toned, and from his posture Phoebe guessed that he was a little shorter than his son too.

His mum had the same face shape – slightly broader and more amiable looking, although the look in her eyes was far from friendly. There was no arguing, however, that in her prime she would have been a fiercely beautiful woman. She was still attractive now – impeccably presented, her shoulder length hair straight and sleek, tinted a rich auburn, her blouse neatly buttoned into wide legged trousers that hugged her trim waist, barely a crease in them considering she was sitting relaxed in a garden chair. Phoebe wondered if she had treated them with industrial grade starch; her own dress was wilting even now and she had taken it from the shop barely half an hour earlier.

'Chicken's almost ready.' Jack clapped his hands together. 'So why don't you get to know each other while I go and sort it out?'

'D'you want some help?' Phoebe asked, hoping desperately that he would say yes.

'It's fine,' he said with a cheerful smile. 'I won't be long.'

As she watched him go back inside, there was a squeal from across the garden.

'Phoebe!' Maria raced over and threw her arms around Phoebe's waist.

'Hey, gorgeous! Having a good day?' Phoebe hugged her back, relieved to have an ally.

She gave an enthusiastic nod. 'I've been helping Daddy.'

'Well, that's good. I bet he was really glad you were here.'

'I put the plates on the table.'

Phoebe gave her a thumbs-up. 'You did a great job of that. What were you just playing?'

'Invisible horses.'

Phoebe nodded. Invisible horses. On a space hopper. Now that she thought about it any old fool could see. She grinned. 'Are you coming to talk to the grownups for a bit? You can join in while we all get to know each other.'

'Ok.'

Jack's dad spoke. 'She seems to like you.' Phoebe looked around to see him smiling at her.

'Children are very trusting,' Jack's mum remarked, crushing the sliver of hope that Phoebe might win them over after all with one concise and cutting observation. 'Come and sit down, Maria,' she added, patting her knee.

Maria obediently skipped over and clambered onto her grandmother's lap.

Feeling awkward and unwanted, Phoebe took a seat at the table.

'Jack tells us you work at the toy store in town,' his dad said.

'That's right. I used to work on the shop floor but I've recently joined the PR team.'

'Is that the scruffy place on the high street?' Carol asked.

Phoebe was a whisker away from reminding her that her own brother owned possibly the grubbiest looking fruit and veg shop she had ever seen, but simply gave a tense smile. 'There are plans to modernise it. Mr Hendry's son is training to take over and he has lots of ideas.'

'Awww, it's not that bad, Carol,' Jack's dad said. 'You spent enough hours in there with Jack when he was young and you didn't seem to mind it so much then. And just look at Fred's place; nobody complains about that.'

Phoebe wondered if he had somehow read her mind. She hoped Jack's mum couldn't do that too because her mind wasn't filled with very complimentary thoughts at that moment.

'Fred's place has character,' Carol replied coldly. 'It's an old world charm.'

'I think Hendry's has character too,' Phoebe replied, struggling to keep the argumentative tone from her voice. She could see that perhaps, in the future, Jack's dad was someone she could get along with. It was a shame he was married to a woman with all the charm of a rusty nail.

To Phoebe's immense relief, Jack appeared at the back door.

'How's it going?' He eyed all three adults, his expression betraying a certain amount of anxiety.

'Phoebe was just telling us about her work,' Jack's dad replied.

'Is the chicken ready yet?' Maria asked, her attention now drawn from the colouring book she had been leaning over while the adults were *getting to know each other.*

'Just about. Are you hungry?'

Maria nodded.

'Good, because there's tons.' Jack grinned. 'I know it was labelled in the shop as extra large but I think Jurassic Park might be missing one of its velociraptors.'

'What's one of those?' Maria asked.

'A dinosaur, spud. How do you like the idea of eating dinosaur?'

'No way, José,' Maria said, screwing her face up.

Jack burst out laughing. 'Where have you heard that saying?'

'Archie.'

Jack's laughter died. He glanced at his mum and dad but said nothing.

Jack's mum stood up. 'Let me come and help get everything to the table.'

'I'm fine, mum, I've got it all under control.'

'I insist. It's the least I can do since you've cooked everything all by yourself.'

The jibe was obviously aimed at Phoebe and it hit its mark. It also set the pattern for the rest of the afternoon. Wherever Carol could dig or snipe, or get one up on Phoebe, she grabbed the opportunity with both hands. Wherever she could squeeze in a comment about how wonderful Rebecca had been at this and that (great singing voice, lovely dress sense, A-levels coming out of her ears, Nobel peace prize, personal friend of the Dalai Lama) she made sure that the remark was delivered loud and clear. Phoebe had always been taught never to speak ill of the dead, but if Rebecca's ghostly form had appeared to them, hovering above the table with beneficent light, Phoebe was pretty sure she'd have thrown a chicken leg at her and told her to sling her heavenly hook. No matter what Phoebe did or said, how complimentary she was, how helpful, how generous, how demure, none of it was enough to stem the onslaught. Lucretia Borgia could have turned up asking Jack on a date and Phoebe suspected that Carol would have danced a jig. The plain and simple truth was that Phoebe wasn't Rebecca. She was only relieved that Jack's dad seemed more tolerant and understanding of the fact that it was possible for other women to exist on earth who weren't Rebecca and that was pretty much ok.

When the time came for them to go, Carol stood at the front door waiting, as if she expected Phoebe to leave with them. Phoebe stood by Jack's side, clearly with no intentions of going anywhere, and his mum let out a huge sigh. She seemed very reluctant to leave herself, until Jack's dad led her gently but firmly to the dark blue Saab they had parked out on the road and made her get in.

'Wow,' Phoebe said as Jack closed the front door and Maria went to tidy her colouring crayons before bath time. 'That was… interesting.'

'It went ok.'

Phoebe stared at him. He thought that had been ok? Had he been at a different meal with a different family? How could she say anything about it now? Turning over replies in her head, she realised nothing she wanted to say was remotely diplomatic enough. She was saved by Maria returning with crayons bundled in her hand and a huge flapping colouring book trying to escape from under her arm.

'Can you manage that, spud?' Jack asked. Maria nodded, her tongue poking from the corner of her mouth, and carried on up the stairs to her room. Jack turned to Phoebe. 'I'd better get madam in the bath and settled before bedtime. You want to grab a coffee and a bit of TV and then we'll talk more later?'

Phoebe nodded as he gave her a quick kiss and followed Maria up the stairs, growling and calling out her name in a monster voice which was followed by squeals and raucous giggling and the thudding of footsteps across the upstairs landing. With a sigh, she took herself back to the kitchen and switched the kettle on.

❧   ❧   ❧

With Maria tucked safely in bed, Jack came through from the kitchen with two colourful glasses.

'Mojitos…' he grinned. 'I figured we'd earned them.' He popped them down on a side-table before snuggling on the sofa next to Phoebe and reaching for the TV remote. He waggled it at Phoebe. 'Want me to switch off so we can talk?'

'She hates me,' Phoebe sighed.

'Who?'

'Your mum. She detests me.'

'She doesn't.' Jack switched off the television and pulled her close. 'She just needs time to get used to you.'

'How can she get used to me if she doesn't even want to hear me speak? It's obvious that she is determined to hate me no matter what I do.'

'It's not you… she'd be the same with any girl.'

Phoebe looked up at him. 'You told me you hadn't had a girlfriend since Rebecca died so how do you know she'd hate anyone?'

'It's just… well, Rebecca was different… Special.'

'And I'm not.' She knew it was unreasonable, she knew she sounded like a whining child, but Phoebe couldn't help the resentment in her voice.

'Of course it's not that,' he replied patiently, not a bit phased by her tone. 'But Rebecca and I… well, we'd been together since school. We started out as friends and she was always at our house from our early teens, and I suppose Mum already saw her as a daughter, even before we started dating. She had dreams of us getting married and getting, in her eyes, the perfect daughter-in-law. Losing her hit Mum hard.'

'But she has gone. No matter how much she loved Rebecca, would she see you alone for the rest of your life?'

He shrugged. 'Like I said, she just needs time. She'll come round.'

'She wouldn't even let Maria sit with me.'

Jack bit back a grin. 'I think you're more upset about that than the fact that she doesn't like you dating me.'

'So you do admit that she doesn't like me!'

'No… no. I didn't mean that.' He squeezed her shoulder and kissed her hair. 'The first, and worst, meeting is over now – think of it that way. It's got to be easier from now on, right?'

'I don't think I want to do it again.'

'At least you didn't get squished half to death by a giant in the middle of a crowded restaurant.'

'I think that would have been less painful.'

'Drama queen.'

Phoebe couldn't help a smile. But it was a grudging one. 'Don't make me do that again for at least six months.'

'Dad loved you, if it's any consolation.'

'Dads always do. It's the mums you have to do battle with. I suppose I'll be the same when I have kids of my own.'

'There's no one here now…' Jack said, sliding a hand to the nape of her neck. 'You do look lovely in that dress and there's no need to be respectable any more… how about we get up to something that my mother definitely would not approve of?'

'Seriously?' Phoebe raised her eyebrows. 'After the day of torment I've endured?'

'All the more reason to do something to take your mind off it…' he kissed her, that special kiss that he knew did strange and wonderful things to her and she melted into it. It wouldn't have mattered if Genghis Khan had come storming through the living room at that moment – she was Jack's and his completely.

⚜ ⚜ ⚜

'We have totally got to have lunch at Pizza Express. And I'm ordering the biggest, most expensive pizza on the menu.' Midnight leaned on the table between them and gave Phoebe a manic grin. Phoebe tried not to return it with a grin that was just as mad and turned her gaze to the landscape rushing past the train's broad window. Much as she was going to enjoy today too, she had to be the voice of reason.

'We get expenses for essential things. I think that means a sandwich deal from Subway and not a slap up lunch. If we take the piss we won't be allowed out again.'

'I can't believe we've been let out this time,' Midnight replied, her grin spreading, if it was anatomically possible, even wider than before. 'Steve's face was classic when Adam Hendry spoke to him about letting me out for the day, an absolute picture. I wish I'd had my camera with me; that was one memory I'll treasure forever.'

'You're terrible,' Phoebe laughed as she turned back to Midnight. 'You know you could do a lot worse than Steve for a boss.'

'Like Mr Hot-Lips Hendry?'

'Ugh! What am I, a coffin botherer?'

'Not the old dude, you simpleton! I mean Adam.'

'He's ok, I suppose... although he's not technically our boss yet.'

The sign for Manchester Piccadilly flashed by the window and the train began to slow. Around them other passengers collected phones, books and tablets from their tables, stuffing them into bags and backpacks.

'He's not far off,' Midnight said. 'I wouldn't pick a fight with him anyway.' She tilted an open packet of mints at Phoebe, who took one and popped it into her mouth.

'I guess so...'

'And you're well in there for when he does take over.'

'How do you work that out?'

'Because he totally fancies you.'

'He does not.' Phoebe's laugh was rather more awkward and forced now.

'Oh. My. God! Wake up and smell the coffee! The way he looks at you it's like he wants to gobble you up. And not in a Hans Christian Andersen way. Are you really that blind?'

'Don't be ridiculous. He could have his pick of posh girls – ones that daddy would approve of. Besides, I have a boyfriend.'

'You'd really take Mr Stalker over Adam-hot-and-incredibly-rich-Hendry?'

'I love Jack. Money has nothing to do with it. It doesn't make you happy.'

'No, but it bloody well makes you less miserable.'

'Well, I don't fancy Adam Hendry, so you can try to catch his attention if you like and you have my blessing.'

'It must have been him that approved this research day and expenses. Old Mr H would never have done something like that.'

'Maybe…'

Phoebe had been troubled by this herself for a few days now. At first she'd been excited and happy that she was being trusted with the whole venture. But Midnight was right – nothing like today had been sanctioned at Hendry's before, certainly not for anyone below senior management level. Much as she didn't want to see any truth in what Midnight had teasingly remarked upon, she had to wonder how much influence Adam had brought to bear on the situation. And if it had been him, what were his motives?

The train slowed to a halt.

'This is us,' Phoebe said. 'Grab your stuff.'

'We can do H&M before we head to the museum, right?'

'No we can't. Museum, toy store, sandwich, home. That's it.' Phoebe pulled on a denim jacket and smoothed it down.

'Spoilsport.' Midnight grinned.

'I don't want to be a party pooper but if there's a sniff of us doing anything other than what we've been sent to do then we'll never be trusted again and I need to do stuff like this for ideas. So you'll just have to behave.'

Midnight rolled her eyes. 'I suppose it beats standing at the tills all day next to Veronica Small and her sinuses.'

As they stepped onto the heaving platform, Phoebe caught sight of the giant ornate arches that led out onto the main station. Whenever she was here, she always felt like she'd been away from Manchester for too long. There was a cosmopolitan vibe in this city to match London but she never felt like a country mouse as she did whenever she visited the capital. The people here were friendly and cheerful with a wicked, stoic northern humour. And, of course, the shopping was amazing.

Today, the weather was perfect too – fresh and sunny with a cool breeze that chased fluffy cotton clouds across a blue sky.

'What, exactly, do you need to find out today?' Midnight asked as they walked.

'I want inspiration, you know?'

'And you're going to find it at the Museum of Science and Industry?' Midnight's tone held disbelief.

'It might sound dull but, actually, it has some cracking reviews online. I think it's a big hit with kids because the exhibits are fun and interactive. And then we'll head to Hamley's… well, that goes without saying really, doesn't it?'

'Ok… But how is all this going to help with the cosplay event you're planning?'

'It might not help with that, but it will give us ideas for other events.'

'Ok. So you've got all the details sorted out now?'

'God, no! I wish we had!'

'What is it, about four weeks away?'

'Don't remind me. I would have given it more time but Adam is really keen to get this strand of the business up and running. He and Dixon are calling in favours to get council permission for the street space and Adam is getting town traders involved doing food and stuff. I think it's doable if everything goes to plan.'

'I can't wait; it'll be awesome if you pull it off.'

'We have to. Jack's got contacts and he's going to help too. It's going to be hectic, but weirdly fun.'

'Fun? Bloody hell, you have a different idea of fun than the rest of the world.'

'Actually, there was something I wanted to ask you.' Phoebe held the door open for an old lady as they exited the station into the sunshine. 'How do you fancy mingling in the crowds… you know, like a representative of the store?'

'I said from the start I would. You'd have to lock me in a cupboard to stop me.'

'I know, but this is in a more official capacity so you wouldn't be quite as free to do what you liked as before. And you'd need to dress in something more recognisable, I'm afraid, a character that ordinary punters will know. So that means no obscure anime or debauched game characters.'

'For you, I think I can do that.'

Phoebe smiled. 'I was hoping you'd say that. You're an absolute star.'

They stopped at the Metro timetable outside the station. Phoebe squinted up at it while Midnight tapped on her phone.

'Google Maps says the museum is close to the Coronation Street tour. Please, please, please, can we go there?'

Phoebe gave her a sideways look. 'You don't watch Coronation Street.'

'How do you know?'

'Because you've never mentioned it. And because it really isn't you at all.'

'Just because I have some unconventional tastes, doesn't mean I can't appreciate a good bit of northern soap.'

'It's still a no,' Phoebe said as she looked up at the board again.

'Awww, come on…'

'We can't. I've already told you – work and nothing else.'

'I'm sure we can make it about work.'

'No we can't.'

'But we might not get a chance to come to Manchester again for ages.'

Phoebe turned to her. 'Look... I'll treat you one weekend, I promise, my thank-you for all your help.'

'I thought you spent every weekend with Mr Stalker.'

'Not every weekend...' Midnight raised her eyebrows. 'Ok, every weekend. But I'm sure he won't mind if I take one day off to spend it with you.'

'I'll hold you to that!'

Phoebe pointed to a bus stop across a short stretch of road. 'That's where we need to be for our bus.'

'So, what do you think I should dress as?' Midnight asked as they made their way to the stop.

'Just think mainstream. And any other ideas you can bring to the table will be rewarded with a tall, cream-covered mocha later on.'

'You need stunts!' Midnight said with a yelp.

'What do you mean?'

'You know, role play? That would be soooo cool! I've seen them at 'cons; they get proper actors to dress up and replay fight scenes and stuff for the crowds. The rest of the time they walk around and mingle in character.'

Phoebe was thoughtful for a moment. 'I suppose that could be fun.'

'We'd have to do something really cool to make people sit up and take notice. Like have Spiderman climbing the side of the store or something.'

'You know Spiderman isn't real, right? You know that's an actor? And that no one can actually scale buildings using sticky webs oozing from their fingertips?'

'Ha ha. Do you want me to help or not?'

'Yes,' Phoebe grinned. 'I want to hear your amazing ideas. Are we also going to get a guy in a cape to fly over us and shoot lasers from his eyes?'

'No... but you'll be flying over the road when I kick you up the arse in a minute.'

Phoebe giggled. 'Sorry, but for someone who takes the piss all the time you're very easy to wind up.' Midnight folded her arms and pouted at the road. 'I actually think that all sounds great, in principle,' Phoebe continued. 'I have no idea how we can make any of it real, and we definitely don't have the budget for real actors – not that I'd know where to find them if we did – but if you can come up with something doable I'll love you forever and ever.'

'Till death do us part?'

'I'll be haunting you long after I'm gone.'

A slow smile spread over Midnight's face. 'But you have to trust me, yeah? You have to let me run with some ideas even if they sound crazy.'

'Um, I think I'd have to run them by Dixon first. He is my boss, remember? And he'd probably have to run them by Mr Hendry.'

'And Adam.'

'And Adam...'

'Who will totally go for it if you say you think it will work because he loves you.'

Phoebe rolled her eyes.

'He does!' Midnight insisted. 'He has the hots for you. He wants to handcuff you to the Barbie shelves and have his wicked way.'

'Here we go again! He's not remotely interested in me. I'm a shop girl and way beneath him.'

'He'd like you to be beneath him.'

'Mid –'

'Anyway, not a shop girl now, a PR executive. And *I'm* a shop girl, if you don't mind. There's nothing low about it.'

'I'm a promotions assistant. In a shop. So technically I'm a shop girl too. And I didn't say that there was anything wrong with that. It's just that Adam Hendry mixes with the great and the good of Millrise. His wife will be a girl whose daddy is a member of the county polo club, is intimately acquainted with the Masonic handshake, and will have known the Hendry family since their days at a select and expensive public school.'

'Whatever. Anyway, nobody mentioned marriage. I just think he fancies you and that's a totally different thing.'

'As a bit of rough? That's even worse. I'm never going to be anyone's bit of rough.'

'I'd be a bit of rough for him.'

'Be my guest.' Phoebe pointed towards the road ahead. 'This looks like our bus.'

Her tone invited no more discussion on the matter. Phoebe didn't want to talk about it, think about it, or have it penetrate even the outer limits of her subconscious. Part of the reason for this, as her subconscious was trying to tell her, was that she was afraid she really rather liked the idea, and that disturbed her. She loved Jack, didn't she? So why were thoughts of Adam unsettling her like this?

Half an hour and a bumpy, overheated bus ride later they were outside the newly-expanded and renovated Manchester Museum of Science and Industry. If the name suggested a fusty old building full of crankshafts and Wankel rotary engines attended by myopic middle-aged men dressed in corduroy and tweed, the reality was very different. Walking into the vast foyer of the main building, the first thing they saw was a huge ball of TV screens suspended from the ceiling playing snapshots of the day's visitors so far. School parties full of wide-eyed, giggling children (primary school) and not so wide-eyed but still giggling children (high school) were everywhere, being yelled at by exasperated teachers who had about as much chance of being heard as a laryngitis stricken gnat during the Proms.

Phoebe had wanted to see how somewhere that seemed so functional and purely educational still managed to wow its guests and make them want to return time and time again. Because if they could do it, then surely Hendry's, with its added attraction of being a toy store and not a museum, would be onto an irresistible winner. Phoebe didn't think they needed exhibits, exactly, but she did need to know what fired the imagination of an age group she felt she'd lost touch with.

She and Midnight visited a booth that played musical notes as you broke various beams of light within it by leaping about, a recycling quiz played over a giant dance mat, and a bicycle connected to a skeleton that replicated your movements as you peddled. Midnight seemed to enjoy herself more than the kids as she hollered into infinite wells, cranked up an old Mini attached to a huge crane whilst pretending to be The Hulk and played with a giant, spinning model of Saturn. They settled on a surprisingly good lunch in the museum café before heading back out into Manchester to search for its biggest toy store.

❧ ❧ ❧

Midnight gave a low whistle as they stepped through the massive doors of Hamley's. 'OMFG! This place is amazing!'

'It's certainly how a toy store should be,' Phoebe agreed. She glanced towards a pair of burly security guards standing sentry at the entrance. 'Do you think it'll look dodgy if I take notes as we walk around?'

'Nah. I'll just whip out my phone and take photos if it makes you feel better. They'll think I'm some toy loving weirdo having an orgasm in here.'

'You *are* a toy loving weirdo,' Phoebe laughed.

'Thanks. I'll take that as a compliment,' Midnight grinned.

The toy store visit was a success. Just as the museum had done, it gave them some fantastic inspiration and before either had even consulted a watch, two hours had passed as they checked out impromptu events, hidden play corners and epic-looking displays linked to all the latest film and TV blockbusters. After a quick discussion about what time they wanted to get home for various evening plans (Midnight: a re-watch of *My Neighbour Totoro*, which she could already recite line for line, with a group of college friends. Phoebe: Jack, of course, Midnight greeting the revelation with a roll of her eyes) they decided to head back to the station. Another hour filled with animated chat, biscuits and tea, notes and laughter, and they were back in Millrise. A hug goodbye, a bus ride, and Phoebe was home, too wired to stay on her own for long. She showered and changed quickly, desperate to get to Jack's and tell him about her day. She'd be an hour earlier than she'd said, but he'd be pleased to see her, like he always was, and she could help with Maria's tea and bath time. Without another thought, she headed out into the mild evening air to catch her bus.

⚜ ⚜ ⚜

There were raised voices when she arrived at Jack's, clearly audible even from outside. Phoebe's hand hovered over the doorbell. But then, filled with anxiety, she rooted in her handbag and let herself in with her key.

Jack and Archie were in the kitchen, toe to toe, yelling at each other. It looked as though they were close to blows and Phoebe wondered, with some degree of alarm, whether that would have been the outcome had she not turned up in time. Instead, they both turned at her entrance.

'Phoebe!' Jack exclaimed, 'I wasn't expecting you this early.'

Archie's expression was dark with resentment and Jack looked shamefaced through his rage.

'What's going on?' Phoebe asked

'We're… it's something we need to sort out.' Jack glared at Archie, who simply shoved his hands in his pockets and lowered his eyes. An awkward silence descended.

'Where's Maria?' Phoebe asked after a few moments. She was concerned about such a fracas going on with Maria in earshot but she also needed something to say and nothing else came to mind.

'She's still in after school club,' Jack replied. 'I had to phone them to keep her a bit longer when this… *situation* arose.'

Phoebe looked at her watch. 'Doesn't it close soon?'

'Um… yeah…' Jack looked from Phoebe to Archie and back again, clearly having some sort of internal debate.

'D'you want me to go and fetch her?' Phoebe asked. 'It's only ten minutes away and it's a nice evening for a walk.'

Jack looked relieved. 'That would be great.' There was another beat of silence. 'Sorry...' he added.

'For what?'

'Just...' he sighed. 'Thanks.'

'You phone ahead to let them know I'm coming and I'll get off.'

'I will... thanks again.'

With one last searching glance, Phoebe headed out to fetch Maria.

Taking long, brisk strides, she turned the situation over in her head. Had Archie sunk to a new low with his gambling problem, or were they just going over old ground again? Archie didn't usually stay long once it stopped being fun and the lectures started and with a bit of luck, today would be no different. Perhaps, when Phoebe returned with Maria he would already be gone. It wasn't that Phoebe was callous about the situation, or that she didn't care. Of course she did. She cared that Jack was worried about his brother and frustrated by it in equal measure. It was a problem without end and until Archie admitted that he had one (which wasn't about to happen anytime soon as far as anyone could see), they just went round in circles. And Phoebe hated to see Jack get so stressed and upset. It couldn't be good for Maria either, whose short life had been complicated enough as it was.

When Phoebe arrived at the club, Maria was beside herself with excitement to see her. The reaction that a change in routine elicited in children never ceased to amaze Phoebe and the novelty of someone other than her dad collecting her sent Maria into a frenzy of sentences without end and without breath, rolling into one another like waves onto a beach as she recounted her day. Phoebe listened patiently, nodding and smiling in all the right places but at the back of it, still worrying about their return home and what she might be taking Maria into.

'Hey… how about we have half an hour in the park before we go home?' she asked.

Maria gave a squeal of delight.

'I take it that's a yes?' Phoebe smiled.

'YES, YES, YES!' Maria cried as she bounced up and down like a deranged frog.

Phoebe hoped it would wear Maria out for an early bedtime and give her and Jack space to talk. Archie had never done anything to upset or offend Phoebe, but something about him made her uncomfortable whenever he was there. Maybe it was the fact that his moral code seemed to be the opposite of everything Jack stood for. Maybe it was that she had already, rather depressingly, reached an age where she no longer understood teenagers, especially nineteen-year-old boys. Maybe it was all the trouble he seemed to bring with him whenever he turned up. Whatever it was, she was happier when he wasn't around, although that did make her feel guilty. How would she feel if she knew Jack was thinking the same about her brother? Pretty wretched, she supposed, but that didn't make it any easier to like

Archie – at least not all the time. When he was behaving, Archie could be almost as charming and funny as his brother; the problem was he didn't behave very often, or not to her eyes, anyway.

A quick phone call to Jack, letting him know where they were and that they'd be in late, revealed that Archie was still there. Phoebe let Maria race about for an hour, then took her for a burger and milkshake (which she was certain Jack would not approve of but desperate times called for desperate measures) and then, when she really couldn't keep her out any longer, began the walk home with a very tired little girl riding piggyback most of the way.

Phoebe was pretty exhausted too, after stomping the streets of Manchester for hours on end and then coming home to more walking. Whatever happened when they arrived back and however early Maria went to bed, all Phoebe wanted was to snuggle down too. She always kept spare things at Jack's – toothbrush, pyjamas, hairbrush etc – and it might be just as easy to stay over as go home. A lovely evening falling asleep in Jack's warm arms would be just the ticket. It didn't sound like she was going to get that for a while, though.

At the house, Phoebe let herself in and slid Maria to the ground. The place was quiet – an unnerving kind of quiet after the scene she'd left earlier. Maria seemed to gain her second wind immediately and raced down the hallway.

'DADDY, DADDY!'

They found Jack at the kitchen table nursing a coffee. He looked up at their arrival and Maria threw herself into his arms.

'Did you have a good day, spud?' he asked.

'Uh huh. I played and then Phoebe got me strawberry milkshake!'

'Sorry,' Phoebe mouthed, but Jack simply gave her a weak smile. He sat Maria on his lap and gave her an absent kiss on the head.

Phoebe sat opposite him. 'Where's Archie? Has he gone home now? Did you sort –?'

'Actually…' Jack ran a hand down his face, as if somehow trying to iron the tension from his expression. Before he could finish, there was a shout from upstairs.

'Hey, Jack! Is this the only shower gel you've got? It's a bit poncey for me.'

Phoebe raised her eyebrows.

'Archie's staying with us for a couple of days,' Jack said.

'Archie!' Maria shot to attention. 'Is he going to sleep here?'

'Yeah, spud. A little holiday with us. What do you think of that?'

'YAY! Can I see him now? Is he upstairs?' Maria leapt from Jack's knee but he held her back from running to find her uncle.

'He's having a shower right now. Why don't you go and watch some telly while you wait for him to finish?'

'I want to stay in here,' Maria replied.

'Just go to the living room for a little while. I need to talk about some grownup stuff with Phoebe.'

'I don't care if you kiss her; I've seen it.'

'I know,' Jack smiled. 'There will be no kissing, only talking. Promise.'

Maria slouched off without another word. Seconds later they heard the jangling theme tune of her favourite kids' TV show, of which she had hundreds of episodes on DVD. Usually, Jack gave a look of comical desperation when the music filled the house. But not today.

Phoebe turned to Jack. 'What happened?'

'Mum's kicked him out. It'll blow over in a couple of days, I'm sure, but he's got nowhere to go in the meantime.'

'Your mum's done that? Does she know about the gambling?'

'I don't think so, not yet. But she'll find out now.'

'Bloody hell,' Phoebe said in a small voice. 'Are you going to tell her?'

'I might have to. Someone's got to talk some sense into her and she needs to know.'

'Do you think she'll let him go back?'

'He'd have to do some pretty impressive grovelling first. And she needs time to calm down.'

'What about your dad? He'd stick up for Archie, wouldn't he?'

'I expect he's tried, but even he doesn't have enough influence with mum to diffuse one of her moods once she takes the hump about something. He'll be working on it, I'm sure, and I'll have to talk to him when I can get him alone to find out how far he's got. That's why I thought Archie should stay here just for a while, where I can keep an eye on him until it's sorted. You don't mind, do you?'

'How could I mind? He's your brother and you need to look out for him.' Phoebe did mind, of course. Archie being around threw out the delicate balance of her blossoming relationship with Jack. It made him tense and irritable. It meant she couldn't relax in Jack's home – what she had come to think of as home herself. But family was family and it was only for a couple of days. How could she kick up a fuss about that? She knew she'd do the same for her brother. She reached across the table and gave Jack's hand a squeeze. 'Are you very upset about it all?'

He gave a long sigh. 'I'm tired of it all. I wish he'd sort himself out,' he replied in a low voice. 'He can't go through life like this; he'll end up with nothing and nobody.'

'He's young. There're plenty more years for him to put right any daft mistakes he makes now.' She paused, uncertain whether her next question would overstep the mark. 'What did he do? To upset your mum, I mean.' Having met Carol, Phoebe didn't imagine it would take much. But Archie was her son. Surely she'd be a little more tolerant in his case? To throw him out was a big thing.

'He won't tell me, exactly,' Jack replied. 'He says he *borrowed* something and when she found out she went mental. He says she overreacted. I'll have to find out what happened when I speak to Mum and Dad later.'

'Do you think your dad will be able to talk her round? I mean, she always seems very unforgiving to me.' Phoebe gave an apologetic smile. 'Or perhaps that's just because it *is* me.'

'I honestly don't know. I've told Archie to be prepared for the possibility that he'll have to find a flat. To be fair, I don't necessarily think it's a bad thing. There's nothing like a bit of independence to make someone grow up fast. It could be the best thing that's ever happened to him.'

'I'm glad you're still being positive about it,' Phoebe replied in an encouraging tone. But she wished she could agree with him. Her version of his independence was Archie gambling away his rent every month and coming to Jack for more. But she didn't think now was the moment to articulate it. Perhaps there would never be a right time to speak such a painful truth.

'I can't do much else. I've told him he'll have to put college on hold, or at least get some kind of job that fits in with his studies, especially if he's going it alone. He's a bugger for not speaking to his lecturers about things that are hindering his studies and he's in enough trouble there as it is, so I've told him he needs to go and see them, at least see the student

counsellor and talk through his options with someone who knows what they are. Whether he will or not
is a different matter. I don't want to treat him like a
ten-year-old and drag him along to the right office
myself, but I might have to if he doesn't go and do it.
Otherwise, he may lose his place on the course. He
probably doesn't care that much to be honest, I'm
not sure he's all that keen on it anyway. But I'm worried if he does he'll lose the one thing that grounds
him and go completely off the rails.'

'It'll iron out, one way or the other; especially
now he has his awesome big brother on his side.'

'I wish I could have your confidence in me.' He
gave her a tiny, hopeful, rather adorable smile. 'I
don't suppose you can have a word at Hendry's about
a job for him?'

Phoebe would love to say yes. But she could think
of nothing worse than suggesting wayward and unreliable Archie as an employee at the store where she was
working hard to make a name for herself. Thankfully,
there was no need to lie. 'I'm afraid they're laying off,
if anything. They didn't even fill my old job when I
left the shop floor.'

'I'm sorry for asking. It was a shot in the dark.'

'Just you wait,' Phoebe said with an encouraging
smile, 'this time next week everything will be forgiven
and back to normal and Archie will be home.'

'Yeah... I suppose you're right.' He got up and
kissed her. 'Listen to me... I should be asking you

about your day. Let me make you a drink and then you can tell me all about it.'

Phoebe watched him fill the kettle. She didn't much feel like talking about her day anymore.

❧ ❧ ❧

Phoebe counted the notes again. She was certain she'd had a ten and a twenty in her purse when she'd left work the previous evening, and now there was only the ten. She marched through into the living room where Archie was still in Jack's towelling dressing gown reading the sports pages of the *Echo*. She held back a deep sigh of irritation. Two weeks had passed since he'd moved in and he had not shown the slightest inclination of getting himself a job or a flat of his own. Often, he didn't get out of bed until Phoebe had left for work and God knew how Jack managed to get his own work done with his brother's constant and demanding presence every day. There were times, at first, when he had been good company despite the baggage he brought – a breath of fresh air in the house – and they'd had a laugh around the dinner table. But those times became less frequent the longer he stayed and the worse the friction between them became. Archie's only redeeming feature now was that he was extraordinarily good with Maria and she seemed to love having him around. Even that would only take him so far, though.

'Where's Jack?' she asked. 'I thought he was in here with you.'

'The old woman next door shouted him over to change a bulb or something,' Archie replied, his eyes not moving from the paper. Phoebe wanted to snatch it from his grip and shove it in the bin. Chances were he was looking for something to bet on anyway so she'd be doing him a favour really, not to mention it being immensely satisfying.

'You mean Doreen?'

'Yeah, her.'

'So, where is Maria?'

Archie shrugged.

'Did Jack ask you to keep an eye on her if he was going around to help next door?'

'Yeah, but I thought she was with you.'

'I was in the shower!' Phoebe stormed out. Maria wouldn't be far away but it didn't stop Phoebe's annoyance at his lack of consideration. It wasn't good enough for him simply to assume that Maria was ok; it was Archie's job to check if Jack had entrusted her care to him, no matter how long it was for and how close Jack was to home. She marched back into the kitchen. 'Maria!'

There was no reply. Phoebe ran to the bottom of the stairs. 'Maria!'

Still nothing. Shit, where was she? Phoebe glanced at her watch. She was going to be late for work if she didn't get a move on, but she couldn't go out and leave things as they were. She raced upstairs to check but every room was empty.

'Archie!' she yelled as she clattered downstairs again. 'I can't find her!'

Archie ambled out from the living room. 'Chill… she'll be outside or something.'

'Outside? What for? She ought to be getting ready for school.' Phoebe pushed past him and through to the back door. Sure enough, the key was in the lock and it had been opened.

Maria was in the garden digging up the marguerite patch with an expression of intense concentration. She sang as she worked, lost in her own little world. Her hands were filthy and next to her lay a pile of blooms complete with roots and clumps of earth.

'What are you doing?' Phoebe cried.

Maria looked up and smiled. 'Getting some flowers for Miss Poxon. She's having a baby and she's leaving today but Daddy forgot to get some yesterday. He said I could take some from the garden.'

'I'm not sure he meant like that; I think he was going to help you cut them.' Phoebe rushed over to take the trowel from her. It looked as though Maria had managed to get into the locked shed somehow too, and God only knew what was in there that she could kill or maim herself with. Three adults in the house and still Maria had managed to get into danger. But the real culprit here was Archie. 'Come on…' Phoebe led Maria back into the kitchen to wash her muddy hands. 'I'll cut you some flowers when we've cleaned you up. You should have come to get me or Archie.'

'Archie said he would come in a minute but then he carried on reading the paper. You were in the bathroom. I knew where the keys were so I could do it.'

'I know you could, spud.' Phoebe pulled a chair to the sink and ran the tap as Maria clambered up to wash. 'But there are dangerous things in the shed and a grownup should be with you in there.'

'I didn't touch anything dangerous.'

Archie's voice came from the doorway. 'You're not dumb like all the other kids, are you?'

Phoebe spun around. He folded his arms and leaned against the door frame, directing a challenging glare at Phoebe. She shot one right back.

'You were supposed to watch her,' Phoebe growled.

'Nothing happened.'

'That's not the point.'

Archie shrugged. 'What do you care? It's not like you're her mum or anything.'

Phoebe's mouth dropped open. In any other situation it might have looked comical, but there was nothing funny about the simmering resentment that filled the space between them, so strong it was almost palpable.

Phoebe glanced at Maria. She was watching the exchange, a look of confusion on her face. 'It's alright,' Phoebe said, trying to smile for her. 'Why don't you go and fetch your shoes and we'll go next door to tell Daddy you're ready for school?'

Maria nodded before climbing from the chair and running from the kitchen.

'That was a vile thing to say!' Phoebe snapped as soon as Maria had left the room.

'True.'

'Of course I'm not Maria's mum. But right at this moment I'm about as close as she's got.'

'Don't flatter yourself. You're nothing like Rebecca and you'll always be a poor substitute.'

'What's that supposed to mean? I've never tried to be Maria's mum. All I meant was there was nobody else looking out for her just then.'

'It means that you think you can come into our lives and fix everything. Well, you can't.'

'Nobody can fix the problems you bring, it seems,' Phoebe said to Archie in a low voice.

'I'm not the one kicking off over every little thing…' He began to mimic her. '*Jack, this isn't right, Jack, that's not proper, Jack, I'm so OCD I can't stop moaning at you…* How he manages to get you to shut up long enough to screw you is a mystery.'

'That's uncalled for!'

He jabbed a finger at her. 'No… *you're* uncalled for! Jack was just fine before you turned up messing with his life.'

'You mean he was a pushover who lent you money whenever you called and didn't ask any questions?'

'You mean like you do?'

'I don't borrow from him.'

'Yeah, but I don't see you paying the mortgage and you practically live here too. Maybe we're not that different.'

Phoebe stared at him, blood rushing to her face and completely lost for words. What, exactly, was he trying to say?

The front door slammed and Phoebe looked past Archie to see Jack make his way up the hallway. 'Come on, Maria!' he shouted up the stairs as he passed. 'Nearly time for school!' His gaze fell on Archie and Phoebe. 'What's going on?'

'I found Maria digging up the garden.' Phoebe glared at Archie, daring him to argue. He simply shrugged.

'Sorry about that, dude. I didn't notice her slip out.'

'Where is she now?' Jack asked.

'Upstairs getting her shoes,' Phoebe said. 'Luckily I found her before she got into any trouble.'

'What do you want, a medal or something?' Archie sniped. 'She wasn't wrestling Godzilla, she was just in the garden.'

'She'd also been in the shed with all the pesticides and sharp tools.'

'She's not stupid,' Archie growled.

'She's five!' Phoebe shouted.

'Woah!' Jack stepped between them. 'No harm has been done, right?'

'Right,' Archie said.

'Then what's this about?'

'He should have been watching,' Phoebe said, fighting to keep her temper in check.

'I know, dude.' Archie turned to Jack. 'And I said I was sorry.'

'I know you are.' Jack laid a hand on his shoulder.

'What!' Phoebe stared at them both now. 'He gives a half-assed apology and it's all forgotten?'

'I'm sorry you had to get stressed before work,' Jack replied. 'But Archie's explained it and no harm was done and I can't keep banging on about it, can I?'

'What is wrong with you, Jack?'

'Wrong with him?' Archie cut in. 'What the hell is wrong with *you*, psycho girl?'

'That's out of order,' Jack said. 'Don't speak to her like that.'

'Whatever. She started it.' Archie didn't wait for a reply. He turned and sloped off towards the stairs.

'Where the hell are you going now?' Jack called after him.

'Bed,' Archie shouted back.

'Archie!'

'Leave it,' Phoebe said. 'There's no point. You have got to speak to him about responsibilities though. If I hadn't asked him where Maria was there's no telling what she might have got up to.'

'Don't labour the point, Phoebe. She didn't come to any harm and things are hard enough as it is.'

'Then tell him to leave. You said it would only be for a few days but he's a part of the furniture now. Why can't he go home?'

'Because Mum still hasn't forgiven him and Dad hasn't managed to talk her round yet. You know all this; we've been over it a thousand times already. I'm doing my best here but it would help if you and Archie could just get along.'

'We do get along… most of the time.'

'You used to. It would make life easier for everyone if you both just tried a bit harder.'

'Maybe your mother shouldn't let him back home. Maybe it is time he got a place of his own. You said you would talk to him about that.' It was probably the first and last time she would ever side with Carol Andrews but after checking her purse this morning she had good reason.

'What does that mean?'

Phoebe hesitated. Did she dare voice her suspicions? 'It's just… well, some money has gone from my purse… I mean, I'm sure I had thirty pounds yesterday and now –'

Jack lowered his voice. 'Are you accusing Archie of stealing from you?'

'Not stealing, exactly… it's like you said, he borrows –'

'Don't you dare!'

'Jack?'

'I don't want to hear it Phoebe! Not another word! I know he's getting under our feet and I know that things are strained but what you're accusing him of is bang out of order.'

'But…' Phoebe's glance went to the floor. What was the point? It seemed that the only person who was allowed to criticise Archie was Jack and if anyone else dared to point out his flaws they got blasted. 'It doesn't matter.'

Jack drew a steadying breath and took her in his arms. 'I know you're finding this hard. I'm trying to sort it. You have to trust me, ok?'

She nodded. 'It just seems that you're not getting anywhere.'

'I am. It's going to take time.'

'I wish we could be how we were before.'

'We will be. Just be patient, huh?' He kissed her hair. Phoebe's frustration subsided in his embrace. How could she stay angry when she knew how hard he was working to make things right? She just wished that waiting for the end result wasn't so stressful. He looked down at her. 'Need a lift into work?'

'Sure, thanks.'

'I'll call Maria and drop you off first if you don't mind being in a bit early. And I'll sort this stuff, I promise.'

Phoebe had to believe that he would. Much more of this and someone was going to blow, and it would probably be her.

❧   ❧   ❧

Four weeks had never gone by so quickly. And the damage had been insidious and relentless. Archie was still hanging around like an increasingly bad smell, steadfastly refusing any hints that it might be time for him to move on. Phoebe should never have stayed over last night either. Today was the biggest day of her life, and already it was sliding away from her. She and Archie had sniped at each other all evening and she'd drunk too much and stayed up too late as a result. It had been made worse by her foul mood on waking and Jack's stubborn refusal to admit that something now had to be done about Archie. He kept promising that he was doing all he could, reminding her that these things had to be handled properly and took time. Archie had a recognised addiction, he said, and it had to be treated as such if it wasn't going to be his undoing. All that Phoebe could see was a sarcastic youth who actively enjoyed causing tension between her and Jack. She had seen the evidence of Jack's words – leaflets around the house about local help centres for people like Archie, scrawled notes on phone pads from counsellors that Jack was trying to persuade Archie to see – but gambling addiction or not, all she wanted was for Archie to stop making her life so difficult. Just like the rest of the family, he seemed intent on driving Phoebe out because she wasn't Rebecca. Or maybe he was that contemptuous of everyone. And, the longer things dragged on, the more stubborn Jack seemed to become in his defence of his brother. It was as though Archie was getting under his skin, gradually becoming a normal part of his existence, and Phoebe could see a day looming where Jack wouldn't want him to leave even if he offered. There had been spats, of course, and stern words full of disapproval, but even those seemed fewer these days. Phoebe had to face the truth that Jack liked having Archie around. Increasingly, she'd started to wonder whether he actually preferred Archie being there to her. It was crazy to be jealous of a brother, but there it was.

Today, however, she needed to focus on the thing she and Dixon had been planning for weeks, and she had to get it right.

Jack peered around the bedroom door as she got ready. 'Would a coffee help? It's freshly ground... your favourite with the cinnamon in...'

Phoebe tried to smile. It was his way of making up without either of them having to admit there had been a problem in the first place. It was how things always were nowadays. 'Sounds amazing.'

He left the cup on her bedside cabinet and came up behind her as she stood at the mirror. He reached to kiss the back of her neck, but Phoebe shook him off. It was a sudden and instinctive response. In that instant she couldn't bear him to touch her. She was still angry and frustrated and bringing her a coffee wasn't going to fix that so easily. She could see his reflection in the mirror as she buttoned her blouse. He looked hurt, and she knew she had wronged him in a way he didn't deserve, but she couldn't help the anger she felt. She tried constantly not to direct it at him, but instead at the situation they found themselves in. She knew Jack was a good, kind man who could never kick Archie out, and she didn't really expect him to. The fact remained, however, that Archie's continual presence was disrupting their lives more and more each day, and as Phoebe couldn't be angry at anyone else, poor Jack was getting the full force of her frustration.

'Archie and I had a talk after you'd gone to bed last night. He'll leave as soon as he gets a job and finds somewhere to live,' Jack said, stepping back from her.

Phoebe turned to face him. 'He's been saying that for four weeks.'

'He's sorry, and he means it this time.'

'Really? Somehow I don't see it happening. He's never going to get a job and he's never going to get anywhere else to live because he knows you're daft enough to let him live here rent free.'

'The guy's on the ropes. He's my brother and I have to look out for him.'

'He has no one to blame for that but himself. I've been on the ropes but I never scrounged and I certainly wouldn't take advantage of my brother.'

'It's what families do, isn't it?'

'Use each other?'

'Help each other.'

'You're the one doing all the helping. He does little of anything except enjoy your hospitality.'

'It's not like that.'

'That's how it looks.'

'You can't judge from the outside.'

Phoebe planted her hands on her hips. 'That's just it, though. I'm not on the outside anymore. And right now, I spend so much time with Archie, I feel like I'm dating him as well as you.'

'You don't have to come over.'

'You don't want me here?' Phoebe squeaked.

'Of course I do! I just mean that you don't have to come over if you're sick of seeing him.'

'And what's the alternative? Is this you dumping me?'

'Phoebe… you're overreacting. I'm not saying anything of the sort.'

'So now I'm unreasonable and overreacting? Great! Anything else you want to throw at me? Perhaps I'm crap in bed too! Let's get all the insults out of the way in one go, shall we?'

'Keep your voice down!' Jack hissed.

'You don't want Archie to hear this?'

'I don't want Maria to!' Jack's voice, despite his own warning, crept up in volume too. 'She's downstairs, in case you hadn't noticed, being given breakfast by Archie – who never does anything according to you – so that I can have this pointless conversation with you.'

'Wow! So you're defending him again! This is the boy who got himself kicked out of his home because he stole from his mother–'

'Borrowed…' Jack cut in.

'Borrowed very long term… Why am I the bad guy for wanting our life back the way it was?'

'Nobody says you're the bad guy.'

'Then why does it feel like I am?' Phoebe's vision blurred as she fought the tears welling in her eyes. Damn it, she didn't want to cry, but it was so hard to hold her emotions back.

Jack turned her gently to face him, hands resting on her shoulders as he held her gaze. 'I want it back too,' he said softly. 'And I know you think otherwise but I miss the way things used to be. You must be able to see how hard it is to sort this? Archie is struggling to find work and Mum won't listen to reason. I've tried to persuade him to get professional help but he simply won't admit that he needs it. I can't just kick him out now that he has no money and nowhere to go, especially when what little comes his way will end up in the bookie's purse... What would you do?'

And there it was – the sucker punch. What would Phoebe do? Jack knew what the answer was. She would do exactly what he was doing; she'd try to help and would never abandon her brother. She turned back to the mirror.

'I'd better get ready or I'll be late for work.'

Jack was silent for a moment as he watched her.

'Do you still want me and Maria there tonight? At the superhero event?'

Phoebe sniffed and ran a hand across her eyes. 'Of course I do. Do you still want to come?'

'Of course. We wouldn't miss it for the world.'

Never had anything sounded less like the truth.

❧ ❧ ❧

The day had been a frenzy of last minute organising and thankfully Phoebe had no time to dwell on the argument with Jack that morning. There were suppliers to call, guests to confirm, decorations to inspect and staff to brief. That was all on top of her normal workload and trying to calm her own nerves as well as soothe an unusually jittery Dixon. It didn't help that Adam Hendry had chosen this day to hang around poking his nose into everything Phoebe did, constantly asking questions and then posing alternatives that he believed were better. They might have been better, and had he aired his opinions weeks earlier, they might even have adopted some of them. But telling her on the day of the event that fireworks would have been a great idea was beyond infuriating. By mid-afternoon, she could think of nothing more satisfying than ramming a firework up his well-dressed backside and watching him shoot into orbit.

As the store prepared to close, Phoebe's anxiety was in danger of swallowing her whole. She took herself off for a brisk walk round the block to check on the preparations and clear her head a little. Outside the shop, the first vans were arriving to set up. Radio Millrise had turned up, Phoebe was pleased to see, having been warned by several local businesses that they often didn't even when they'd promised. A couple of lads who looked like they'd only just finished their GCSEs were lifting a panel from the side of the van to reveal the sound stage inside. There were a couple of fairground attractions setting up too, and passers-by were gathering to point and discuss what they thought was going on. That was a good sign too – perhaps those who weren't already aware of the party would come by later to see what was happening.

And at least the weather was perfect too, Phoebe reflected as she passed Applejack's to see Jack's Uncle Fred watching her through his vast windows. She gave him a little wave but he merely scowled in return. She did see his jaw twitch slightly though, so it could have been a smile. It was hard to tell on a man who looked as though a smile might crack his face. Jack definitely got his charm and easy humour from his dad's side of the family.

When she arrived back, Phoebe had to get one of the security guards to let her into Hendry's again. A small chatty army of staff waited with Dixon and they all turned at her approach. Phoebe took a deep breath. This was it – her first ever big event. Tonight was the night that would make or break her. She had a sudden urge to shout some freedom speech like Mel Gibson in *Braveheart* – either that, or run and hide in the nearest toilet until it was all over. Dixon gave her an encouraging nod.

'Ready to crack on?' he asked.

Phoebe gave him a salute that made her look far more confident than she felt. She wasn't ready at all.

⚜ ⚜ ⚜

Dixon marched across to Phoebe where she stood with Adam watching the crowds grow. She had hoped for a reasonable turnout but could never have imagined the numbers that were gathering now. She had also never seen so much black leather, vinyl, spandex and false hair in one place and doubted that she ever would again. Many people were armed with fake weapons of various descriptions – and although she had seen many of her dad's re-enactments where fake weapons were plenty, she was pretty sure she'd never seen any of them seen them wield lightsabres and laser guns before. She couldn't deny that the atmosphere was incredible, though, and it was another thing that she had never experienced the likes of. If all conventions were like this no wonder fans loved them so much. As they recognised each other's characters complete strangers were high-fiving, taking photos, swapping internet details; people whose characters belonged to the same show or comic were hugging and squealing with excitement. One or two, in an attempt to go the extra mile, were wearing massive fake creature heads, perched precariously (and perhaps somewhat painfully) on top of their own heads. A PA system blasted out film themes from classics like *Indiana Jones*, *Back to the Future* and *Star Wars*. Hobby photographers, professionals from newspapers and websites, and film cameras mingled with the crowds clicking away at each new and impressive sight as it arrived. From a row of stalls at the far end of the gathering the smells of popcorn, crepes and hot dogs wafted through the throng.

'Cracking turnout,' Dixon boomed as he drew level.

'I know, I can't believe it!' Phoebe replied. 'Let's hope they all spend lots of money.'

Dixon laughed. 'As long as they know about us now, that's half our job done; even if they don't spend it tonight there's a chance they will at some point. That's really our goal.'

'I won't complain about a few sales while we're at it,' Adam cut in. 'It would certainly make dad happier about all this.'

Phoebe felt her good humour evaporate. 'He isn't pleased?'

'He doesn't believe that this is an effective use of funds. I happen to disagree but I had a devil of a time persuading him to let it go ahead.'

'That's made us feel a whole lot better,' Dixon said with a wry smile.

'Don't worry about it. We have to move with the times and business is all about calculated risks. If not this then we'll hit on something else to bring the money in, but if you don't try you don't know.'

'Is he coming tonight?' Phoebe asked, silently praying that the answer would be no.

'He might. But I suspect he won't because if it's a success he won't be able to stand the fact that he's been proved wrong.' Adam threw Phoebe a knowing sideways glance and smiled. She didn't like it when he did that; it made her feel all sorts of things that she knew she shouldn't. Instead, she turned her attention to the crowds, searching for Jack. Then she heard Dixon give a bellow of delight.

'Would you look at that!' he shouted, pointing up at the front of Hendry's building. 'Bloody hell, that looks fantastic!'

Phoebe and Adam turned as one to see a huge searchlight trained on the storefront, the circumference of its beam taking up almost half the area. Projected onto the wall was a huge Batman symbol. They watched as it travelled the building and then morphed into the shadow of a spider, followed by a round shield bearing a stars and stripes design.

'Jack found this company online,' Phoebe said, a swell of pride in her chest. 'They're amazing, aren't they?'

The crowd had turned their attention to the light show too, and there were oohs and ahs from the audience as they watched, rapt.

'I've never seen anything like that,' Adam said approvingly. 'I know who I'll be hiring for my next birthday party.

Phoebe had seen the bill presented to Hendry's for this particular entertainment. She couldn't imagine being wealthy enough to pay for such a thing as a birthday treat. Part of her resented the frivolous nature of his comment. Here they were, trying to save an ailing business – one that he was set to inherit – and he was making light of how much money he had to spare. He was obviously used to being privileged and having everything he wanted but, under the circumstances, Phoebe thought he should keep his profligate ways to himself. It seemed that Dixon was thinking along the same lines as he kept a tactful silence on the subject.

'Dixon Montague?' A good-looking man, young but with thick grey hair swept up into a quiff and a camera slung around his neck, looked enquiringly at both Adam and Dixon in turn.

Dixon held up a hand. 'At your service.'

'Brilliant! I'm Patrick from the *Millrise Echo*. I wondered if I could get a couple of photos of you and your team.'

'Wouldn't the cosplayers be more interesting?' Phoebe asked, slightly panic-stricken by the idea of her photo appearing in the paper.

'Oh, I have everything I need from them. But I want to get some of the organisers too. You know it's not all about the words; the photos can be half the story if done well, and I try to get as many angles as possible.'

'Why not?' Dixon beamed. 'Adam? Would you like to be in the photo too?'

Adam inclined his head and moved closer to Phoebe. His aftershave was having a strange effect on her. It filled her senses, like inhaling incense or some hallucinogenic tribal drug. She felt his heat against her as he moved in. Not for the first time that evening she willed Jack to turn up.

The photographer chatted amiably as he clicked away, making subtle alterations to their poses as he went. Then, the lens cap went back on and his notepad came out.

'Can I take some names for the captions? Dixon, of course,' he said, jotting it down. Phoebe gave hers and then Adam, which provoked a raised eyebrow from the photographer. 'Hendry as in *Hendry's*? Are you set to take over the business then?'

'Eventually. Dad isn't ready to abdicate just yet and I wouldn't want him to. I'm going to be a lot more involved now though.'

'Interesting... do you fancy doing an interview about that some time? I have a colleague at the *Echo* I think would be very interested in featuring you.'

'Can't hurt to get a little extra publicity, can it?' Adam dug in his breast pocket and handed Patrick a business card. 'Here's my number whenever you're ready.'

The photographer shook hands with all three of them. 'I'll leave you to it.'

'That could be good,' Dixon said to Adam as the man left them.

Adam nodded agreement. 'I'll run it by Dad first, make sure he's happy with it.'

Phoebe wondered how much influence Adam would have over his father in the months to come. His support of her ideas was valuable, but if he was set to become as powerful as it seemed (assuming the business survived that long) then it might be crucial. She realised that she needed to stay in his good books if she was going to succeed at Hendry's – and she had a better chance of doing that with him than with his father, who didn't seem to care for her or her ideas very much at all.

'Here comes trouble,' Dixon said, nodding his head at a buxom Catwoman rushing their way.

'Enjoying it so far?' Phoebe asked.

'Yeah… great,' Midnight panted.

Phoebe frowned. 'You don't sound so sure of that. Is something wrong?'

'It's just…' Midnight glanced up at the roof of the building.

'What?' Phoebe asked, a sense of unease bubbling up.

'I'm so sorry… you know when I said I was totally ok to go on the roof with Batman…'

'Yes…'

'I'm not.'

Phoebe stared at her. 'Oh God, why wait until now to tell me?'

'I thought it would be alright… I got carried away, I didn't want to let you down… I don't know; all of the above. But when I look at it today there's just no way. It's so high!'

'Of course it's bloody high! That's why I asked you to think really carefully before you said yes!'

'There will be a guard rail up there,' Dixon put in, calmly, 'if that makes you feel more confident. There is no way you can fall.'

'I know…' Midnight wailed. 'I'm so sorry. I really didn't think this through properly, but the thought of going up there fills me with terror. I'll freeze; I won't be able to do a thing.'

Phoebe chewed her lip. She could tell that Midnight was genuinely distressed, even though her face was almost completely obscured by her mask. It wasn't fair to insist that she go through something that would clearly be a trauma, but what was she going to do? She could call the stunt off, of course, but it was the one she was particularly excited about, the one she knew people would talk about for weeks to come. They had spent a great deal of the budget on it too.

'We can't make the girl do it if she doesn't want to,' Dixon said.

'Quite,' agreed Adam.

'But what about the stunt?'

'It'll have to be cancelled.'

Tears burned at Phoebe's eyes. She needed this day to be perfect, she had to prove her worth and there was only one thing for it. She took a deep breath. 'I'll do it.'

'Go on the roof?' Midnight squeaked.

'Why not? I'll put on your costume and get up there. I'm not afraid of heights and it's, like, ten minutes, tops. How hard can it be?'

'Oh, great,' Midnight said, 'make me feel like a total loser.'

'Of course you're not. You can't help having a phobia.' Phoebe raised her eyebrows and tried to smile. 'Although I do wish you'd told me before.'

'Sorry, honey…' Midnight replied in a sheepish voice.

'You're really going to do this?' Adam asked.

'Totally,' Phoebe said.

He gave a low whistle. 'I have to say I'm impressed. Who's your Batman?'

'Gareth…' Midnight nodded towards a rather weedy looking specimen dressed in black from head to toe, cape hanging like a limp sail around him, trying to impress a group of teenage girls all wearing space suits from *Ender's Game*.

'Right…' Adam rubbed a hand across his chin, 'and this is happening in the next half an hour?'

Phoebe glanced at her watch and nodded. 'In which case, I'd better get that costume off you,' she added, looking at Midnight.

'I suppose,' Midnight said, the reluctance obvious in her voice.

'Don't worry.' Phoebe smiled. 'You can go and get something else from the stock. Can't have you wandering around in civvies, can we?'

'Won't this be a bit big for you? Midnight glanced down at herself and then Phoebe's diminutive frame.

'I'll grab some pins from somewhere. Come on, let's get a move on.' As Phoebe turned to go, she called back as an afterthought. 'This is ok, isn't it, Dixon?'

Dixon gave her a thumbs up. 'If you're mad enough to do it, that's fine with me.'

❧ ❧ ❧

With minutes to spare, Phoebe found herself pinned into Midnight's suit and up on the roof. In the short time since she'd decided to do the stunt herself dusk had already began to gather over the city. The timing was just as they had planned it, of course, because fabulous as the spotlights had been earlier that evening, they were going to look truly awesome trained on the enigmatic figures standing above the crowds in the dark. But now up on the roof, darkness suddenly seemed like a very bad idea. There were lanterns, and coloured strips like cat's eyes so that people could find their way safely to and from the stairs into the building, but there was still room for error. For someone as clumsy as Phoebe there was room for error in situations far less dangerous than this one.

She had briefly explained the swap with Gareth, and had arranged where to meet him before she headed to the toilet to get changed. Having assumed that he understood her instructions, she was perturbed to find she was now alone on the roof. She paced up and down for a few minutes, muttering under her breath and hardly daring to approach the edge of the building to see what was going on below. Now, she realised just why Midnight had been so afraid.

Just as she was about to run back into the building and give Gareth the bollocking of his life, an imposing figure appeared on the rooftop, his cloak flapping in the wind as he strode towards her, every inch the Dark Knight. All it needed was a ton of dry ice and some stirring incidental music and the scene would be epic.

Phoebe stared at the figure standing before her trying to work out what was weird about it. Maybe it was the sudden onset of vertigo, but Batman looked a lot more buff than he had done down on the ground. In fact, he was filling his suit rather pleasingly, and this thought prompted a little kick of guilt. What the hell was wrong with her? How did a spotty, weedy youth suddenly turn into a dark and dangerous caped crusader with only the addition of a mask and suit? She shook the thought away.

'Where have you been?' she hissed, but there was no reply. Perhaps he hadn't heard her and she didn't suppose it mattered now that he had arrived. 'The spotlight is ready to shine up here any minute now. Midnight said we're supposed to jog up and down a bit, wave and look generally super. Is that ok?'

Batman gave a silent nod. Phoebe tried not to roll her eyes. Talk about getting into character. This had to be the most ridiculous situation she had ever been in.

'Let's just get it over with,' she added, as she made her way across the roof, mustering all her determination to face the ledge.

She let out a squeal as Batman pulled her back and spun her into a grip with his arm around her neck. Unable to respond for the shock, Phoebe let him lead her to the ledge where the spotlight swept over them and the crowd below roared. Instinctively, Phoebe stamped on his toe and he let her go with a low chuckle.

'What the hell are you doing?' Phoebe squeaked. 'We're supposed to stand and wave, not fight!'

She ducked as Batman swung a theatrical punch. 'Gareth!'

There was another low chuckle from her adversary as she ran across the rooftop to get away from him. He gave chase and caught her easily. Then he let her go and she ran back. It wasn't the plan Midnight had outlined to her, but it seemed safer than getting herself in another wrestling grip. The spotlight followed them wherever they went. He reached to grab her again but she leapt out of his way.

'Don't even think about it, sonny!'

Laughing, he shrugged and stood alongside her. With a sweeping glance across the crowds below, he held his arms aloft. The crowd cheered.

What a dick, Phoebe thought as she watched him. She inched away. God only knew what he was going to do next. What if he tried to shove her off the roof? There was a safety rail, but it didn't look as though it deserved its name. With great caution, she waved at the crowd too, and elicited another wave of cheers. She couldn't help but smile – just for a moment, she understood why celebrities craved their fame. She waved again. Then she glanced at her superhero partner and chanced a small smile. Perhaps he'd just been reacting to the adoring audience too.

But then, in a movement so fast she barely had time to scream in shock, he had whipped her into his arms and was kissing her. And in that brief moment, a scent filled her head, something intoxicating and dangerous and far too expensive for the likes of a spotty shop-floor boy like Gareth.

'Jesus! What the hell are you doing?' she gasped as she wrenched herself from Adam's embrace.

'Relax,' he replied, in his familiar easy tone, 'I'm just putting on a show. Look – they're loving it.'

'But I'm not!' she squeaked.

'Watch…' he grabbed her again.

'Will you get off!'

'You're making a scene,' he laughed.

'I'm not the one making the scene!'

'Anyway, I thought that was the whole idea.'

'ARGH! You're so infuriating!'

'I'm also your boss.'

'Which gives you the right kiss me whenever you feel like without my permission?'

'Don't you like it?'

'No! I bloody don't!'

'Not even a tiny bit?'

'Sod off, Adam!'

He grinned and turned to wave at the crowd who roared their approval. 'I could get used to this kind of adoration,' he said.

'Then why don't you go down and snog some of them instead?'

He turned to her, his grin just showing just beneath his mask. Now that she looked properly, it was obvious who had been on the roof all along. His full lips were instantly recognisable. 'I'm sorry if I've offended you.'

'You don't sound very sorry.'

'I didn't mean any harm.'

'Then what did you mean, exactly? What was I supposed to do with a whole crowd of people watching? What will people think?'

'Relax. Nobody knows it's us in these costumes.'

'Everyone who works for Hendry's does.'

'Nobody but you, Dixon and your friend know that you swapped at the last moment and nobody knows that I did either. As far as anyone's concerned we're the original staff members who were asked to perform this stunt.'

'What makes you so certain that Gareth or Midnight won't tell everyone?'

'I'll make sure they don't.'

Phoebe thought about this for a moment. She supposed he had the power to make good that promise but she didn't like the idea of it. Was it right to abuse his position in that way? But even more worrying – what were his motives for doing the stunt? And why had he kissed her? In reality, he'd taken a huge risk. She had the right to bring up the issue of sexual harassment. She wouldn't dare, of course, and he probably knew that. A small part of her wouldn't want to either, but he couldn't know that. Or was she giving him signals that told him he was safe? And if she was, even inadvertently, what did that say about her feelings for Jack?

She shook herself as he nudged her. 'Stop sulking and wave to your public.'

She waved automatically when all she wanted to do was ask him what his game was.

On cue, her dad's re-enactors entered the fray down on the street. She could see them working their way through the crowds in their costumes. Her dad had been so pleased to get an invite and only too happy to help provide some entertainment. It wasn't exactly superhero sci-fi stuff, but the crowd seemed delighted to see them all the same. They took their positions for a fake skirmish in an area cordoned off from the throng.

'I suppose we'd better go down now,' she said as the spotlight finally swung away and plunged the roof into unnerving darkness.

'You go first. I'll follow in a few minutes.'

Of course he wants to sneak away to get changed and melt back into the crowds, she thought. In fact she agreed it was a good plan, and if she went down first she could distract anyone who mattered. Phoebe nodded and wandered slowly back to the stairway that led from the tiny section of flat roof to the main building.

❧ ❧ ❧

Phoebe changed quickly in the deserted staffroom, her mind brimming with everything that had happened. Overlaying it all was a stain of guilt that she couldn't quite explain. She had nothing to feel guilty about. Did she? Somewhere in the crowd, Jack had watched the scene unfold on the roof, oblivious to who the figures were. But it wasn't like she'd done it on purpose. And it wasn't like she'd enjoyed it. Was it? So why did it suddenly feel so important that Jack didn't find out?

Back in her normal clothes, Phoebe checked her phone. There was a text from Jack telling her that he and Maria had arrived and asking where she was. He'd sent it only half an hour ago, so he probably hadn't yet had time to grab anyone she worked with to ask. But he would definitely have seen the rooftop show.

Racing down to the street, she clumsily texted him back saying she was on her way and to meet her by the store entrance. Then, amidst all the noise and chaos, she spotted him smiling across at her through a sea of faces. She rushed over, fighting the blush that spread across her cheeks. She stopped in her tracks as she saw that Archie stood with him and Maria. She hadn't expected him to come to something like this, especially when it was organised by her. Maybe he was trying to make an effort. The thought cheered her a little and took the edge off her anxiety.

'Everything ok?' Jack asked as he kissed her lightly. 'You look a bit flustered.'

'It's all this…' she waved a hand over the crowd and gave a self-conscious laugh. 'I just can't get over it.'

'Well, if it makes you feel better it's bloody amazing.' He looked down at Maria. 'What do you say, spud?'

'Yeah!' Maria shouted with a huge grin.

Phoebe's gaze rested on Archie. He shoved his hands in his pockets and grinned. 'I have to say, it is pretty cool. And there are some totally fit women walking around here.'

'Thank you, I think,' Phoebe laughed. She wondered whether it might be a good idea to find Midnight after all, perhaps she could keep Archie entertained as he admired her curves. But then, annoying younger brother or not, she knew she'd feel guilty about the fact that Midnight wouldn't just eat him for breakfast, she'd swallow him whole and wash him down with a neat whiskey.

'You've played a blinder, honestly,' Jack continued. 'If this doesn't get Millrise talking nothing will. What does Hendry say? Is he pleased?'

Phoebe's flush burned even harder and she tried valiantly to think about Old Mr Hendry's stern face glaring down at her instead of his son grinning at her on the rooftop.

'I think so. It's hard to tell at this point.'

'I think he ought to give you a pay rise,' Jack replied. 'At the very least he should treat you.'

He already did that, Phoebe thought. 'It's part of my job, isn't it? I doubt he'll even give it a second thought next week.'

'Midnight was great in the rooftop show too.'

'Yeah,' Archie agreed. 'She was pretty awesome. I'd like to meet her.'

'Be careful what you wish for,' Phoebe smiled. 'Once met, never forgotten.'

Jack clapped Archie on the back. 'From what I've heard I think you'd be in way over your head.'

'Still,' Archie sniffed, 'I'd take my chances.'

'I bet you would,' Jack said. He looked at Phoebe. 'Where is she?'

'Not sure. Getting changed I expect. I haven't seen her yet.' Phoebe scanned the crowds wondering where on earth Midnight could be. She was in there somewhere, dressed as who knew what. With a bit of luck she would stay in the crowds and avoid a meeting with Jack. Why couldn't Phoebe just tell him that it had been her up there? She had nothing to hide. She and Jack were adults and in a loving, trusting relationship, so they ought to be honest with each other and able to avoid petty jealousy. Phoebe had been doing her job and he'd understand that. Her mum would say that she was behaving like a silly teenager. Right now she wondered whether any of her teenage years had given her quite this much angst.

'Soooo, Maria…' Phoebe said brightly, 'have you seen the radio van? They're giving out amazing lollies.'

'We haven't made it over there yet,' Jack said as Maria's expectant grin spread across her face.

'In that case, we must go right now!' Phoebe said. 'Come on…'

'Don't you have to be on duty?' Jack asked.

'Dixon can handle everything for a bit. There's not much to do right now other than supervise the stuff other people are running.'

'Ok then…' Jack swept Maria up into his arms and onto his shoulders.

'I can see EVERYTHING up here!' Maria giggled.

'That's the idea, spud.'

'If it's all the same to you,' Archie said as they began to work through the crowds, 'I might just check out that beer tent and see what they've got on offer.'

Phoebe turned and gave him her brightest smile, one that told him he was forgiven – for now at least. 'No problem. We'll catch you up later.' Whether Archie was making an effort or not, whether he was forgiven or not, she was still happier when she had Jack and Maria to herself, just like it had always been; things were far less volatile. 'Is that ok with you, Jack?'

'Yeah…' Jack waved a vague hand, 'just stay out of trouble, eh?'

'Trouble?' Archie said with a grin. 'Me? As if!'

❧ ❧ ❧

She didn't know how she'd managed it, but Phoebe succeeded in keeping Jack out of Midnight's way. She hadn't really tried, thinking that a meeting was inevitable, but it had just happened and she certainly wasn't going to complain about Lady Luck cutting her a break for once. They spent time with her dad, who was delighted to introduce Maria to the rest of his re-enactment society and she was fascinated by everything that they showed her. They chatted to Dixon and other members of Hendry's staff, and then waited patiently in the wings while Phoebe was collared by a local reporter who wanted a few words on the plans for Hendry's. They ate every conceivable type of junk food they could get their hands on until Phoebe started worrying for Maria's health. Amidst it all there was blasting music, vivid spectacle and a buzzing atmosphere. After a couple of hours Maria was too tired to stay any longer so she and Jack hugged her goodbye before disappearing off to find Archie (who was probably drunk on hormones somewhere doing his best to impress any girl with a pulse) and take him home with them. As she waved them off, Phoebe realised that after everything that had happened, the argument that had seemed so disastrous that morning had shrunk to nothing. They had been as comfortable this evening as ever, and she didn't want anything to jeopardise that.

❧   ❧   ❧

Phoebe spent the rest of her weekend fulfilling a promised and overdue visit to her parents, and cleaning her flat. Despite the fact that she and Jack had parted on good terms after the cosplay event, there had been an unspoken agreement that a bit of space might be good for both of them. She had even enjoyed not seeing him, and couldn't decide if this was a good or bad thing. But on Monday morning, although she felt rested and happy, she woke feeling uncomfortably queasy.

Dixon pulled her into a hug as she walked into the office. She was surprised and flattered in equal measure but wished he wasn't squeezing her quite so enthusiastically.

'Here she is! My Golden Girl! What an event, eh? I haven't been able to stop thinking about it all weekend. Do you know how much money we made on the night? We sold almost everything!'

'How much?' Phoebe hung her jacket on an antiquated coat stand in the corner of the room.

'I have no idea! But I'm sure it's a lot. Steve is doing the sums now.'

'Christ, I bet that's made him happy.'

Dixon chuckled. 'Adam is thrilled with how it went too. I wouldn't be surprised if we get a little visit from him and his dad today.

'Hmmmm.' Neither prospect filled Phoebe with joy. She still hadn't forgiven Adam for taking advantage of her on the roof. Nor herself for liking it. The less she saw of him the better.

'He wants more of the same – as much as we can give him,' Dixon continued.

'I bet he does,' Phoebe muttered as she switched on her PC. The queasiness she'd woken with was now causing her some actual grief. She began to wonder if she'd eaten something dodgy or picked up a bug. The timing couldn't be worse. She was far too busy to be ill.

The door burst open and Sue from HR stood in the gap, legs virtually buckling under the weight of a bouquet that was almost larger than her. It was bursting with exotic tiger lilies, roses, gerbera and lush greenery. It looked like a very expensive and exclusive arrangement.

Sue peered around them with a manic grin.

'Wow, Phoebe said, trying to muster the appropriate enthusiasm, 'somebody really loves you.'

'I wish! They're actually for you, you lucky thing.' Sue tottered over and dumped them on Phoebe's desk, looking mightily relieved to have unburdened herself.

'Me?' Phoebe blinked at the flowers. Jack really couldn't afford to spend this sort of money, even if he did feel he had something apologise for. Which he didn't.

'Aren't you going to read the card?' Sue asked breathlessly.

Phoebe reached for the tiny white envelope nestling amid the blooms. The flap was closed but not sealed. She hoped that Sue hadn't already peeked at the card inside, but she wouldn't have put it past her. Phoebe opened it up.

Holy cow, that was one hell of a party!
Let's do it again soon!
Batman.

If she'd felt queasy before, nausea now swept over her. She read the note again. It was such a simple, innocent, even playful message, and yet there were so many complexities hidden in the subtext. Why was he doing this? It could be a harmless token of friendship, of course, and Phoebe wanted to believe that. But men like Adam Hendry didn't need to make gestures of friendship. A part of her was flattered, but the sensible thing to do would be to throw the flowers in the bin. She certainly couldn't take them home and she absolutely had to destroy the card.

'Who are they from?' Sue asked as Dixon stood with his arms folded, a huge grin on his face.

What could she say? If she told the truth the office gossip machine would crank into overdrive in seconds. If she lied she was risking the fact that Sue had already read the card and the gossip machine would get a turbo boost. She plumped for a semi-truth.

'I'm afraid I don't know, as they haven't signed it. Perhaps it's a secret admirer?' Phoebe tried to give an impish and secretive smile hoping they might enjoy being part of the mystery.

'Ooooh, how exciting!' Sue cooed, already in. 'Nothing like that ever happens to me.'

Phoebe wished she could say the same. Her nausea lurched and she took a deep breath. 'I'm not actually feeling that great today…' she announced to Dixon. 'Can you just excuse me for a minute?'

She bolted from the room and arrived in the bathroom just in time to hurl into the nearest toilet.

Afterwards, she gave her face a quick splash and stood at the mirror, pulling herself together. Normally, she felt better after being sick, but not today. Perhaps she'd be better off at home? But she had so much work to do and there was no one else to do it but her. Could things possibly get any worse?

Through the door, she heard Adam's voice on the stairs, and with that, she had her answer.

⚜   ⚜   ⚜

PART THREE
THE PARENT TRAP

M idnight handed Phoebe a glass of water. 'Have you done that test yet or what?'

They were on a rare break together. Phoebe grimaced as Midnight sat next to her with a coffee.

'Ugh! That's so disgusting.'

'See... my mum always said she couldn't stand the smell of tea or coffee when she was expecting me. This is why you need to do a test.'

'I know, I know. If anyone knows it's me. You don't have to keep going on about it.'

'So why aren't you?'

Phoebe stared into her glass.

'Phoebe...'

'I will, when I get a minute.'

'You've had plenty of minutes. You've been throwing up for two weeks.'

'I don't exactly throw up... not all the time anyway.'

'How is that better? If you were hurling your insides out you might be able to say it was food poisoning or something. But feeling sick and not always being sick...'

'Look, it's not that easy,' Phoebe cut in. 'I can't just pee on a stick and that's the end of it.'

'That's exactly what you do. These test kits have very simple instructions, you know. Simple enough, even for you.'

'Ha ha...'

'Seriously, isn't it better to know for sure?'

'I...' Phoebe glanced up as the staffroom door opened and Veronica Small came in.

'Alright?' Midnight greeted.

'Steve's on the warpath. He's sent me to find you.'

'You found me.'

'He says you're to get your arse back on the shop floor.'

'I've still got ten minutes of break left.'

'He says you were due back ten minutes ago.' Veronica looked distinctly nervous as she relayed her boss's words. Everyone who worked at Hendry's knew that although Midnight was the perpetual party girl, she also had a sharp tongue and could more than handle herself. Her appearance reinforced the impression. Not many wanted to get on the wrong side of her.

'I went late,' Midnight huffed. Veronica inched back towards the door. 'You can tell Steve that next time I'll drop everything and leave the customer I'm helping if he wants exact break timing.'

Veronica gave an apologetic shrug. 'Don't shoot the messenger.'

'Tell him I'll be down in ten minutes when I've had my actual break!' Midnight called after Veronica as she turned to leave. 'Honestly, the guy is such a douche.'

'Yeah…' Phoebe agreed in a vacant tone. She checked her watch. 'I suppose I ought to get back to it anyway.'

'You've barely been here two seconds yourself.'

'I know, but I have loads to do.' Phoebe went over to the sink to tip her water away.

'Don't think going upstairs will get you out of this conversation we've just been having,' Midnight said. 'If you can give me a valid reason why you shouldn't just take the bloody test and get it over with I'll give up. But I bet you can't.'

Phoebe turned to her with a heavy sigh. 'I'll do it later. I promise.'

'Personally, I don't give a rat's arse whether you do or not so there's no need to promise me like my life depends on it. I'm just telling you, as a friend, that you need to.'

'I know, and you're right. It's just…'

'Pretending it's not happening won't make it go away. Not confirming you're pregnant doesn't make you not pregnant. The baby will still be there, whether you acknowledge it or not.'

'It's easy for you to sit here and spout. It's not your whole life about to get ruined.'

'Hey… don't do the crime if you can't do the time.'

Phoebe gave a wan smile.

'Do you really think it will be all that bad if you are?' Midnight asked. 'You're ok with sprogs now that you know Maria?'

'Of course. It's scary though. I mean… it's not exactly how I imagined it would happen.'

'These things rarely are. If it helps make you feel better I'll totally babysit for you.'

'I think I'd rather get Beelzebub himself to baby-sit, but thanks.'

Midnight laughed. 'Go on; piss off back to your office. I have coffee drinking to get on with here. And I need to take my time and really savour it so that I'm at least ten minutes late back off break.'

Phoebe raised her eyebrows.

'If Steve wants to hassle me about being late back I'll give the twat something to hassle me for.'

Phoebe gave a bemused shake of her head but she couldn't help smiling. When it came down to it, Midnight would arrive back on duty and Steve wouldn't say a word about where she'd been. She'd always been a handful, but these days Midnight was a force of nature. She'd probably end up being the store general manager – people like her usually did. With a wave, Phoebe headed back to her own office at the top of the building.

Everything her friend had said was true, of course. Phoebe already knew the answer. She was sick every morning, or at least queasy, cried over the most ridiculous things, and – most importantly – couldn't remember when she had last had a period. But knowing the truth in your heart and seeing the evidence in front of your eyes were two very different situations and Phoebe honestly didn't know if she was ready for that point of no return. As things were now, at least she could kid herself that it wasn't really true, that there might be another, more easy to swallow explanation for her symptoms.

She hadn't dared mention it to Jack either, and it had been tough pretending everything was fine when all she wanted to do was hurl into her cornflakes at the breakfast table every morning. In fact, she hadn't told anyone but Midnight so far. Perhaps not the most reliable confidante, but Phoebe hoped that she'd keep the secret and in the end, she'd had to tell someone just to make the burden seem that little bit lighter. Out of everyone Phoebe knew, Midnight was the only person likely to remain neutral on the subject and she didn't care enough about anything to judge. Phoebe's parents would blow a gasket when they found out. With a bit of luck she could raise the kid in secret until it was eighteen and then send them out to announce their own existence to their grandparents on the day they came of age. As for Jack... well, she had no idea how he would react and right now she was too afraid to find out. Archie was still living with him, his mother still hated Phoebe, and Maria, naturally, demanded to be the centre of Jack's universe. There were too many reasons to keep this to herself and not nearly enough to announce it right now.

❧   ❧   ❧

Phoebe was in the seventh circle of hell. Otherwise known as Sunday lunch with the possibly-one-day-prospective in-laws. She could think of worse things she could be doing, of course: extracting her spleen through her belly button, cleaning the London sewer network with her toothbrush, sitting through double maths... It wasn't the lunch bit, although that was a real task these days when all she wanted to eat was ginger biscuits. But Jack's mum still detested her, and had zero conscience about making her feelings known. Whatever Phoebe said, she contradicted, or dismissed, or sneered at. Whatever Phoebe did made her roll her eyes and mutter under her breath.

Right now, Phoebe was looking longingly at the salt located next to Carol and wondering how best she could phrase a request for it without causing her nemesis to vomit in disgust. After a few moments of hesitation, she decided it was probably easier to go without.

'So...' Jack's dad began, 'Jack tells us you're doing really well at Hendry's these days, Phoebe.'

She caught the tiny, irritated sigh Carol emitted. But at least she had one ally in the parent camp, and she was grateful for his genuine friendly interest. If only he could persuade his wife to like her a fraction of the amount he seemed to, it would make her life so much more bearable. She couldn't think what it was about her existence that irked Carol so. Phoebe had never been anything but polite and friendly, and she had tried – Lord knows she'd tried – everything to make Jack's mum like her. It wasn't that she particularly cared about Carol, but she cared deeply about Jack, and if they could only get along it would make his life easier too. She swallowed her frustrations, and turned to Jack's father with a bright smile.

'I think it's going ok. Dixon seems happy anyway and the events are a success, for the most part. We have the odd disaster, of course...'

'Pass the mustard, Jack,' Carol said in a loud voice across Phoebe.

Phoebe trailed off and gave up. What was the point? Excruciating silence descended over the table again. Even Maria was diligently sawing at a slice of beef in absolute quiet. The only thing that could possibly make this worse would be the arrival of Archie, who had promised to stay out for the afternoon, having about as much desire to see his mother as she had to see him. Phoebe reflected that since they were harbouring the son that Carol had denounced as a thief and ejected from the maternal home, it was a miracle that she had deigned to grace them with her saintly presence at all.

'This beef is wonderful, as usual,' she continued. 'You're such a fabulous cook.'

'I had a fabulous teacher,' Jack said.

Phoebe wondered how much longer she could go without hurling. She took a giant swig of water to prevent her saying something that she wouldn't be able to unsay.

'Maria, darling... do you need some help with your meat?' Carol asked.

Maria looked up and shook her head.

'I could help, spud,' Phoebe said.

Maria looked up again and blew her fringe away from her head. She offered her knife and fork to Phoebe. If Carol had been irritated before, this would be enough to provoke all-out warfare. It probably would have done too, but at that moment there was an almighty crash from the front of the house as the front door burst open, slamming against the hall wall.

'Well... this is very cosy!' Archie exploded into the kitchen. The overwhelming stench of beer that followed in his wake set Phoebe's already delicate gag reflex on overdrive.

'Archie!' Jack shot up from his chair. 'I thought –'

'That I would be a good boy and stay out of the way while my big brother plays happy families for the inheritance? I changed my mind.' Archie lurched towards the table and snatched a roast potato from the dish.

'You're steaming drunk!' Jack dashed around the table in a bid to usher him from the room, but Archie ducked out of his way with a slurring laugh.

'Not fast enough, bro.' His hand darted for the table again and another potato disappeared into his mouth. 'So, how's it going?' He looked at his mother as he chewed. 'Missing me?'

'About as much as I miss shingles,' Carol replied tartly.

'That's better than I'd hoped for.'

The atmosphere in the room was so over-charged it was almost visible. Things were about to get ugly. Phoebe glanced across at Maria, who was watching proceedings with a wide-eyed look somewhere between confusion and outright fear. She was just about to suggest a walk in the garden when Jack's father beat her to it.

'Maria, sweetheart, shall we go and pick some of your dad's strawberries for pudding?' Without waiting for a reply he swept his granddaughter into his arms and headed for the back door. Phoebe half-wondered whether he would have been better refereeing his sons, but it wasn't her place to suggest it and, even as the thought ran through her head, he was gone.

'Go and sleep this off, Arch. We'll talk about it when you've sobered up.' Jack started to shepherd him towards the kitchen door, but it was like trying to herd cats.

'I want more potatoes... man, you're good at those. Remind me, how is it you're banging an actual girl?'

There was a sharp intake of breath from Carol, and Phoebe resisted the insane urge to giggle.

'Shut up, Archie!' Jack snapped. 'You're pissed and making an idiot of yourself.'

'Coz you never do that, do you, Mr Perfect? God it must be hard being so amazing.'

'You'll always be a bad seed,' Carol hissed.

'If I am then you made me that way,' Archie slurred back. He began a slow, sarcastic round of applause. Phoebe had to be impressed he could coordinate his hands to achieve this given the state he was in. 'Good work, mother.'

'Get out!'

'I can't, mother, since I live here now. Or have you forgotten that you threw me out?'

'Archie, you said you wouldn't do this.' Jack glanced at Phoebe. 'Not now.'

'Oh yeah, don't want your girlfriend to find out how dysfunctional your family really is. Not when you've put so much work into making her think you're the perfect man. It's a shame Rebecca isn't around to put her right.'

'Don't you dare bring Rebecca into this,' Jack growled.

'She's already in it. She was in it the minute she met you.'

'She's dead you idiot.'

'Yeah... you had quite a lot to do with that, didn't you?'

Jack's jaw twitched and in the same instant, his arm pulled back to fire a punch and Phoebe leapt up to grab it.

'Don't!' she yelled. 'He's drunk.'

'Thanks, doll face,' Archie gave a hollow laugh, 'but I think I can take this loser on if he wants a go.'

'I'm not protecting you,' Phoebe shot back. 'I'm protecting him from the guilt he'll feel afterwards.' She yanked on Jack's arm. 'Think about this, Jack.'

'Leave it, blondie,' Archie sneered. 'If the tough guy wants a pop I'm game.'

'Stop being so ridiculous,' Carol snapped.

'*You're* ridiculous, you bitter old cow,' Archie returned. 'You've never had time for me and I've never been able to make you happy so what's the point in trying anymore? It was always perfect Jack and his perfect Rebecca. I think you'd have been happier if I'd died instead of her. You'd much rather have had her as a daughter than me as a son.'

'That's bollocks, Archie!' Jack shouted.

'At least Rebecca didn't steal from her own mother!' Carol shook as she spoke and Phoebe could see that he'd hit a nerve. She wondered whether Archie was sober enough to have noticed, but doubted it.

'Whatever… I don't need this.' Archie glowered at Jack and then at his mother in turn.

'Neither do we.' Jack shook his arm from Phoebe's grip. She held her breath, but he didn't swing for his brother again, as she had feared. Instead, he shoved him towards the kitchen door.

'Go and sober up. You can come down when you've decided to stop being a dick.'

Archie gave a savage salute. 'Yes, sir, boss, sir!' he replied in a mocking tone. 'You carry on being Perfect Peter down here and I'll go to my room and think about what I've done.'

'Archie!' Carol yelled, but he simply threw her a contemptuous grin and then swivelled himself clumsily out of the doorway, weaving down the hall towards the stairs.

When Phoebe looked at Jack again he was shaking more than his mother had been. 'I'm sorry, Mum,' he said in a low voice.

'You've brought it on yourself, Jack.'

'What?'

'You've always known what he's like and yet you were still foolish enough to give him house room. Now you're reaping the rewards of that decision.'

Jack's eyes widened. 'You're serious?'

'Deadly.'

Phoebe looked from one to the other. She couldn't believe what she was hearing. Jack looked even more incredulous.

'He's my brother – your son! Are you suggesting that I ought to have left him to fend for himself on the streets?'

'Don't be so melodramatic.'

'Anything could have happened to him!'

'I'm sure he'd have managed. One of his no-good friends would have put him up in a dosshole somewhere.'

'And that would have been ok?'

'He's relied on this family for far too long and he's played us all for fools. He's still playing you.' Carol folded her arms and held Jack in a scornful gaze. 'In future, I'd rather not see him here when I come to visit you and Maria.'

Phoebe couldn't hold her tongue any longer. 'Hang on a minute!' she cut in. 'Jack never wanted this to happen. He tried to protect you by making sure Archie wasn't here. He's looking after the boy you refuse to. He's trying to be the good guy –' her speech was cut short by Carol slamming her hand on the table.

'I'll thank you to keep your nose out of our affairs.'

'Mum, Phoebe's only trying to –'

Carol held a hand up to silence him. 'Phoebe should remember,' she said coldly, 'that she is not a part of this family and therefore has no right to pass judgement on us.'

'As far as I'm concerned she has as much right to an opinion as anyone else,' Jack fired back.

'I can actually speak for myself,' Phoebe cut in.

'Not if Mum gets half a chance to shut you up.'

'I beg your pardon!' Carol gave an indignant snort.

'You heard him,' Phoebe returned. Dire as the situation was, she experienced a sliver of triumph watching Jack bring the mother from hell down a peg or two. But he turned on her now instead.

'Don't…' he warned. 'Leave it alone.'

Phoebe stared at him. 'You're having a go at *me* now?'

'Of course not. Perhaps you should go outside for a bit with Dad and Maria.'

'I don't believe it!' Phoebe squeaked. 'I'm the only person here who has done nothing wrong and I'm being banished from the room like your naughty little brother?'

'You're overreacting,' Jack said.

If eyes could actually pop out of heads then Phoebe's would be rolling around the floor right now. 'After everything that's gone on in here you say I'm overreacting? You have a very weird idea of what's normal behaviour.' She hooked a thumb at his mother. 'What about her?'

'How dare you...' Carol began.

'Oh, shut *up*!' Phoebe snapped, her temper now getting the better of her. She knew, even in the heat of the moment, that she'd regret it, but she'd been pushed to the absolute limit. 'You hate me whatever I do or say so what's the point in trying to be nice? I might as well tell you how I really see it. I think you're a silly cow who ought to be helping her youngest son when he's clearly crying out for that help. You have a totally black and white view of the world...' she waved away Jack's interruption. 'I'm not Rebecca so I can't be right. Archie is not the perfect grade A son so you can't love him. He's made a mistake so he has to move out of your house and you don't care where he goes and there are no second chances. You'd rather your older son stayed alone forever than find a girl who doesn't fit your perfect criteria but loves him all the same. That's what I think. And it makes me wonder just what kind of mother you are.'

Carol was open mouthed. 'Jack… are you going to let her talk to me like that?'

Jack looked helplessly from one to the other.

'Jack.' Phoebe countered, 'are you going to let her talk to *you* like that?'

'Or are you going to grow a pair and tell her where to get off?' Archie stood at the kitchen door again with an inebriated but delighted grin on his face. All three spun round to face him.

'What the hell…' Jack snapped. 'What do you want now?'

'Potatoes,' Archie said. 'I'm starving.'

Before anyone could argue, Archie dashed in and whipped the dish from the table. He ran for the stairs again with a derisive laugh as he went.

'That's it – he has to go,' Jack muttered.

Phoebe winced. All the time Archie had been living with Jack she had wanted him to leave. But not like this. This wasn't Jack. The Jack that Phoebe loved would never throw his brother out and no matter what Archie did, Phoebe wanted that wonderful, kind, forgiving Jack to be the one to deal with it, not this furious, reactive Jack who faced her now.

'You can't do that,' Phoebe said quietly. 'He needs you.'

'What would you know?' Carol cut in. 'You think you have the answers?'

'No, but –'

'You've been with Jack for a few months and you think you know everything. You think you can cure

Archie?' Carol let out a scornful laugh. 'I'd like to see you try.'

'Well maybe I will,' Phoebe replied stubbornly. 'I think he just needs some focus and a little self-respect.'

'And how do you propose to achieve this miracle?' Carol asked coldly.

'I'll… I'll talk to him. He needs someone to take an interest, to find out what he wants from life.'

'Money to squander is the answer you'll get.'

'Perhaps. But you need to look deeper than that, at why he's doing what he does.'

Phoebe glanced at Jack. He was gazing at her thoughtfully. He looked calmer, which she was thankful for, but he also looked hopeful, which worried her. She thought she knew what he was thinking. He believed that she might be able to get through to Archie and that what she'd said in irritation and self-defence to get back at Carol was something she actually believed was possible. There might be some truth in it, but where on earth did she begin trying to get through to someone like Jack's brother? He wouldn't open up to Jack or his parents so he certainly wasn't going to pour his heart out to her, someone he seemed to have very little respect for.

'I can't make any promises,' Phoebe said, pre-empting any request Jack might make for her to talk to Archie. 'He might not even listen to me. In fact, he almost certainly won't.'

'But he might,' Jack replied. 'You're neutral ground. And he likes you.'

There was a derisive snort from Carol that they both chose to ignore. Although Phoebe was inclined to agree with what it meant – she wasn't sure Archie liked her at all. She suspected he tolerated her the way she tolerated him. If he did like her and had told Jack as much, he had a strange way of showing it. 'Perhaps not such a good idea today, though,' Jack added.

'Probably not,' Phoebe agreed with obvious relief in her voice.

Jack rubbed a hand through his hair. He gazed at the detritus of lunch littering the table and now rapidly cooling. 'Do you think we can finish our meal without someone committing actual murder?' There wasn't a sound from upstairs – not a tap running, or footsteps on the landing – nothing. Phoebe could only assume Archie had fallen onto his bed and passed out.

Carol had already taken her seat and was arranging her napkin across her lap. The action was so ridiculously prim that Phoebe didn't know whether she wanted to laugh out loud or slap the woman. If there was one thing putting her off a future with Jack it was his mother. Her thoughts wandered momentarily to the baby she was almost certain she was carrying. What would Carol make of that? Phoebe and Jack had been together for a little over six months now. But when Rebecca fell pregnant, even though she and Jack were still young, they had been together since school. Sometimes, when she reflected on the tragedy of Rebecca dying so young, she could understand why everyone worshipped her the way they did. A life cut short like that had a way of making a dent in the soul of all who knew them.

'You want me to fetch Maria and your dad in?' Phoebe asked.

Jack nodded. 'I think the coast is clear.'

The rest of the meal was completed in an even more awkward silence than it had begun in. By the time Jack's parents left, taking Maria with them to spend the night at their house, Phoebe really just wanted to go home too. Jack seemed a little hurt and offended when she announced her intentions, but she didn't fancy a second round with Archie when he woke up and she explained this as subtly as she could.

'You probably need to talk to him without me in the way,' she said.

He tried to smile, pretending – not very well – to make light of the situation. 'I'm more sensible when you're here.'

'I don't think so. You can be more honest when I'm not here.'

There was a pause. 'I thought...' he began, 'I thought you were going to talk to him...'

She shook her head slowly. 'I'm not sure if that's such a good idea after all. It was something I said in the heat of the moment but your mum was right. I'm not part of your family and it's not for me to stick my nose in.'

'She's wrong...' Jack took Phoebe into his arms as they stood in the hallway, trying to stop her from leaving. 'You're a part of *my* family and I want you to continue to be that. She's going to have to get used to it and she will… All I ask is that you give her more time.'

'I'd be surprised if she ever accepted me. I will try though, if only for you.'

Jack planted a tender kiss on her forehead. 'Thank you. I'll talk to her.'

'God, no!'

'I won't make it obvious, don't worry. And I won't make it sound as if you've complained about her.' He smiled. 'I can do diplomacy, you know…'

'Ok.' Phoebe leaned into his embrace. 'Good luck with that.'

Jack laughed. Phoebe could feel it vibrate through his chest as she lay her head against him. 'You're sure you won't stay?' he asked.

'I…' Phoebe paused. With his arms around her, holding her in a safe, warm bubble of love, she felt braver. She wanted to tell him the thing that was troubling her above all else – more than the family squabbles and the one-woman hate campaign –the thing she had been keeping back for fear of his reaction. But the moment passed as quickly as it had arrived and her courage left her. Perhaps, on reflection, this wasn't the time. And perhaps she ought to be certain of the news before she announced it. If she was wrong, there was no point in stirring things up even more.

She looked up and kissed him. 'I have some things to do. I'll call you tomorrow.'

There was a chemist on her way home that kept out-of-hours opening for emergencies. As far as Phoebe could tell, her situation had now escalated into at least a minor emergency. It was time she took charge of her future.

❧ ❧ ❧

Lunchtimes were always a rush, but this particular Monday was even more fraught than usual. Perhaps it was Phoebe's agitated mood, or the extra work that Dixon had dumped on her desk without warning while he went off to a meeting with the editor of the *Millrise Echo*. Or perhaps it was the fact that Adam Hendry had been stalking the place like a cheetah waiting to separate a gazelle from the rest of the pack so that he could pounce, forcing Phoebe to hide in any room he wasn't likely to be in as soon as Dixon left the premises. So, while it had been a relief to get out into the sunshine with Midnight when their break came, Phoebe wasn't exactly relaxed.

As they stood at the cash machine, Phoebe punched in her pin and snatched the money from the slot, hardly giving it time to eject the notes.

'Oooh, totally saw your number then,' Midnight said, peering over Phoebe's shoulder with a grin.

'In that case you will have totally seen my bank balance,' Phoebe said as she turned to face her, tucking the money into a purse, 'which is poor enough but is certainly not going to be enhanced by the arrival of a baby.' She started to walk in the direction of the imposing frontage of Hendry's toy shop, clearly visible towering over the smaller buildings that hugged its shadow along the high street. The sight gave her that dull ache in her heart again. She wasn't ready to give up all that she had worked so hard for, and would have continued to fight tooth and nail against competitors, financial difficulties, long hours, overbearing bosses – anything that was thrown at her. But how could she fight what was going on inside her own body? Whatever happened now, this baby was coming and despite her very mixed feelings, the alternative was unthinkable. She had new priorities now, ones that she hadn't planned for and didn't know how she felt about, but there was no shirking them. Everything was going to change, whether she liked it or not.

'It'll be alright, you know,' Midnight said.

Phoebe eyed her silently, wondering whether she'd voiced her feelings out loud without realising or Midnight had actually read her thoughts. The day felt that kind of weird.

'Loads of women carry on working with babies,' Midnight added.

'Yeah, I know that. But I'll have to take a break, and just when we're starting to turn things around for Hendry's. I don't want to miss anything. I won't have to be off work for long before I'm out of the loop and not needed anymore, then they'll never need me like they do now.'

'They might get maternity cover in but it'll prob-ably be someone shit. I wouldn't sweat it.'

'It's not just work,' Phoebe continued. 'My flat is hardly big enough for me let alone a baby and a whole load of weird and wonderful equipment.'

'Can't you move in with Mr Stalker?' Midnight asked, a faint note of surprise in her voice.

'He's already got a house full. And I can't say I'm enamoured with the idea of living with Archie, who isn't going anywhere soon, as far as I can tell.'

'Surely a baby will change all that?'

'Maybe...' Phoebe sounded unconvinced.

'You could apply for a council house,' Midnight said brightly.

'I could, but they're much further out of town and as I don't have a car it would make life difficult. Not only that but I don't think I'd like feeling that isolated. I thought about moving back in with mum and dad for a while, but I don't know if I could stand my mum telling me how wrong I'm doing everything every time I change a nappy...' she shuddered. 'Ugh, listen to me... I'm actually talking about changing nappies.'

'So?' Midnight raised her eyebrows. 'You will have to, you know.'

'I just never saw myself as a mother. Not like this, anyway.'

'But you are going to keep it?'

Phoebe looked at Midnight who was wearing the most serious and anxious expression Phoebe had ever seen on her face. It seemed that she really was concerned about the answer to the question.

'Of course,' Phoebe said. 'There's no question of me not keeping it. I suppose I just don't feel ready.'

'When are you going to tell Jack?'

'I want to see the doctor first, get a midwife appointment and find out everything I need to know.' Phoebe sighed. 'I'm so bloody crap at keeping track of my not very reliable periods that I don't know for sure how far gone I am. I wish I'd kept up with writing them on the calendar, but as it is, I need the midwife or a scan or something to tell me.'

'You must have some idea.'

Phoebe shook her head. 'Obviously I know I'm nowhere near full term and can't possibly be more than about four months because me and Jack... well, you know...'

'Yeah, yeah, I get it.' Midnight glanced at Phoebe's midriff. 'I don't think it's many weeks at all because there is literally no bump yet.'

Phoebe looked down at herself. She was wearing a neat blouse and slacks – more or less her standard work kit now. She couldn't see any difference either but she'd certainly felt the fabric pull a little more on her trousers this past week. She'd tried putting it down to contentment or too many of Jack's cakes, but there was no denying the truth now. Two little blue lines and a sleepless Sunday night could testify to that.

'I'll know more later in the week, I suppose,' Phoebe replied. 'Please, Midnight, keep this to yourself until then.'

'Of course I will. Aren't you just a little bit excited, though?'

Phoebe thought about that for a moment as the front door of Hendry's came into view. Was she excited? Was the sheer terror that had coloured her initial reaction masking the fact that the idea of having Jack's baby was a tiny bit attractive? It was hard to tell.

'God knows what I think. Right now, all I can think is that I hope Dixon is back from his meeting, because otherwise I might have to customise a light sabre from our new cosplay section to fight off unwanted attention this afternoon.'

'Need any help with that?' Midnight grinned.

'The customisation or the unwanted attention?'

'Both.'

'I think I have it covered. I suppose I could just whisper the P word and he'd be off like a ferret down a pair of Y-fronts, but I'd better keep that to myself for the time being.'

Midnight lowered her voice as they entered the building. 'You must be the only woman in the country who'd complain about the fact that Adam Hendry is trying to get off with you.'

'It's the getting off bit that worries me. I'd be concerned about a bit of chivalric wooing but getting off is a definite no.'

Midnight's reply was cut short by the sight of Steve storming in their direction like a disgruntled head-master. All he lacked was the funny hat and the cane.

'Oh God, he's on the warpath again,' Midnight hissed.

Phoebe glanced at her watch. 'You're not late.'

'It doesn't matter with Steve. I've probably brought too much ozone back in with me or some-thing and it's against company policy.'

Phoebe laughed as she swerved off towards the stairs, leaving Midnight to deal with whatever barrage of abuse Steve was intent on launching at her. It was funny, but talking about it over the last half hour, away from the confines of work and with someone as neutral as Midnight had actually made her feel a lot brighter about her current situation. If only Midnight could weave her magic over the next eighteen years and make those as easy, bringing up a child would be a doddle.

⚜   ⚜   ⚜

When she reached her office, Dixon was still missing and Adam was swivelling in his seat from side to side as he pored over a spreadsheet on Dixon's computer screen. At her entrance, he looked up and gave a rather too satisfied smile.

'You're here. I'd almost given up on you.'

'I went for a quick walk; blow the cobwebs out – you know?'

'Where did you go?'

For half a moment Phoebe was torn between telling him that it was none of his business and the truth that she had gone to draw the last of the money from an account that would not be topped up until payday, which was ten days away. She decided that he would probably struggle with either of those concepts.

'It was such a nice day so I wandered down the high street and back.'

'Ah… shopping, eh?' he said in a voice that suggested he thought shopping was the only thing women did apart from cook, clean and bear children.

'No. Just a walk.' Phoebe wriggled out of her jacket and hung it on the old coat rack. 'Is there something I can help you with?'

'Actually, there is…'

As Phoebe sat at her desk he gave her such a penetrating look that she couldn't help the violent blush that spread up from her neck. He wasn't just undressing her with his eyes, he was clearing the desk and ravishing her on it. If she hadn't already been pregnant it was the sort of look that might have done the job even from ten feet away. All she could bring herself to say in reply was, 'Oh.'

'I'm struggling to work out what Dixon is doing here…' he inclined his head at the computer screen, 'and I wondered if you could enlighten me.'

'You want me to come and have a look?' Something that involved standing close to Adam was the last thing she wanted to do.

'I'd appreciate it,' he said.

Phoebe hesitated for a heartbeat before shuffling over. Leaving a respectable distance she peered over his shoulder. But then he moved his chair, ever so slightly and subtly, and closed the gap.

While he had never yet tried to repeat the kissing incident on the rooftop – what Midnight had christened Bat-Gate when Phoebe had filled her in – Adam had made his intentions towards Phoebe very clear. Any clearer would have involved him wearing a ruby-encrusted codpiece and carrying a huge sign saying: *PHOEBE – GET IT HERE*. She had stubbornly dismissed it at first, despite his blatant interest, but it was now so painfully obvious that she couldn't deny it any longer. She just wished he would get the message that she wasn't interested without having to offend or insult him. Even if she *was* interested (which she wasn't, she kept reminding herself) she had a boyfriend and Adam knew that.

As these thoughts ran through her mind, that intoxicating scent of his clouded everything. God only knew where he bought this stuff but she was convinced that it was some voodoo doctor in a seedy backstreet in New Orleans rather than an actual shop, because it had the strangest effect on her. Was this part of his power? It seemed that every woman working in Hendry's was attracted to him and even though Phoebe was not (she definitely was not) there was no doubt that his attention was extremely flattering. She just wished he would be attentive from a distance… Peru ought to do it.

'See this column here...' Adam pointed a finger at the screen. Damn, even his fingers were lean and muscular, his nails manicured to manly perfection. Phoebe blinked away the thought and concentrated on the computer monitor. She blinked again and wished she could concentrate on the finger once more. She had always been crap at spreadsheets and databases at school, unable to see the point and unable to care enough to try. She hoped that whatever followed wouldn't be too difficult for her to understand or explain. She gave a tiny, silent nod. Adam looked at her.

'Well?'

What was she supposed to be looking at? He seemed to be labouring under the impression that she knew what he meant.

'Erm... perhaps you want to wait until Dixon is back? This is his work and I'm not sure that it's finished yet anyway, so I might be giving you incomplete information...'

'You'll be able to tell me this much. Just lean in here...'

Phoebe reluctantly inched forward, his scent wrapping its sexy tendrils around her common sense a little bit tighter.

'Come on...' His voice was low and husky. It was sexy, if you thought the wolf from Little Red Riding Hood was sexy. Dangerous would be a better word, the kind of danger that made women weak at the knees. 'Don't be shy. Come and look properly...'

Phoebe moved closer, some compulsion that overrode her rational thoughts driving her. She could feel his breath on her cheek. Where was Dixon when she needed him? 'What am I looking at?' she asked, her voice struggling above a whisper.

He turned slowly to face her, his lips inches from hers. What would she do if he tried to kiss her again? She chased the image from her head and tried to concentrate on the screen.

The door burst open and Dixon bowled in, whistling some unrecognisable tune. Phoebe leapt away from the desk and even the unflappable Mr Hendry looked vaguely ruffled.

'Alrighty there?' Dixon called cheerfully as he went to hang his coat on the rickety old stand.

'We were…' Phoebe mumbled as she hurried back to her desk.

'Dixon…' Adam's composure returned as he greeted his employee smoothly. 'I had hoped that Phoebe could explain a section of this spreadsheet to me but now that you're here you can assist me instead.'

'My pleasure,' Dixon smiled. 'Just let me grab a spare chair and I'm all yours.'

Phoebe heaved a silent sigh of relief. Another few moments and she might have been Adam's too.

⚜　⚜　⚜

Bloody hormones. Phoebe sat on the bus watching the town rush past her window. The sun from earlier in the day had given way to a leaden drizzle that washed the colour from the streets and left people hurrying home coatless and without umbrellas.

Phoebe didn't know these days whether she was up or down, left or right – bastard hormones had to be the only explanation for her weird behaviour today in the office with Adam. Her face burned every time she thought about how, if Dixon hadn't arrived when he did, she might have found herself kissing Mr Hendry the Younger. Not the behaviour of a woman who was supposed to be in love with the man whose baby she was carrying.

That wasn't the only weird thing to happen that day. Sue Bunce, the HR boss, had been whispering to Office Lady when Phoebe walked in to ask if she could borrow their printer while Dixon, elbow deep in cyan toner, tried to fix their own. As she entered the office they immediately broke off, turning to her with awkward, sheepish expressions. Phoebe wasn't normally the paranoid type, and she wasn't narcissistic enough to think that people cared about what she did enough for her to be a source of juicy office gossip, but there was no mistaking that they had been talking about her.

Then there was the knowing smirk from Gareth Parker later on the stairs. She had tried to dismiss that too; after all, Gareth was full of knowing smirks, but this one really did seem very knowing indeed.

Phoebe had missed Midnight at the end of the day and so hadn't been able to see whether her friend could shed any light on the puzzling events. They were probably unconnected and more than likely only in her head, but if it continued then she would have a word. If there was some scandal concerning her, Midnight would know about it.

Her musings were interrupted by the bleep of her phone. She fished it from the sweet wrapper-filled depths of her bag and read the message from Jack.

Did you have a good day? I've made far too much chilli if you want to come over and help me out! x

Phoebe locked the screen again and stared out of the window. She felt weird, stressed, and very, very tired. In her current mood, it probably wasn't a good idea to go over there, but she would have to give him a better reason than feeling weird for not going.

The bus ground to an abrupt halt, throwing her forward in her seat. Phoebe watched as people got off, and more people got on to fill their seats. A woman with a tiny baby and a huge pram struggled up the steps with both in her arms. A middle-aged couple dashed to her aid, taking the pram from her while she paid the fare and then helping her stow it in the little section for buggies and wheelchairs at the front before she took her seat. She kept saying thank you, over and over again as they helped. She seemed so utterly grateful that Phoebe wondered if, at some point, she was going to offer them her soul.

God, was that what life would be like for Phoebe soon? Would it be dominated by the logistics of buses and the arbitrary kindness of strangers? Would the real Phoebe Clements disappear under a mountain of nappies and sleepless nights, never to be seen again?

The engine roared into life again, but the rocking and juddering as it chugged along made Phoebe feel queasy. All she wanted to do was go home, lie in her bath for an hour… maybe three… and then go to bed.

Her phone was still clutched in her hand. Unlocking it, she sent Jack a brief text apologising that she felt unwell and that she couldn't come over. His response, moments later, was so typically Jack that Phoebe almost changed her mind. He was worried, and wanted to bundle Maria in the car and come over to the flat to make sure she was ok. She reassured him that everything was fine and that she was just overtired, and after some to-ing and fro-ing they agreed that she would call round to see him the following night.

Phoebe stashed her phone back in her bag as the bus drag-raced towards a set of red lights. Jack really was the most wonderful boyfriend. So why did her mind keep wandering back to her close encounter with Adam Hendry? She ought to forget all about it and make careful plans to defend herself against his peculiar and deadly form of attack. She needed to make sure it didn't happen again.

Bloody hormones.

❦ ❦ ❦

The giant monkey shaped piñata had a frozen grin that was less *Curious George* and more Chucky from *Child's Play*. The delivery driver couldn't have failed to see the look of distress on Phoebe's face when she signed for it, but not a word was said and it was too late to do anything about it by the time it arrived anyway. Besides, in an hour from now it would be lying in tatters on the floor of Hendry's store, battered to death by twenty psychotic, sugar-fuelled nine year olds, and the smile would be well and truly wiped from its demonic face.

As Midnight shoved another handful of sweets up its backside, Phoebe couldn't help a small sense of triumph at her revenge on the offending monstrosity. Sitting next to her, cross-legged on the floor, she turned her attention back to the balloon she was trying, with a great deal of muttered cursing, to tie.

Hendry's newly opened *Party Central* zone had been another of Phoebe's brainwaves. The idea was to create bespoke birthday parties for kids based on their favourite toys or shows. Dixon had loved it, and Adam had taken very little persuading to give the go-ahead, not even bothering to consult his father. A space had been allocated in the store, advertising had gone up, and bookings were coming in thick and fast. So fast, in fact, that Phoebe was having trouble keeping up with them. Steve had been unhappy, of course (when was he ever happy?) when Phoebe had been forced to poach some of his staff to help with the preparations from time to time, but had been silenced by one word from Adam, and forced to glower in Phoebe's direction every time she walked past.

There had been teething problems, as with everything. One particular highlight of the first party that had almost called a halt to the whole enterprise was the appointment of Jeff the sometimes-Santa-janitor as chief party entertainer. Midnight had found him passed out in the stockroom with an empty hip flask when he failed to show up for his first performance and the arrangement had had to be quickly terminated. Despite this inauspicious start, the parties were a hit. The secret was in the different packages. Phoebe had a flair for putting together a fantastic event for even the smallest budget and word had quickly spread through the local schools. The area of the store that *Party Central* occupied was a relatively unloved one and Phoebe had given alteration instructions to the store maintenance crew, which had worked really well to make the best use of the small space.

'I don't suppose you could stay on tonight to do this party?' Phoebe asked Midnight as she finally won the battle with her balloon and batted it over to a pile of others.

'Why?'

'I said I'd see Jack tonight and if I stay it will make me really late for him.'

'But you always like to see that everything is running according to your OCD plans.'

TILLY TENNANT

'I'm not that bad; I just want everything to be right. Anyway, they pretty much go ok now and I think it would be fine without me for one night.'

'You're going to tell him about the…' Midnight lowered her voice, 'you know what?'

'I don't know…'

Midnight's normal tone returned. 'What makes you think I don't have plans?'

'Do you?'

'No. But you assumed that I don't and it bugged me. Why would I want to spend my evening at a kids' party, even if I didn't have plans?'

'Because you love parties.'

Midnight grinned. 'True. I want double time, though.'

'Time and a half is the best I can do.'

'Throw in first dibs on the party leftovers and you have a deal.'

Phoebe reached over to give her a quick hug. 'Thanks, gorgeous.'

Midnight gave a subtle flick of her head in the direction of an approaching figure as Phoebe let go. 'Speaking of gorgeous…'

'Shit!' Phoebe muttered. Her hand dived into a box of sweets at Midnight's feet. She fished one out and pretended to read the wrapper intently. 'No nuts in these!' she announced in a staged voice, never taking her eyes from the sweet. Perhaps, if he thought she was far too busy to talk, Adam would leave her alone.

276

'Afternoon, Mr H!' Midnight called cheerfully.

Phoebe's heart sank. She looked up to see him smiling down at them. It wasn't the sort of smile to put her at ease, though; it was sardonic, calculating, hungry. Today, she looked as unattractive as it was possible for her to look but still he persisted. Tomorrow, she would turn up for work with a bag over her head, preferably one that smelled of rotting vegetables. Although she'd probably discover he was kinky that way and liked it.

'How's it going?' he asked.

'Fine. We're just super busy right now getting everything ready for a party at six.' Phoebe reached past Midnight to stuff a handful of sweets up the monkey's bum, to demonstrate how super busy they were.

'Don't let me stop you.' Adam crossed his arms and continued to stare down at her.

'Ok,' chirruped Midnight. Phoebe gave a quick glance her way to see that she was clearly holding back a grin. As she looked away, her gaze swept across the shop floor beyond the party area, and she could see other members of staff now watching proceedings with interest too. If Adam really had to play out this little obsession, then why did he insist on doing it as publicly as possible all the time? He might as well call a staff meeting and snog her in full view of everyone. It couldn't be any more humiliating than this. Her gaze returned to Adam. He was still looking steadily at her – or rather, as it felt, straight through her clothes to her naked body. She could ask him if there was anything he wanted but after the previous day alone with him in Dixon's office that seemed a little too much like an invitation. Instead, she returned silently to her task. And then, Midnight did it for her.

'Is there something you need?'

Phoebe held back a groan as she looked up again.

'Actually, I'd rather like to see what goes on at one of these parties. I'll stay in the background, of course, watch things from our end; not actually attend the party.'

'You want to be like... a member of staff?' Phoebe asked incredulously. But if he wanted to stay and observe proceedings he would have to be. A man standing in a suit watching a load of nine-year-olds larking around would have the parental paedo alarms ringing in minutes – even Adam had to be able to see that.

'Why not?' he replied.

Phoebe blinked at him. And then another plan popped into her head.

Ten minutes later the heir to the Hendry family business stood before Phoebe and Midnight, dressed in the stock uniform of his employees.

'Suits you,' Phoebe said.

His red polo shirt (a little snug around the shoulders and short in length and definitely in need of a hot date with a washing machine) looked deeply incongruous teamed with his expensively-tailored trousers and leather-soled shoes. The addition of a red peaked cap bearing the words *Team Party Central* was enough to make Phoebe laugh out loud. He looked completely ridiculous. It was only a small victory, but she was willing to grab it and enjoy the hell out of it.

Adam didn't seem quite so enthusiastic about the transformation and was clearly trying to retain his last shred of dignity by not reacting to the silent shoulder shaking of his staff.

'I know it doesn't really fit,' Phoebe added, 'but it was the best we could find...' It wasn't, but he didn't need to know that. 'And,' she continued, 'it is regulation party team wear.'

'Of course,' he replied stiffly.

'And we couldn't have you dressed incorrectly for the party.'

'Quite,' he replied.

'Because that would rattle the parents... you know? They wouldn't be able to identify you as a member of staff and they need to do that... for Hendry's reputation. You understand, don't you?' Phoebe felt a tiny bit bad about how much she was enjoying this situation. But not for long. It was just too funny not to milk, and the next part of her master plan would be even better. Plus, there was no way he could be angry with her – after all, she was following company procedure and protecting their reputation. Whatever he thought about his current state of dress he would have to keep to himself. 'Although, we might need to keep you in the background because the uniform isn't the best fit and doesn't look that great and the other party team members are far more experienced at this sort of thing by now...' He gave a grim nod. 'So...' Phoebe concluded, 'I'll leave you in Midnight's capable hands. She'll tell you what to do once the party guests arrive and explain anything you need to know.'

He stared at her. 'You're not staying?'

'Oh no,' Phoebe said airily. 'I'm not on shift tonight. Midnight is very kindly covering this one.' She gave him her brightest, most innocent smile. 'You're in good hands with her. I do hope you have a lovely time and gain a valuable insight into what the parties are all about.'

Midnight threw her a delighted grin. Phoebe suspected that Adam would meet his match in her tonight; she just hoped that her lovely friend wouldn't push his buttons too far. But the satisfaction in being able to get one over on Adam was too good to be diluted by any other worries – at least for now. Maybe she'd regret it in the morning, but right now she was going to enjoy her evening with a man who was worth twice what Adam Hendry was to her.

❖ ❖ ❖

Archie opened the front door to Phoebe, Maria standing beside him. On the way over she had been full of high spirits and eager to tell Jack and Maria all about her day. Her little victory over Adam had filled her with a sense of mischief that had chased away the fatigue and nausea that were now a part of her daily routine, and she felt almost like her old self again. But she had been brought back down to earth again with a heavy bump as she caught the knowing grin on Archie's face. Something was up.

'Phoebe!' Maria squeaked as she threw her arms around Phoebe's legs.

'Hey, spud, how's it going?'

Archie sauntered back up the hallway. 'You're in for a night and a half,' he said carelessly without looking back. 'Too bad me and Maria are heading out.'

Maria always ate tea with them when Phoebe visited on weeknights and then they played or watched TV with her before she went to bed at around seven-thirty. It was their thing, what they did. And Archie was taking Maria out? On his own? Jack didn't trust Archie to be a responsible adult at the best of times, as far as she could tell, but now he was allowing him out with his precious daughter? Why the sudden change of heart? 'Is everything ok?' Phoebe followed Archie down the hallway. He stopped at the cupboard doorway under the stairs to pull out a jacket for him and one for Maria.

'Not that one,' Maria said. 'I want the pink one because I have my pink pumps on.'

Archie gave an impatient sigh and waved the yellow jacket at her. 'Does it matter? We're only going to MacDonald's.'

'But the pink one is the right one. Daddy always gives me the pink one with my pink pumps.'

'Daddy would,' Archie muttered as he hung the offending coat back on the peg and searched for the right one.

'You're going to MacDonald's?' Phoebe asked, still waiting for an answer to her previous question.

'Bloody hell, you're quick.' Archie shoved a pink jacket at Maria.

'I thought Jack was cooking.'

'He was. But he changed his mind.'

'It's all chopped up,' Maria added, 'but he said he didn't feel like doing it after all and Archie could take me for burgers and milkshake. Do you want to come?'

Phoebe frowned. 'Not right now, honeybun.' She peered past Archie to the empty kitchen. 'Where is he?'

'In the garden,' Archie said. Phoebe nudged past him, heading for the back door.

'Bye, Phoebe!' Maria called, and then the front door slammed leaving the house silent.

Phoebe found Jack sitting at the patio table staring at a can of beer. 'What's the matter? Archie says you're feeling under the weather.'

'I'm perfectly well.'

'Then what's wrong?' Why have you sent him out with Maria to get tea? You hate Maria eating MacDonald's and she always eats tea with us.'

Jack's gaze met hers. He looked empty. 'I need to talk to you and I wanted to do it alone.'

'About what?'

No reply.

'Has something happened with your mum?'

'Not exactly.'

There was another heavy silence while Phoebe waited for him to expand on his reply.

'For God's sake, stop being so cryptic!' she snapped.

Another silence, shorter this time. And then:

'At the cosplay launch event, it was you on the roof, wasn't it? Why did you tell me it was Midnight?'

Phoebe suddenly felt sick, and it was nothing to do with her hormones this time. She dropped into a seat opposite him and hugged herself.

'I'm right?' he asked.

'Yes.'

'So it was you kissing that man?' Jack didn't shout. Instead he looked sad and disappointed. In many ways, this was far worse. She wished he *would* shout, and then she wouldn't feel like such a turd. If he did she could shout back, defend herself against something that she'd actually had no control over. But she felt guilty. Why? Was it because, despite the nature of Adam's trick on the rooftop, a little bit of her had liked it?

'Is it true?' he asked quietly.

'I can explain –'

'So it is true?'

'Yes, but...'

'Why did you lie to me?'

'It was an act... it didn't mean anything...'

'If it was an act then why did you have to lie?'

'I... I don't know.'

'And why did your boss pay the original guy who was supposed to be playing Batman fifty quid to swap with him at the last minute? Was it some weird sex game you'd cooked up between you?'

Phoebe's mouth fell open. 'How dare you!'

'Ok, that was a bit harsh,' he said. 'Perhaps you can explain it to me, because I'm struggling here...'

'How did you...'

'Find out?' Jack finished for her. 'It doesn't matter, does it?'

'It bloody does! Even I didn't know Adam had bribed Gareth to do that.'

'Adam? First name terms, eh? More than just a boss, then.'

'Have you never called a boss by their first name before?'

'We're not talking about me.'

'What the hell, Jack! This is stupid! He kissed me, not the other way around, and it didn't mean anything.'

'It does now, to me. I can't understand why you never told me.'

'Because I knew you'd react like this!' Phoebe bit her lip. That wasn't fair and she knew it. To this day her motives for acting so irrationally that evening and for keeping it all from Jack were as clear as an advanced algebra paper. And if she had told him there and then, he might have been a bit miffed, but they would soon have laughed it off as a wacky misunderstanding and moved on. He was right – now it looked a whole lot worse and it felt like she had something to hide. She sighed. 'Ok, my turn to be sorry. That was a bit harsh too.'

'How could you do that to me? In front of all those people like that? For God's sake, Phoebe, Archie saw it... and Maria!'

'Nobody knew it was me up there...'

'But I was there, and now I know it was you! Archie knows it was you as well! You say you want respect from him but then you go and do something like that. What kind of message is it sending out?'

'Look I was only filling in for Midnight because she got cold feet about the whole rooftop thing, and if I hadn't done it the whole stunt would have had to be cancelled. I'm sorry that Archie and Maria had to witness it but that's the truth. I didn't know it was Adam I swear – not at first anyway. He tricked me, and before you go off with a hatchet to take him out, you cannot say anything. He can have me sacked from Hendry's quicker than you can say P45 and he would.'

'He'd have an unfair dismissal case on his hands, and probably sexual harassment to boot,' Jack growled.

'Maybe. But my career would still be over. Even if I won and got my job back, how could I continue to work there under those circumstances?'

'It's not right.'

'I know it isn't. But I can handle it my own way without making a fuss…' she moved closer, emboldened by his apparent understanding, and looked up into his eyes. 'You trust me, don't you?'

He paused. 'Yes. But sometimes I feel I hardly know you.'

'When have I ever given you cause to feel like that?'

'I… never. It's me. Don't listen to me, I'm just an idiot. It hurt so much last time I lost someone I loved that I don't think I could go through it again. I've only just learned to trust fate and let my guard down with you after all those years alone and… please don't let me down.'

'Jack… you have to know that I would rather cut off my own arm than hurt you. Not knowingly anyway. This business with Adam, I promise it's nothing to me. He's just an idiotic jock who thinks he can get whatever he wants. But he didn't bargain on how much I love you.'

'So we're safe?'

Phoebe nodded. 'We're safe.'

He hooked a thumb beneath her chin and tilted it up to kiss her. 'I have a long way to go, I know. I was shocked when I heard but I should have realised there would be a good reason behind it all. And I should have known that mum would twist it to make it sound as terrible as possible. I know I can trust you.'

Phoebe didn't want to reopen the wound again, but she had to know. 'It was your mum who told you?'

'That's the bit you're not going to like...'

'No shit Sherlock.'

'My thoughts exactly.'

Phoebe was happy to see that Jack seemed to have accepted her explanation and was as keen to draw a line under the episode as she was. He might have been jealous but he wasn't the sort of man to hold a grudge and he certainly wasn't vindictive or petty. His mother, however, was a different matter entirely. Any excuse to besmirch Phoebe was too good to miss. 'I bet she loved that,' Phoebe muttered. She paused as another thought occurred to her. 'When was this?'

'She called me about an hour ago.'

'But how did she find out? I mean, I could understand Hendry's gossip getting around the store, but as far as your mum?'

'Uncle Fred.'

'Oh...' Phoebe shook her head with a puzzled expression.

'Linda told him,' Jack elaborated. 'You know, the woman who works for him. She overheard it in the Bounty according to mum.'

'I bet that went down well, too,' Phoebe said.

'You could say that.'

'Bloody hell,' Phoebe said, 'you'd have thought there was more important stuff for the shopkeepers of Millrise to talk about.' Phoebe chewed her nail as she mused on the situation. 'How come Archie knows? Does that mean she's speaking to him again?' Perhaps something good could come from this mortifying situation. It was a forlorn hope but there had to be some positive to counteract all the crappiness.

Jack shifted in his seat. 'That was me. I know it was probably a bad move but I just lost it – I needed to talk it through with someone and he came back from college after she'd gone.'

'Oh. I bet he was complimentary about me, wasn't he?'

'If it makes you feel any better, he did actually stick up for you.'

'He did?'

'Hard to believe, eh? He said there'd be a simple explanation. He said you'd have to be pretty dumb to cheat on me in front of the whole town. He also said he believed you *were* pretty dumb, just not *that* dumb...' Jack gave her a strained smile, one which she returned. Archie was probably right – she did feel pretty dumb right about now.

She was also beginning to wonder whether Midnight had had something to do with this information leak. Midnight loved to share titbits of gossip in the Bounty when she went for her lunch. 'Are we ok?' she asked Jack.

Jack reached across the table and laced his fingers in hers. 'I want us to be ok,' he said. 'I have to know you won't keep stuff like this from me in the future. I'd rather hear it from you than my mum, you know? How can we build a rock solid relationship if we can't trust each other?'

And there is was. Phoebe was keeping something massive from him; something that would make the kiss on the rooftop seem like an ant compared to a huge hairy mammoth of a lie. No, not a lie exactly, she told herself, but an omission of the truth. And as truths went it was a whopper.

She took a deep breath. Jack needed to know. But where did she even begin? He would want to know how, and then she would have to tell him about the days she had forgotten her pills and told him everything was fine. He would want to know when, and she would have to tell him that she didn't know because the whole forgotten pill situation had happened more than once but Phoebe had been convinced that everything would be fine. Where she was normally so careful and methodical, his caresses in the heat of passion had made her throw all common sense aside and she had never uttered a word to stop him, never once heeded that warning bell in her head. It would be ok, she had told herself as another pulse of desire had rippled down her spine; what were the chances of her getting caught?

When she had revealed all these lies and omissions, he would start to wonder how much of a liability she was. But she couldn't keep her secret any longer, not after all that had happened today.

'There's something else,' she said slowly.

His grip on her fingers tightened. She tried not to wince even though it was close to uncomfortable. Just to be safe, she prised her hand from his. There was no knowing what a shock like this would do to him and she found her digits rather useful the way they were.

'I'm pregnant.' She held her breath and waited for a response. He stared at her.

'Say something,' she faltered.

Jack pushed his chair away from the table, got up and walked across the garden. He stood with his back to her and stared into the depths of the leylandii, the same hedge where he had hidden Phoebe's special Easter egg, back when they were happier than any couple had ever been. So much had gone wrong since then, at times it felt as though some invisible machine had steamrollered over their lives. Phoebe watched him. She sensed that he needed time and space and she should leave him for a while. Wrapping her arms around herself, she shivered in a sharp breeze that rattled across the patio.

Time passed and stretched like an eternity, a silent emotional wasteland filled only with the low hum of an aeroplane high above them and the intermittent barking of a neighbour's dog.

When she could stand it no longer, Phoebe went to him.

'Are you angry?' He shook his head, his back still turned to her. 'Then why won't you say something?' She laid a hand on his arm. 'Jack?' Tightening her grip, she tried to pull him to face her, but he shook himself free. Phoebe tried again. 'Jack, please…' her voice was husky now, broken by tears that she tried to suppress.

But then he turned around and she saw his own tears rolling down his cheeks. Phoebe took a sharp breath. She had expected many reactions, but not this. She felt her heart would break to see it.

'Jack?'

'I can't do it again,' he said. 'I just can't…'

'Jack…?'

'I'm going to lose you too.'

All at once, understanding flooded in. Phoebe threw her arms around his neck. 'God, no! We'll be fine; you'll see!'

Jack buried his face in her shoulder and she clung to him. Over and over she promised it would be ok. But it wasn't a promise she could make and they both knew it. Hadn't Rebecca looked forward to years with Maria and Jack? Hadn't Jack thought she would always be there to share Maria's childhood? Life had a way of screwing up your plans when you least expected it and you'd never even see the crash coming.

❧ ❧ ❧

Phoebe knew it would be a long time before Jack really came to terms with her shock news. Even as she left him that evening, when they had talked and cried till they could talk and cry no more, the pain and fear still shone in his eyes and no amount of reassurance could banish it. They had decided not to tell Maria or Archie, not until Jack had got his head around the news himself at least. Which meant that they couldn't tell anyone else either. That wasn't necessarily a bad thing as far as Phoebe was concerned – apart from anything else she wasn't remotely ready to deal with Carol's response. Jack's mother needed no excuse to think the worst of Phoebe, as the Bat-Gate incident had clearly demonstrated. They would have to tell his parents eventually, of course, but a little more time was definitely the sensible approach.

Bat-Gate had also taught her that she couldn't afford to reveal her news at work either. Gossip had flown around Hendry's like a racehorse with a pitchfork in its backside, but it had apparently spread up and down the high street as well. News of her pregnancy would reach Carol's ears long before she and Jack had a chance to tell her properly if she wasn't very careful. She was sick, she was tired, she was moody and irritable, but Phoebe would have to hide it from everyone – at least for a little bit longer.

The evening with Jack had been so exhausting that Phoebe had gone home late and fallen into bed. As the alarm went off the following morning, she realised that she hadn't moved position since she had drifted off to sleep. It was incredible how tired crying could make you. For the first time in weeks she actually felt like she'd had a proper night's sleep, and she dressed quickly so that she could get into work early and catch Midnight before anyone arrived.

❧   ❧   ❧

Phoebe had greeted plenty of people as they came and went from the staffroom but by nine o'clock there was still no Midnight. With a slight itch of annoyance that she wasn't here when Phoebe most needed to speak to her, she was forced to take the stairs to her own office and begin her working day. After an hour of vague answers and preoccupied gazing into the distance, she excused herself from the office and headed back down to the shop to try and find Midnight again.

On the stairs, however, she met Adam. That man seemed to be omnipresent, like an aftershave-soaked god. Phoebe was beginning to suspect that one day soon horns would sprout from his head and he'd whip out a contract for her to sign.

'Good morning!' he smiled. His hand went to his jacket pocket and Phoebe wondered whether this was the moment he would try to bargain for her soul.

'Hi...'

'Are you in a rush?'

'Sorry... yes... something I need to sort out...' Phoebe replied, her gaze drifting towards the stairs as she searched for an escape route. In fact looking anywhere but at his face was good.

'Do you mean the rumours?'

Phoebe looked sharply at him now. 'What rumours?'

Adam lowered his voice and leaned into her. 'About us.'

'How did you...?'

'I hear all sorts in that stockroom when I'm doing my secret inspections.'

Phoebe blinked at him. He didn't appear to be angry or embarrassed at all. In fact, he seemed unconcerned by the whole thing.

'Can't you do something?' Phoebe asked. 'To stop them.' As soon as the question left her lips she realised how stupid it was.

'What can I do? People will talk whether I tell them to or not.'

'But you're not angry about it?'

'Workplace scandal is like giving a budgie a mirror to play with. It keeps everyone entertained and happy.'

Phoebe suspected that his analogy said a lot about what he really thought of his staff – her included.

'But the way I see it,' he continued, moving forward so that Phoebe was forced back against the wall, 'is that you may as well be guilty, if everyone thinks you are anyway.'

'What do you mean?'

'If people want to gossip, and they will, then you might as well give them something to gossip about.'

Phoebe ducked around him. 'I have to go...' she ran down the stairs as fast as she dared. She'd probably pissed him off by running away mid-conversation, but at that moment she really didn't care. As she hurried away she was sure she could hear chuckling from the top of the stairs.

A quick inspection of the shop floor and a word with Steve revealed that Midnight had taken the day off. She'd probably mentioned it at some point but Phoebe must have forgotten with everything else jostling for attention in a brain that was ready to explode as it was. Intending to return to her desk, but then looking up to see Adam stalking the shop floor, she took the only course of action she could to avoid him, which was to dash out through the shop entrance. Agitated now beyond reason and huddled in the shadow of one of the huge pillars as rain started to soak the high street, Phoebe pulled out her phone. Midnight might still be in bed if it was her day off, but right now Phoebe didn't care.

Sure enough, shortly after Phoebe had dialled the number, a sleepy voice answered.

'Have you no respect? Seriously, Clements, it's not even midday yet.'

'Everyone knows about me and Adam,' Phoebe hissed. She hadn't planned to take Midnight to task in quite this way, but the morning's events had soured her mood and addled her logic.

'You and Adam?' Midnight asked carelessly. 'I thought there *was* no you and Adam… that's what you keep telling me anyway.'

'You know what I mean!'

'The kissy kissy moment?'

'It wasn't a kiss!'

'It looked like one from where I was standing. It probably looked like that to the rest of the town too.'

'I was conned! Did you tell everyone?'

'I didn't need to. Or have you forgotten that you were on a roof at the time with a rather large audience?'

'Very funny. No one knew it was us other than you.'

'Gareth Parker did.'

'He knew about Adam.'

'He knew about you too. I bumped into him on the way to get changed. When I asked him why he was in his normal clothes he told me that Hendry had given him fifty quid to swap and keep his mouth shut. I told him I'd have done it for twenty. Anyway, he wanted to know why I wasn't on the roof so I told him you wanted to do it… I didn't think it was a secret.'

'Yeah, but I was only doing it because you were too scared. Now it looks like Adam and I both decided we wanted to be up there together!'

'I was hardly going to tell him that I was too chicken, was I? And Gareth is too thick to have come to that conclusion anyway.'

'Other people will have done though.'

'Ok… I'll concede that might be true…'

'Shit,' Phoebe muttered. 'Jack knows too,' she added.

'Jack? That sucks.'

'It does more than suck. He got it from his mother, of all people, who told him she got it from Jack's uncle Fred.'

'The Applejack's guy?'

'How did he find out?'

Phoebe could almost hear Midnight's nonchalant shrug. 'I dunno. News just gets around this town.'

'So nobody was blabbing about it... say... in the Bounty when they went to get their lunch?'

'Is that what this phone call is really about? You think I blabbed to everyone?'

'Not everyone. But you do tend to tell Stav things... And if that Linda woman who works for Fred was there...'

'So you think it's my fault?'

'I didn't say –'

'I'm tired of being your hapless and amusing side-kick, Clements, and I'm tired of your dramas. You're pregnant, Adam Hendry fancies you, your new job is so tough... deal with it like other people do because I don't want to hear you whine anymore. Now if you don't mind I want to go back to sleep.'

Before Phoebe had time to reply, Midnight ended the call. Phoebe stared at the phone screen as it faded to black. What had just happened? Somehow, she was now to blame for all the stuff that was Midnight's fault. How could Midnight simply absolve herself of all responsibility like that? Phoebe knew her so well now – how much she loved to gossip, how easily she lost any sense of discretion when she had a juicy titbit to share. Even if Gareth Parker did know (or thought he knew the truth, which he didn't) there was no way that rumour reaching Applejack's could be down to him. It had to have been Midnight. How dare she cut Phoebe's call short without so much as an apology?

Phoebe was the injured party here and she had every right to be angry.

So why, as the townsfolk of Millrise hurried past beneath umbrellas and hoods and folded newspapers, did Phoebe feel so hollow about the whole thing? Why had her initial rage now turned to an uncomfortable niggle in the pit of her stomach that she had been unfair to her friend? In a subconscious movement, her hand fluttered to her belly. She and Jack had agreed that they wouldn't tell anyone yet, but perhaps if she made it public at Hendry's, the news would be enough to put Adam off. The rumours certainly hadn't been.

The more she thought about it, the more miserable Phoebe felt. Perhaps Midnight was right after all: this mess was of her own making and she was wrong to blame everyone else. If she grew a spine and told Adam straight then he'd have to leave her alone. If she'd been honest with Jack from the start he wouldn't have been so shocked at the news his mother had so gleefully delivered and then she would have been able to tell him about the pregnancy under much better and kinder circumstances. And perhaps Phoebe would still have the support of a friend who had quickly become her rock, someone who brightened even the darkest days. Hendry's without Midnight would be a much lonelier place.

Phoebe redialled her number. Unsurprisingly, it went straight to answerphone.

'Midnight...' Phoebe swallowed hard, fought to keep her voice from cracking. 'It's me... I'm sorry... I shouldn't have blamed you...' There was nothing else to say. She ended the call and rubbed her eyes, head down so that nobody passing by would see her tears. Taking deep breaths she tried to get herself together. She couldn't stay out here all morning but she couldn't go back into the shop in this state.

'Are you alright?'

Phoebe looked up to see Sue Bunce, water dripping off her hood, balancing a tray of take-out coffees as she held an umbrella over them, a look of concern on her face.

'Having one of those days?' Sue asked.

Phoebe gave her a watery smile, still too choked to speak. She hated it when people were kind, it always made her want to cry more.

'I know those well,' Sue said. 'When you've worked here as long as I have they come around with every full moon. Anything a coffee and a chat would help with?'

Phoebe shook her head. 'I don't think so,' she managed to utter in a strangled voice.

Sue gave a sympathetic smile. 'Well my door is always open if you change your mind.'

'Thanks...'

With an encouraging nod, Sue continued on her way. Phoebe stared out onto the street again. She took a deep breath. There were a million things on her desk that needed sorting and feeling sorry for herself would achieve nothing.

⚜ ⚜ ⚜

Every time Phoebe was there around bath time, Maria now insisted that Phoebe did it. Sometimes Jack protested, saying that Maria shouldn't keep nagging Phoebe who was a guest and shouldn't be asked to do chores. Sometimes he relented. Tonight was one of those nights, after much cajoling from both Maria and Phoebe (who insisted privately she now needed the practise).

So Phoebe found herself perched on the side of the bath, staring into space as Maria collected all the suds she could find into a giant bubble island, chattering through some imaginary scenario to herself as she went about her work with solemn concentration.

Midnight had returned to work and whilst she'd greeted Phoebe civilly enough as they'd passed on the stairs, there was a new frostiness that told Phoebe she was far from forgiven. Phoebe took her to one side and apologised again and Midnight told her not to worry and that the spat was forgotten, but it wasn't true. For the rest of the day Midnight had been conveniently missing or too busy to talk whenever Phoebe went to look for her.

'You're sad,' Maria said.

Phoebe shook away her melancholy thoughts to see that Maria had paused in her game and was watching her with a look of uncanny comprehension. Phoebe gave her an absent smile. 'What makes you say that?'

Maria shrugged. 'I just know.'

'I'm ok.'

'Daddy has been sad too.'

'Has he? What makes you think that?'

Maria shrugged again. 'His face.'

Phoebe couldn't help a little laugh. 'Has he told you he's sad?'

Maria shook her head. 'I haven't told him I know about it.'

'Why not?'

'Um… I don't know. But Archie did.'

'What did Archie say?'

'He said daddy was a miserable sod.'

'Oh… perhaps you shouldn't repeat that last bit to anyone else.'

'Is it rude?'

'A little bit.'

'Ok…' Maria hummed to herself as she went back to her bubbles. 'Archie shouldn't say that because he's sad too.'

'He is?' Phoebe had never seen evidence of this but, on reflection, she didn't doubt that he had plenty to be sad about. Maria nodded.

'Yesterday he was sad at the table with Daddy.'

Phoebe was silent as she mulled this over. But when Maria didn't offer further explanation she probed a little more. 'Do you know why he was sad?'

'No. But Daddy said he would talk to granny again and he would go with Archie to the college to talk to them too.'

'What about?'

'About Archie's lessons, I think.'

'How did you hear all this? Were you at the table with them?'

'No. But I heard it when I came in to get some milk. Archie pretended he wasn't crying and he started being funny but I could tell.'

'What else did you hear?'

'Not much. Daddy gave Archie a piece of paper and said he had to phone someone.'

'Who?'

'I don't remember.'

'Was it the college?'

'No. Daddy said he'd go there with Archie and not to worry about it. Someone else.'

Phoebe stared into the water as she turned this information over in her mind. Jack had told Archie to phone someone? Perhaps it was the gambling support group. Phoebe sincerely hoped so, although they had been down this road before and there was nothing to say that Archie would take Jack's advice this time. She could only hope that eventually Jack would wear him down. She might not always see eye to eye with Archie but he was still a vulnerable young man working through a lot of problems right now, despite the front he always presented. Maria had also said Jack was going to see someone at Archie's college? Archie had missed a lot of lectures at college and he made no secret of the fact that the course choice – something Carol had apparently pushed him towards – was not one that made him happy. He was already a year behind too, after failing many of his modules. Perhaps the situation there now felt untenable to him? She would have to try and talk to Jack later, find out what was going on.

'Why are *you* sad?' Maria asked.

'Me? I'm not sad.'

'You look sad,' Maria insisted.

Phoebe paused before she answered. She could deny it, of course, and that would be the easiest thing to do. But somehow, she felt that Maria, as young as she was, deserved a little bit of the truth. After all, she was being lied to enough right now and clearly, she had some inkling of that.

'Lots of things are hard for me right now.'

'What things?' Maria looked up from her bubbles again.

'Well… some people at work are making things a bit tricky.'

'Have you broke friends with them?'

'Um… yes… I suppose I have.'

'I broke friends with Grace once.'

'Oh dear. Were you upset?'

'I cried to Miss Latham and she helped me make a sorry card for Grace because I'd shouted at her.'

'And then Grace was friends with you again?'

'Yup.'

'So I should make a sorry card for Midnight?

Maria nodded. 'Or you could buy her some sweets if you can't draw.'

'We all know I can't draw.' Phoebe laughed. 'Did you think of that yourself?'

'Uh huh.'

'It's a good idea.'

'I know.' Maria prodded a hole in her bubble island. It was obviously a deliberate design feature and, judging by the concentration on her face, served an important purpose in her game.

'So you think we'll be friends again after that?' Phoebe asked.

'Yes.'

Phoebe smiled down at her. A child's logic was so black and white. It was a pity that adults didn't view the world with as much pragmatism; it would make life a lot simpler. To make Jack's mother like her, get Midnight talking to her again, persuade Archie to sort his life out, stop her parents lecturing her, convince Jack that everything would be ok once the baby was born, all she would need was a box of sweets.

❧   ❧   ❧

The trick was getting Midnight alone, especially as she had been so careful to avoid Phoebe whenever possible over the last few days. In fact, not only was it difficult to get her alone, it was difficult to get her at all.

Phoebe had been struck by the simplicity of Maria's solution. A peace offering, something from the heart, in this case a box of Midnight's favourite jelly beans was what Phoebe had decided on to apologise. And she wanted to apologise, because she was truly sorry. Whether Midnight had been the source of the gossip or not, it would eventually have got out and, besides, Phoebe missed her friend like crazy. Midnight could be infuriating, irreverent, uncontrollable and scary, but she was always fun and she had a heart as big as Millrise itself.

In the end Phoebe had been forced to resort to drastic measures, lying in wait outside the shop doors to ambush her as she left to get her daily sandwich.

'Boo!' Phoebe leapt from behind a pillar. After planning on such a military scale – covertly checking Steve's rota and then ensuring she got across the shop floor and outside before Midnight spotted her – it was not her most inspired moment, but it did the job.

Midnight spun around, hand to her chest. She didn't look pleased.

'Sorry…' Phoebe said. 'Did I make you jump?'

'What do you want?'

'A word –'

'I've already told you I'm not bothered about your stupid phone call so you don't need to keep apologising.'

'I want us to be friends again.'

'We are friends.'

'No we're not. We're acquaintances who happen to work in the same store. Friends don't avoid each other.'

'Friends don't phone and blame the other one for the fact that people have found out that the boss, who is making no secret of it anyway, fancies them.'

'Ah! So it *is* still bothering you! I knew it.'

Midnight hunched her shoulders in a shrug that looked casual but was loaded with meaning. 'Whatever.'

'Come on,' Phoebe pleaded. 'Don't let's be like this. I'm miserable without you.'

'You should have thought about that before.'

'I know. I didn't think. My head is a sea of not thinking with a tiny little raft drifting about on it holding my brain. There is so much not thinking that my brain doesn't stand a chance.'

'You're so weird…' Midnight said.

'You have every right to be angry,' Phoebe continued.

'Damn straight I do.'

'So what can I do to make it up?'

'Leave me alone.'

'Apart from that.' Phoebe gave a hopeful smile as she pulled the box of jelly beans from behind her back. She'd tied a black bow around it and covered the box in glitter. Midnight's frown cracked into a slow smile as Phoebe held the box out to her.

'That's the saddest thing I've ever seen.'

'A little bit,' Phoebe agreed. 'I'm crap at arts and crafts. But the sweets will taste ok.'

Midnight took the box. ‘Ok…’ she sighed, ‘you win. You’re forgiven this time.’

Phoebe pulled her into a hug. ‘There won’t be a next time, I promise.’

‘And don’t think I’m sharing these with you either,’ Midnight continued, shaking the box at Phoebe, who simply gave a delighted grin.

‘I wouldn’t dream of it.’ She knew she would later, though.

⚜ ⚜ ⚜

Everywhere she looked, there were bumps of varying sizes. Women who looked tired, radiant, nervous, and some as though they were waiting at the supermarket checkout. A couple were with friends or female relatives, others with what seemed to be the expectant father, and one or two on their own. A box of toys in the corner of the room had drawn a crowd of hustling toddlers, negotiating in that strange toddler language for their playthings of choice. There was a cloying mix of scents – different deodorants and perfumes mixed with hospital cleaning fluid, and Phoebe was quite certain she detected the whiff of freshly filled nappy too – all of which wasn’t helping her nausea.

She glanced up at the clock on the wall again. Dixon had given her the morning off without any questions but his patience would only stretch so far and Phoebe didn’t want to push her luck.

'Looking at it won't make it go any faster,' her mum said.

'I know. It's just so bloody hot in here it's making me feel sick.'

'It must be your turn soon,' Martha replied in a reasonable tone that made Phoebe want to throw something at her. 'I think most of the people here now came in after us.'

'God, I hope so,' Phoebe said, savagely fanning herself with a tattered magazine swiped from a pile on a nearby coffee table. 'I don't want to whine about it but I'm pretty sure I'm going to pass out if I have to wait much longer.'

Martha let out a heavy sigh. 'It is a bit warm,' she agreed in a rather less dramatic voice. 'I could get you some water.'

'Mum, I've already drunk what they suggested for the scan. Any more and I will pee myself with such force that I'll wash away everyone here.'

'I'm just trying to help,' Martha replied tartly.

Phoebe dropped the magazine to her lap. 'I know… I'm sorry.'

'You seem tense.'

'Do I?' Phoebe said, unable to keep the sarcasm from her voice.

'It should be me that's tense. I might have known this would happen.'

'What?'

'You getting into trouble.'

Phoebe rolled her eyes. 'It's not the fifties, Mum. No one says that any more.'

'It's a bit soon for a baby. Even you agree with that.'

'True…'

'And why isn't your partner in crime here instead of me? He should be mopping your fevered brow and listening to you complain. After all, it is his fault.'

'You should have said if you didn't want to come.'

'I didn't mean that. I just think he ought to be here supporting you, especially for the first scan.'

Phoebe had thought a lot about the reasons Jack had given for not coming with her today. She'd been hurt by how unimportant they sounded, though she tried not to show it. He was so obviously avoiding the situation and couldn't share his reasons. In fact, he'd been extremely evasive about the whole thing. After their initial difficult discussion, he appeared to get his head around the fact that Phoebe was pregnant. But he had closed up again, carefully avoiding any conversation where the mention of babies was likely to come up. This was understandable when other people were around, as they had decided not to share their news yet, but when they were alone surely there was nothing more important to talk about? It was as if the very idea of it offended him in some way, and the silence was forging a chasm between them that Phoebe felt more each day.

She only wished that her mum could be as reticent. Despite her promise to Jack not to tell her family, Phoebe had blurted the news out in a low moment, desperate for the emotional support she wasn't getting from him. Sadly, Martha had spent the next week lecturing her at every opportunity on how she should have been more careful or how she should have given the relationship more time before she rushed into motherhood, how everything would change with the arrival of a baby (as if Phoebe didn't know that), how she and Hugh wouldn't be on call to babysit every five minutes when Phoebe fancied a night out… etc, etc.

Phoebe's dad, on the other hand, whilst appearing to agree with his wife, showed a secret sort of pride and pleasure in the whole thing that surprised her a little. She had always imagined he would be the more disappointed of the two – he had always seen Phoebe as his precious little girl. But he seemed rather happy about the whole thing. Phoebe wondered whether, in his head, he had already gained a grandson who would be inducted into the re-enactment society the moment he grew big enough not to buckle under the weight of a musket.

The problem Phoebe had created for herself now was that she had made a new lie. She'd promised Jack she wouldn't tell her family, and now she had to make them promise not to tell him they knew. She hated all this lying, but it seemed impossible to stop.

'Jack's got so much work on at the moment he'll get behind if he takes a morning off – especially with how long they take in here. Besides, this is only a dating scan. He can come to the important ones with me.'

'When are you going to tell his parents?'

'Mum… we've been through all this…'

'I think it's wrong, that's all. They should know.'

'And they will, soon.'

'Are we going to meet them? We'll be practically related in a few months so I think we ought to.'

Phoebe didn't agree. In fact, she couldn't think of anything more horrific than the prospect of Jack's parents meeting hers. She adored her mum and dad, of course, but she knew for others they could be an acquired taste. She wasn't sure what prim and proper Carol would make of her father's hobby and his plain-speaking ways, but she was pretty sure she wouldn't approve. And she certainly didn't need any more reasons to hate Phoebe. If, God forbid, Carol dared display her obvious contempt for Phoebe in front of Martha then it would be handbags at dawn and there was no telling where that would end. Martha might appear to be a nag and she might not always approve of Phoebe's choices in life, but any-one stupid enough to hurt her daughter did so at their peril. In those situations, Martha was like a lion-ess protecting her cub: no mercy and no forgiveness. It was hardly going to make for a future of peaceful Christmas lunches.

'Give us a bit more time,' Phoebe said. 'There'll be plenty of opportunities once the baby arrives and things that both sets of parents will have to attend.'

Phoebe ran through a list in her head: Naming ceremony or christening (depending on what Jack wanted), birthday parties, school plays, awards ceremonies – all of them would have to take place in a secret bunker somewhere under the Swiss Alps so that nobody but she and Jack would know about them. It was the only way to keep all-out war at bay. Even Maria would have to sign the official secrets act.

Phoebe looked up at the sound of the scanning room door opening. A young couple practically skipped out, hand in hand, their expressions alive with happiness and expectation. Phoebe was filled with a pang of envy. They looked barely old enough to have finished their GCSEs and weren't dressed in a way that suggested a lot of money, and yet they seemed so happy. She and Jack would be in a much better position in many ways, but that happiness was so absent from their lives right now it was painful. She tried to block the sadness that crept into her heart. Jack would come round eventually, wouldn't he? He was such a fantastic dad to Maria; how could he not be the same with their child?

And then her darkest thoughts pushed their tendrils of doubt into her heart. Maria was Rebecca's daughter. Sweet, clever, funny, perfect Rebecca. Jack had loved Rebecca for almost his whole life and then she had died. His family never seemed to tire of reminding Phoebe of that. What if Jack had loved Rebecca in a way that he could never love anyone else? Rebecca might be dead, but she would always own his heart. What if Phoebe was always on the out-side looking in?

'Phoebe Clements…'

Martha nudged her daughter and nodded towards a woman in a white tunic and shapeless navy trousers standing at the open door of the scanning room.

'Come on, let's find out what's going on.'

Phoebe took a deep breath. This was it, the first time she would see her child. She was both excited and terrified at the same time. As she walked towards the smiling sonographer, she reached for her mum's hand, suddenly feeling like a little girl again. Martha gave her hand a reassuring squeeze. There was a kind of calm, stabilising influence that only a mum could give, no matter how old you got. Phoebe was so glad to have hers there. She only wished that she had Jack with her too.

❧   ❧   ❧

Phoebe had barely been able to keep her mind on anything for the rest of the day. She desperately wanted to tell Dixon about her scan. In fact, she wanted to climb onto the roof with a megaphone and tell the world. But she had gone about her day, having a quiet meltdown in the privacy of her own brain whilst pretending to get on with her job. What on earth she'd written in emails, what figures she'd sent to Old Mr Hendry, what she'd said on the phone to a new costume supplier who wanted to discuss sponsorship, she had no idea. She just hoped she had sounded reasonably sensible and not promised anyone rainbow-striped kittens and unicorns.

After much internal deliberation, she'd decided to call at Jack's with the scan photo, now carefully slotted inside a laminated cover purchased from the hospital shop and stowed in her bag. If nothing else had moved him so far, perhaps this would. He knew this was the day of the scan, but she hadn't phoned ahead to warn him she was coming so he wouldn't be able to come up with an excuse to put her off.

On the bus now, she clutched the photo, gazing at it. Yet again she wondered how a grainy monochrome image, barely recognisable as anything but perhaps a baked bean or a squished prawn cracker could have such a profound effect on her. But this was the life she had helped to create, growing inside her. For all her fears, her doubts, her moments of resentment over the past weeks, the sudden rush of love that had overwhelmed her as the image took shape on the screen of the scanning room – the tiny fluttering heartbeats barely visible inside a sea of grey and black shapes that would become arms and legs and a beautiful face – had knocked Phoebe's world out of orbit. She hadn't expected it, and even now it took some getting used to, but she felt it every time she looked at the picture, so it had to be real.

Would Jack feel the same way? Her fear of rejection was double now that the maternal instinct to protect her baby had jolted violently into life. It would be hard to enough to take rejection of herself but Phoebe would get over it, eventually. Rejection of her child was quite another thing.

The bus stopped, and Phoebe looked up to see a mother and her toddler make their way up the aisle. They came and sat down in the seat next to Phoebe. The toddler, a little boy, struggled to get off his mother's lap but the woman held him tight, cajoling him to sit still with promises of chocolate at the other end. Phoebe watched for a moment, forgetting that she was still holding the picture of her own child.

'Yours?' the woman asked, turning to Phoebe now with a smile and nodding at the tiny square of paper. Phoebe nodded. 'First one?'

'Yes.'

'How far are you?'

'Ten weeks.'

'Lovely. Not long until you get another snap for the family album then.' The toddler twisted around in her arms again and made a grab for the photo. As tactfully as she could, Phoebe moved it out of his reach.

'No, Leo,' the woman said, pulling his sticky hands gently away. 'It's not a toy.' She dug in her bag for a dummy and gave it a quick blow before shoving it into the child's mouth. The effect was instantaneous, like she had given him a magic sedative, and he stared into space in a peaceful trance as he sucked at it. Then she turned back to Phoebe. 'Are you looking forward to it?'

'Sort of,' Phoebe smiled.

'I suppose you're nervous.'

'That would be an understatement.'

'It's only natural. This little terror is my third. The first birth was horrific, like a scene from a Hammer film or something. My husband said watching *The Exorcist* was like *Antiques Roadshow* after seeing me in labour. By the time I got to my third it was like shelling peas. I could have done the ironing at the same time. Leo was a home birth and he was out before the midwife had arrived and got her gloves on.'

'Does it hurt?'

'Like nothing else, no doubt about it. But you soon forget. If God let us all remember how bad it was, we'd never have a second. I'm sure you'll be just fine.'

'I think I'm more scared about afterwards than the birth,' Phoebe replied. Her own honesty had taken her by surprise, but somehow she found it easier to open up to this complete stranger than anyone else so far. 'I'm scared of getting it wrong. I mean, how do you know what the baby wants? How do you know if you're doing things wrong? What if you cock it up?'

The woman gave her son an affectionate kiss on the head as he snuggled into her arms. 'I can't explain it, but things just slot into place. People will offer you all sorts of advice and they'll tell you you're doing things wrong and how their way is better. Sometimes they'll be right and sometimes they'll be wrong. In the end, you'll just know and you'll wonder what you were ever scared of.'

'Really?' Phoebe couldn't imagine that day at all.

The bus juddered to a halt. Phoebe looked up in some surprise to see that she had reached her destination already. 'This is my stop.'

'Oh, right…' the woman stood to let Phoebe squeeze past before sitting her son on the empty seat and easing herself down next to him again. The little boy pulled himself up at the window and began slapping the glass with squeals of delight.

'Thanks,' Phoebe added. 'It was lovely to talk to you.'

'No problem. And if you want to find me after the little horror arrives, I'm a helper at St Alban's Street Playgroup. Come along any time with junior for a cup of tea and a chat.'

'I will,' Phoebe smiled.

'Good luck!' the woman called as she made her way down the bus. It was a funny thing, but Phoebe felt more like a mum after that short conversation than ever before. Maybe she wouldn't stink after all.

⚜   ⚜   ⚜

The walk to King's Road was short and balmy and Phoebe blinked, half-surprised to find herself there as she looked up at the street sign. Familiar faces passed her and smiled their greetings as she walked to Jack's house. It was amazing how quickly people accepted you as part of the community if you stalked the same street often enough. Most of them looked as if they had just finished work too – suits on, briefcases at their side or wearing paint-spattered overalls. Work... what was she going to do about it? It was another thing to figure out and she would, just as soon as she got her head around the fact that she was going to be a mum.

When she got to Jack's there was no reply. She knocked again but still nothing. Frowning, she dialled his number and he didn't answer his phone either. She wondered whether she ought to let herself in, but it seemed weird to sit alone in his house.

After wandering the street again a couple of times, hoping to bump into him returning from a walk with Maria or something similar, and phoning him again to no avail, Phoebe gave up. She had been so excited to see him tonight, especially after her chat on the bus, and had been determined to infuse him with some of her new-found optimism too. She left feeling oddly flat. *That's what you get for arriving unannounced*, she thought, although it was strange for him to be missing at that time on a weekday evening when he would usually be busy with Maria's tea and bedtime routine. Not to mention the fact that she often paid him impromptu visits and he normally let her know if he wasn't going to be in, just in case.

Not wanting to go home, and not wanting to bother her parents for a second time that day (or give them any excuse to suspect that things weren't all rosy in the garden with Jack), Phoebe found herself wandering slowly back towards the centre of town. It was a long haul in bad weather but this evening, in the warmth of the sun, it was a pleasant walk that gave her space to think.

The landscape of her life had changed beyond recognition in the last twelve months and sometimes she forgot that her emotions needed to catch up with the pace of progress. This time last year she had been working as a barmaid, drinking away most of her shifts with the customers in a bid to forget the despair that each day waking up without Vik brought.

Thinking about Vik brought her up short. With every day that passed now he occupied less and less space in her life. But how could she forget? The old guilt pricked at her. His Sikh parents had erected no memorial she could visit, and had forbade her to attend his cremation. His ashes were probably miles away now, drifting on some foreign tide. What would he think if he could see her now? Would he think her fickle and inconstant, moving on so soon? Was that why Jack struggled so much? He had seemed so happy to give his heart to Phoebe, but that was back in the beginning when it was all just fun and games. Now that their future had become so serious, did he feel he was being unfaithful to Rebecca's memory, as she did to Vik's? Phoebe wished he would talk to her, that they could work it out together, but whenever she approached the subject he closed up tight. They had both suffered losses, and surely it was right that they should be granted just a little happiness?

'PHOEBE!'

She turned to see Maria racing down the street towards her. 'PHOEBE!' she cried again, running so fast she almost tripped over her own feet.

'Careful!' a woman called after her.

As Maria threw herself into Phoebe's arms, giggling, Phoebe looked up to see the woman coming towards them at a brisk walk. She was in her fifties, a willowy and elegant figure dressed in a flattering long skirt and fitted jersey top with coordinating scarf. Phoebe could tell that her shoulder-length hair was once strawberry blonde but now washed silver-grey; there was a sprinkling of freckles over her cheeks, the skin so fine it needed no foundation.

Phoebe stared at her. She recognised the features instantly, but from photos of a much younger face, one gone now from all but memory.

'Hello…' she greeted warmly. 'You must be Jack's friend. Maria has told me lots about you.'

'Um…' Phoebe's brain struggled to process a reply.

'Are you coming to our house?' Maria asked. 'Granny May is coming.'

So this was Rebecca's mother. She gave Phoebe a warm smile that took her completely by surprise. She had never expected to meet May, although perhaps that was rather foolish. If she'd been asked, she would have assumed that May would be cold towards her – not unlike Carol in fact. This warmth was too weird and Phoebe wondered if she would actually prefer May to be rude to her.

'Jack's not at home,' was all that Phoebe managed to get out.

'That's odd,' May said, her smile fading. 'He knows to expect us.'

'That's what I thought. I tried to phone him but he's not answering…' She paused before continuing, wondering whether it would be ok to mention what she was thinking? 'I have a key…' she said, finally. 'If you need to drop Maria off at home I can stay with her until Jack gets back.'

'That's very kind of you, but there's nowhere I have to be and nobody to get home to. I'm happy to stay with Maria.'

Phoebe had no idea how she was supposed to respond – what she should and shouldn't say about the situation they all found themselves in. Would they both creep around the elephant parked on the pavement between them and pretend not to see it?

'Perhaps I should try Jack again,' she said eventually.

'You do that and I'll phone Carol to see if she knows anything.'

While Phoebe dialled Jack, almost certain that he wouldn't answer, May pulled an old mobile phone the size of a brick from her straw shoulder bag. A quick conversation with Jack's mum revealed that she didn't know where he was either, or Archie, for that matter (although that was less worrying as nobody knew where Archie went and what he got up to half the time). From this half of the conversation, it was clear that May was having a tough time persuading Carol not to leap into her car and head straight over.

'Phoebe's here,' May said, giving Phoebe an unexpected and very disconcerting wink. 'She has a key and can let us in.'

Phoebe could only imagine Carol's reply. Perhaps that was why May was winking. Whatever was being said at the other end of the line, she seemed unperturbed by it. As Phoebe watched her, she decided that she loved May already and cursed her rotten luck that this perfectly sweet woman had to be the mother of her nemesis and not Jack's own.

May ended the call and slipped the phone back into her bag. 'Carol says we should call her when we find out where Jack is. She tried him too and got no reply.'

Phoebe wondered whether Carol had swallowed her pride enough to try Archie too, but guessed from the fact that May didn't mention it that there would be an ice-rink in hell before that happened.

May looked down at Maria. 'How about we make good use of Phoebe's key and let ourselves in? Knowing your dad there'll be a cake in the larder with our names on it.'

'Can we go to the park, Phoebe?' Maria asked.

'You've just come from the park!' May laughed. 'I'll bet after a day at work what Phoebe needs is a cup of tea, not a race round the park trying to keep up with you.'

Maria giggled. 'I won't run fast.'

'The only place we want to go fast is home...' May held out a hand, 'come on little madam. Time to head back.'

'Ok...'Maria grumbled, reaching up to hold onto May's hand.

'You work in the big toy shop in town, don't you?' May asked Phoebe as they began to saunter back in the direction of King's Road.

'I do. Started there at Christmas.'

'And you like it?'

'Some days. It's not exactly a high-flying career but I'm happy enough there.'

As they continued to exchange small talk, Phoebe felt the irrational urge to answer every question with a question of her own about Rebecca. It probably wouldn't be the best ice-breaker though, so she bit her lip and forced herself to think of other things.

'That's a lovely hairclip,' May continued, gesturing towards an azure butterfly pinning back one side of Phoebe's hair.

'Oh, thank you!' Phoebe put a hand up to feel the shape and remind herself what it was she had chosen to wear that morning. 'I got it in Ibiza.'

'It really suits you.'

Damn it, why did this woman have to be so bloody nice? She felt guiltier than ever for being in Jack's life instead of her daughter. If Rebecca had been alive, it would have been her walking home with May, Maria swinging between them with each of her hands clasped in one of theirs. For the rest of the journey, Phoebe tried to focus the conversation on Maria and school; it was much less of an emotional minefield.

As they walked up the path to Jack's front door, Phoebe with her key in her hand, Jack's neighbour, Doreen, came rushing out and called to them over the fence.

'Hello,' May said amiably.

'I saw you leaving the first time,' Doreen said a little breathlessly, 'but I couldn't get out quick enough to catch you. The old arthritis, you know...'

'I do know.' Phoebe gave an encouraging smile. Doreen obviously needed to get something off her chest, but knowing her it could take a while. Phoebe prepared for a bit of verbal tennis before they got to the bottom of it.

'Only I thought you ought to know that Jack and his brother are out,' Doreen said.

Phoebe nodded patiently. 'Did he pop in to tell you where he was going?' Phoebe asked, trying to prompt Doreen to focus.

'No... no he didn't.'

'Oh...'

'But before he went out three men hammered on the door.' Doreen lowered her voice and shot a furtive glance around her garden, as if the three men might still be hiding in the gladioli. 'They didn't look very nice.'

'How do you mean?'

'They were polite enough when I came out. But I could see by their faces they were trouble.'

Phoebe wondered why on earth Doreen would come out of her front door to face them if she thought they looked like trouble, but then she was so congenitally nosey that there was no telling what she'd do once curiosity took hold.

'And they wanted Jack?' Phoebe asked, glancing at May now with the first stirrings of real fear nibbling at her. She handed May her key and suggested that she take Maria inside.

'No, they were asking after Archie. They looked like wrong 'uns, they did.'

'When was this?'

'About an hour ago. You probably only just missed him. Jack came to the door and they said they wouldn't leave until Archie came to speak to them. Jack told me to go in but I stayed just inside the front door to listen. Jack said Archie couldn't come out because he wasn't living there anymore. Well, I know that's not true and I wondered why Jack would lie about it... but they said they didn't believe him either.'

'What did they do then?'

'They said they wanted to go inside and Jack told them he would call the police. Then they said that Jack could call the police all he liked but they would wait and grab Archie when they could and take him for a friendly chat. They didn't look like they wanted a friendly chat though...' Doreen shook her head. 'Such a shame... such a nice family to be in trouble.'

'We don't actually know that it is trouble yet,' said Phoebe, although she knew she was fooling no one. 'So, Jack went with them?' she asked, still struggling to get to the bottom of things.

'No. But then Archie came to the door and said he would go with them. Jack shouted for him to come back but Archie shouted that he didn't need Jack to fight his battles all the time and told Jack to go inside and leave him alone.'

'And Jack did that?'

'Yes.'

'But if he went back inside then where is he now?'

'I don't know,' Doreen said.

Phoebe wanted to shake her. She took a deep breath. 'Did you see him go out afterwards?'

'Oh yes! A couple of minutes later he hopped into his car and drove off. I think he must have gone after them.'

'Probably,' Phoebe agreed. 'Were the three men who took Archie in a car?'

Doreen nodded.

'Thank you Doreen. You've been a big help.'

'Do you need me to come over?' Doreen asked. It was clear she was not yet ready to relinquish her role in the drama.

'I really don't think there's any need,' Phoebe replied with a firm but diplomatic smile. 'You've done quite enough for us already,' she continued, 'and I'm sure you have things you need to be getting on with.'

Doreen looked crestfallen, but nodded and shuffled back behind her own front door. 'Let me know if you hear anything,' she called as she closed it.

Phoebe rushed through the door that May had left open for her, and found her and Maria in the kitchen. She looked at May. She was a strange ally to find herself with but right now May was all she had. Then, with an encouraging smile for Maria she said, 'Spud, how about you get out of that school uniform and into something snugly and comfy?' Maria gave a solemn nod and then disappeared upstairs. Phoebe quickly filled May in on the rest of Doreen's story. 'What do we do?' she asked.

'I'd better call Edward.'

'Ok.' Phoebe didn't relish the idea of bringing Jack's parents into this mess but she understood that they didn't have much of a choice.

May put her phone down after a brief conversation. 'Edward says he's going to call a few friends – the ones he knows of anyway – and then he'll meet us here if he gets no joy from that.'

Phoebe wasn't sure what Jack's dad could do apart from stand around pondering the same scenarios they were, but the idea of him being there was still oddly comforting. She just hoped he would come alone.

'Don't worry,' May added, 'whatever is going on, I'm sure Jack has enough common sense for the both of them.'

'What do you think has happened,' Phoebe asked in a low voice.

'Well, you see Jack a lot more than I do now. He was always so reliable but, of course, he's changed over the years…' She didn't elaborate on the reasons for this. Phoebe had considered him reliable as he was now, but he must have been rock solid during his relationship with Rebecca. Archie would have been a lot younger then, too, Phoebe reasoned. Perhaps he'd had less to distract him. 'Even I can see that things are not right with him and his brother,' May concluded.

So Jack had not told May about Archie's problems, and neither had Carol, despite her alleged closeness to May. What did that say about their relationships, Phoebe wondered?

'Carol hasn't even mentioned that Archie moved out. I only found out from Maria that he was living here. If Carol hadn't mentioned it then I didn't think it was my place to quiz her, but I did wonder.'

'He's been here for a good few weeks now,' Phoebe replied, her mind running over just how many problems that situation had caused.

'Why's that?'

Phoebe chewed on her lip as May found two cups and laid them out. 'Not for me, thanks,' she said as she noticed her open the coffee jar.

'Tea?'

'No thank you.' What response could Phoebe give? It wasn't up to her to share the information that the rest of the Andrews family had seen fit to keep a secret and yet, May was now involved and it didn't seem fair to keep the truth from her. 'I think there was some sort of family argument,' she said carefully. 'You know how teenagers can be.'

'I do that,' May said with a chuckle. 'But I'm sure he'll be moving back in with them once they make it up. Carol adores her boys and she wouldn't let that situation last for long.'

Phoebe almost snorted. That wasn't the Carol she knew. Was there more to the ice-queen than met the eye? It was hard to believe. 'It does seem a bit drastic to throw someone out over a family disagreement,' Phoebe conceded. She knew the truth, of course, that Archie had taken money from his parents to gamble. But Jack had explained that his intentions had been honourable, if his morality a little muddied, and that he had honestly believed he would be able to make their money back with a healthy bonus on top. So why was Carol still refusing to forgive Archie? Surely, she shouldn't even need it explaining – Archie was her son and it should be her priority to understand his problems. Phoebe felt more awkward by the minute as the lies and half-truths stacked up.

'I suppose a bit of distance will help everyone to see sense.' May poured some boiling water into a cup for herself.

'Do you think we ought to call the police?'

May shook her head. 'I don't think they'd do anything just yet; the boys haven't been missing long enough.'

'But, what Doreen said –'

'Sounds bad, I admit. But for all Doreen knows it could have been a bunch of rowdy friends calling for Archie. I think we'll have to wait until we're sure there's a problem before we take it any further. Besides, I don't think Jack would appreciate a full scale police search for him if it turns out he's only gone to the supermarket or something.'

Phoebe wished she could share May's calm optimism. 'Perhaps we should check the hospitals,' she added after a moment. 'Just to be certain.'

'Will it make you feel that you're doing something useful?' May asked with a smile.

'Something like that. Sitting here doing nothing is driving me insane.'

'Edward will be here soon and you and he can take a drive around the streets to see if you can spot them.'

Well yes, but only if Carol's not in the car too... Phoebe chewed on a fingernail. 'I just wish Jack would answer his damned phone. Even a quick text would be better than nothing. If it's something simple and straightforward going on here I won't be happy about the lack of contact.'

'I'm sure there's a good reason for it.'

'That's what I'm worried about.'

'Come and sit down. Are you sure you don't want a hot drink? It might make you feel better.'

Phoebe flopped into a seat at the table. 'I just want him to call.'

For the next twenty minutes, May took charge and Phoebe was happy to let her. After rustling up a quick tea for Maria and doing a fantastic job of keeping her mind off Jack's absence by quizzing her about school, she made sure that Phoebe ate a slice of toast. The more time Phoebe spent with May, the more she liked her. She was a natural mother hen, an emotional rock, and Phoebe was almost jealous of her fortitude and calm. How strong she must have been when Rebecca died, what a warm and gentle soul. Phoebe wished she could be half the woman May was rather than the snivelling wreck who sat at the table watching her and Maria chat whilst fighting back pointless and stupid tears. As May had pointed out more than once, they didn't even know if there was anything to worry about yet. Phoebe rubbed her eyes and silently concluded that it must be those pesky hormones to blame again.

A knock at the front door made them both jump. May hurried to answer it and returned with Jack's dad. He gave Phoebe a brisk nod.

'No Carol?' May asked.

'She's staying at home in case they turn up there.'

'Good idea. What do you think we ought to do?'

'Have you tried to call them again since you phoned me?'

'More than once. Although only Jack; neither of us has Archie's mobile number.'

'I tried that before I left home and it's switched off.'

'Jack's is just ringing out,' Phoebe said.

Edward nodded. 'I know. It's a hell of a nuisance.' He ran a hand over his chin thoughtfully. 'I'll go around to the usual haunts, see if anyone has seen them or knows anything about these men. What exactly did Doreen say about them?'

'I'm surprised she didn't come out when you arrived to tell you herself,' May said.

'It's probably a good thing she didn't,' Phoebe said. 'What she told us wasn't a great deal of use and you'd have been there all night. She didn't like the look of them though.'

'I don't like the sound of them either,' Edward said. 'Knowing Archie he's mixed up with something he shouldn't be.' He turned to May. 'I'm sorry you had to be involved in this.'

'Don't be silly. I think of you all as family and I want to help.'

'It's appreciated. Are you ok to stay here?' He looked at them both in turn and both women nodded.

'Didn't you want to go out with Edward?' May asked Phoebe.

'I think I'll stay here actually.' Phoebe didn't have much faith in Edward finding his sons by driving around the town looking for them in pubs and betting shops. There was no way Jack would be sitting in a pub with his brother and not answering his phone if he knew he was expected to be home for Maria. She voiced her original thoughts to May again. 'I'll call the hospital, see if they've turned up there. And we should call the police now.'

'Don't involve the police just yet,' Edward said. 'It's too early and there might be a simple explanation for all this.'

'Another hour or so and we'll have to call them,' Phoebe insisted.

Edward looked at his watch and nodded his agreement. 'You're probably right. Let's give them a chance to turn up first, though.' He glanced around, as if suddenly realising something was missing. 'Where's Maria?'

'Bed,' May replied. 'It's a tad early but I thought it was the best place for her to be right now, away from the drama. I wondered if I'd have trouble getting her off but she must have been exhausted from racing around the park because she fell asleep half way through her bedtime story.'

'Bless her,' Edward said. 'Look, I'll get going. I have my mobile phone with me if there are any developments here.'

'No problem. We'll hold the fort.'

He left them and May joined Phoebe at the table. 'Are you sure I can't get you a drink? You must be parched.'

Phoebe looked up. 'I'm fine. I don't much care for tea or coffee these days.' The remark had slipped out before she thought about it. But if May attached any significance to it she let it pass.

'Water maybe? Or something more to eat?'

'Thank you, but the toast you made has done the trick. Besides, I can't have you waiting on me.' Phoebe scraped her chair away from the table and went to run herself a glass of water. 'Do you really think they're ok? It's half seven and there's no way Jack would miss Maria's bedtime without arranging it first. This is just not like him at all.'

'It's not,' May agreed.

Phoebe turned to her as she leaned against the sink and sipped her water. What sort of relationship had she had with Jack before Rebecca died? Had she viewed him as a good son-in-law? Was she as fond of him as Carol had been of Rebecca? How had she felt when Rebecca died leaving her with only the man who had, effectively, brought about her demise? Did she blame Jack at first? Had she hated him?

'Maybe I'll try his phone again,' Phoebe said, snatching hers up from the table. She didn't expect it to do any good but it was better than doing nothing.

She dialled the number and listened to the ringing tone. Just like before it rang and rang but no one answered. Phoebe turned to the window to hide her tears. They weren't tears of sadness or fear, but of frustration. How could Jack behave like this? She could believe it of Archie, but not Jack. Didn't he know that everyone would be scared to death for him? Didn't he realise he should have left a note, sent a text, anything before he went dashing off after Archie, knowing that there may well be trouble waiting for them both? She felt a gentle hand on her arm.

'Don't worry,' May said. 'I'm sure everything will be fine. We'll probably be laughing about this tomorrow when it turns out they've just been to Sainsbury's.'

Phoebe turned and gave her a watery smile. 'You're right. It's one hell of an introduction for us, though, isn't it?'

May returned the smile. 'It is. I felt as if I knew you already, though. Maria talks about you all the time and I can tell she adores you.'

'Is that ok?' Phoebe asked. It was hard to understand what had suddenly made her desperate for May's approval, but she was. She needed to know that it was ok to be here, where Rebecca should have been.

'I think Maria is an excellent judge of character, even at her age. And it's more than ok.'

Phoebe silently wondered how much Carol had told May to try and undo Maria's good work. Would she pull any punches when reporting her dislike of Phoebe? Phoebe doubted it. If that was the case, it was good to see that May was happy to make up her own mind.

'I'm glad Jack has found someone,' May continued. 'He won't say it, but he's been so lonely since we lost Rebecca.'

Was there an etiquette for a conversation like this? Was Phoebe supposed to say she was sorry? Should she ask about Rebecca? Was May expecting a reply to the remark at all?

'My boyfriend died too,' she blurted out, not even sure where it had come from. 'And I was so lonely. Maria and Jack…' God, all she wanted was to see him walk through the door with a smile on his face and a funny anecdote to explain his disappearance. The thought that he might not really terrified her. She'd already mourned the loss of one lover, what if she lost Jack too? She didn't think she was strong enough to do it again.

'That must have been awful,' May said. 'I suppose it helps that you and Jack both know how it feels though.'

Phoebe nodded.

They both spun around at the sound of a key in the front door, Phoebe beating May in a race down the hallway. Jack and Archie both staggered over the threshold.

'Where have you been?' Phoebe threw herself at Jack, who winced as he gently prised her arms from around his neck.

'Steady…' he mumbled, placing his hands on her waist to stop her wrapping her arms around him a second time.

'What the hell…' Phoebe saw now what, in her relief and desperate need to hold him, she had missed.

May's hand flew to her mouth. 'What happened?'

Archie gave a rueful smile. 'There was a bit of a disagreement in a pub car park.'

Jack glared at him. 'Go and get cleaned up.'

Archie held out his hands. Both sets of knuckles were covered in dried blood. His left eye was swollen shut and his coat was torn. He looked as though he was going to argue with Jack for a moment, but then stomped up the stairs without another word.

'Quietly!' Jack added in a loud hiss. He glanced at May and Phoebe in turn. 'Maria's in bed?'

'Yes,' May replied. 'She was exhausted so I think she'll sleep through.'

'Was she ok?'

'She was a bit upset, but I think it was more that she'd caught the worry from us than her being unduly worried herself about the fact you were missing.'

'I'm glad she's not up now. I wouldn't want her seeing this.'

'She's going to see it tomorrow whether you like it or not,' May said. 'You're going to have one hell of a bruise on the side of your face there.'

'I think I fared better than Archie,' Jack returned, his jaw clenched. 'I definitely fared better than the bastards who tried to do us over.'

Phoebe's eyes were wide with apprehension. 'What if they come back for you?'

Jack took a moment. 'Back here?'

'Yes. Well we know they know where you live.'

'Ah...' Jack said, understanding illuminating his features. 'Doreen told you.'

'About the three men looking for Archie, yes,' May said.

'There's not much else to say,' Jack said briskly.

'Then it won't take you long to fill us in,' May said.

Jack's hands moved to his ribs with a grimace as he held them. 'Some dispute,' he said as he started to walk to the kitchen. 'I don't even know what it was over; it was someone Archie had managed to upset somehow. I mean, I had to go and bail him out, didn't I?' He took a seat at the table. Phoebe could see that his hands shook slightly as he lifted his shirt to reveal an area of his flank already dark red with bruising. She hoped it looked worse than it was, because it looked pretty bad from where she stood. But if she'd learned one thing about Jack in the last few months, it was that he wouldn't tolerate molly-coddling. She could tell him to get himself checked out at the emergency department and he'd promptly ignore her. 'I'll live,' he said, letting the shirt drop back over his chest. And that was exactly what Phoebe was expecting him to do.

'You should go to the hospital with that,' May chided, airing Phoebe's thoughts for her.

'There's no need,' Jack insisted. 'Apart from cuts and bruises we're both fine. It was all a bit of a cat-fight really. In fact, I've seen worse at milk time in Maria's class.'

He wasn't telling the whole story; that much was obvious to Phoebe. Was he keeping it back for May's sake? 'Your dad's out looking for you,' she said, anger starting to build now that the initial relief had subsided. 'We've all been panicking here. You need to call him and tell him you're both safe.'

'Um... yeah...' Jack replied looking awkward. 'I can't really do that right now. I've sort of mislaid my phone.'

'I suppose that explains why you weren't answering. Couldn't you have got Archie to call us once you were safe? We've been worried sick.'

'I think his is broken.'

'I'll call your dad now,' May said. She went through to the living room and shut the door. Phoebe suspected it was to give the two of them some privacy.

'What the hell actually happened?' Phoebe hissed. Tears where threatening to fall again. 'I was so scared.'

'Archie got himself mixed up with a bit of money lending. They came round after their payment but it was nothing I couldn't handle. They were only bits of kids themselves, playing at gangsters. They didn't reckon on us being able to hit back.'

'If they came for Archie how did you end up getting a pasting?'

'I couldn't very well let him go off and get his head kicked in, could I? I went off after them.'

'How on earth did you find them?'

Jack gave a half-smile. 'They weren't driving the subtlest of cars. An N reg yellow Fiesta XR2i with go-faster stripes kinda stands out these days. When I found it round the back of the Nag's Head it was either them, or the National Chav Museum had lost an exhibit.'

'You could have got yourselves killed!' Phoebe squeaked, ignoring his attempts at humour.

'We didn't. We had a little chat, they didn't like what we had to say and they nicked our phones as payment for Archie's debts – or down payment was how they described it but I'm damned if they're getting any more out of us. If they'd just taken the phones and left it at that I might have let it be myself. But I wasn't having them threatening to come back. So we gave chase as they went back to their car and exchanged a few blows, but then they got away.'

'So where have you been until now? You've been gone for hours! What if they come after you for the rest?'

'That's why I dragged Archie to the police station. I'm not sure what they can do but I thought we should report the theft at least. Archie didn't want to, of course, and he told them he didn't have any names even though he must have known who they were.'

'What did the police say they could do?'

'They took statements. Said they'd do what they could to look into it and have a patrol car pass by our house a few times over the next couple of days to see that all was well. That was it. It didn't help that Archie was playing silly buggers and wouldn't give them all the facts.'

'They didn't need all the facts.' Archie stood at the kitchen door now. 'And those bastards won't come back, not now we've shown them we can handle ourselves.'

'Unless they come back with crowbars and baseball bats next time to do the job more efficiently,' Phoebe replied.

Archie was about to reply when May spoke from behind him. 'Your dad says he'll be back in ten minutes.'

'Can't wait,' Archie said. He joined Jack at the table, fingering the swelling around his eye.

'You want some ice on that,' May said.

'There's a bag of peas in the freezer.' Jack inclined his head towards it. 'That should do it.'

As May went to fetch it, Jack shot Phoebe a look that she interpreted as a plea to keep things to herself. Phoebe supposed he had good reason; May would hardly be reassured if she thought that he was bringing danger to his door or, more specifically, to Maria's door. She was frankly surprised that Jack hadn't already come to that conclusion himself and given Archie his marching orders, brother or not. Supporting him with a gambling problem was one thing, but dealing with thugs who came by demanding recompense for his gambling debts, was quite another.

'I'm so sorry about this,' Jack said as May handed Archie the bag of peas. 'And Maria really wasn't too upset about tonight?'

'Honestly, you don't need to worry, she's fine. She was a bit upset when you weren't home to put her to bed but when I said you'd be here in the morning and that Phoebe and I would stay with her until then, she settled down.'

'Thank you.' Jack ran a hand through his hair and gave a heavy sigh.

'And that's it?' May replied with obvious disbelief in her voice.

'What do you mean?'

'The story you've given us about where you've been? That's all there is to it?'

'Honestly. It was a misunderstanding, wasn't it, Archie?'

Jack's brother nodded from behind the huge bag of peas clamped to his face.

Further interrogation was halted by another soft knock at the door. 'That'll be your dad,' May said as she hurried off to get it. They returned moments later, Edward thundering down the hallway and into the kitchen.

'Bloody hell!' he cried as he took in the scene at the table. 'What's all this?'

Jack went through the edited version of the story again, complete with apologies for the worry and covert glares at Archie to keep quiet while May made them hot, sweet tea and went to check on Maria who was, miraculously considering the hullabaloo downstairs, still asleep.

'I think it's about time you came back home,' Edward said to Archie as Jack finished.

Hallelujah! It was the first positive thing to come out of the evening as far as Phoebe was concerned. The wonderful morning she had shared with her mum, seeing her baby for the first time, the encouraging and inspiring conversation she'd shared with a stranger on a bus, meeting May and finding a lovely woman – it had all been overshadowed by the fear and anxiety Jack's disappearance had brought and Phoebe could barely remember what happy and relaxed felt like right now.

'You can't tell me what to do,' Archie said. 'I'm nineteen.'

'And yet you behave more as though you were nine. Tonight has proved that.'

'What if I don't want to come back to live with you? What if I like it here? Don't I get a say? Doesn't Jack get a say? He likes having me here.'

I bloody don't, Phoebe thought. *Please, for once, lay down the law, Edward.*

'This has nothing to do with Jack,' Edward said. 'And quite frankly it doesn't have very much to do with what you want either. This is about me saving you from your own stupid self until you're old enough to know better.'

'Jack doesn't treat me like a kid, Dad. That's why I want to stay with him.'

'Jack has enough to contend with already. He doesn't need to be babysitting you.'

'What!' Archie yelped. 'It's always my fault, isn't it?'

'Yes, actually it is. You've only got to look at what happened tonight to see that. I don't need any more phone calls like that. You've disrupted everyone's evening and had us all running around like idiots worried to death.'

'Jack was part of it too,' Archie replied stubbornly.

Phoebe resisted the impulse to throw something at him. Had she and her friends been this idiotic at nineteen or was Archie a special case?

May cleared her throat, a subtle reminder to all that, perhaps, this argument was one they might not want her to witness. 'Now that the boys are back safe I should think about going home, let you all settle down.'

Edward pushed his chair away from the table. 'I'll run you back.'

'There's no need –'

'Yes there is. I'm not having you walking home alone.' He grabbed his keys from the table where he had tossed them and turned to Archie. 'Don't think I've finished with you yet. I'll be back in five minutes.'

'Of course you haven't.' Archie threw the peas onto the table and leaned back in his chair wearing a sardonic grin.

Once they had said their goodbyes to May, and Jack had apologised and thanked her yet again, she followed Edward out to his car.

Jack let out a long breath as the front door closed behind them. Archie went to the fridge, grabbed a bottle of milk and proceeded to gulp directly from it. It was a move that usually provoked a torrent of abuse from Jack, but if Archie was doing it deliberately to taunt him tonight it didn't work. He simply turned to Phoebe.

'I suppose that was a bit weird for you... meeting May like that, I mean.'

'No weirder than my boyfriend being kidnapped by a bunch of Kray wanabees and going AWOL for two hours. It's been a weird sort of day, if I'm honest.'

Jack stared at her. And then he suddenly clapped a hand to his head. 'Shit! Of course... this morning...' he glanced at Archie and then back at Phoebe. She understood his meaning perfectly but was beginning to tire of being the last in line for his attention these days. 'You can tell me about it later, yeah?'

'What happened this morning?' Archie asked as he drained the milk and dumped the empty bottle back in the fridge.

'Nothing important,' Jack replied.

That was it. Phoebe could not hold back any longer.

'Nothing important?' she spat.

'I didn't mean it like that,' Jack began, reddening, but she shot him down with a burning glare. She rummaged in her bag and slapped the scan photo onto the table.

'Sure... nothing important at all!'

Jack tore his gaze away from the picture, as though it was painful to look at it. But Archie leaned over.

'Shit... is that....?'

'Yes!' Phoebe snapped. 'It is!'

Archie turned to Jack. 'Bloody hell, you kept that quiet.'

'Yes...' Jack replied in a low voice as he glanced back at Phoebe, still refusing to look at the photo.

'We were both supposed to keep it quiet for the time being.'

'We might have noticed sooner or later, dude,' Archie said with a laugh. 'Am I supposed to congratulate you or give you the name of a better brand of condom?'

'Shut up!' Jack snapped. 'Why is everything a bloody joke with you?' He looked at Phoebe, a slew of emotions so vast swimming in his eyes that she couldn't see what he was feeling at all. She could only wonder why he hadn't answered Archie's question; in the end, it was the only one that really mattered to her. Why wasn't he telling Archie how happy he was, how excited he was for the baby to come?

Before she knew what she was doing she had run for the door, Jack calling after her. His silence had been his answer. She had never been anyone's burden, not even in her darkest hours, when she had been so bereft that she barely saw the point of living anymore, and she wasn't about to start now.

She could still hear her name being called as she ran along the street, but she couldn't look back. It was only when she realised, somewhere in the margins of her thoughts, that the voice calling her wasn't Jack's, that she stopped and turned around.

Archie jogged towards her holding his side.

'Where are you going?' he panted.

'Home.'

'Are you really having a baby?'

'Yeah. It looks like it.'

'Are you moving in with Jack?'

'I don't think so. It looks like you win,' Phoebe said, 'you get to stay and I go.'

'Come back and sort it out.'

'I don't think so.'

'But you're having a baby.'

'I don't want to come back in.'

'Whatever. It's stupid though.'

'He doesn't want me to.'

'I reckon he does.'

'Then why isn't it him chasing me instead of you.'

Archie shrugged. 'I'm faster?'

Phoebe looked along the empty street behind him. 'Nice try, but I know he doesn't want to come after me.'

'Because he thinks you won't go back in.'

'And that's reason enough not to try? It's a funny way of showing someone you love them.'

Archie shrugged awkwardly. He looked torn.

'I knew it,' Phoebe said in a dull voice.

'I guess he's freaked out by the baby is all.'

'Seriously? Don't you think it's me who should be freaked out by all this crap going on?'

Archie scuffed the toe of his trainer against the protruding edge of a paving stone. 'Yeah, I get that. I'll probably go home with Dad later, get out of your way.'

'I shouldn't bother. It's me who needs to get out of the way. Jack's made his feelings perfectly clear.'

Archie's gaze slipped to his feet. Phoebe turned and started to walk towards home. She felt numb.

She couldn't begin to get her head around how this day could have begun with such hope to end like this, and it had all happened so fast. It was just another of life's curve balls and she was getting used to ducking them by now.

'You won't get far without your keys,' Archie shouted. 'Your bag's still on the table.'

Phoebe stopped and turned to face him again.

'Right.'

'So much for your grand exit, eh?' Archie's expression betrayed nothing – was he being sarcastic or sympathetic? Phoebe couldn't work him out.

'I suppose I'd better get them…'

'You want *me* to get them?' he asked carelessly. It was possibly the most helpful he'd ever been to Phoebe, and it had come at the strangest and most unexpected moment. She blinked at him. It was just another one of those curve balls.

'Um, yeah…'

She watched him jog back as she waited, staring down the street as night fell in a lilac and orange haze over the silhouetted rooftops.

In a few minutes he had returned with her bag, jacket, and the scan photo. Phoebe's eyes welled up as Archie handed it to her. She had hoped that even if Jack didn't come back out instead of Archie, then he'd at least want to keep the photo. But he had apparently relinquished it without a fight. Was this really it? Were they through?

'What do you think?'

'About what?'

Phoebe shrugged helplessly. Even she wasn't sure what she was asking Archie.

'So... are you coming back in or what?'

'Thanks, but I'm tired and I want to go home.'

'You're walking home? Alone?'

'Yeah, it looks like it. At least to the bus stop.'

Archie's hand went up to his swollen eye. He scuffed his feet on the pavement again and he looked at Phoebe with an expression that told her he didn't know what to think or say. Perhaps he was out of his emotional depth. If the truth was told, so was Phoebe.

She turned away. 'Bye Archie.' She began to walk. If Jack didn't want this baby then she would do it alone.

⚜   ⚜   ⚜

Phoebe stared up at the ceiling as she lay flat on her bed. Her fingers gripped the corner of the scan photo at her side. What had just happened? Had she and Jack split up? She was still struggling to understand any of it. Her phone had rung four times since she'd arrived home but she couldn't bring herself to talk to him. Maybe he wanted to apologise but Phoebe wasn't in the mood to accept it with any grace. She didn't care what he felt or how much he was hurting. In fact, she hoped he was, because then he would know how it felt to be rejected. Sure, he had been subjected to a difficult night, but hadn't they all?

And nobody else had behaved with such utter disregard for her feelings. It wasn't just tonight either; ever since she had told him about the baby he had become a totally different person from the man she thought she knew. Well, if he didn't want their baby then he would get his wish. There was no need to involve a man who didn't want to be involved. Loads of mothers got by just fine on their own and Phoebe didn't see why she should be any different. As far as she was concerned, there were no half measures: either he acted like a proper father or he stayed away for good.

She looked at her phone again. It had been silent for twenty minutes now. As the anger subsided, fear and sadness took its place. It was late now, too late to call her parents. But she needed them and the protective bubble that only they could weave around her to make her feel safe. She dialled the number, hoping they hadn't yet gone to bed.

'Mum…' Phoebe's voice cracked but she took a steadying breath. 'Do you mind if I come over?'

'Phoebe…? It's half ten…'

'I know. I'm sorry. If you're going to bed it can wait –'

'Don't be daft. Is everything alright?'

'No…' Phoebe began to sob. 'No, Mum, it isn't…'

'Right,' Martha replied briskly. 'Give us twenty minutes and we'll be there to pick you up.'

❧ ❧ ❧

Martha already had a pan of milk on the stove when Phoebe followed her dad through to the kitchen. True to Martha's promise, he had arrived exactly twenty minutes after Phoebe's plea for help and ushered her into the car. The drive back to her parents' house had been quiet, the silence only broken by the occasional stifled sob from Phoebe and her father clearing his throat. He knew from experience that driving and having deep, meaningful conversations didn't really go together and that once they arrived back home they would be able to talk things through properly.

'I'm making you cocoa,' Martha announced.

'Mum... there's really no need. I just wanted... I don't know what I wanted.'

'I want to know what that lad has done,' Hugh said.

'He hasn't hurt me if that's what you're worried about,' Phoebe said.

'So why are you here looking like your world has ended?'

Phoebe let out a sigh. 'Watch your milk doesn't boil over, Mum.' She angled her head at the pan as she dropped into a seat at the table.

Martha removed the pan from the hob and poured milk into two mugs. 'You'll stay here tonight, and I think it would be a good idea if you take the day off tomorrow.'

'I can't do that, there's far too much to do at work,' Phoebe replied.

'In your state? I should think a day off will do you good. Do they know you're pregnant yet?'

'No. I'll tell them soon. But we have a full day of story sessions tomorrow and I need to be there.'

Martha turned and planted her hands on her hips as Hugh took a seat at the table next to Phoebe. 'Are you telling me that if you died today they'd have to cancel all future story sessions because you wouldn't be there?'

'I'm not dead, though, am I?'

'You know what I mean. If you need a day off then you should take one. Let someone else worry about what's going on at Hendry's for once.'

'I'm not taking the day off.' What she wanted to add was that if things didn't improve with Jack then her job would be all she had left. And she'd need the income with a baby to raise on her own. But she didn't.

'Don't worry, love,' Hugh cut in. 'I can run you into work in the morning, no problem.'

'Won't that make you late?' Phoebe asked.

'Don won't mind if I'm a bit late. He knows I'll always make the time back.'

Phoebe gave him a grateful smile. 'Thanks.' Right here in her childhood home felt like the safest place to be right now. Tomorrow was another day but tonight she could lie in her old bed and pretend everything was as simple and uncomplicated as it been back in the days when she lived here.

Martha placed a mug of cocoa in front of Phoebe. The sweet, heady smell wrapped itself around her frayed nerves like a soothing balm. Whenever there had been upset throughout her teenage years, Martha had always made cocoa for her. Phoebe couldn't remember exactly when it had started, but it had become something of a tradition. There had been a lot of cocoa, right about the time Vik had died, and a lot of it had gone cold as Phoebe wept into it. But without it, she knew that her mourning would have been even more painful than it was. It wasn't about the drink, but what it symbolised. Her parents couldn't protect her from all of life's injustices, but they would be there to comfort her, no matter how dark things got.

Martha slid another mug over for Hugh and joined them at the table.

'Aren't you having one?' Phoebe asked.

'I'm trying to cut down,' Martha replied.

'Really?' Phoebe raised her eyebrows.

'That's what I said,' Hugh chuckled. 'There's not much of her to start with but she keeps telling me she's filling out.'

'I am,' Martha replied. 'You're just not looking properly.'

'Oh… I look alright,' Hugh winked.

Martha rolled her eyes. 'For pity's sake; you're such a brute.'

'I know,' he grinned. Then he turned to Phoebe. 'Are you ready to tell us about it, love?'

'Not especially. I suppose I'm just feeling a bit lost at the moment. Jack and I had words tonight and I don't know what's wrong. He won't share what he's thinking about the baby. He says he is but I know he's keeping things back from me and he's changed since I told him. He tells me he's happy but I can see that he's not. And the situation with his brother isn't helping; it's putting a lot of strain on us both. I'm only glad now that I stood my ground over moving in with him. It would have been twenty times worse if I'd been living in the middle of it all.' Phoebe didn't like keeping secrets of her own, but there was no way she could tell her parents everything that had gone on with Archie and his *pretend* gangsters. Harmless or not, her mum would have been worried to death and her dad would have been straight round to sort Archie out himself.

'Aye… it's always good to have a bolthole,' Hugh agreed.

'Like your shed?' Phoebe smiled.

'Exactly.'

'I think I might need a bit more than a shed,' Phoebe mused. 'Maybe another universe.'

Martha reached across the table for Phoebe's hand. 'You know that we'd be upset if you split from Jack and found yourself living as a single mum, but that's only because it would be a struggle for you. We'd back you all the way, though. Anything you need, we'll be here. So if that's what's happening now and you're afraid, don't be. You have to do what you feel is right.'

'That's just it. I don't even know myself how I feel about it all. Maybe I just need some space, time away from Jack to think it through.'

'Good idea. It's good to see you thinking clearly about this.'

'I don't know about that,' Phoebe said. 'I know one thing, though, I hadn't realised cocoa would agree with me quite as well as it does. I haven't been able to stand tea or coffee since I started having morning sickness but this is perfect. I may have to move in so that I can have it on tap.'

'You know you'd always be welcome. And I mean that in all seriousness, love.' Hugh let out a wide yawn. He clamped a bear paw of a hand to his mouth. 'Well! I didn't see that one coming!' he laughed. 'I should think it's your mother's cocoa working its magic on me too.'

'You did get up at six today,' Martha reminded him.

'Aye, I suppose I did and this old body can't stand the pace like it used to.'

'Go to bed, love,' Martha said.

Hugh looked from one to the other and then gave a knowing grin. 'Woman to woman chat now, is it? You're going to tell Phoebe how men are all terrible and that she should burn her bra and get straight to a nunnery.'

'It's a bit late for the nunnery,' Phoebe said.

'You great daft lump,' Martha added. 'I'm going to talk to her about extended labour, pelvic floor collapse and stretch marks.'

'Oh blimey! In that case I'm off!' Hugh drained his mug and smacked his lips like a cartoon character. 'Bloody good cocoa, that.' He bent to kiss them both – Martha on the lips and Phoebe on the head. 'Don't worry, love,' he said to Phoebe. 'I'm sure it will all look better in the morning.'

'Thanks, Dad. You're probably right.'

Hugh placed his empty mug in the sink before leaving them with a cheery goodnight.

'You're so lucky,' Phoebe said to her mum. 'Dad's brilliant.'

Martha smiled. 'You're right. He's a good man. But it's taken work, just like it does for everyone else.'

'It's not the work that bothers me,' Phoebe said. 'I know good, solid relationships don't happen by magic. I'm prepared to give and take and I want to be with Jack, but it's like…' she sighed. 'I don't know. It's like his heart is a house. I can wander around there, go in any room I like, but I know there's one little trapdoor that he just won't open for me. I want to know what's down there but at the same time I'm too scared to force it.' She grabbed her cocoa and stared into it. 'I suppose that doesn't make a lot of sense.'

'More than you know.' Martha smiled. 'Wait here.'

Phoebe looked up as her mother disappeared from the room. She returned a few moments later and pushed a book across the table towards Phoebe.

'What's this?'

'Help… at least I hope so.'

Phoebe picked it up. The pages were well thumbed and the cover and spine creased. 'What have you been doing with this, washing the windows?

'You may laugh, my girl, but that's the secret of my success. I read that book fifteen years ago and since then your dad and I have never been happier. Every time I lose sight of its advice I read it again.'

'Seriously?' Phoebe asked in a sceptical tone, turning it over in her hands. '*Men Are from Mars, Women Are from Venus* saved your marriage?'

'Not saved, exactly. More like enhanced it. There was no danger of us ever splitting up but we had definitely reached a point where it had become hard work.'

'It's not about sex, is it?' Phoebe asked with a grimace. The last thing she wanted to visualise as she turned off the light after her bedtime read was her parents *doing it.*

'Don't be daft. It's advice, about what makes us tick and how women are different from men.'

'From some overpaid American shrink?'

'Fifteen million readers can't be wrong.'

Phoebe placed it on the table and pushed it back. 'I think I'll sort out my problems the old-fashioned way.'

'By ignoring them?'

'I'm not.'

'So why did you run away?'

'He pretty much made me leave,' Phoebe said in a defensive tone. 'And I wasn't the one in the wrong.'

'Did he try to apologise?'

'Sort of…'

'And did you let him?'

'Sort of…'

'That means no. I know you. Once you close up there's no getting through again.'

'Is that one of the phrases from your book?'

'If you're going to poke fun then I won't try to help.' Martha looked genuinely hurt.

'Sorry,' Phoebe replied. 'Of course I'll read it.'

Phoebe pulled the book towards her again and read the back cover. She didn't think for a moment that a book was going to help her and Jack, unless she could beat Archie with it. He had told her he would go home to his parents. Phoebe wondered whether he had gone through with it after all. Perhaps Jack was alone there now. She could go to him, sort it out. It was silly to sit here and cry when they could be together, talking it all through. But even if Archie had gone home, it still didn't change the way Jack had hurt her. The truth was, right now, she didn't want to go to him. She believed she was worth more than that.

⚜ ⚜ ⚜

PART FOUR
AND BABY MAKES FOUR

W hen Phoebe woke, the book her mum had given her was lying on the bedside table. As her eyes focused on it, she tutted under her breath, still unconvinced that it contained the secret of saving her relationship with Jack. Did her relationship even need saving? Perhaps she had overreacted the night before, already stressed by a very long and weird day, and today she would find everything that had seemed so big and scary yesterday now looked unimportant in the light of a new day. Her gaze travelled the room as she mused on the idea. Accompanying the odd yet familiar scene of old bedroom furniture, decorated with stickers of long-forgotten bands and childhood crushes, was the gentle tick of her old Mickey Mouse alarm clock. The soothing, rhythmic sound made her smile. Her brother, Josh, had bought it for her during one of his many gap-year stopovers. Phoebe had left it with her parents when she moved out, believing herself too grownup and sophisticated for Mickey Mouse clocks. How silly she thought that version of herself now. Sometimes, the best way to deal with the present is to cling on to the comforts of the past, and never had she seen that more plainly than now, as she lay in her little room – a space captured in time. She silently gave thanks that her dad had been stubborn in his refusal to let Martha clear it out and give all Phoebe's old stuff to charity. Not this year, he kept saying, until she had given up asking. As Phoebe stared at the clock, watching the minute hand inch around the face, she wondered whether Maria would like to have it. Perhaps Maria would then pass it on to the baby?

Her mind went back to the awful argument with Jack. Well, less of an argument and more of an explosion on her part, now that she really thought about it. What if she had gone too far after all? Only time would tell but she wasn't entirely sure that her dad's insistence everything would be clear after a good night's sleep was true. Of course, to really test that hypothesis one had to have had a good night's sleep... Phoebe had spent the night drifting from shallow sleep to wakefulness in a frustrating cycle. It was to be expected in the circumstances, she supposed, but fatigue wasn't going to help her get through a day at work that promised to be trying enough as it was.

There was a gentle tap at the bedroom door and then Hugh's head appeared.

'You're awake then. I was doing a bacon sandwich and I wondered if you wanted one.'

'Ummm… I'm not sure bacon is what I need this morning. Thanks anyway, Dad.'

'You can't go to work on an empty stomach, lass, especially not in your condition.'

Phoebe gave a rueful smile. 'What condition would that be? The pregnancy or the terminal stupidity?'

Hugh seemed to wince slightly. He let himself in and sat on the edge of her bed. As he did so, his gaze fell upon Martha's book.

'Oh. I see she's tried to dump that daft bit of wisdom on you.'

'Mum says it's the secret of your good marriage. She says she has everything figured out thanks to that book.'

'*Thinks* she has,' Hugh chuckled. 'Let me tell you a secret... the only thing that makes our marriage so good is that I love your mum more than life itself. And I like to think she feels the same way about me.'

'I think she does.' Phoebe smiled as she pushed herself upright. 'So all that rubbish about men in their caves and elastic bands isn't true?'

'I wouldn't say that, exactly...' he gave her a sheepish grin. 'I don't have a cave but I do have my shed, I suppose. As for an elastic band, I'm too caught up in your mother's apron strings to get far enough for her to need to flirt me back.'

'It doesn't look as if you're doing too badly on it.'

'I'm not. We've had a good life together.' Hugh patted a giant hand on her knee. 'Now, what about your Jack? You love him?'

'I think so. I'm so confused lately that I'm not even sure I know what love is. It shouldn't be this hard, should it?'

'Do you feel like you can't breathe without him?'

'Yeah, a little bit. But I put that down to my asthma.'

Hugh laughed. 'That's my girl!' Then his expression became serious. 'Are you sure it's a good idea to go into work today? Wouldn't it be a better plan to stay in bed a while, think about what you really want and, if it is Jack, go and talk to him?'

Phoebe rested her chin on her gathered knees. 'Probably. But I really have to be in work today. Even if I don't do the story sessions, I like to be on hand while they're going on and I wouldn't be able to relax at home knowing that I'm not available. Maybe I'll go and see him tonight.'

Hugh raised his eyebrows as if in disagreement but he remained silent.

'Is that what I should do, Dad?'

Hugh didn't answer straight away. Then he began a measured reply. 'He seems like a decent bloke to me, and I wouldn't trust any old Tom, Dick or Harry with my precious daughter. Aye, I get a good feeling about him. These arguments you've been having, perhaps they're just teething problems. You don't really know each other yet and now you've been landed with all these extra pressures.' He stroked his beard thoughtfully. 'Did I ever tell you that me and your mum split up for two months during our first year together?'

'You did? How come neither of you told me?'

'It didn't really matter before. It was something and nothing and it all blew over a long time ago.'

'What did you do to fix it?'

'I'm not even sure why, but one weekend I just needed to see her. Of course, there was no text messaging in those days and your grandmother wouldn't call her to the phone to speak to me. So I got in my car, drove all the way down from Leeds one Saturday night with a bunch of flowers and my fingers crossed at the wheel. Luckily I got to see her and she took pity on a pathetic lovelorn man. She's been stuck with me ever since.'

'I like that story,' Phoebe smiled. 'But it feels more complicated than that for me and Jack. For a start, Mum wasn't pregnant and you didn't have his little brother breathing down your necks every minute you were together.'

'That's true enough. All I'm saying is think carefully before you throw it all away. It's not easy living with a lifetime of regret. If you've done all you can to save it and it still fails, at least that's one regret less; easier than knowing you let it go without a fight.'

Phoebe nodded as she gazed past him, mulling over his words. It was possibly the first time her dad had been this open and frank about affairs of the heart. She had always seen him as this huge, gruff, ale-swilling man's man – loveable in his own way but no room in his life for girly stuff like emotions. But the man beneath the carefree dad she'd always known was deep and insightful. She wouldn't be surprised if his next confession was that he'd written her mum love poems in their youth – in fact, she wondered if he still wrote love poetry for her now. In many ways, although Jack and her dad were very different on the surface, they were also the same. Maybe that was why she'd been attracted to Jack. He was intelligent, thoughtful, creative and articulate. He was sensitive (usually) and very, very kind. His favoured form of expression might have been cooking rather than poetry but in the end it was sort of the same. Was he really the perfect man for her? Would she later regret any rash actions she took now? There was still anger for the way he had treated her, of course, and she still held a strong conviction that he was completely in the wrong, but maybe he deserved more effort from her to help him put it right.

Hugh patted her knee again before standing up. 'I'd love to sit here all day but if either of us is going to get into work we need to crack on.'

'I'm getting up now, Dad.' Phoebe threw her covers back and swung her legs out of bed. Hugh nodded and went for the door.

'Oh, and Dad…' Phoebe called him back. 'I should say thank you.'

'Anytime, love. I only hope you make the right choice.'

Without conscious thought, Phoebe's hand went to her belly. 'Me too, Dad. Me too.'

✤ ✤ ✤

'Bloody hell!' Midnight sucked on a cola lollipop as she and Phoebe sat on a low wall skirting the ornamental gardens that marked the exact town centre of Millrise.

To call them ornamental gardens was, perhaps, stretching the definition. While it was true that the gardens contained plants, many of them were of the dandelion and thistle variety, interspersed by the lesser-spotted crisp bag and hardy beer can. The council had done their best for many years and had tried to bring tourism to the area by improving parks and green spaces, but there had been a slow and steady decline to many parts of Millrise that echoed a prevailing and hopeless apathy borne from a lack of money. Sadly, the gardens were one of the victims of that downward spiral. Today, it wasn't looking too bad, and Phoebe had only actually seen one beer can nestling in its chavtastic greenery.

From their perch, they could see the civic hall – dignitaries and council admin staff scuttling to and from their daily business – the *Echo* building further down the road looking similarly busy, and a small selection of local businesses such as solicitors, accountants and recruitment agencies. Midnight had chosen this spot to play her new game, 'Hot or Not', and as she listened to Phoebe offload, was diligently labelling each man she saw. Phoebe didn't take offence at this distraction – she was used to Midnight's inability to focus on one task at a time and she knew she was listening despite appearances to the contrary.

'So, Archie has gone?' Midnight asked before yelling 'Hot!' in the direction of a man coming out of Lycett and Lycett Accountancy.

'I don't know,' Phoebe replied, her gaze following the direction of Midnight's as she sucked on an identical lollipop. Although many foods still set off the nausea, Phoebe had found that sugary sweets agreed with her way more than was healthy. So she was eating them in large quantities as she would possibly never have an excuse this good again.

'Not!' Midnight swung her legs out in the direction of a man so bald and skinny he looked like an egg perched on top of an empty suit. 'Haven't you called Jack to find out?'

'It didn't seem like the best idea. As the whole argument started with Archie and the way Jack was protecting him, I didn't think the phone call I should be making was: *hey, how are you? I know that your brother almost got beaten to a pulp last night but has he gone now?*'

'Why not?' Midnight sucked on her lollipop and continued to scan the street for game. 'It's not like Jack doesn't know your feelings about his brother and, besides, it's sensible to get things out in the open.' She sat a little straighter as she caught sight of a floppy haired youth dressed in chain adorned jeans on a skateboard. 'Hubba, hubba, HOT!' she shouted. The youth spun around, looking for the source of the exclamation, and Midnight collapsed into giggles.

'It seemed a bit insensitive,' Phoebe said, 'that's all. I know it's sensible. Anyway, I don't know that I necessarily want to yet.'

'I thought you were all loved up with Mr Stalker?'

'I was… I mean, I am. But sometimes love isn't enough, is it? Does love mean I should let him treat me unfairly? Does it mean I have to stay with him no matter what he does?'

Midnight rolled her eyes. 'Jeez, you're always over-complicating things. If you like him and he likes you, then sort it out. That's all there is to it. If not, then give him the elbow and move on.'

Phoebe spun the lollipop around in her mouth as she gazed into the distance. 'Kind of hard to move on with a baby in tow, though, isn't it?'

'Having a baby isn't the end of the world. The dating market is full of single parents.'

'When you put it like that it all seems simple.'

'That's because it is. Although not as simple as you.' Midnight nodded towards a man in his forties wearing a charcoal suit. 'What do you think about him? I can't decide. A bit of an oldie but he looks like he's wearing well.'

'Sort of lukewarm,' Phoebe said. 'Maybe if he was one of last people on earth and we had to reproduce he wouldn't be too much of a hardship.'

Midnight nodded a sage agreement. 'Good call.' Biting into her lollipop with a loud crack, she proceeded to crunch it like a contented cow chewing the cud out in a field. 'You want to know what I think?'

Phoebe shot her a sideways glance. 'You've changed your score on the lukewarm guy?'

'Nope. In fact, he's a definite meh. I mean what I think about you and Jack.'

'Ok…' Phoebe replied slowly, wondering what pearl of wisdom she was letting herself in for now.

'I think you're both a bit thick. Although I'm leaning towards you being thicker than him right now.'

'Explain.'

'Well, he's obviously going to freak out about you being pregnant because the last woman he got up the duff ended up dead.'

'Right… Not exactly how I would have put it but I take your point. I already knew that, though. We talked about that when I first told him I was pregnant. He was upset but we sorted it.'

'Doesn't look like you sorted it to me, otherwise we wouldn't be having this conversation.'

'We talked about how it was really unlikely to happen again and how I'd be super careful and so there was no need to worry. He said he was fine with all that and he knew that he was being silly.'

'Yeah. I can say I'm Scarlett Johansson, but that doesn't make it true.'

'You think he's not ok with it? Why would he tell me he was?'

'Because he's thick.'

'How am I thicker?'

'For believing that it was all sorted when the evidence against is right in front of your eyes.'

'But all the coldness directed at me… like he didn't want me around. That was nothing to do with the baby…'

Midnight shrugged. 'Men are weird; they don't know how to react to emotional stuff and they push it away rather than deal with it.'

'Like Martians?' Phoebe smiled.

'Huh?'

'Nothing. Mum was trying to persuade me to read a book that says pretty much what you just said. The shrink who wrote this book reckons that men need to sulk in caves when things are bothering them but women like to talk so when there's trouble between the two, neither party naturally takes the approach that's right for the other. When men have been in their caves long enough they'll come out and be ready to discuss their problems.'

'Do you think Jack has been in his cave for long enough?'

'Maybe.'

'Then smoke him out, girl.'

Phoebe grinned. It was amazing how Midnight's seemingly skewed view of the world often made more sense than any other, and how much better Phoebe always felt after just a short time in her company. She'd barely known Midnight longer than the few short months she'd known Jack, and the relationship, in its own way, was just as important to her. Often, when Phoebe thought back to the punch she'd thrown in the Rose and Crown that had got her sacked from her job there and sent her in desperation to Hendry's Toy Shop, it was hard not to believe that some divine providence had been sticking its nose into her life.

Midnight hopped off the wall. 'Are you going to phone him now? You've just got time while we walk back.'

'Not now…' Phoebe glanced around. The street felt too busy, too intrusive. 'It's too noisy here. I can phone him later.'

'Don't make excuses to put it off. I always say do it now and regret it later.'

'Like shouting at random passers-by?'

'Not shouting, merely observing and showing my appreciation for the male form.'

'Try telling that to the ones you just insulted by shouting *NOT* at them. I hope you never observe me like that, it'd be terrifying; I dread to think what score you'd give me.'

'You'd definitely get a hot.'

'Even when I have my huge baby belly?'

'Even more so. Quit stalling and get to a nice quiet spot so you can sort your idiot out.'

Phoebe dropped down from her perch and threw her now empty lollipop stick into a nearby bin.

'What I don't get is how you're still single,' Phoebe said as they began to walk back towards the high street. 'I mean, you're stunning, you have a figure to die for, you're dead funny and dead smart. Isn't there anyone you fancy?'

'If you'd met my friends you'd see why I'm single,' Midnight laughed. 'They're great but hardly eye candy. And you've seen what we have to contend with

370

at work. Adam Hendry's a bit of alright, but we all know he only has eyes for you.'

'Ugh, don't remind me.' Phoebe did a theatrical shudder.

'I honestly think I'll have to look further than Millrise.'

'You're probably right about that. I don't think the small town mentality suits you. You think you'll move away?'

Midnight shrugged. 'Who knows? Maybe I'll take off on an adventure one of these days.' She gave Phoebe a sly, sideways look. 'Where did you say your brother was living?'

'Queensland.'

'Maybe I'll go and look him up.'

'He's spoken for, I'm afraid.' Phoebe was strangely relieved by this fact. She couldn't decide whether the idea of her brother dating Midnight was the most exciting or the most terrifying prospect she could imagine. It would certainly make life interesting – for Phoebe and for Josh.

'If he looks as much like you as you say then he's probably not my type anyway. I like my men a bit more… manly. If you know what I mean.'

Phoebe's phone buzzed in her pocket. She lifted it out to check.

'Jack?' Midnight raised her eyebrows.

'I have another voicemail from him.'

'What's he say?'

Phoebe dialled the number to retrieve the message and held the phone to her ear. It wasn't the first missed call from him that day or, indeed, since the argument of the previous night, but she hadn't been in the right frame of mind to listen to any of them. Somehow, she felt stronger after a morning at work; just like her dad had said, distance from the problem and a chat to Midnight had helped everything fall into place. She knew now what she needed to do, and she'd even been able to see so far ahead that she knew what she would do if that didn't pan out the way she hoped. Strangely, that prospect didn't seem all that scary now either. As Midnight had also pointed out, Phoebe owed it to Jack to save him from his cave if she could. After all, he probably didn't even realise he was in there. But if he still refused, she had other priorities to worry about and she would simply have to get on with them.

The message began to play:

'Phoebe… Please, pick up … Phoebe?' There was a loud sigh, a heartbeat's pause, and then: 'I know I was a dick last night; I know I upset you. Archie's really sorry too. You were scared for us and I realise now how insensitive to that I was. But I was wrapped up in my own problems and… Phoebe? Oh… what's the point? You'd be right if you never called me again but don't do that. At least until you've given me a chance to try to explain and change your mind. So… call me, yeah?'

The line went dead. Phoebe stowed her phone back in her pocket.

'Well?' Midnight asked.

'He wants to talk. He says he knows he's been a dickhead.'

'At least he's got something right.'

Phoebe smiled. 'He does sound really sorry.'

'See, you're forgiving him already.'

'I am?'

'Yep. And you can't wait to see him.'

'I can't?'

'As we all know, a minute away from Mr Stalker is like a year to you.'

'I'm not that bad.'

Midnight fired an impish grin at her. 'You know what I said about calling him now? Scrap it. If he's as sorry as you say then you should totally make him sweat for the rest of the day. At least until teatime if you're too pathetic to manage the whole day.'

'Oh my God! You're so mean! Now I know why you're single: you're too evil to date real actual people!' As Midnight laughed, Phoebe pulled her phone out again. 'I should probably call him back...'

This time, Phoebe was the one talking to an answering service. 'Hi, Jack... Ok, this is weird. We should probably talk at some point actually to each other rather than to a tape recorder. I'll call you again when I get my afternoon break.'

'That was even weaker willed than I had bargained for,' Midnight said as Phoebe ended the call.

'Sorry. I guess I really am that pathetic.'

Midnight shook her head in mock solemnity. 'And to think, I let people see you in my company.'

As they wandered through the entrance doors of Hendry's, Phoebe feeling lighter and happier than she had done in what felt like years, Steve was ready to pounce.

'Midnight…' he always said her name as if the very sound of it offended him. It probably did; as Midnight had often asserted, something like an unusual name for Steve was like the sun being kicked out of orbit for anyone else. 'You're late coming back from your break.'

Midnight gave her watch a nonchalant inspection. 'Not according to my watch.'

'Well, you are according to mine.'

'*Well…* as I left by the time on my watch I should come back by the time on mine too. In fact, this watch says I have two minutes left which I fully intend to enjoy before resuming my duties. So… if you'll excuse me…' Midnight folded her arms and gave him a wide smile, as if she intended to pass the next two minutes exactly where she stood and love every second of it. He snorted like an enraged bull then, unable to respond to Midnight, he jabbed a finger at Phoebe. 'Mr Hendry is looking for you.'

'Mr Hendry?'

'The young one…' Steve flapped his hand as if to dismiss her. He began to mutter about people who were in nappies when he started out as store manager meddling where they weren't wanted and stalked off in the direction of Gareth Parker, who suddenly looked like a startled rabbit despite the fact that he was doing nothing wrong, unless you counted actually doing his job as something wrong.

Phoebe shot a helpless glance at Midnight.

'You'd better go and see what he wants,' Midnight said.

'Bloody hell...' Phoebe grimaced. 'It'll be another ruse to get me alone. I don't know how much longer I can keep putting him off without being downright rude. He knows I have a boyfriend and it still doesn't stop him.'

'A little thing like a boyfriend won't bother him. For men like him it's all about winning and if there's an obstacle like another man in the way it makes the sport that bit more exciting.'

'I don't think I like being sport.'

'Everything is sport to him. You should be loving it. Girls in here would kill for five minutes on the roof with him.'

'It's flattering and everything... I have to admit he's attractive too... But he's just making life so damned difficult all the time. All I want is to come to work, do my job, and go home without having to worry about all this extra crazy stuff. God knows I have enough things outside work to worry about. Is that too much to ask?'

'You know what would put him off?' Midnight added.

'The baby?'

'Exactly.'

Phoebe stared across the shop floor at where Steve was running his finger along the top of Gareth's till and gesticulating about something it was obvious only he could understand as Gareth stared at him blankly. Phoebe assumed he was complaining about cleanliness, but as it wasn't Gareth's job to clean the tills it seemed a bit unnecessary. Perhaps Steve was having a mini-breakdown, just one of the weekly occurrences Phoebe now missed as she worked upstairs. 'I suppose it's going to have to come out sooner or later,' she said thoughtfully, her eyes still trained on Steve. 'I only kept it to myself because Jack said…'

'But, it's not up to Jack, is it? This is your life and your call. If you want to tell people then you go for it.'

'You know what?' Phoebe turned to her and smiled. 'I actually really do want to tell people.'

'Then do it.'

Phoebe pulled Midnight's wrist towards her and looked at her watch. 'Half an hour until the next story session. I don't know if that's enough time to make the announcement.'

'What are you going to do, organise a marching band? Stop making excuses. Go up there and tell Dixon. That's all you'll need to do; it'll spread like wildfire after that anyway.'

'I suppose you're right.'

'Of course I am.'

They were interrupted by a shamefaced and rather shell-shocked Gareth. 'Um… Steve says –'

'I know what Steve says,' Midnight snapped. 'I'm coming.'

'Hey...' Gareth backed away.

'No need to shoot the messenger,' Phoebe cut in, cocking an eyebrow at Midnight.

'I'll do more than shoot him if he doesn't piss off,' Midnight returned as they watched him scuttle back to his till.

'I think he's rather hoping you will,' Phoebe said with a mischievous smile.

'Gareth? I don't think so. You know that amazing guy I said I wouldn't find in Millrise? He's exhibit A. If you ever needed more evidence than that I don't know where you'd find it.'

'He's not that bad.'

'He's not that good either and I'm not desperate. Not yet, anyway. Now, vamoose!'

'Ok, ok... I'm going. God, you're so bossy.' Phoebe headed for the stairs. 'Wish me luck!' she called.

'You're going to need it,' Midnight muttered as she smiled and waved.

Phoebe ran so fast up the stairs that she almost didn't see Adam on the blind corner until it was too late. He was partly the reason she was running that fast in the first place, hoping to make it to the relative safety of her and Dixon's office before she bumped into him anywhere he could make more of his increasingly obvious advances. Far from curbing his behaviour, since the rumours about their kiss on the rooftop had emerged, he didn't seem to care too much for discretion at all. So, while she was expecting to have to do her customary ducking and diving on the stairs as she tried to negotiate a way out of the situation, she didn't expect what actually followed.

'Oh, I'm so sorry...' she mumbled, hand on her chest. 'I was rushing... back from lunch... you know how it is, something to talk to Dixon about...'

'Right.' Adam dug his hands in his pockets. 'I'm glad I bumped into you, actually. Not this literally, of course.'

'Really?' Phoebe glanced past him, but her escape route was well and truly blocked by his frame. Perhaps deliberately. Not that it mattered, of course, even if there was enough space to squeeze through she didn't suppose for a minute she'd get away with it. 'Is it anything important, only I have a story session in about twenty minutes or so and –'

'Doesn't Melissa Brassington do those?'

'Yes, but –'

'And perhaps one of the other shop floor staff would step in and look after the café and till?' he added, pre-empting her fallback excuse. The fact was that she had already arranged for all those things to be done. She only liked to be on hand, watching from the sidelines, just in case she was needed. It had been that way from the start and it was hard to let go of the habit. Adam had obviously noticed the usual pattern.

'It's just that I like to be there. Something might need sorting or go wrong.'

'It's commendable that you do. Can you spare five minutes, though?'

'Um... I suppose I could.' Phoebe didn't really see that she had a choice.

'Good. We'll use my dad's office.'

'Won't it be locked?' Phoebe asked. Old Mr Hendry had a grand office along the corridor from HR but it was seldom used these days and was always locked. Adam seemed to prefer working from various other offices and bases around the store, presumably to keep a closer eye on his empire, everyone supposed, but Phoebe often thought that if she was forced to spend her time in a room like old Mr Hendry's she'd probably choose to work from other places as often as she could too. She'd only ever been in there once, and recalled that the overwhelming smell of damp in there was even stronger than in the office she shared with Dixon. That, and the fact that there were a lot of faded portraits too.

As soon as she had asked the question, she knew how stupid it was. Adam shook the offending article in front of her. 'It won't take a minute.'

Phoebe wondered vaguely what the *it* he was referring to was. And if it was only going to take a minute, then she didn't rate it much. However, unable to come up with a convincing excuse to escape, Phoebe had no choice but to follow him up the stairs, past the sanctuary of Dixon waiting behind a closed door, and along to the empty office in question. He rattled the key in the lock and it swung open on squeaking hinges to release the fusty smell of old wood and damp carpets.

'After you,' Adam said as he reached for the light switch. Phoebe stepped in, and then the door was closed. She noted that the blinds were down but Adam didn't attempt to open them, preferring to keep the daylight and the outside world from their meeting. It didn't really seem like a good sign, but Phoebe couldn't quite grasp why. She tried to comfort herself with the idea that he wasn't bothering to open them because he wasn't planning to use the room for long. He turned to her, digging his hands in his pockets again.

'First off, I'd like to thank you for the hard work and loyalty you've shown to the store over the past few months.'

Odd, Phoebe thought as she wondered how to reply. No *please sit down*, no preamble – in fact, no real need to thank her when you considered that her loyalty and hard work amounted to half a year with the company that others had spent half their lives faithfully serving. Was he going to bring them all up here one by one, make them stand in a dark office and thank them?

'Thank you,' was the best she could do. She hovered uncertainly by the door. Was that it? Could she go now?

'The new revenues from your story sessions and themed events aren't enough to pull us completely out of the danger zone yet, and I suspect we may have many more tricky years ahead of us,' he continued, 'but I'm confident that you've helped us make strides in the right direction.'

'Good,' Phoebe replied. 'It's what Mr Hendry hired me to do so I'm glad that my work is helping.' She glanced around the room so that she wouldn't have to look at him. It looked dusty, even though she knew that the other person who had a key was the cleaner, who came up here every night to give it the once-over. These sorts of rooms always looked dusty, though. Perhaps it was the bad rap they got from old horror films and period dramas. Not that any of that was important now, of course. Just what was going on here? Usually, at this point in a room alone with him, Adam would have been breathing down her neck in an attempt to get close. But now he was standing feet away from her, hands in pockets, wittering about the business with a look like a lost puppy. This wasn't Adam Hendry, at least, not the one she knew. Or, perhaps this was more like the real one than any version she'd met before. Either way, she felt almost sorry for him in this state. She also rather liked this Adam, who seemed fallible and uncertain, and, well... human.

'And how is everything with you?' he asked. Phoebe couldn't help a slight disbelieving raise of her eyebrows. 'I mean,' he continued, 'it's just that... I hope you don't mind me saying but you haven't seemed always completely content over the last few weeks. It's nothing to do with your job here, is it?'

'God, no! I love my job! I had a few personal issues, but it's all fine now.'

'That's good.' Another uncertain hesitation. 'I'm your boss but I like to think I can be a friend too. And so I want you to know that you can talk to me anytime you like about anything that's troubling you.'

'Oh… thanks,' Phoebe said. She wondered when the hidden camera crew was going to leap out and start patting her on the back while she cried tears of relief mingled with embarrassed laughter and repeatedly called them all bastards. Because this situation couldn't be real.

'When you say your personal life…' His hands came out from his pocket, brushed through his hair, and then shot back where they had come from. 'You're still ok with…'

'My boyfriend?' Phoebe finished for him. She had guessed that this was where the conversation was leading. In one way or another, any interaction with Adam ended up at this point. But it had never gone quite this way before. Why the sudden uncertainty? It was a new and difficult to believe revelation, but perhaps Adam genuinely liked her rather than seeing her as another conquest. Something had changed, or at least, it felt that way. Phoebe almost preferred the old Adam, the predatory letch; it was easier to say no to him, especially back in the days when she was more certain of Jack. This Adam was really rather sweet. If he'd been like this from the start, who knew where things might have ended up?

Phoebe took a deep breath. 'There's something I need to tell you –'

'Come for a drink with me…' Adam blurted out before she'd had a chance to finish.

'What?'

'You know, a drink.'

'But I'm –'

'Seeing someone, I know. But you could give it a try, couldn't you, a night out with me? If you have fun then we could… well, you could…'

'Dump him for you?'

'All's fair in love and war, right?' He gave her a guilty smile that held glimpses of the Adam she knew of old, a faint look of superiority that assumed she wouldn't be able to resist. It was absolutely all she needed to resist.

'That's true. But it wouldn't change the fact that I'm carrying Jack's baby.'

Adam stared at her. It wasn't the way she had wanted to break the news to him of her pregnancy – not to anyone, in fact – but what else could she do? Midnight was right; it was the only way to put him off once and for all. If it didn't, then he needed therapy.

'Oh…' he replied stiffly. 'Congratulations.'

'Thank you.' Phoebe inched towards the door. 'Sorry…'

He gave her a tight, forced smile.

'Maybe, though…' she added, 'it would have been fun to go out…' *Get out, Clements! What the hell are you doing; you're making it worse!* The moment was awkward as hell and she found herself filling the chasm of silence with platitudes that she knew were idiotic to say the least. But he had been so uncharacteristically sweet that she simply wanted to make him feel better about it all. 'I probably would have said yes…' she continued, ignoring the Jiminy Cricket voice in her head telling her to stop, 'had things been different…'

'Of course you would.'

'I'll go then….'

'Phoebe!' he called as she turned to leave the office. 'I hope you're going straight to HR to make the necessary arrangements. I'm quite certain that the health and safety rules change when you become pregnant. You're not supposed to keep information like this from the company.' In that moment, the Adam of old had returned, the familiar arrogance in his voice.

'I will. I've only just found out,' Phoebe lied.

'Good. Then I'll see you tomorrow.'

'You're finished for the day?'

'Meetings this afternoon… very important meetings off site. One more thing…'

'Yes?'

'I can rely on your…'

'Discretion? Yes, of course.' He nodded his thanks and Phoebe let herself out.

She went straight to the bathroom, too stunned to go and see anyone else just yet. She needed to collect her thoughts and she wanted to keep her promise to Adam that she wouldn't tell anyone about what had just happened, not even Midnight. Especially not Midnight, now that she came to think of it. She had a feeling that her face would betray a certain drama if she talked to anyone before she'd had time to pull herself together. She turned over the events as she splashed water on her face. It had been lovely to see that Adam was a real human being after all, but horrible all in the same breath to have to dash his hopes. Phoebe had always assumed that his interest in her was purely about sexual power, that she was just another potential notch for his bedpost. Now she wondered whether his feelings had indeed been more genuine, while being Adam Hendry, he'd simply had no way of expressing them other than playing the letch. If that was the case, the fact that she'd had to refuse him in such a blunt way upset her more than she could fully comprehend. She had never wanted to hurt anyone in life, not even a man like him. Now, right at the back of her mind, was a new foreboding that she may well have sealed her doom at Hendry's by humiliating the future CEO, no matter how unintentional it had been. Only time would tell and she would have to deal with it as it happened.

But at least there was no way she could keep her pregnancy secret now. And she really didn't want to anymore.

❧ ❧ ❧

For a short while her problems with Jack were pushed out of her mind as colleagues around the store congratulated her. Once she began telling everyone about her pregnancy, she wondered how she had thought the idea so scary before. One or two offered dated but well meaning advice, while Tania Simpson, proud mother of five children, told her horror stories about childbirth and childrearing. No horror story could compete with the one she already knew, of course – Rebecca's story – but she tried to put this out of her mind and enjoy the good wishes that everyone was sending her way. Dixon had been the hardest to tell, because Phoebe felt keenly how much he had come to rely on her and just how much he'd miss her help when the time came to go on maternity leave. He'd never say it, of course, but he didn't need to. They'd grown very fond of each other in a short time, and Phoebe would miss not seeing him every day at work. She'd already decided that she would return to work (not that a decision ever really had to be made there) but she'd still have to be away for six months at least. She told Dixon that she'd stay in touch and that she still wanted to contribute in an unofficial capacity, even if she couldn't be at work. He told her that they'd tick over just fine in her absence and he'd hear nothing of the sort. Her baby needed her more than Hendry's, he said. She knew that his sentiment was heartfelt and honest, but underneath it all he was feeling just a little lost.

She'd been so wrapped up in the various conversations around the store that there had only been time for a brief check on the first story session of the afternoon. By now it was two-thirty and she still hadn't had the opportunity to phone Jack either. It was all very well shouting about motherhood, but perhaps she ought to sort out the father too. And someone else occupied her thoughts now that things had calmed down a little as well. She kept telling herself that Adam wasn't and never would be her type, but she couldn't stop thinking about him. If only things had been different; who knew what might have been? If only he hadn't been so damned vulnerable and normal during their last meeting, perhaps she wouldn't be feeling this strange, wistful sort of guilt now.

Still, she had work to do and all that would have to wait. She forced thoughts of both men from her mind and tried to concentrate on the pile of paperwork currently heaped on her desk.

'It certainly explains a lot,' Dixon said. It was actually the fourth time he had said this since Phoebe had broken the news to him. 'I had wondered why you looked so washed out all the time but I didn't like to ask. And those funny turns you kept having when I brought in certain food for lunch.'

Phoebe silently wondered who wouldn't have a funny turn when faced with the stench of mackerel and red onion sandwiches right under their nose. She simply smiled.

'I'm so sorry I couldn't tell you sooner, but I had to be sure, you know.'

'Yes… quite. It's very sensible to make certain before you announce anything. And I'm grateful that so many of your projects are pretty much self-sustaining, you've set them up so well. It shouldn't be too difficult to keep them up and running when you go off to have the baby.'

'I hope so.' Phoebe chewed on the end of her pen as she turned her attention back to a fancy dress catalogue. She flicked a page and began circling some prices.

'Can I get you anything?' Dixon asked.

Phoebe looked up. She didn't need anything now and she hadn't needed anything the previous three times he had asked. She hoped this wasn't going to be a recurring theme for the rest of her working time or she might start to find it irritating, no matter how well-intentioned.

'I'm fine, honestly. There's really no need to worry about me.'

'But if there was anything you need you'd tell me? I feel terrible about all those times you must have needed a window open, or felt faint, and I didn't do anything about it.'

'You couldn't have known if I didn't tell you,' Phoebe smiled. 'How is that your fault?'

'I know... but you can tell me now. You will, won't you? I don't want you suffering in silence.'

'I will. Thank you.'

'And you will tell me about any little twinges, won't you?'

'Twinges?'

'You won't ignore any warning signs?'

'Warning signs of what?'

'The baby coming!' Dixon's expression was almost comical in his exasperation.

'Labour?' Phoebe blinked. 'Dixon, I've got six months to go. It's highly unlikely I'll go into labour here in the office. I don't think you need to worry about it.'

'I'm just saying, for later on. Just so you know. And if you happen to be at home when it starts and you can't find Jack, you just call me and I'll be straight over.'

'Thank you.' Phoebe replied. While she was touched by the gesture she was a little bemused. Surely he knew how many other people she could call on before she had to resort to him. She liked Dixon, but as a birthing partner... maybe not. She wasn't sure that he fully understood what he was offering either. Perhaps now wasn't the time to explain it. She gave her brightest, most grateful smile before she bent back to her work again. Since she had spent such a long time this afternoon filling in forms for her maternity leave and inevitably chatting about it at the same time, she was really behind with her workload. Another story session was due in half an hour and she had a stack of market research to get through before she went down to oversee it.

Dixon's voice spoiled her concentration again. 'How are you getting home tonight?'

'The same way I always do – the bus. Why do you ask?'

'No reason. I just wondered if you ought to be travelling on public transport in your condition.'

Phoebe resisted the impulse to laugh. In her condition? She was pregnant, not an unexploded bomb. 'I'm sure it will be ok. Lots of pregnant women use the bus.'

'Yes, but all that pushing and shoving, the bus shaking, all those potholes in the road... won't they do damage? Isn't it better to avoid it if you can? I could take you home.'

'That's kind of you but I'm fine.'

Dixon paused. He looked mortally wounded by her refusal of his offer. He really was taking this baby business a lot more seriously than Phoebe had expected him to. 'It was just a thought,' he said finally. 'That's all. What does Jack think of you taking his baby on the bus?'

Jack. Phoebe still hadn't called him. Despite the conversation with Midnight at lunch, the positive message from him on her phone and the optimism she'd felt then that they could fix things, she still didn't really know for sure. With all the other drama since then, the moment had somehow come and gone. She would have to face him sooner or later but for all her bravado earlier, her courage had failed her again. What would Jack think of Dixon's worries? Would be even care? Midnight's assertion that he avoided the baby issue out of fear made sense, but was it really at the root of the problem?

'We haven't properly talked about it.'

'Well,' Dixon said, wearing a frown, 'I can't understand why he wouldn't have thought of it. You should let me run you home.'

'Dixon… you can't run me home every night for the next six months or however long I have left here.' Lovely Dixon was driving her mad and she didn't want to be rude but she did wish he'd shut up now.

'I wouldn't mind at all,' Dixon insisted cheerfully.

Phoebe's smile contained every grain of the patience she had left. 'I'd better get downstairs. The last story session of the day is about to start.'

'You'll have a seat, won't you?' Dixon asked. 'You won't be standing up all the way through?'

'I've been standing up for all the others and nothing has gone wrong.'

Dixon looked as though he was reaching for an argument, but then he seemed to give up. 'Don't overdo it. If you feel tired come straight back up here.'

Phoebe stood to leave. 'I'll see you later.' Sooner, rather than later, she suspected, as she fully expected him to come and check on her over the next hour or so. It was going to be a long six months.

As Phoebe made her way down to the shop floor, she met Adam on the stairs again. Her bloody timing, as always, was perfect. She gave him an awkward smile, but his expression was now stony, rather like the one his father always wore. Perhaps something similar had happened in old Mr Hendry's youth to make him look so sour all the time. Perhaps this was how Adam would always look from now on. Either way, he seemed neither pleased nor embarrassed to see her, only coldly neutral.

'Sorry,' Phoebe stammered as she passed. She didn't even know what she was apologising for. He gave a curt nod and continued on his way.

So much for her ally in the Hendry family. She had the feeling her proposals would be rather harder to get past old man Hendry from now on. It was just another thing she was going to have to try to move past in a life that was becoming more and more complicated. And there was no way she was giving this job up, not now, no matter how tough Adam made things. All the same, she hoped he wouldn't cause too many problems.

✤   ✤   ✤

Melissa Brassington was depositing sock puppets of various animals on each of twenty floor cushions when Phoebe found her.

'How's it going?'

'Good,' Melissa replied with a nervous smile. She always looked nervous around Phoebe, which was weird. It was hard to imagine that Phoebe could make anyone feel that way and although she was older than Melissa and more senior in the company, most days she didn't feel that different from the very young and inexperienced store assistant. 'By the way,' Melissa added, 'a lady was in asking for you.'

'Oh. I wasn't expecting anyone. Did she say who she was?'

Melissa's huge green eyes were wide as she shook her head. She was pretty, delicate looking, and Phoebe suspected this was part of her appeal to the young audiences, who must have felt she was on their level in a very instinctive way. She looked barely older then them herself.

'Did she say what she wanted?' Phoebe asked.

Melissa shook her head again. 'I told her she could ask one of the till staff to page you but she said she would come back when you were available.'

'Ok. What did she look like?'

'Nice. Well dressed.'

'Anything else?'

'Sort of old.'

Phoebe frowned.

'I didn't really notice that much,' Melissa excused.

Phoebe got the impression Melissa had noticed more than she was letting on but for some reason she was keeping the knowledge to herself. Was she afraid that whoever had come looking for Phoebe wasn't welcome and she'd find herself in the middle of it all? Had the woman not been very nice, perhaps a little intimidating? There was no reason to think these things, but there was no other explanation that Phoebe could think of either. It also appeared that the mystery woman was being cagey about how much information she shared. Most people would tell Melissa who they were or simply leave a message. She pulled her phone from her trouser pocket. Her mum would have called ahead to warn her she was coming but there was no voicemail. Based on all this, Phoebe was beginning to form a strong suspicion about the identity of this woman, but she hoped she was wrong. If she was right, then the conversation they might have wasn't one she wanted to have at work. She tried not to dwell on it.

'Did the kids like Chicken Licken?'

'They loved it. Quite a lot went away and bought puppets too.'

'That's brilliant. You were ok with Valerie helping?'

'Yes. She's great.'

'I must remember to thank her.'

Melissa looked past Phoebe towards the first parents who had started to trickle in with their children. Phoebe followed her gaze.

'They're keen.'

'We had to turn them away from the last one,' Melissa said, her nerves evident again. 'They must have waited around for this session.'

Phoebe felt proud that people were willing to wait around for two hours to get into one of her sessions. It had happened on the odd occasion before, but it seemed to happen more often now as word got round the playgroups and nurseries of the town.

'I'll offer the parents a free drink, just to keep them sweet,' she said.

'That's what I told them. If they came back, I mean.' Melissa blushed. 'I hope you don't mind me doing that but I thought you would offer them anyway if you'd been down here.'

'Not at all. That was well handled.' Phoebe gave her an encouraging smile.

With her news out in the open, Phoebe felt that she could now plan ahead for her maternity leave without worry or guilt. She had already earmarked Melissa as someone she could trust to look after the storytelling sessions. Now, she just needed to find people for each little project that she had up and running. Midnight was an obvious choice, of course, but it would take more people than just her. Another thing to think about on her ever-growing list.

❧   ❧   ❧

With the story session in full swing, the specially-constructed space was alive with a cacophony of squealed animal noises and raucous giggling from the children gathered around Melissa as proud parents looked on. Phoebe felt a little like a proud parent herself as she watched Melissa perform. She was constantly surprised by how the shy girl changed when given a storybook and a rapt audience and it was a lovely thing to see.

'The sky is falling in! Melissa cried before giving the cue for more animal noises from around the room.

But the involuntary grin that stretched Phoebe's face faded as her phone buzzed in her pocket. She rushed from her spot leaning against a post to a quieter corner to take the call.

'Jack...' she said, the squeals and laughter from the story room, although muted, still making it difficult to hear him. 'I was going to call you.'

'I'm sorry,' he said into her tiny pause.

'No... I'm sorry, I just –'

'Phoebe, my mum is coming to see you.'

She held in a groan, her suspicions confirmed. 'Here? At work?'

'I told her about the baby. I had to, Archie would have done anyway.'

'I know. I don't care about that. I've told people at work now anyway. Was she angry?'

'With me, yes, for not telling her sooner. What she has in store for you I've no idea.'

Phoebe couldn't help a smile. He'd called, not only to apologise, but to warn her, as if they were naughty kids in trouble together. It made them feel somehow solid again. 'Does this heads-up mean we're speaking?'

There was a pause from the other end. 'I suppose it does,' he said finally and Phoebe could hear the smile in his voice.

'Then I can deal with whatever your mum throws at me.'

'That's good, because she's on the warpath big style. You should have heard the roasting she gave Archie.'

'I'm glad I didn't. I'd have felt sorry for him and that would never do.'

Jack laughed, and Phoebe felt that peculiar kick of excitement deep in her gut that only the sound of his laughter could bring. She was suddenly desperate to see him, but she had to bottle it up and take a breath. She had a long day to get through first and if the second half was going to be anything like the first she was going to be emotionally exhausted by the time it was over.

'Archie's packing, by the way,' he added.

'He has a place to go?'

'Yes. It's called home. Mum decided she needed to keep an eye on him. In all honesty, he seemed only too happy to let her. He acted like the tough guy last night but I think when he realised this morning how bad it had actually been, he was scared shitless.'

'Do you think those guys will come back? To finish what they started?'

'No, I don't think they will. They were as pathetic as Archie when it came down to it – just more kids playing at tough guys. I'm only glad that things didn't get out of hand. Playing or not, someone could have been seriously injured. Or worse.'

'I'm trying not to think about that,' Phoebe replied, the memory of that cold dread creeping over her again. She shook herself. Perhaps Jack was right, perhaps they wouldn't dare come back again now that they knew Jack could handle himself. And he'd been to the police too and they must have realised he'd do that. Jack certainly sounded confident enough. 'I'm almost sad Archie's leaving, though. I'd just decided he was ok after all.'

'Oh, he'll still bug us every five minutes. He seems to have this weird idea that you and he are best buddies now.'

'He's ok,' Phoebe said, thinking back to how Archie had tried to act as a go-between for her and Jack the night before. It had been a rather inept performance, but she realised now that Jack hadn't asked him to do it and he'd behaved out of genuine concern. He had meant well and, ultimately, he wasn't as much of a pain as he'd have people believe. 'Oh…' Phoebe was snapped from her musings as a familiar figure headed in her direction. 'Jack… I'll have to call you back.'

'What's wrong?'

'Your mum.' Phoebe never got to hear his reply. Carol drew level and stared her down as if they were enacting a scene from High Noon. Phoebe put her phone away and waited silently for the onslaught. The woman had never been pleased to see Phoebe, but right now she looked as though someone had shoved a wasp in her mouth and glued it shut.

'Phoebe…' Carol began.

'Carol. What brings you here?' It was a very stupid question, under the circumstances. What Phoebe didn't know was how much detail Jack had gone into about their row the previous night.

'Jack tells me you're pregnant.'

Phoebe nodded.

'How far along?'

'Ten weeks.'

'What do you intend to do about it?'

Phoebe was thrown, momentarily, by the question. 'As I understand it, the traditional aim of a pregnancy is to give birth.'

Carol didn't flinch. She didn't acknowledge Phoebe's sarcasm at all.

'I want to know if you intend to marry Jack.'

The smug smile, such as it was (smug was not really in Phoebe's repertoire even when she tried) was wiped from her face. 'Marry Jack?' she spluttered. 'I've only just got my head around being pregnant! Anyway, why is it important? He wasn't married to Rebecca.'

'Not for the want of trying. Rebecca was a headstrong girl, very modern values. Her refusal seemed a bit silly to me.'

Phoebe stared at Carol. Was she hearing this right? Marrying Jack would make Phoebe an official part of the family, and there'd be no getting rid of her then. Carol hated Phoebe; surely she couldn't want this? Was her sense of propriety so strong, so out-of-date that she would put all other feelings for Phoebe aside to see this happen? If it was true then it was ridiculous. 'I think it's for me and Jack to decide, don't you?'

'That's my grandchild you're carrying. I think I get a say.'

Phoebe could have pointed out that Carol clearly hadn't been able to influence Rebecca. She could also have added that she didn't see why Rebecca should have been afforded that luxury whilst Phoebe was not. But she held her tongue. To drag Rebecca into it would be a cheap shot. Phoebe wasn't going to sink that low. She was, however, going to make her feelings clear, once and for all.

'With respect, your involvement in the life of my baby will be on my terms, grandmother or not.'

It was Carol's turn to stare and Phoebe was filled with a tiny sense of triumph. She had finally stood up for herself; she'd been assertive and hadn't had to resort to the shameful passive-aggressive backbiting that had been the main feature of their relationship so far. Was Phoebe Clements finally growing up? She could see by Carol's face that she'd scored a point. Ok, maybe scoring points was still a bit childish, but she supposed she couldn't grow up all at once.

Carol drew herself up to her full height. 'Since I don't have a lot of choice in the fact that you are the baby's mother, I want to offer my support. I can only hope that in time you will do the right thing by the baby and my son.'

'You want to offer support?'

'Of course. It's what families do.'

Some families also tricked and poisoned each other; Phoebe had watched enough *Dallas* re-runs in her time to know that. But she tried not to let her distrust of Carol's motives get the better of her. 'It's very kind of you. I'm sure we'll be glad of it once the baby comes.'

'So, there'll be no more of this nonsense between you and Jack?'

Phoebe held back her reply, trying to glean any clue she could from Carol's tight-lipped expression about how much Jack had revealed of their row and the state of their relationship. Carol would have made a fantastic poker player, however, because Phoebe wasn't getting a thing. 'We plan to talk about it,' she said finally.

'Jack and I have done a little of that ourselves.'

'Oh?'

'Quite simply, I don't think you realise how traumatic this is for him.'

'He said that to you?'

'He doesn't need to. I'm his mother, I know it. He's terrified that he's going to lose you the way he lost Rebecca. Why do you think he was on his own for so long after she died?'

'But that's silly. We've already been over all that,' Phoebe said, hearing echoes of her earlier conversation with Midnight.

'Not to him it isn't. Do you have any idea how a death like that can affect someone?'

'Yes,' Phoebe shot back. Carol knew about Vik and her accusation wasn't fair.

'Then you must be able to understand his feelings.'

'Of course I do. But he knows that the chances of the same thing happening to me are tiny.'

'They still exist, no matter how tiny. Jack will find it difficult to get past that.'

'But we discussed it –'

'Discuss it all you like. That fear won't go until the baby arrives and all is well.'

Phoebe folded her arms. 'So no matter how moody he is or how he shrugs me off I have to put up with it?'

'Don't be stupid, I didn't say that. But you have to understand it. Denial of the baby is the only way he can keep from worrying himself sick. He has Maria to think of too and he has to keep his anxieties at bay for her sake.'

Phoebe nodded slowly. She couldn't argue with that. With all that had gone on, it was easy to forget poor Maria and how things would be affecting her. Phoebe vowed to make it up to her somehow. 'Archie is back home with you now?'

'Yes.'

'What's going to happen? About his problems, I mean.'

'I don't think you need to concern yourself with that.'

'I do if he ends up back with us. That situation wasn't exactly helping Jack's stress levels either.' Phoebe held Carol in a steady gaze. She waited for the backlash but none came.

'He won't end up back with you. He'll be staying at home with us where he belongs.'

'Right...' Phoebe waited for some elaboration from Carol but she didn't get any.

'So I can rely on you to do the right thing? You'll go and straighten out this mess with Jack?'

Phoebe could have explained that trying to straighten things out was what she'd been doing all along if only everyone else had let her. But she didn't think it was wise to jeopardise what seemed to be the makings of a fragile truce between her and her future mother-in-law.

'We're going to talk it through later.'

'You've spoken to him?'

'We're not completely useless, you know. We can actually sort some things out for ourselves.'

Carol gave a tight smile, the first one Phoebe could ever recall being aimed at her. They were hardly bosom buddies, but it was a start. She was beginning to wonder whether someone was handing out personality transplants today. First there'd been humble Adam and now an apologetic and almost friendly Carol. What was next? Steve handing out sweets and hugs and calling everyone darling?

'I only want what's best for Jack and Maria,' Carol said.

'And you weren't sure if I was it?'

'No. And I'm still not. But as they both seem very fond of you and you are now carrying my second grandchild, it seems we must make the best of things.'

'It does.'

Silence fell between them. Was that it? Was Phoebe's interrogation over now? 'I'm sorry,' Phoebe began, 'but I have –'

'Work to do. I understand.' Carol glanced at her watch. 'I have an appointment to get to as well.'

Phoebe half wondered whether she was expected to offer a hug or a kiss on the cheek. But then, to her relief, Carol turned and strode away. Perhaps the hugs and kisses would come, Phoebe mused, but she wasn't in any hurry for them either.

A pair of hands suddenly slammed down on Phoebe's shoulders. She spun around to find Midnight grinning at her.

'Where the hell did you come from?' Phoebe squeaked. 'You gave me a heart attack!'

'Was that Maggie Thatcher's evil twin?' Midnight nodded her head in the direction of Carol's retreating figure.

'Yeah. Lucky me, eh?'

'What did she want?'

'To make friends, I think.'

'Won't her face need extensive re-plastering if you make her smile too often? She needs to watch out for that if she's going to go around making friends with people.'

Phoebe laughed. 'I'll tell you one thing; it's been a very weird day. I'm starting to believe anything is possible.'

❧ ❧ ❧

Thankfully, the rest of the afternoon was rather less eventful than the earlier part had been and Phoebe was able to go about her duties with a broad smile on her face. The news of her pregnancy was still filtering down to all the staff, and she even got a stiff word of congratulations from Steve, which was surprising to say the least, followed by the offer of a quick nip of whisky from Janitor Jeff who insisted that it would make the baby sleep when he or she arrived. Jeff had never quite been coherent enough for Phoebe to ascertain how many children he had or, indeed, whether he had any at all, but if he did she sincerely hoped he hadn't offered that sort of advice to their mother, and that she wasn't daft enough to take it. All in all, however, it had been a long time since Phoebe had enjoyed an afternoon at work quite that much.

And she had Jack to look forward to afterwards. She had run through the possible conversations in her head all afternoon, and while she was uncertain how it would go, she knew one thing for sure – she wasn't going to let it turn into another argument. Every moment with him was precious and she didn't want to fill a single one with harsh words ever again.

As the sounds of slamming shutters, burglar alarms being set and goodnights filled the high street of Millrise town centre, Phoebe stepped out into the warm evening, a sense of excitement building. She didn't need to go far before the cause of it came running towards her with a bouquet and a sheepish grin. Jack thrust the flowers towards her. 'I thought I was going to miss you coming out.' Phoebe took them and held them to her nose, a familiar warmth spreading through her. 'I know they don't even come close to the apology I owe you, but will they make a start?' he said.

She looked up at him with a watery smile. How could she have even contemplated giving him up? 'I think they're more than a start.' But then her smile faded. 'You're not here because your mum told you to come, are you?'

'No,' he laughed. 'I know I'm a mummy's boy but I'm not that bad. Although, if she had have done I would have been too scared to refuse.'

'Me too,' Phoebe smiled, 'and she's not even my mum.'

He rubbed a hand around the back of his neck and gave her an awkward smile. It was so endearing that Phoebe could barely stop herself from dragging him into the nearest bus shelter and kissing his face off. 'Did she give you a hard time today?' he asked.

'Not as hard as she gave you, by the sounds of things.'

'Probably.' He dug his hands in his pockets. 'We're ok, right?'

'More than ok. But we do need to talk.'

'I know. I've got the car parked on the spare ground near Uncle Fred's shop. Want me to take you home? We can talk on the way.'

'Your home or mine?'

'Ours… if you'll have me.'

'You're asking me…'

'To move in. Don't say anything just yet. But think about it. I promise not to rush or hassle you if you promise to give it some proper consideration.'

Phoebe smiled. 'I will.'

⚜ ⚜ ⚜

After a couple of detours Phoebe hastily changed at her place, and then Jack whisked her off to a little bistro in a nearby village complete with a pianist and portions of food so tiny that it must have cost him a small fortune. Ordinarily, she would have scolded him and told him that he needed to spend his money on more practical things. But she knew that he needed this more than she did; it was a way of making good and easing his guilt, so she simply took the evening in the spirit it was intended. The journey to the restaurant had been full of stuttered beginnings, heavy pauses, clumsy explanations, sentences that didn't go anywhere. At times it still didn't feel as if they were getting to the root of anything but the fact that they were talking at all felt like progress.

Afterwards, they headed back to Jack's house, and as he opened the front door to let Phoebe in, she expected to see Maria race down the hall to greet her. But then she remembered the time; Maria would be in bed. Still, the house was unusually dark and silent; there was clearly nobody there.

'I thought you said May was looking after Maria?' Phoebe said.

Jack gave another sheepish grin, one of many aimed at Phoebe that evening. 'She is. I never said they were here, though. They're at May's house.'

'Oh… so it's just us?'

'Yeah.' Jack kicked the door closed behind him and grabbed the flowers from her arms, dropping them onto the hall table. 'Is that alright?' He pulled her close. 'I thought it would be better for talking.'

'This isn't talking where I come from,' she murmured as his lips brushed hers.

'This is the warm up.'

A lazy smile stretched her lips as his hands ran down her body. It felt like years since they had been this intimate.

'We're supposed to be sorting things out,' Phoebe insisted, trying, but failing, to chastise him.

'We are. I'm sorting out the need to see you naked in my bed.'

'You're impossible,' Phoebe grinned as he began to lead her to the stairs. 'I'm still starving after that meal and you said you'd cook supper for me.'

'Don't worry. I have sausage for you.'

Phoebe let out a shriek of laughter. 'That's the corniest thing I've ever heard!'

'Hey… I'm trying to be seductive here.'

'I HAVE SAUSAGE FOR YOU!' Phoebe snorted. 'You're hopeless!'

'Hopelessly in love.' He halted on the stairs, took her hands in his and held her in a smouldering gaze. 'I love you.'

'I love you too.'

'Let's never forget that again.'

'No, let's not.' Phoebe leaned in to kiss him. 'Now... about that sausage you promised...'

✤ ✤ ✤

Phoebe rested against the bonnet of Jack's car and wiped a film of sweat from her forehead. The sultry heat of an August afternoon wasn't helping her fatigue. As she watched Jack and Archie carry boxes from the hired van into the house, she wondered how such a small flat like hers could have contained so much stuff and how many hours, exactly, it was until bedtime. She had been told by her midwife that the second trimester of her pregnancy (her midwife loved to use big words for everything) would be the best, that she'd be full of energy and blooming. Right now, she felt distinctly wilted. The decision to move in with Jack had come hard on the heels of Archie leaving them to go home, but with notice to give on her flat and other sundry setbacks, it had taken almost two months to finally get to this day. Phoebe was beginning to wish she'd stayed put and waited for a nice cold, winter's day to do all this running to and fro.

'Oh yeah, that's right,' Archie shouted over as he spotted her, 'you just take it easy and we'll move all your stuff.'

Phoebe grinned. She liked Archie a lot more since he wasn't living with Jack and he seemed to like her a lot more too. 'I'm supposed to take it easy. I'm pregnant, in case you'd forgotten.'

'I'm beginning to think it's all a ruse to get people running around for you. Seriously, I can't even see a bump.'

'Trust me, there's a bump.' Phoebe ran a hand over the gentle curve of her belly.

'I don't know where you've been looking, Arch…' Jack called over as he made his way to the van to pick up another load, 'you can see it a mile off.'

'Oh, thanks,' Phoebe pouted. 'You know how to make a woman feel good about herself.'

Jack threw her an impish smile and a blown kiss. He almost bumped into May as he lugged a box of old CDs up the garden path.

'Oops!' he called cheerfully. 'Nearly had you then.'

May smiled. 'We've made cold lemonade if anyone wants some.'

'Is lemonade code for beer?' Archie asked. May showed him her best schoolmistress frown. 'Oh, actual lemonade then,' Archie laughed.

Maria appeared at the front door, her legs almost buckling under the weight of a huge ice-and-lemon-filled pitcher.

'Whoa!' Phoebe hopped from the car and raced with surprising speed up the pathway to the front door. May turned around and took the jug from Maria.

'Close one, eh?' she smiled at Phoebe.

'Sorry…' Phoebe blushed. 'I see you've got it under control here.'

'You need to learn to relax,' May said. 'When your baby comes there'll be more trouble for him or her to get into than jugs of lemonade. Besides,' she tapped the side, 'it's plastic, so a sticky floor was the worst we'd have got if Maria had dropped it.'

'I wasn't going to drop it,' Maria piped up.

'I didn't think you were,' Phoebe replied. 'I was being silly.'

'I was bringing you a drink,' Maria added. 'The baby is thirsty.'

'The mummy certainly is,' Phoebe said. 'It's actually a good job Granny May was here to take this or I might have drunk all the lemonade straight from the jug and then what would everyone else have had?'

'Milkshake,' Maria returned in a serious tone.

Phoebe looked at May. 'No need to worry then. You'd better hand over that juice!'

Jack came out to the step again, empty handed this time. 'That looks good,' he said.

'I'll get some glasses and we can take a break.' May took the jug back inside, Maria chattering away as she followed.

Jack turned to Phoebe. 'If I'd known how much stuff you were going to bring I wouldn't have begged quite so hard for you to move in.'

'Thanks...' Phoebe raised her eyebrows and he laughed. 'Anyway, I've been trying to help all morning. It's not my fault you won't let me carry anything heavier than a Sugar Puff.'

'I can hardly ask you to lug boxes around, can I?'

'I'm not that big yet. I am still able to walk around and look at my own feet and everything. It wouldn't have hurt me to carry some of the smaller boxes.'

'Even so…' Jack pulled her into a brief kiss. 'I just want to keep you safe and you promised you'd let me… remember?'

'I am safe. I'll be even safer tonight when I'm ensconced in your safe home. In fact, I'll be so safe that The Queen will hear about it and pop round with the crown jewels for me to keep an eye on, as they'll be much safer here with me than in the Tower of London.'

'You know you're beautiful when you're being sarcastic? It does funny things to me.'

'Really? Then I shall drive you mad with desire from now on.'

Archie made his way up the drive. 'I'm going to hurl if you two don't stop being so loved up in public. There are laws against that sort of thing.'

'You're just jealous.'

'Of you, bro? Phoebe's easy enough on the eye, granted, but she must have a screw loose if she's moving in with you.'

'Oi! You're not too big for a cuff round the ear!' Jack laughed.

'You've got to catch me first, old man.'

Phoebe watched the banter with a broad smile. It was nice to see them getting along – at least, better than before. While Archie was far from cured, he had at last agreed to seek help for his gambling habit, reluctantly forced to see sense that any hobby that got him beaten up was probably out of hand. There was still tension, and sometimes there were still heated exchanges but, for the most part, things were a lot better. It certainly helped that Carol and Edward had taken back some responsibility for him too, leaving Jack free to worry about Phoebe and Maria, which was quite enough for anyone.

May returned with a tray. She plonked it down on the front lawn and everyone dropped to the grass around it, not worrying about stains or cat poo or anything else that might ruin a good pair of jeans. Spirits were high and everyone's mood was too good to care.

'It's so good of you to come over and help.' Phoebe took a glass from May. Some might say it was a strange situation to be in, but Phoebe was getting used to having Jack's dead girlfriend's mum around the place. She was easy to get along with, kind, patient, tolerant and seemed really keen to be involved in Jack and Maria's lives, to the extent that she had welcomed Phoebe warmly from the first moment they'd met. This was probably the last reaction Phoebe could have predicted had someone asked her beforehand, and more like the one she felt she should have got from Jack's own mother.

'I had nothing else to do,' May said with a shrug. Phoebe knew that probably wasn't true and May was just making light of the gesture.

'You're a superstar,' Jack agreed. 'And this lemonade is amazing.'

'I helped!' Maria squeaked.

'You practically made it all yourself,' May said, winking at Maria.

Phoebe glanced at Jack, but he wasn't following the conversation now. Instead, he was frowning at Archie, who was looking at his watch.

'What's with that, Arch?' he asked.

Archie looked up. 'What?'

'Checking your watch every five minutes. You need to be somewhere?'

'I'm just keeping an eye on the time.'

'What for?'

'I might go out tonight.'

'So… you're not waiting for anything to finish? A game result or –'

'Jack…' Phoebe cut in. 'Leave it.' She forced a carefree smile for Archie. 'I bet he has a date he doesn't want to tell us about.'

Archie took a long swig of his drink, content to let Phoebe's explanation stand. Phoebe heaved a silent sigh. If they needed to discuss this then they could do it later when May was gone and Maria in bed. *So much for getting on better.* Getting on better didn't always mean getting on.

'We'd better crack on or we'll still be moving this stuff when the baby comes,' Phoebe announced, pushing herself to her knees before standing.

Archie drained his glass and jumped up too. 'Good idea.' He ruffled Maria's hair. 'Thanks for the drink, gorgeous.'

As they walked to the van, Phoebe glanced back to see that Jack was helping May collect the empty glasses. She looked around again to see Archie swing himself up into the back of the van.

'Does it matter what I bring in next?' he asked.

'Not really...' she pointed to a box. 'But that one's heavy so I'd wait until Jack's finished before you try to pick it up.'

'No worries...' He lowered his voice and leaned closer. 'Thanks, Phoebe.'

She smiled. There was no need to ask what he was thanking her for; she was just happy to know that it was not only Archie and Jack who had finally learned to understand one another.

❧ ❧ ❧

'I should be doing this for you, not the other way around.' Phoebe let out a contented sigh as she lay stretched across the sofa, Jack massaging her bare feet.

'If you touch my feet right now your hands would burn off. I'm not the one carrying an extra person around, anyway.'

'But you have carried most of my belongings around all day today. That's got to be worth my gratitude.'

Jack grinned across at her. 'I'll think of a suitable repayment that you can give to me later.'

'I don't think so. Later is reserved for bath and bed. I'm shattered.'

'Tomorrow, then?'

'Tomorrow when I wake up and it's the first morning in my new home, you mean?'

'That's the one.'

'Maybe I can stretch to a little reward then…'

They were quiet for a while, watching some programme on the TV about internet scamming. At least, Jack was watching, but Phoebe was so tired she was only staring at the screen. It didn't matter, because she was content to lie there in Jack's company, easier now than ever before.

'Oooh,' she pushed herself up, hand to her belly.

'The baby?' Jack asked, concern darkening his features. 'Is everything ok?'

'I think it's just wriggling, that's all.'

'Can I feel?'

'I don't know if it's strong enough yet… here…' Phoebe took his hand and pressed it to her bump. He was still for a while, but then he took it away with a disappointed frown.

'I didn't feel anything.'

'See, the little bugger is running rings around you already,' Phoebe grinned. 'I don't think you'll be able to feel until it's bigger.'

'All this stuff I'd forgotten. It feels like another lifetime now, Rebecca expecting Maria, like a dream that I can't quite remember.'

'Are you happy now, though?' Phoebe asked. 'Do you think you made the right decision?'

'Asking you to move in?'

'Having me at all?'

'God! Phoebe!' Jack pulled her into his arms. 'How can you ask me that? Of course I made the right decision! I'm lucky you had me back, not the other way around!'

'I was just… well, sometimes I wonder. You can't blame me if I have a little wobble every now and again.'

'Of course not.' He held her at arms' length and gazed at her. 'Would it help to stop the wobbles if I asked you to marry me?'

'Jack… don't be daft –'

He rolled off the sofa and got onto one knee. 'I don't have a ring – I wasn't expecting to do this tonight – but will you marry me?'

'I've only just moved in –'

'Say yes. Please say yes.'

How could she say no? But equally, how could she shake the conviction that she just wasn't ready for marriage yet – that neither of them was? They hadn't even been together a year. The moving in had been quick, but this… it was too soon, wasn't it? Marry in haste, repent at leisure, wasn't that what people always said? But then she looked into those blue eyes – love, desperation, anxiety, hope in every amethyst fleck, and she knew she couldn't refuse him.

'Yes.'

Jack pulled her into an embrace that was fierce with all the love and protection his proposal had promised her for the future. But she pushed him gently away.

'What?' he asked.

'Not straight away,' she said.

'Ok. I can do that. When?'

'I don't know, exactly. But after the baby is born.'

'If you're worried about organising it, I can do that. Or if you're panicking about looking fat you needn't, you'll look beautiful.'

'It's none of those things. I just think we should wait. What's the rush?'

'I can't wait. I want to be married to you. What about a Christmas wedding?'

'Christmas! I'll be almost ready to pop by then!'

'No you won't, you'll still have four weeks. It's the perfect way to get rid of all our bad Christmas memories and it gives us around four months to arrange it – give or take a week.'

'That's not much time at all. How do you know I don't want a huge meringue of a dress and a castle in Scotland?'

'Do you? Because if you want those things I'm sure I can –'

'No, Jack, I don't. I'm happy with a quiet affair but that's not the point. The point is that you're rushing it for no good reason. I love you, I've said yes – be happy with that and let's enjoy the idea for a while. We'll have the baby, let things settle down and then we'll do it.'

'That's really what you want?'

'Yes.'

He looked disappointed, but he kissed her and nodded. 'You have to let me buy you an engagement ring, though.'

'Naturally,' Phoebe smiled.

'First thing tomorrow.'

'Tomorrow? But it's Sunday and we have a million things to do here.'

'I don't care about that.'

'Nowhere decent will be open. You can't get a ring at Sainsbury's.'

'We'll find somewhere.'

'I don't need a ring straightaway. In fact, I can wait for months, I really don't mind.'

Jack shook his head. 'No way. We're getting one this week and that's that. I could take you to the jewellery quarter in Birmingham. In fact, I bet loads of the dealers there will be open tomorrow...'

'Jack...' she began, but he got to his feet and grabbed their empty glasses from the mantelshelf.

'You want some more juice? Not exactly champagne but I can make a nice juice cocktail for you.'

Phoebe gave him a weak smile and watched him stride from the room, a bundle of nervous energy. She'd heard of Bridezilla, but Groomzilla? It didn't bear thinking about.

❧ ❧ ❧

Jack's proposal should have been the most glorious moment, but it continued to trouble Phoebe for some days afterwards. Since they'd got back together and he'd laid his fears about the baby bare, he had gone from disinterested to almost obsessed with Phoebe's welfare at all times. At first she had thought it sweet that he couldn't do enough for her, but now she was beginning to wish she could just have her normal Jack back.

The morning after he had asked her to marry him, Phoebe had been forced to feign illness just to stop him from bundling her and Maria into the car and driving them to Birmingham to choose a ring there and then. While the romance of that was exciting, and the thought of marriage equally so, she couldn't suppress the practical feelings that they had more pressing concerns to worry about first – namely the arrival of their baby. She supposed that she had to be glad he hadn't taken offence at her refusal to get married right away – some men would – and that for now, at least, he had agreed to be content with her promise to let him buy her a ring some time after she had finished work for her maternity break.

Maria, of course, had been bouncing up and down at the news that her dad was going to marry Phoebe and was already planning a bridesmaid dress that would make Cinderella's look like a dishrag. Phoebe did feel a bit guilty that she was forcing Maria to wait for the big day – after all, asking a five-year-old to wait six months is like asking them to wait ten lifetimes. But then Phoebe reminded her that in that time her birthday would arrive, closely followed by Christmas and then her new brother or sister. It seemed to do the trick, and Maria's disappointment, whilst still palpable, was not quite so keen.

Monday came around and Phoebe met Midnight during their lunch break, taking their seats on the walls of the ornamental gardens in the centre of town.

'So, he wants to get married?' Midnight offered Phoebe a jelly bean.

'Yep.'

'And you want to get married?'

'Well… yes. Eventually.'

'What's the problem?'

Phoebe popped the sweet into her mouth. 'It's his rushing that's the problem.'

'You want a big, million pound wedding?'

'God, no! I couldn't stand all the stress.'

'You want a big fat wedding frock?'

'I'll be fat enough without one of those after the baby.'

'So it doesn't really matter if you get married before or after the baby.'

'It does.'

'Why?'

Phoebe paused. Midnight's response was so typically Midnight that she was beginning to wonder why she'd expected anything else. Why did it matter? How could she make Midnight understand why it mattered when she couldn't even articulate it in her own mind? 'It just does.'

'Not good enough.'

'It's too soon.'

'Why?'

'We haven't even been together a year yet.'

'You've moved in and you're having a baby together. I think the question of premature commitment is a moot point, don't you?'

'I… um… don't know.'

'I think you do know. I think you know I'm right.'

Phoebe let out a sigh.

'Besides,' Midnight added, 'I want to shop for wedding dresses. I fancy trying a few on.'

'You're not getting married.'

'Yeah, but the shops don't know that, do they? It'll be a laugh.'

'You can go and try wedding dresses on any old time, you don't need me for that.'

'Yes I do. I'm going to pretend we're marrying each other and really freak them out when we ask for a dress each.'

'I'm pregnant!'

'I know. That'll really confuse them! I can't wait!'

Phoebe shook her head wonderingly as Midnight leapt from the wall. How lovely it must be to inhabit Planet Midnight. What she wouldn't give to live just one day there, where everything was a game designed especially for her and nothing ever had real consequences.

But as they walked slowly back to work, Phoebe had to admit that, put so simply, Midnight's argument actually made a lot of sense. Why, exactly, was she panicking at the thought of marrying Jack sooner rather than later? Common sense dictated they wait, but she was just about sick of being ruled by common sense, and it never got her anywhere anyway. Maybe Jack understood it better than even he realised. While he was better, every now and again Phoebe caught him watching her, a faraway look in his eyes, and she knew he was thinking about Rebecca. Not about how he loved and missed her, although Phoebe was sure he did those things too in private moments, but about how he might lose Phoebe in the same way, about how he could have saved Rebecca if he'd been wiser and stronger, about how he needed to be ready to save Phoebe. Maybe, by marrying Phoebe, he would feel ready.

Or maybe he thought life was simply too short to wait.

⚜   ⚜   ⚜

Maria was clasping a bedraggled bunch of dandelions in her hand. As Phoebe left Hendry's at the end of the day, she ran forward to hand them to her.

'Wow! For me?' Phoebe gave Jack a knowing grin as she took them.

'We got them down there…' Maria pointed to a grassy verge bordering the car park at the top of the high street. 'There are lots of them there. Do you like them?'

'I do. They're very… yellow. And a bit squishy too. But yellow and squishy is good.'

'Daddy said we didn't have time to get more. But we can get some now if you like.'

'You know what?' Phoebe waggled the bunch at her. 'This is just the perfect amount. I really don't think we need any more.'

'How are you feeling?' Jack asked. Before Phoebe could reply he frowned slightly and peered closer. 'You look tired.'

'Thanks for pointing that out. Time for some new make-up, eh?'

Jack gave her a sheepish grin. 'Did I say tired? I meant beautiful. Beautiful and only a little bit tired.'

'I'm glad we got that straightened out,' Phoebe replied with a wry smile.

They began to walk in the direction of the car park. 'What brings you here anyway?' Phoebe asked. 'I did say I was ok to get the bus home.'

'Aw, you know, we just thought we'd come and get you anyway. It gives us an excuse for a run around, get some fresh air.'

'On Millrise high street? Good luck with finding your fresh air here.'

'We looked at rings!' Maria bounced up and down as if she had just answered a tricky question in class.

Phoebe glanced at Jack, who immediately blushed. It would have been adorable if she hadn't been mildly annoyed by the reasons behind it.

'We only looked,' he said, 'just to see what sort of money I'd need.'

'The lady showed Daddy a reeeeaaaally sparkly one and he said that one was perfect and he wanted the lady to put it away for him so no one else could have it and the lady said she needed some money and Daddy got his card out and she said that will do nicely and they both laughed and then the lady put the ring in a box and took it in the back of the shop and I don't know where it is now...' Maria said all this, apparently without the need to breathe at any point. Jack grimaced as he listened to his plans come flooding out, and then he looked at Phoebe with a hopeful kind of plea for forgiveness in his face.

'You're not angry, are you?' he asked.

'Hmm, and why would I be angry, I wonder?'

'Because I said I'd wait and I didn't?'

'Wow, you're sharp. Nothing gets past you, does it?'

He gave her the second incredibly sheepish grin of the afternoon. 'Nothing gets past this one, either, apparently...' he ruffled Maria's hair, who gazed up at him with a serene expression, clearly oblivious to the problems she'd caused him.

'At least someone is keeping me in the loop.' Phoebe grabbed his hand and smiled at him. All he wanted to do was show her his love. After all they had been through to get to this point, how could she be angry about that? 'So, you've bought it.'

'I've half bought it. Does that count?'

'It's close enough. Please don't stretch yourself, though. There's no rush and so many other expenses coming soon.'

'Always the voice of reason.' He gave Phoebe's hand an affectionate squeeze. 'It's a good job I have you to sort me out.'

'Well, I have to bring something to the partnership. As I can't cook, won't clean and make a terrible racket when I sing, the voice of reason is the only thing I have left.'

'Daddy says you can't sing,' Maria cut in.

'Oh, he does?' Phoebe threw Jack a questioning glance.

'Maria…' he began in a tone that was tinged with a mix of humour and warning, but it was too late; she was already in full swing.

'He was laughing with Archie when you were in the shower one day. He said the ceiling was cracking and Archie said his eardrums were cracking.'

'Oh, he did, did he?' Phoebe tried to look stern but it was no use. 'Just wait until I see Archie; I'll crack his eardrums for him.'

'But I thought you already did that,' Maria said.

Phoebe laughed. 'Some more, then.'

'I'm sorry about the ring,' Jack said as the laughter died down. 'I probably should have waited for you to come and choose with me. I just got carried away. I mean, it's so perfect and so you that I didn't want it to get sold to anyone else and I'm sure you'll like it –'

'Jack… I don't care what it looks like. If you've chosen it then I'm sure it's gorgeous. My only worry is the money, but as you seem determined…' She stopped walking. 'What we talked about, you know, dates for the wedding… I've been thinking. You're right, there's no point in waiting. If you want to do it this year then lets do it.'

Jack beamed at her. 'You mean that?'

'God help me but yes, I do.'

'That's the best news!' Jack pulled her into his arms and kissed her. 'I'm going to make you so happy, just you watch!'

'You already have,' she smiled.

Jack bent down to pick up Maria. 'You hear that, spud? You won't have to wait for that bridesmaid dress after all.'

'Can I get it tomorrow?' Maria asked, legs swinging as if she was subconsciously running to the nearest shop already.

'Maybe the day after,' Phoebe laughed. She looked at Jack. 'Low key,' she warned, although she couldn't keep a serious face. 'Don't go crazy with the costs and please not loads of guests. I hate all that formal stuff and I hate being the centre of attention.'

'Whatever you want you can have.'

'Not *too* soon, either. We need some time to get a bit organised.' They began to walk again.

'No problem,' Jack said. 'When do you think is good?'

Phoebe arched an eyebrow as she threw him a sideways glance. 'I have absolutely no idea. I've never arranged a wedding and I don't have a clue how long things take to organise. I only know that we can't just pitch up at the church tomorrow morning and get hitched. At least, not if we don't live in Las Vegas.'

Jack grinned. 'We could do Vegas.'

'A vicar dressed as Elvis? Maybe not.'

'Mum will help. She's going to be thrilled when we tell her.'

'No mums,' Phoebe said. 'Not a single bit of mum involvement until the day.'

'Really? I don't think she'll like that.'

'I know. And neither will mine but their complaining will be a breeze to handle compared to their involvement.' And then it hit her. 'Oh God! Our parents will have to meet!'

'Oh…'

'That's going to be… interesting.'

'You could say that. On second thoughts, how about we just run off to Gretna Green and tell everyone after we've done it?'

'Where's that?' Maria asked. Phoebe had almost forgotten she was still listening. She hoped she wouldn't repeat any of this to either set of parents, as she seemed to be developing quite a talent for that sort of thing these days.

'It's in Scotland,' she replied. 'But we're not going to go there, Daddy's just joking. We'll just have to be very firm with everyone and tell them that we'd like our big day to be exactly our way.'

'Will I still be bridesmaid your way?'

'Of course.'

'And I can choose the dress?'

'You can totally choose the dress.'

'How about yours?'

'You want to choose mine?'

'Yes. I'll pick a nice one.'

'Um... I'm sure you would. But maybe I should choose my dress. You can come with me and help – give me thumbs up or thumbs down when I try some on.'

'I can do that. Is your mummy coming?'

'I expect she'll want to,' Phoebe said, realising that her no mum rule wasn't likely to last very long when it came down to it.

'I like her.'

Phoebe smiled. 'She likes you too.'

As they passed Applejack's, a portly man, hardly taller than Phoebe, was pulling the window shutters down with the aid of a long hook.

'Uncle Fred!' Jack hailed. 'How are you?'

'Run ragged by the staff that are supposed to do this sort of thing for me,' he huffed. 'Five-thirty comes and they just bugger off, whether the shop's ready for closing or not.'

'Linda's still misbehaving?'

'Even worse now Bonnie's gone and we've got this new girl in her place. I ought to sack the whole bloody lot of them.'

'You'd miss them really if you did.'

Fred snorted a reply. At least, it could have been a reply but it was hard to tell. He ran his eyes over Phoebe before giving her a curt nod, which she took to mean hello.

'Uncle Fred!' Maria yelled before anyone could stop her. 'Daddy and Phoebe are getting married!'

Jack gave an awkward laugh. 'We don't have to put an ad in the paper with you around, do we spud?'

Fred sniffed. 'Congratulations, lad. What's your mother said about it?'

'She…um… doesn't exactly know yet. We've only just settled it this afternoon.'

'Well, I think you'd better tell her.' His slightly unnerving stare rested on Phoebe as he spoke. 'News in this town has a habit of getting around whether you like it or not and I doubt she'd want to hear it from other lips than yours first.'

Phoebe reddened. He was obviously referring to Bat-Gate and his part in relaying the gossip he'd picked up via his employee. It didn't seem to occur to him that he was at fault for this in any way, though; he just held her in a stern gaze. If it was designed to make her feel uncomfortable then it was doing a great job.

'We're going to phone and tell her as soon as we get home,' Jack said. 'In fact…' he glanced at Phoebe for approval, 'I suppose we could go straight there now.'

Oh glee! While Phoebe had come to a certain understanding with Carol, she still couldn't say she liked her, and she was sure the feeling was mutual. The last place she wanted to be right now was in that woman's company. She gave a noncommittal shrug. 'We could, I suppose.'

'Great! She'll be so pleased to see us with this news.'

Phoebe doubted that. But she didn't doubt that the next thing Carol would do was start to meddle in their plans. If she did and Jack took his mother's side, there might be a divorce before there'd even been a marriage.

'We need to tell my parents too, don't forget.'

Jack's face fell. 'Oh, am I supposed to ask your dad's permission or something before we can go ahead?'

'Maybe if this was 1915. As it isn't, I think we're ok. But we do need to tell them as soon as we can. I'd hate them to think they were second best.'

'Of course... But we can't do both at the same time.'

There was a deep chuckle from Fred, who had been following the conversation while they'd almost forgotten he was there. As Phoebe looked around in surprise, she wondered if that was the first time she'd seen genuine humour of any kind displayed on his features. 'Good luck, lad.' With that, he let himself back into the shop and locked the door behind him, still laughing as he did so.

Phoebe put on a bright smile for Jack. 'Let's go and see your parents first – I don't mind, honestly.' She wanted to add, *let's get the harpy over and done with*, but she managed to stop that bit coming out.

✤   ✤   ✤

While Edward had given Phoebe an affectionate hug and kiss on the cheek, the best Carol could do was a stiff display of teeth that Phoebe presumed was meant to be a smile. What on earth had attracted Jack's dad to her was a mystery that the greatest minds would never solve. Whatever it was, she kept that particular virtue well hidden from anyone else. But at least they seemed pleased, and although they'd offered their opinions on dates and venues, they hadn't tried to take over. Not yet, anyway, but there was time enough for that. They had discussed the virtues of an autumn or a winter wedding, versus simply waiting until the baby had arrived, and whilst Phoebe thought it was none of their business what date she and Jack chose, she was content to let them. It seemed to make Jack happy and she figured they would have time alone later to thrash it out properly.

Far later than they had planned to leave, Jack bundled a now sleeping Maria into the car. He gazed fondly at her. 'We're so going to pay for keeping her up past her bedtime when she has to get ready for school tomorrow.'

'It's a special occasion, though,' Phoebe said. 'Although you're right. You might struggle with me too; I'm shattered.'

'Lightweight,' Jack grinned.

'It's your fault.'

'We had to come, though, especially with Fred knowing. Mum would have been really upset if she'd been the last to know.'

'I know.' Phoebe eased herself into the passenger seat.

'I still think December would be good,' Jack said as he climbed in beside her.

'As good as anything, I suppose.'

'It's just that I like the idea. It seems fitting, in many ways. I mean, we've both had terrible Decembers full of tragedy, but we've also had great things happen too. We met in December, for a start. There seems to be a certain significance around that month. Why not make it stick with our wedding anniversary too?'

'So, you want our wedding, Maria's birthday and Christmas all in the same month?'

'Why not?'

'Then you'll have another birthday in January, as long as this little tyke behaves and comes out on time...' Phoebe stroked her belly, 'you know how to pack a schedule, don't you?'

'We may as well get it all out of the way at once,' Jack laughed.

'Ok...' Phoebe gave him a wry smile. 'I must need my head examining but it looks like December wins after all. I just hope we don't live to regret it.'

❧ ❧ ❧

Dixon nudged the office door open. He placed a mug of sweet smelling fruit tea down on Phoebe's desk, and then took one to his own. Phoebe picked hers up and held it under her nose.

'Blackberry and vanilla, if I'm not mistaken,' she smiled. 'Thank you.'

'No problem. I've got the same. I haven't tried that flavour before but it smells nice.'

Dixon had taken to buying boxes of herbal and fruit teas instead of their normal caffeine-fuelled supplies as soon as Phoebe had explained she couldn't stand the smell of tea and coffee during her morning sickness phase. But when she had told him that she felt better and could probably drink it again, he warned her that caffeine was no good for the baby and insisted they both continue with the alternative brews until after the birth. So the flavours had changed every week, and the tasting sessions had become a cute little ritual for them to share. Phoebe rather looked forward to being surprised by what he had bought for them whenever he went out for more. Quite why Dixon needed to carry on drinking them was a mystery, however, but Phoebe was beginning to wonder whether he might start with sympathetic Braxton Hicks at some point too.

'I've just seen Sue Bunce on the stairs,' Dixon added. 'She says she's still waiting for a date.'

'She wants to go out with me? That's lovely but I'm already engaged.'

'Very funny. You know what I mean.'

'I gave her a ballpark weeks ago.'

'She needs more than that. Phoebe, I'm not sure whether you've noticed but it's October and you don't have that long left.'

'I can work for ages yet, right up until the birth if I want to.'

'You can but you know my feelings on that. We still need a date from you anyway and there's no point in putting it off. Will I have to tie you to a forklift from the stockroom and drive you off the premises myself when the time comes?'

'Don't be silly...' Phoebe sighed. 'You're right, as usual. I'll go and see her later.'

'Are you still worried you won't have a job to come back to?'

'No.'

Dixon raised his eyebrows.

'Ok, yes. A little. It doesn't help that Adam hates me now. I get the impression he'd rather I didn't come back.'

Dixon sipped at his drink. 'It is a funny business, that. He went from everyone's best friend to the incredible sulk overnight. It makes you wonder whether his father ended up having a word with him about appropriate employer/staff boundaries, that sort of thing. If it's any consolation, I don't think it's only you he's stopped talking to.'

True to her word, Phoebe had never told another soul about what had transpired between her and Adam in old Mr Hendry's office the day he had gambled on a yes from her. But Dixon was right – not only had Adam stopped hounding Phoebe, he'd also removed himself from any social interaction with the staff as a whole and it had been the source of much gossip; at least, until everyone had got bored and moved onto the next scandal.... So for about two weeks really. That change of heart couldn't be down to Phoebe alone, could it? She hated to think so and had thought many times about trying to get Adam to talk to her about what had changed but, in the end, she'd been too scared to. Perhaps it was best to let things run their own course now.

The office door was flung open and Midnight strode in with a carrier bag. These days she was almost as much at home in that room as Phoebe, as she spent so much time there preparing to help Dixon after Phoebe had left. Steve had been horrified when it had been agreed over his head, and Midnight had asserted that although he was always complaining about her, his distress meant that really he had a secret crush and would be bereft without her on his tills every day. Whatever his reasons, he had kicked up quite a stink about losing Midnight from his staff but his complaints had fallen on deaf ears. Pretty soon after, Midnight had already begun to assimilate herself into the dynamic of Dixon's team. Phoebe wondered sometimes whether Dixon was going to survive the assault.

'Your weekly delivery has arrived.' Midnight dropped the bag onto Phoebe's desk and took a seat at the opposite side.

Phoebe peered inside. She groaned as she confirmed what she already knew she would find in there. 'Oh God, not more fruit.'

'I bet you preferred it when Jack's family hated you, eh?' Midnight grinned.

'How can he possibly expect one woman to eat this much in a week? I'm eating for two, not the Welsh rugby team.'

'It's nice that he wants to give it to you. Shows he cares... in his own weird fruity way.'

Phoebe pushed the bag towards her. 'You take it then.'

'No way! I didn't get this figure from eating greens. I like my strawberries processed in a vat of sugar and E numbers before they pass my lips.'

'It was worth a try,' Phoebe said, pulling the bag back towards her. 'Jack's just going to have to tell him.' She turned to Dixon. 'I don't suppose you want any of this?'

'I've already done my weekly shop, I'm afraid. It looks as though you're going to have to eat it. Anyway, all those vitamins are good for the baby.'

'That's what Fred says. I suppose Jack can make some pies or something.' Phoebe stowed the bag underneath her desk.

'You can totally bring those back in when they're done,' Midnight said airily.

'I think it's kind of him to send you all that free stuff every week,' Dixon said mildly. 'Show's he thinks a lot of you.'

'He must *love* you,' Midnight added, 'because everyone says he's a tightwad. It must be killing him to give stock away.'

'I'd rather he cracked me a smile every now and again,' Phoebe said. 'He sends me fruit but when I go in to thank him – and I have to go in every time – he looks at me like I've drooled on his shoes.'

'He can't help his demeanour,' Dixon replied. 'Some people just aren't gifted with natural charm.'

'You can say that again.'

Dixon turned to Midnight. 'You might want to step up your hours in here – Phoebe is going to set a leaving date today.'

Phoebe opened her mouth to argue but Dixon's smug expression closed it again. She knew when she was beaten. 'I'm going to see Sue Bunce to sort it out.'

'Brilliant!' Midnight said. 'So I get your desk?'

'Yes, but don't wreck it.'

'As if!'

'And try not to break Dixon either.' Phoebe shot him a smug grin to match the one he'd sent her and he looked up with an argument of his own hanging from his lips.

'Roger that,' Midnight said. 'Anything else is fair game though? I can't wait to start on Steve. There's going to be some serious revenge around here.'

'Try to behave,' Phoebe said.

'I don't know any other way.' Midnight's manic grin completely contradicted the statement she had just made.

Phoebe swallowed her misgivings and prayed she'd still have a job to come back to once her friend had been let loose.

❧   ❧   ❧

There was a definite feeling of *déjà vu* as Phoebe stood and stared at Jeff in his Santa costume. She was only relieved that she didn't have to dress up as an elf and stand around in the grotto with him this time. 'It looks a bit tired, don't you think?' she asked Dixon who stood alongside her. 'We should probably get a new one this year if we have time.'

'I don't think it's that bad.'

'Really?' Phoebe turned to him. Sort of. She was finding it rather difficult to tear her eyes away from the disturbing bump in Jeff's trousers. For once, she hoped he'd got a whiskey bottle in there.

'We've had that suit for as long as I've been here.'

'That's why it's knackered,' Phoebe said.

'It looks traditional.'

'If traditional is another word for knackered then yes, it does.'

Dixon looked hurt by her reply. It was then that she realised he was one of those people who dragged the same tired Christmas decorations from the loft, year in, year out, just because he always had. They'd be faded, the glitter worn away, the edges of stars snapped off, but he wouldn't notice. All he'd see were fond memories of all the other Christmases he'd spent with them. She supposed it was quite a nice way to be, and maybe, one day, she'd feel the same about decorations she put up with Jack as their children grew. But it wasn't right for a toy store that was supposed to be impressing its primary demo-graphic. Christmas these days was a rather more glitzy, high-tech affair than when Jeff's suit had received its first grotto guest.

'I think we need a new one,' Phoebe insisted, doing her best not to get dogged by sentiment. 'Trust me on this. And the elf costumes need updating too.'

'What!' Midnight, who had been standing at the other side of Phoebe trying not to laugh at Dixon's admonishment, now had to defend herself. 'But I love the old ones!'

'So do I, but they're worn out.'

'They're well loved,' Midnight pouted.

Phoebe shot her a sideways smile. 'I'll let you choose the new ones with me?' she teased.

Midnight grinned. 'OK!' she cried, her argument gone from her brain like a dandelion clock on the wind.

'The grotto will have to be repainted too,' Phoebe continued.

'The closer your maternity leave gets, the bossier you become,' Dixon said, folding his arms. 'God help your child.'

'I'm not being bossy. I just want to leave things in order. It means I have to do as much as I can before I go. We've come so far this year and we've done so much to change the way people in Millrise see us that we can't ruin it all by sticking this old stuff out at the busiest time of year. It'll be like one step forwards and two back... you understand that, don't you?'

Dixon sighed. 'Ok, you win.'

'We'll have to put in the order soon, though. It's the beginning of October now and we'll run out of time for the stuff to arrive if we don't.'

'Remind me again what date you're leaving?' Dixon asked with a wry smile. 'Because I'm not sure how much more of this I can take.'

Phoebe laughed. 'Christmas Eve. So you'll have to put up with me for a while yet.'

'Can't you make it sooner?'

'No, I can't. I'm looking forward to seeing the elves in action and not being the one wearing the costume this year – I wouldn't miss that for the world!'

Jeff raised a hand. 'Um… can I go now?'

'Yes… sorry, Jeff…' Phoebe waved him away.

'What about me?' Midnight asked as Jeff scuttled away to get changed back into his janitor overalls.

'Not yet. I need your awesome brain a while longer.'

'Can you manage without me for an hour?' Dixon asked. 'I have that monthly report to get ready for Adam and it's late as it is.'

'We wouldn't want to keep God waiting, would we?' Midnight said.

'Of course,' Phoebe replied, choosing not to comment on Midnight's jibe. 'Midnight and I are going to look over the Christmas stuff in the storeroom anyway so you'll have the office to yourself for an hour.'

Dixon nodded and made his way to the doors of the stockroom where they had met at Jeff's request. Phoebe had been a little surprised when Jeff had brought up the matter of his suit to Phoebe, but now that she had seen it, she was glad he had. It seemed that he took more pride in being Santa than he let on.

It was reassuring to know. And although he had always seemed like a rather unsavoury character during her day to day dealings with him, she remembered from her stint working in the grotto the previous year that he was never anything less than professional when the children filed in to see him. She had no qualms at all about letting him continue in his role this Christmas, and she quite agreed that he needed a new suit.

'We'd better have a look at this other stuff,' Phoebe said. She and Midnight made their way to a small storage area off the main stockroom. As she flung open the door, the smell of damp assailed her, having such an immediate effect that she wished her asthma inhaler wasn't lying on her desk up on the top floor.

'So,' Midnight began in a tone that was only pretend annoyed, 'you got a dress at the weekend?'

'Yes… I'm sorry about that, Midnight, I really am. But my mum wanted it to be just us and I couldn't very well say no, could I? You understand, don't you?'

'Course I do, you daft cow. My mum would be the same. After she'd regained consciousness from the shock of me wanting to get married, of course.'

Phoebe smiled. 'Your prince is out there, there's no doubt about that.'

'I don't want a prince. I want a hot rock god with a penis the size of a Boeing 747.'

Phoebe erupted into a fit of giggles that quickly gave way to a coughing fit. Once she had composed herself again, she threw her arms around Midnight and gave her a hug.

'Steady on,' Midnight grinned. 'You don't want to get too close, I haven't made up my mind about whether I like girls too, yet, and there's no telling where it might lead.'

'I just love you. And not in that way, before you get any ideas. I'm so glad you're ok with the dress shopping.'

'What did you end up with?'

'Something quite traditional and white. You'll find it terribly boring.'

'Probably.'

'It's got a gorgeous blood red trim, though, to spice things up. I thought, you know, with it being a winter wedding it would be good. And I've got an adorable little hooded cape with a fur trim to go with it and keep me warm.'

'Not real fur I hope.'

'Don't worry, it's fake. And no tiny nylon nymphs were harmed in the making of it.'

'Is the dress huge?'

'No, it's pretty sleek actually. I thought my bump didn't need making any bigger.'

'You're probably right,' Midnight said, not bothering to offer the usual platitudes that she was pregnant, not fat. 'You do realise I had to turn down a lot of awesome New Year parties to come to this wedding?'

'Jack and I really appreciate it. We'll make sure we still sing Auld Lang Syne especially for you when the clock strikes twelve.'

'I'll be too pissed to care by then.'

'I'm so excited now I can hardly wait two more months.'

'Three, really. At least you'll have finished work by then.'

'Yeah, I just hope I can get everything straight here before I go.'

'Don't sweat it, you've got me. So, you're glad you said yes to Mr Stalker after all?'

'I am. I can't believe I ever thought about saying no.'

'I think you had a pretty good excuse at the time.'

'I suppose.'

Midnight dragged a box from a shelf and blew a layer of dust from the top. There was a lot of jangling and tinkling and what sounded suspiciously like breaking glass as she let it drop to the floor. Phoebe tried not to wince as Midnight bent to open it. 'Is the boy wonder still behaving?'

'Archie?'

'Yeah, him.'

'I think so. It all seems to be quiet on that front. Jack says that he's going to his gambler's support group.'

'He's going or he *says* he's going? There is a difference.'

'I think Jack's dad drives him there and waits for him to come out, so I'm pretty sure he's going. How much good it's doing is anyone's guess. He's still a massive pain in the arse at times, especially when he turns up at all hours without letting us know first, but

I'm just grateful he's not asking us if he can move in again.'

Midnight held up a string of bedraggled tinsel and raised her eyebrows. 'I think you may have a point about these decorations.'

'I know, but I do wonder whether we'll be allowed the budget to change them all.'

'Now that Adam's not your best friend anymore?'

Phoebe glanced around and lowered her voice. If he was eavesdropping somewhere out of sight it wouldn't be the first time. 'Exactly.'

'I wouldn't stress about it,' Midnight returned, her voice at its usual indiscreet volume, 'I heard he's dating someone from the *Echo*.'

'He is? How do you hear all this stuff?'

'Stav. Why else do you think I walk there for my dinner every day? It's not for the exercise, I can tell you.'

'Who is she?' Phoebe asked, unable to name the strange emotion that was pulling at her. Was it just the tiniest smack of jealousy?

Midnight shrugged. 'I think she's head of advertising or something. She bumped into him with a coffee and tipped it all over him. I guess he must find that attractive because she came away from the scene of the crime with his phone number. Lucky cow. If I'd know that was all it took I'd have done it months ago.'

Phoebe smiled. 'Good for him. I'm glad he's not dating the daughter of a Lord something-or-other.'

'What does it matter to you?'

'It doesn't. But I think, underneath that posh and scary boss veneer, he might secretly want to be a pleb, just like us.'

'We certainly have more fun,' Midnight agreed as she clamped a faded Santa hat on her head. 'So, you don't regret missing your chance when you had it?'

Phoebe pondered the question. There had been the briefest moment when she had almost imagined that she did fancy Adam Hendry. But it would never have lasted. She had been right to fight for Jack and put Adam firmly out of her mind, she was certain of that now. She had never been more certain of anything.

❧ ❧ ❧

All day Phoebe had wondered how on earth it was that people still needed to buy toys. It was Christmas Eve, and surely if they hadn't already got what they needed it was time to give up. Janitor Jeff had been kept busy in the grotto too, with hopeful last-minute requests from those kids still naïve enough to believe that Santa could manufacture and deliver their gifts in less than twenty-four hours and had realised a glaring omission from their already never-ending list of gift demands. Thank goodness for a Christmas Eve early close, Phoebe thought to herself as she wandered the heaving shop floor. Really, there was very little for her to do today, with most promotions already nearing their end or set up for the New Year, and everyone kept telling her she should have made the most of the option to end work before today, but she had wanted to be there. Now she wondered why – she was exhausted just looking at how busy everything was. By the time four o'clock came, she was positively looking forward to the moment she had been dreading up to then – finishing work for her maternity leave.

As Steve locked the door behind the last customer, Phoebe was already making her own way to the exit, shrugging her coat on.

'Hey, where do you think you're going?' Midnight called across the shop floor as she hurried towards her.

'Home.' Phoebe had said her goodbyes throughout the day as she crossed paths with all the people she knew, and that had been emotional enough. She had decided to avoid further trauma by slipping quietly out while no one was looking. It seemed that Midnight had other ideas.

'No you don't, Clements. You need to come back up to the staffroom and say a proper goodbye to everyone.'

'Midnight… I've said goodbye and no one is going to care that much anyway. It's Christmas Eve and people want to go home too, they don't want some weeping pregnant woman stopping them from getting to their eggnog. Besides, Jack is waiting to pick me up and it's freezing out there. I don't want to keep him longer than I have to.'

'Ten minutes. He won't get hyperthermia. I have something for you so you need to come up with me. We can take the lift if your bump is wearing you out.'

Phoebe sighed. 'Ok, ten minutes.' While it was sweet of Midnight to make a fuss, it wasn't like she wouldn't have another opportunity to see her before the baby was born. In fact, she had a feeling she'd be seeing Midnight a lot.

Phoebe started towards the stairs.

'No, you can't.' Midnight grabbed Phoebe's arm and began to steer her towards the rickety trade lift. It wasn't a contraption that Phoebe was particularly fond of and she usually avoided it for fear it would break down with her inside. Today, that fear was doubled by the knowledge that if it broke down with her inside in her current state there would be a puddle of wee on the floor within half an hour, because that was just about how long she lasted these days before she needed to go.

'Do we have to?' she groaned.

'Humour me, ok?' Midnight almost shoved Phoebe through the doors as they slid open before punching the button for their floor with such force that Phoebe wondered if she might put a hole in the control panel. It seemed safest not to mention it; Midnight actually seemed rather agitated about the whole business, as if taking Phoebe up to the staff-room was a chore.

'You know it's really lovely that you have a gift for me but if it's a hassle you can give it to me after Christmas,' Phoebe said.

'It's no hassle.' Midnight drummed on the control panel with her fingers as she leaned against the wall.

'Maybe I'll text Jack, just to let him know I'll be a few more minutes,' Phoebe said. She rifled in her bag for her phone just as the lift stopped with a jerk.

Phoebe looked up sharply. 'Don't tell me it's broken down…'

'Looks like it,' Midnight said, now seeming far more relaxed despite their current predicament. If Phoebe hadn't known better she'd have thought Midnight was actually pleased the lift had broken down.

'What are we going to do?'

'Don't stress, someone will come and get us in a minute.'

'Have you even pressed the help button?'

'Oh, yeah…' Midnight gave the button a whack and then leaned against the wall again.

'I hope everyone hasn't gone home for Christmas. What if there are no engineers to come and rescue us?' Phoebe could feel her chest tightening. She reached into her bag for her inhaler and took a puff.

'That's not going to happen. Steve has to check the lift before he locks up for the holiday and he's such a jobsworth about everything that there is no way he won't. Someone will come for us.'

'But how long will they take?'

'I don't know. You've got your mobile – phone someone.'

Phoebe lifted up her phone. 'Actually, the signal is crap in here. I don't know whether I'll get through but I'll try.' She dialled a number and put the phone to her ear. 'No reply from Dixon,' she said after a few moments. 'I don't have Steve's number or Jeff's.'

'You'll have to try Jack and see if he can get security to open the doors for him.'

'Right…' Phoebe dialled again. 'No reply from Jack either. Shit, this is not good.'

Midnight shifted position slightly, so that the control panel was behind her. Was that a grin Phoebe could see her trying to hide?

Phoebe narrowed her eyes. 'Are you doing this on purpose?'

'Why would I do that? I know you get baby brain or whatever but even you can't be stupid enough to think I'd trap us in a lift on Christmas Eve deliberately.'

No sooner had she said this than the lift groaned into life. Phoebe frowned at Midnight as it clanked its way to their floor, but Midnight merely shrugged. 'Well, that was lucky, wasn't it?'

Then the lift ground to a halt and the doors juddered open far more stubbornly than Phoebe was comfortable with. The feeling of relief that washed over her was almost palpable – even if Midnight, for reasons best known to herself, had stopped the lift on purpose, Phoebe had still not enjoyed the idea of being trapped.

'Come on,' Midnight said cheerfully.

Valerie Cox was at the staffroom door as they reached it. She looked red and very out of breath.

'Oh,' she said, glancing at Phoebe and then at Midnight.

'Don't worry about it,' Midnight grinned. 'She'll have guessed by now anyway.'

'Who will have guessed what?' Phoebe asked, but as Valerie pushed open the door, Phoebe didn't need to ask any more. As far as she could see, the entire staff of Hendry's had stayed behind to give her a proper send-off and were now squashed into a room that was far too small to hold them comfortably.

'SURPRISE!' everyone shouted before a wave of laughter rolled around the room.

'What...?' Phoebe stared at them.

'Bloody hell,' Midnight said, 'you're very hard to get somewhere when you don't want to go. Not to mention the fuss you make about being in a lift for ten minutes. Anyone would think you wanted to ruin the surprise.'

'You *did* stop the lift, you cow!' Phoebe grinned. 'Come to think of it, the shop floor was very quiet when I was leaving too. I wondered why there wasn't a stampede for the exits.' Her gaze ran over the crowd again, struggling to take in the fact that everyone had waited behind on Christmas Eve just for her.

Then Jack stepped out from behind Dixon. 'Hey...' he smiled.

'Jack! How did you....?'

'I had to sneak him in through the back doors before I fetched you,' Midnight said, looking rather smug about her subterfuge. 'It wasn't easy, I can tell you.'

Phoebe beamed at them both. 'I can't believe all this is for me.'

451

'Well, there's booze,' Midnight waved a hand in the direction of a table groaning with bottles of beer, alcopops and various spirits, 'that's clearly not for you. There may be one or two foodstuffs you can eat but mostly we bought the stuff you're always banging on about not being able to eat – you know, soft cheese, raw eggs, peanuts – so mostly that's not for you either. I was all for a fag table but Dixon shot me down. The breast pump and the lady nappies wrapped up in the gift pile over there… they're all yours, baby.'

Phoebe let out a snort of laughter. 'Wow, I'm so spoilt.'

Dixon took Phoebe by the arm and led her to the centre of the gathering. 'I want to say a few words, and then we can all get stuck into the party food.'

'Hurrah!' Jeff shouted, his eye already on the more potent beverages.

'I know I speak for us all, Phoebe,' Dixon continued, 'when I say that you mean a great deal to us here at Henry's….'

Phoebe could feel the heat rushing to her face. She was really hoping Dixon wouldn't get too carried away with his speech. She didn't deal with public praise or sentimentality well and she'd either start nervous and uncontrollable giggling that made her look like a simpleton, or she'd start weeping. Either way it would be a seriously disturbing sight.

Dixon turned to the gathering. 'Personally, Phoebe has been like a ray of sunshine on a cloudy day. She shook my working life up and made it fun again. Her hard work and commitment to our store has never faltered, even when she wasn't having the greatest day herself. She never complains, never shirks, and always does her best. I'm sure you'll all agree when I say she's a considerate colleague and fun to be around...' he turned back to Phoebe, 'you'll be sorely missed, especially by me. But if you try to do any work at all while you're supposed to be looking after that baby there will be severe consequences!'

The laughter whipped around the room again as Phoebe gave a smile that was full of shy pride. Had she really made that much of a difference? It was a lovely feeling to think she might have done. But as she looked around at the faces in the room again, she couldn't help noting that the Hendry family was not represented at all. Clearly, they had very different ideas about Phoebe's contribution to their business than Dixon had. She tried not to let it take the shine off her wonderful surprise.

'I don't know what to say...' she blushed.

'You'd better make some kind of speech as we've gone to all this trouble.' Midnight replied. 'Although, feel free to keep it short – I'm starving and I want to go home at some point today.'

Everyone laughed again. So many people who were really quite new to Phoebe's life, but they all meant so much to her now.

'Thank you,' she began. 'I love working here with you all and even though I'm going to be busy during

453

my time away it won't stop me from missing you all like mad. I can't tell you what this means to me.'

She stopped, and the room was silent in expectation of more, but she could only give a slight shrug. 'That's it. I don't want to stop you all from getting stuck in.'

'Especially Midnight,' Dixon chuckled.

Sue Bunce stepped forward now with a large box wrapped in colourful paper decorated with a repeated motif of a stork with a bundle in its beak. 'We didn't know what you needed and no amount of digging seemed to get any clues from you – Lord knows poor Dixon tried – so we thought a bit of everything would be fun.'

'Let me...' Jack stepped forward to take the box from her. He balanced it in his arms and nodded to Phoebe. 'There, now you can open it.'

With trembling hands she undid the large yellow ribbon that held the wrapping in place and tore the paper away. Inside the box was a colourful assortment of equipment and treats – everything from rattles to teething rings to mummy pamper products to baby vests. Phoebe's eyes filled as she went through the gifts one by one.

'Oh, God, don't get all emotional on us,' Midnight said.

Phoebe looked up and wiped away her tears. 'Thank you so much, everyone, I couldn't have asked for anything more thoughtful and lovely than this.'

There was a round of applause. As it died down and people's attention now turned to the plates of food ranged along a large table at the far end of the room, Jack put the box to one side and wrapped an arm around Phoebe. 'Are you alright?'

She let her head fall onto his shoulder. 'I'm fine. A bit overwhelmed, I suppose.'

'I don't know why.'

'I just didn't expect all of this.'

He kissed her head. 'When are you going to realise just how amazing you are? Everyone is fond of you. Why should it surprise you that they want to make a fuss about you leaving them?'

'I'm not actually leaving for good,' Phoebe sniffed, 'so it's daft, that's all Although I'm not complaining.'

Dixon came and interrupted them. He shoved the remainder of a sausage roll into his mouth before rifling in the breast pocket of his suit jacket.

'Can I have a quick word?' he asked, glancing at Jack for approval, who simply nodded amiably and stood to the side with his hands in his pockets.

'I have to give you this,' Dixon said in a low voice, 'but you're not to open it in front of everyone.'

Phoebe took an envelope from him. She turned it over but it was blank – no name, no label of any sort. 'Is this from you?' she asked.

'No. You'll understand the secrecy when you find out who it's from. At least, you will if it's what I think it is.'

Phoebe eyed the envelope doubtfully. 'Right…' With Dixon's request in mind, she stowed it in her bag. Her curiosity had been piqued, and the answer to a mini mystery lay inside, but it would have to wait. 'Is that all you needed me for?' she asked.

'Yes… I'll let you get back to Jack.' With that, Dixon wandered off.

'Want some food?' Jack asked as Phoebe rejoined him.

Phoebe looked up at him and smiled. 'You know what? I could actually murder a chicken drumstick!'

For the next hour Phoebe and Jack made pleasant small talk with her colleagues. She couldn't decide if it felt like Christmas as yuletide songs began to fill the room and increasingly drunken voices joined in, or something entirely different when she reflected on the reason they were really gathered here beyond their working day. But she felt good, like she was home, like she had finally been accepted by people who liked and respected her and believed that she was capable of making a difference. It was a nice feeling. Maybe what they all saw was the kind of person she wanted her baby to grow up seeing too. Maybe that was exactly who she ought to be from now on.

Eventually, the gathering thinned as people began to leave, wishing Phoebe and Jack all the best for the baby and the impending wedding as they went home to start their own Christmases.

Dixon grabbed a roll of black bin liners from a kitchen drawer and began to clear away the leftovers.

'Here, let me help,' Phoebe said as Midnight kept Jack busy across the room, regaling him with some lurid tale of a night out in a local rock club.

'You're the guest of honour; you shouldn't be cleaning up.'

'Don't be daft. It'll take half the time if we do it together and I won't feel bad for leaving you with the mess.'

Dixon smiled. 'You just can't help yourself, can you?'

'No, so you might as well give in.'

He tore another bag from the roll and handed it to her. She was distracted from her task for a moment as the last of her other colleagues bid them goodbye and a merry Christmas, and when she returned to it Dixon had almost finished.

'You're a fast worker when you want to be,' Phoebe exclaimed.

'I told you I had it all under control.' He glanced across at Midnight and Jack who were still deep in conversation. 'Why don't you open your envelope while no one is looking?'

'Shouldn't I take it home first?'

'I said you shouldn't let anyone see what was in there,' Dixon grinned. 'That doesn't mean I don't want to know, though.'

'You're impossible!' Phoebe smiled. 'Hang on; it's in my bag over there.'

Dixon continued to clear up as Phoebe went to fetch the envelope he had given her earlier. As she rummaged through her bag, she looked up to see Jack was still holding Midnight's attention. It was probably a good thing. If ever there was a person who shouldn't see the contents of a mystery envelope, it was her. For a moment, Phoebe considered opening it by herself in a quiet corner. She wondered whether the contents would be embarrassing or incriminating, or even both. Did she really want anyone else to see? Why had the person entrusting it to Dixon not written on the envelope? Was it because people would recognise the handwriting? Two and two often made a lot more than four at Hendry's (apart from where the accounts were concerned, which would have been a lot more productive). Phoebe was beginning to guess who had given Dixon the envelope, but what it contained was another matter entirely.

She looked up to see Dixon coming towards her, still holding his rubbish sack.

'Did you get sick of waiting for me?' Phoebe asked.

'I realised that you might want to open it in private after all. So I was going to say take it home with you for later.'

'I'm thinking that might be best. Tell me one thing, though… did Adam give it to you to pass on?'

'Bingo! I think it's sort of a leaving gift, but he didn't say and I'm only making an educated guess. He only said I should let you have it without making it part of the official presentation and he preferred to keep it quiet.'

'I suppose that makes sense,' Phoebe said. It was an unexpected turn of events and she was almost beginning to wish he hadn't left it for her; it posed too many uncomfortable questions. 'What the hell...' she decided. 'I may as well look now.' Tearing open the flap she looked inside. 'It's a cheque.' She pulled it from the envelope to take a closer look. 'One hundred pounds.'

Dixon gave a low whistle. 'Anything else? A card?'

'Just a note.' Phoebe unfolded the slip of paper and read it out. '*Thank you for everything.*' She looked up at Dixon. 'What's this? Is this like severance pay? Is this his way of saying don't come back?'

'Don't be daft,' Dixon smiled. 'It's his way of saying he appreciates what you've done for the store.'

Phoebe read the note again before refolding it. She stared at the cheque. It was a generous gift, perhaps a bit too generous. Maybe Dixon was right, but she couldn't help feeling there was more to it than that. Was it simply Adam acknowledging the feelings he may have had for her, and telling her that he had drawn a line under the episode and they could now return to a normal boss-employee relationship? It would be nice to think so. Phoebe thought she could be very happy with that. She hadn't enjoyed his frosty silence, even though she hadn't particularly been happy with his advances either, and a middle ground would be just fine.

Dixon's voice broke in on her thoughts. 'If I were you I'd take it in the spirit it was intended and just enjoy it.'

'There's no doubt it will come in handy,' Phoebe agreed. She folded the cheque and put it in her purse.

At that moment, Midnight and Jack came to join them.

'You two look very guilty about something,' Midnight said.

Phoebe and Dixon shared a knowing glance but remained silent. Jack put his arm around Phoebe. 'You look shattered. Is it time for home?'

'Yes.' She smiled up at him. 'I think I'm finally ready.'

❧ ❧ ❧

Phoebe gazed out onto the snow covered lawn. Her breath misted the window and she wiped it clear, smiling to herself as she watched the flakes still falling softly. The garden looked as though it had been iced, like some giant living wedding cake especially for her and Jack. It would make transport a nightmare, but somehow the magical sight felt like a good omen for the day.

'Haven't you made a start on getting ready yet?' Martha bustled into the room. 'What am I going to do with you?'

Phoebe turned to her. 'Sorry. I was just thinking.'

'There's a time for thinking…' Martha stepped forward, but her expression was suddenly apprehensive. 'Unless you're having second thoughts about today?'

'No,' Phoebe smiled. 'Nothing like that.'

'You're ok? No baby worries?'

'Not that either. Everything's fine. I was just thinking about life... I mean, it's hard to imagine where my own life was at this time last year. I can't believe how much has changed. It all seems so fast and so good, like it's somehow fake, like I'll wake tomorrow morning and I'll be back in my old flat alone and it will have been a dream.'

'You couldn't dream a bump like that.' Martha angled her head at Phoebe's belly.

'I suppose not. It has grown rather a lot in the last few weeks, hasn't it?'

'I should say there's a whale in there now.'

Phoebe laughed. 'Maria hasn't exploded yet with excitement?'

'She's with May now, having the time of her life parading around in that dress... I bet you're exhausted already, aren't you?'

'Four-thirty wake up calls don't really agree with me but I'll probably run on adrenaline today anyway.'

'Josh just called, by the way.'

'He did? He's in England?'

Martha beamed. 'He is. Carla and the kids send their love too, he says, and she's sorry she had to miss it but... well, we all know how expensive the air fare is, don't we?'

'Oh, that's brilliant!' Phoebe clapped her hands and bounced up and down just like Maria often did. She was possibly as excited about seeing her brother as she was about the wedding.

'Your dad's gone to fetch him from the airport.'

'It's weird to think that Josh and Jack haven't met each other yet and they're going to be brothers in a few hours – well, sort of brothers anyway.'

'I'm sure they'll get along just fine. It's the other one I'm worried about.'

'Archie?' Phoebe smiled. 'He's not so bad these days. Not once you get to know him.'

'I just hope he behaves.'

'He will. Jack has given him a job to do so he'll have to.'

'What's that?'

'Chief Maria entertainer.'

'Let's hope it does the trick.' Martha strode over to the wardrobe and removed the cover from Phoebe's white silk dress. She stroked a loving hand down its length. Perhaps she was remembering her own wedding day. She seemed to shake herself before turning back to Phoebe. 'Come on now, you need to get a move on.'

'Mum, we've got ages yet. I could do with another drink actually.'

'Did someone say drink?' May appeared at the open bedroom door, flanked by Maria who wore enough layers of pink tulle to wrap around the world four times and still have enough left to clothe the population of China. Martha had been horrified when she had gone dress shopping with her and Phoebe, and Phoebe had readily agreed to Maria's request to buy it. It didn't match the winter colour scheme they had chosen for the wedding at all – not the blood red and white flowers, not the cake, not the décor at the venue – in fact, it clashed horribly with everything. But Maria looked so adorable and so very, very happy that Phoebe didn't care about any of that. In fact, she almost felt that the whistles and bells of the day were for others and not for her. As long as she was marrying Jack, she'd do it in a bed sheet with the reception in a shed if she had to. And if Maria wanted to wear a pink monstrosity, then what the hell?

'I can make drinks,' May said. 'I need to make myself useful.'

'You're a lifesaver,' Phoebe said. 'I'd love a cup of tea. How about you, Mum?'

Martha shook her head. 'Not for me, thanks.'

May looked positively thrilled to be at their service. 'Great! Give me a minute and I'll bring one up.'

She left, a pink cloud in her wake as Maria followed.

'One thing I can't understand is why she's here again,' Martha whispered.

'Because I like her.' Phoebe's whispered reply was a little fiercer. 'Besides, she's Maria's grandmother.'

'Maria's, but not yours. She isn't anything to do with you, she's *her* mother. Isn't it a bit strange, all this involvement in your wedding day? Won't she just be thinking about her own daughter, how this ought to be her wedding day and not yours? I know I would be.'

The same notion had troubled Phoebe at first. But May had insisted that she was happy to be involved and she wanted to help. She thought of Jack as family, Maria *was* family, of course, and she felt that she couldn't ask for a better person to share their lives now than Phoebe. She could keep an eye on Maria, leaving Phoebe free to get ready with minimal stress, she said, and she seemed so earnest about it that Phoebe hadn't the heart to refuse. She knew May so well now and liked her so much that, at times, she almost forgot the fact that she was Rebecca's mother. Perhaps today would make May a little sad, but Phoebe believed that she genuinely wanted to be a part of it despite that. And Jack had been delighted when Phoebe suggested they invite her to the ceremony as well.

'May's not like that,' Phoebe said. 'You'd really like her if you gave her a chance.'

'I don't dislike her. I don't have any feelings either way. It's just a little unconventional, that's all I'm saying.'

'Maybe, but I don't care.'

Martha sniffed, a wordless communication that said she didn't agree with Phoebe's decision but could see that an argument would lead nowhere. Phoebe recognised the signal well and was content to leave it at that too. 'Have you checked to see if the groom is up and about yet?'

'He'll be up. It's gone ten and he's not a late sleeper.'

'He might be if he went drinking last night.'

'He wasn't planning to go far. It's been hard, bringing up Maria alone, and it's not exactly conducive to keeping drinking buddies. I think he met a couple of old friends for a quiet hour and took Archie and Edward with him.'

Martha sniffed again. 'He could have asked your dad.'

'Mum, that's a silly thing to say considering Dad was at a society meeting and he'd mentioned it ages ago. Anyway, they hardly know each other really –'

'That's another thing...'

Here we go, thought Phoebe.

'I can't believe we don't even get to meet his parents until today. Who does that?'

'I know, and I'm sorry. We just seemed to run out of opportunities, somehow. But as I've said all along, it will be fine.'

More than fine, Phoebe hoped. She and Jack had placed all their faith in both sets of parents being so drunk by the time they got past exchanging awkward pleasantries that they'd get on without even noticing they had nothing in common. The bigger plan was for them never to meet in a situation without a ready supply of alcohol on hand. Refereeing their parents might turn out to be a more demanding task than bringing up two children.

'It's silly,' Martha pouted, reminding Phoebe very much of one of those children.

'And it's too late to change now so we'll just have to make the best of it.'

May appeared at the door again, but she wasn't holding a mug of tea, she had Martha's mobile phone in her hand. 'It's been ringing and ringing so

I wondered if it might be important.' She handed it over. 'Is Josh your son who's flying in?'

'He ought to be at the airport; my husband has gone to get him.' Martha took the phone and dialled the number to call Josh back. The colour drained from her face as she listened.

'Are you sure?' she asked sharply. 'When did this happen? Where are they taking him?'

Phoebe watched as Martha continued to listen, her frown deepening as the call progressed, and her face almost ashen by time it was over. She could tell that whatever was going on, it wasn't good.

Martha ended the call and turned to Phoebe. 'It's your dad. He took a funny turn at the airport. An ambulance is with them now.'

'Funny? How funny?'

'I don't know. Josh says he had pains, they're treating it as a suspected heart attack.'

Phoebe's hand flew to her mouth. 'Oh God!'

'Josh says they're taking him to A&E.'

'Oh God... this can't be happening...' Phoebe ran to the wardrobe, brushing the wedding dress aside she started to rummage for clothes. 'We have to go to him!'

'Phoebe, you're getting married this afternoon!'

'Not without my dad, I'm not.'

'We don't know for sure whether things are that bad yet. He might be overexcited, you know how he gets. Josh says he's still able to talk and even joke with the ambulance crew so –'

'We can't leave him in a hospital all alone!'

'He won't be alone – he's got Josh. Phoebe, please calm down, getting in a state is not going to help anyone.'

'What are we going to do? Sit here and pretend nothing is wrong? How can I get ready for a wedding when my dad could die?'

'Nobody's said anything about dying, have they?'

Phoebe stared at her. How could she be so calm? This couldn't be happening, today of all days. What had she ever done to deserve the terrible luck that hounded her? Whatever she tried to make good went bad, whatever she tried to make right went wrong.

'Please sit down, Phoebe, you're making me nervous. Josh says he will call us the minute he has anything new to report.'

Phoebe halted with her hand on a shirt ready to tug it from the hanger, and swayed on the spot for a moment before perching herself on the edge of the bed.

May's voice cut through the silence. 'Is there anything I can do?'

'Thank you,' Martha replied, 'but I don't really know that there is.' She glanced at Maria, who was now watching with eyes too solemn for a little girl. 'Perhaps you ought to take our princess downstairs, though.' Martha looked back at May who nodded and then held out a hand.

'Come on, Maria. Let's watch one of your DVDs for a while and let Phoebe sort things out here.'

'Is Phoebe's daddy going to die?' Phoebe heard Maria whisper as they walked away. May's reply and the sound of more questions grew fainter as they went down the stairs.

'Oh, Mum, what are we going to do?'

'You're going to do nothing but stay here and get ready for your wedding. Knowing your dad this is something and nothing and he's got everyone in a flap about it.'

'You don't really believe that, do you?'

'Of course I do.'

Phoebe knew she was lying. But she realised it was the only way her mother could stay strong. That fortitude in a crisis was a quality she often felt she lacked, but sometimes she wondered if it came with age. The amount Phoebe had been through over the last two years, surely she would have acquired some of that stoicism by now? 'I can't get ready,' she said. 'If Dad is having a heart attack then we can't possibly have the wedding.'

'He won't be pleased if you call it off. You know he'd feel terrible if he thought he was the cause of that.'

'Am I supposed to pretend it's not happening?'

'No. But you are supposed to carry on with your plans until we know there's a good reason to call them off.'

'It'll be an awful day...'

'No, it won't. May will help you for now –'

'Why? Where are you going?'

'To find out what's going on. Josh needs to be picked up too.'

'But –'

'It won't take long,' Martha cut in briskly. 'If I use the motorway I'll be back before you know it.'

'I'll miss you,' Phoebe sniffed.

'Don't be daft. I'll be there for the ceremony and I expect your dad will too, even if I have to push him in a wheelchair wired to a drip.' She bent to give Phoebe a kiss. 'I won't be long. Promise you'll get ready and stay optimistic? We're not beaten yet.'

'I'll try,' Phoebe said. And she would, but it was hard to be optimistic when life kept giving you reasons not to be.

She followed her mother downstairs and they tried to explain the plan (such as it was) to May without causing too much alarm to Maria. Phoebe suspected that Maria was already alarmed and that perhaps their attempts at subtlety were a bit too late, but they did it anyway.

'I don't know what I'm supposed to do,' Phoebe said at the door as Martha got ready to leave. 'I mean, I know what I'm supposed to do but I don't know if I can carry on like everything is normal and wait to hear. How do I do that? I can't help thinking I ought to call Jack and tell him we need to put everything off.'

'Just wait. I'll phone the second I know anything and we can make a decision then. I can't say any more than that, can I?

Phoebe shook her head slowly. 'I suppose not. It just feels so silly and pointless sitting here waiting to get married while Dad could be fighting for his life. Everything feels so unimportant compared to that.'

'It would be if we knew for sure that was happening. But we don't. I've tried to get an update from Josh but he's not replying. I'm guessing his signal is bad, wherever he is now.' She kissed Phoebe and stroked a hand under her chin. 'Try not to get in a state; it won't do you or the baby any good.'

'I know. I'll do my best. But please let me know as soon as you can about Dad.'

'I will. I'll see you in a short while, I hope, for a lovely wedding.'

Phoebe tried to smile. She knew that her mother's brave words hid a real fear. Martha left her with more promises and then Phoebe was alone in the hallway. As she shut the door, she let her head fall against it and closed her eyes. She had to be positive and strong, just like her mum. Things looked bad but crying wasn't going to fix anything. But her mother was wrong about Jack. He had a right to know that everything might have to be put off and she wasn't about to keep something this important from the man she was about to marry... although, if her dad was as ill as she feared, there was no way she would be getting married today. Her dad was her rock, her hero, her first perfect man – the one by whom the worth of all other men was measured. To walk up that aisle without him was unthinkable.

May was wrapping a huge apron around Maria when Phoebe went back through to the kitchen. It looked as though she was attempting to give Maria a glass of milk without endangering the bridesmaid dress, but as there was significantly more dress than even Jack's large apron, she was struggling to cover it all. She looked up at Phoebe with a silent question as Phoebe dropped into a chair at the table.

'I should call Jack, let him know,' Phoebe said.

'Do you think it's wise to worry him before you have the facts?'

'I don't know. But I think it will be a nastier shock if I call him ten minutes before we're supposed to be at the register office to tell him it's all off. I want to know what he thinks we should do and I want him to be ready for the worst case scenario.'

May nodded. 'You're probably right. Call him now and discuss it.'

Phoebe had half expected May to put up the same argument as her mother had done, but the lack of this convinced her that May's reply had been the more honest of the two. May was treating Phoebe as an equal, not as a daughter she was still trying to protect from the things that she simply couldn't protect her from anymore.

Phoebe started to stand up. But before she had pushed the chair back she sucked in a sharp breath and dropped back again, her hand instinctively on her belly.

May looked up. 'What's wrong?'

Phoebe took a couple of deep breaths before forcing herself to speak. 'Nothing's wrong. I need my phone…' she winced again, unable to move until the wave had subsided.

May rushed around the table to her and knelt down. 'Something's wrong.'

'I just need to…' Phoebe let out a yelp. She tried to fill her lungs again for another steadying breath, but it was cut short by a bigger, more solid wall of pain that swept over her.

But then all was calm. Phoebe panted as she tried to right her breathing again.

'What's happening?' May asked.

'I don't know… I just… I think I'm ok now.'

'Is the baby coming?' Maria asked in a tiny voice from across the room.

Phoebe tried to give her a reassuring smile. 'No, it's too soon.' She looked up at May whose worried expression was asking the same question. 'I'm sure it's just practise contractions.'

The tone of May's reply was astute. 'Practise eh? That seemed a bit intense for practise. You're sure about that? You've had a stressful morning and it's probably making you ill.'

Phoebe nodded. She felt weak and yet strangely wired all at the same time. The incident had taken more out of her than she cared to admit.

'You need to rest, try to relax,' May continued. 'Let me get you a warm drink. Getting in a state will have your blood pressure sky high and it won't do you or the baby any good.'

'You're right,' Phoebe said, doing her best to pull in regular breaths, her belly feeling as though it was in a vice. Something wasn't right, and even as she tried to convince herself she was being silly for thinking such a thing, she knew that her inner voice wouldn't be silenced. Something was wrong with the baby; she felt it in a way that was primal and instinctive, but she was too afraid to say it.

May stood up, eyeing Phoebe warily. 'You look white as a sheet. I'd better get you that drink. Are you sure you don't need me to at least phone your midwife, ask her what she thinks?'

'It's New Year's Eve; she doesn't want to be bothered by –'

Once again pain ripped through her and Phoebe clutched at her middle.

'That's it!' May cried. 'I'm calling an ambulance!'

'Jack…' Phoebe panted, 'I want Jack.'

'You can have Jack, right after I get help.'

Phoebe nodded, fear making her docile. She wanted help, she wanted someone to come and take all this terror away and make everything alright. What was happening to her? Today should have been that magical day, the one every couple cherishes, but now it couldn't be more wrong.

May hurried off to fetch her phone. Phoebe closed her eyes and tried to be calm. She felt a light touch on her hand, and opened them again to see Maria staring intently at her.

'Granny May will look after you,' Maria said. She looked so utterly convinced of the truth of her words that Phoebe almost believed it. 'I will too,' she added.

'I know you will. You're the best little nurse I know.'

May came back in, concern etched into her features.

'The number for the midwife is in my phone,' Phoebe said.

'No need. I've called for an ambulance; I'm not taking any chances.'

Had it been anyone else, Phoebe would have said it was an unnecessary fuss. But it was May, and so Phoebe didn't argue. 'Don't call Jack,' she said. 'I think I overreacted just then. There's no need to get him rushing over here for a bit of a false alarm.'

'Do you still want to tell him about your dad?' May asked.

In the same instant Phoebe was gripped by another contraction, as fierce as the ones she thought had been down to stress, and she knew now that it was no practise.

'Maria, sweetheart, run to get a cushion for Phoebe to sit on, will you?' May said, and Phoebe understood that the request was more to get Maria out of the room for a moment than because Phoebe needed a cushion.

Maria bolted from the room and May bent down to Phoebe in her place. 'Don't worry; the ambulance is on its way.'

'I'm not worried,' Phoebe lied. 'It's just childbirth, right? Lots of women do it every day and they're fine.' But the spectre of Rebecca filled Phoebe's thoughts, as it must have been filling May's, and neither of them truly believed Phoebe's words.

'How early are you?'

'About four weeks. Four weeks isn't that bad, is it? And my dates could be out, couldn't they? And they might be able to delay the birth, right?'

'One thing's for certain,' May replied grimly, 'you're not getting married this afternoon.'

'Jack! I need my phone…' Phoebe began.

'I'll call him.'

'He's going to be so upset. It's such a bloody mess.'

'He won't be upset. He'll only want to know that you're safe.'

'But I'm not, am I?' Phoebe began to sob, all bravery leaving her at the thought of Jack's fear, as real to her as her own.

May grabbed her hand and gave it a squeeze. 'I won't let anything happen to you,' she said in a fierce whisper. 'No matter what it takes I'll make sure you're ok.'

Phoebe squeezed back, so grateful for May's quiet strength. Of all the people who could have been with

Phoebe at this moment, May was the best she could ask for.

❧ ❧ ❧

The previous twenty-four hours had amounted to little more than a jumble of sights, sounds and smells, of shouted instructions and worried faces, of struggle and exhaustion, until the drugs had softened all the edges of her pain so that only the vaguest impression remained. Phoebe had pushed when they told her, she was sure, although she couldn't now remember doing it. She recalled the feeling of Jack's hand in hers, of his voice – sometimes strong and sometimes choked with emotion. She hadn't been scared – perhaps it was the gas and painkillers – and in the end she hadn't given a single thought to her dignity (as little as she had left), as doctor after doctor examined her, midwives changed shifts and examined her once again, and then the call came for theatre to be prepped and all hell seemed to break loose around her. Someone had pushed a form under her nose and a pen in her hand and told her to sign. Consent, they called it, though Phoebe had always assumed that consent had to be given by someone who wasn't so utterly spent they no longer knew what they were doing. She must have somehow scrawled her name, because now she was awake and it all came flooding back. She had heard the cries, been told she'd had a girl, been given the fleeting chance to hold her baby close, and then they had taken her away again. She'd been too exhausted to cry, she was only filled with an overwhelming but curiously numb type of despair when they had told her that the baby would have to be incubated. Phoebe had somehow failed in the simple task of bringing her daughter safely into the world, and this was the only thought that her head had room for. Jack had stroked her hair and kissed her and as they'd wheeled her from theatre she watched him sob. She wanted to call out, to tell him to stop, to tell him that everything would be ok, but nothing would come out. And then, she fell into the darkest sleep.

❧   ❧   ❧

Someone was calling her name but her eyes wouldn't open.

'Phoebe…'

There it was again. She had been dreaming, of doctors and the smell of freshly laundered scrubs, classical music playing somewhere in the background while her baby arrived into the world, helped along where she had failed. She began to drift back into it when her name was spoken a third time. They must really want her to wake. It sounded like…

Phoebe squinted up. Maria was in Jack's arms and she grinned down at her.

'I wanted you to wake up!'

'I'm sorry,' Jack cut in. I would have let you sleep but you know how it is with our Maria.'

Phoebe swallowed, her throat dry and tight, her head pounding. 'It's alright,' she whispered. 'I didn't want to sleep all day.' She tried to move and winced. It was then that she remembered the long line of stitches across her abdomen. That memory brought everything else crashing back. She was suddenly awake. 'The baby…'

'We've just come back from seeing her; she's doing fine.' Jack's smile was far from genuine. Phoebe could see fear behind it.

'She's in a box to keep warm,' Maria said as Jack lowered her onto a seat. 'And she has a teddy that granny brought too so she won't be lonely.'

Phoebe gave a tiny nod, even the small movement of her head draining her. 'I want to see her. Can I see her?'

'Later, the nurse said. When you've had a bit more rest we'll walk you down to the unit,' Jack said.

Phoebe wanted to argue with this but her body wouldn't let her. For now, she had to be content with his promise. Then something else came back to her. 'Dad?'

Jack's smile was more heartfelt this time. 'He's fine too. The doctors say it was more of a warning shot than a proper heart attack. He's on the ward at the hospital in Manchester, but your mum says he's already looking better and they told her she can take him home in the next day or so. He's got to be careful from now on, though, but your mum says she's been telling him that for years anyway.'

Phoebe nodded again, relief flooding through her. But it was tempered by sadness thinking about what should have been her wedding day. She had ruined it all and Jack must have been so disappointed that everything had been called off. 'I'm sorry,' she whispered, a tear tracking her face and disappearing into the pillow.

'For what?'

'I ruined the wedding.'

Jack dived forward and grabbed her hand in a fierce grip. There was so much love, so much anxiety, such a burning need to protect her in the gesture that Phoebe could almost feel the emotions through his skin. 'You didn't ruin anything. You were brave and amazing and I never, ever want you to think you did anything wrong. I only care that you're here now, safe, and that our baby is safe. We have all the time in the world for another wedding – as many weddings as you like.'

'We should really try to keep it at one,' Phoebe said, a smile itching at her lips.

'Probably. Whenever you want this time... however long you want to take over it is fine by me. We'll get settled as a family and you can get well again and then we'll think about it.'

'Ok.' This was the point at which her heart should have swelled with joy and excitement, but she was too tired. Already she was fighting to keep her eyes open. 'Is the baby really alright?'

'She needs a bit of ventilation and a stay in the incubator but the doctors say that she's going to be fine. She was just a bit impatient to come and meet her mum, that's all.' Jack squeezed her hand. 'I can't say I blame her.'

'That's good,' Phoebe said, her voice trailing away.

'I love you,' Jack said.

It echoed in her thoughts as she drifted back to sleep.

✤　✤　✤

When she opened her eyes again, Phoebe was surprised to find Carol sitting next to her bed. She was reading a magazine, and Phoebe watched her quietly for a moment, waiting for her to notice that she was awake. After a few moments, with still no response, Phoebe cleared her throat.

'Where's Jack?' she asked.

'He's taken Maria for lunch. I did offer, but he seemed to think that I might want to sit here with you instead.'

'Right…' Phoebe replied uncertainly. What was she supposed to say to that?

'I think he's expecting us to make some sort of peace,' Carol added after a brief silence.

'Ok…' Phoebe said, lost, again, for a response.

Carol closed her magazine and folded it into a large, leather bag.

'You don't have to stay,' Phoebe said. 'I understand if you have things to do. Quite honestly, I don't think there is anything to discuss. I have no problems getting along for Jack's sake if you don't.' She was still tired, emotionally spent, and the last thing she needed was a pointless heart-to-heart with Jack's mother. What she really wanted to do, even though every part of her body ached and the slightest movement set her Caesarean wound on fire, was to go and see her baby.

'Have you thought of a name?' Carol asked, breaking into her thoughts.

'A name?'

'For the baby.'

'I know what you meant. It was just…' Phoebe's sentence faded. She had given up trying to understand Carol a long time ago. They had flicked from one subject to a completely different one in a split second and Carol didn't even seem to have noticed they'd gone off track. 'I haven't really had time to decide,' Phoebe continued. 'We thought we had a lot longer to settle on one. It seems that baby had other ideas.'

'Jack took me to the incubator,' Carol said. There was a pause. 'She's beautiful.'

Phoebe couldn't help the tired smile that lit her face. 'You think so?'

'Of course. Absolutely stunning. It would be impossible to look at her without falling in love. She's the image of Jack.'

Phoebe's smile grew. If Phoebe had cloned herself and placed the result in a crib, Carol would still have insisted that it looked like Jack. Besides, looking like Jack wasn't necessarily a bad thing and Phoebe didn't mind what Carol thought as long as she accepted the baby. And it seemed that she was besotted already, which could only be good.

'It's strange,' Phoebe said, 'but I feel as if I can't even remember what she looks like right now. I had the briefest cuddle and then she was whisked away.' Tears welled in her eyes and she rubbed them clear. Stupid bloody hormones.

Carol's expression was one of genuine sympathy. It was the first time Phoebe could ever recall seeing such a tender look on her face. 'Do you think you're well enough to go to the ward?'

'I don't know... I'm a bit wobbly and I'm terrified of bursting my stitches, but I do want to, more than anything. If Jack is back soon then I'm sure he'll help me.'

'How about I help you?'

'Oh...' Phoebe blinked. 'That would be lovely... I mean, if it's no trouble. And I have to apologise in advance that I probably stink... I haven't had a bath in –'

Carol held up a hand. 'You've just had a very difficult birth. I think you can be forgiven a bit of body odour.'

'Right,' Phoebe smiled.

Carol helped Phoebe up to sit, and then arranged her drip and various other bits of tubing until Phoebe was unencumbered enough to walk.

'Where are you going?' A nurse rushed over as they headed for the doors to the ward.

'To the neonatal unit,' Carol said briskly, taking Phoebe's arm protectively. 'You're not going to stop a new mother bonding with her child, are you?'

The woman shrank back and nodded assent. Phoebe could understand why. Carol's old bulldog look was back, and it was enough to strike fear into the the hardiest of matrons.

As they walked, Phoebe couldn't help but reflect on the bonding she was doing with her almost-mother-in-law too. It was an unexpected turn of events, to say the least. She might have thought that Jack had had a hand in it, but Carol's actions were far too warm and genuine to be a mere favour to her son. Perhaps this was the breakthrough, and Carol was finally on the way to accepting Phoebe into their family.

❧ ❧ ❧

On a bright day in June, Phoebe stood under the dappled shade of a rose-draped arbour and looked into Jack's eyes. 'I do,' she said, and the smile she gave him spoke of all they had been through together, of the happiness he had brought her and the future she hoped for. He returned it as he repeated the registrar's words, and then said, 'I do.' She looked down as he slipped the gold band onto her finger. There it was, the tiny contract that bound them now forever. There were so many times over the past few years when Phoebe thought that happiness such as this would never come to her, and she had resigned herself to that life. Now, she almost felt she didn't deserve it.

With tears in her eyes, she turned to all the people assembled to watch them take their vows, everyone who meant so much to her. There was her mum, holding baby Charlotte, the little girl who grew stronger and more beautiful every day, her dad, who had always been her knight in shining armour no matter how muddy he was after a re-enactment, her wonderful brother who had made the journey from Australia, yet again, to see her finally marry Jack, Midnight who... well, she was just Midnight, and May, the woman who had offered Phoebe friendship and love against all expectations. Archie, forever Archie, gave Phoebe a jaunty wink as she caught his eye. They had finally come to an understanding too. He wasn't perfectly behaved, and he probably never would be, but Phoebe had faith that in time he would be a good brother-in-law and an even better uncle. His gambling seemed to be under control, for now, but whatever problems he came to Jack and Phoebe with in the future, she and her husband would help him through them together. It was what families did. Phoebe's gaze came to rest on Maria who was holding May's hand – the living, breathing, prettiest little cupid who was, perhaps, the reason they were all here today. Jack's parents stood alongside and smiled, and Carol even looked close to tears. Looking at them all, Phoebe could almost imagine that Rebecca and Vik were close by, their ghosts wandering the gardens of the register office and giving their blessings to the day.

Life felt brand new again, and it was up to Phoebe to take that gift and make it count.

The End...

... Well, actually, not quite the end... Tilly thought you might be wondering what happened to Phoebe, Jack, Maria and Charlotte (and to be honest she was missing them a bit too), so she wrote an extra short story as a treat for all her lovely readers. So wonder no more! This is what happened next...

THE HOUSE THAT JACK BUILT

When Phoebe and Jack had talked about a bigger house, Phoebe had been thinking more along the lines of a tidy extension on their existing house. In the mellow sunshine of a late summer morning, almost two months after they got married, she and Jack stood hand in hand, staring up at the huge... well, she could only describe it as a terrifying monster of rough bricks, held together by a network of weeds.

'No way,' she said. 'There is just no way...'

Jack looked at her. 'Don't dismiss it. Think about it for a minute. It's an absolute steal and we might not get a chance like this again.'

'It's a steal for a reason. It's a complete wreck! In fact, there's more mould and weeds than house.'

'It's not that bad.'

'I've seen sturdier looking trifles.'

'There's a good framework there. It'll take some hard graft, I know that, but it will be worth it in the end.'

He had that face. Oh God, Phoebe thought, not the face. She could never refuse that sweet, excited,

486

sexy-as-hell face. She had looked at the building and vowed that she wouldn't, couldn't be swayed, no matter what he said. It was a disaster waiting to happen – they had two small children, a pitiful income, very little building skill or knowledge. And yet, he was giving her the face and she knew that all her resolution was about to crumble.

'Go on, Phoebes,' he whispered with that special glint in his eye, the one that made the face the most potent thing on earth. 'Why not? Let's take some risks, live a little… it might just pay off.'

Phoebe frowned at him.

'He who dares wins, eh Rodney?' he grinned.

Phoebe couldn't hold the frown any longer and she let out a giggle.

'You want to,' Jack said, 'tell me I'm wrong.'

'You're wrong.'

Jack's grin spread. 'Yeah? We'll see…'

❧   ❧   ❧

Two Months Later…

'Are you sure this is a good idea?' Jack whispered.

Phoebe gave his arm a squeeze. 'He wanted to help. And let's face it, we need all the help we can get.'

'I know, but…' Jack glanced over to the car again.

'You're not jealous, are you?' Phoebe arched an eyebrow at him.

'Of course not.'

'He is twice the size of you, which means he'll probably be able to do double the workload. We'll get loads done.'

'Are you saying I'm not buff?' Jack grinned.

'I'm saying you're a lover, not a fighter… or a lifter, or a labourer, or any of the other attributes useful when doing up a house… if you can call what we've bought one of those.'

'I'm strong.' Jack flexed his arms as if to prove his point.

'Yes, but he's got muscles on muscles. You've got hotness on hotness – just as valuable but in other ways.'

'I'll take that. But I'm still not sure this is such a good idea.'

'Oh, don't be so insecure. I married you, didn't I?'

'But he's pined after you for years.'

'Hardly!' Phoebe laughed. 'I think it was because I was the only woman under thirty and not related to him that he ever talked to, not because I was some special goddess of beauty.'

'I think you're a special goddess of beauty.'

Phoebe nudged him. 'No you don't. I just let you get into my knickers occasionally so you put up with me.'

Jack held a hand over his heart and grimaced. 'I'm mortally wounded by that remark.'

Phoebe gave him a sideways glance. 'Still true though.'

The car door slammed shut, and they both turned their attention back to the imposing figure now striding over the weed-choked gravel of the driveway towards them. Phoebe gave him a bright smile. 'It's so lovely to see you, and we really appreciate the help... don't we, Jack?'

Jack gave a weak smile of agreement. 'Yeah, we do.'

Geraint nodded, and his soppy grin was completely at odds with his disconcerting size. 'I'm happy to help. As soon as your dad told me what you were planning I offered to come straight over. There's nothing I like better than a bit of hard graft – makes me feel alive, you know?'

'Right...' Jack said.

'Dad not with you?' Phoebe added, glancing over, or rather, trying to glance over, Geraint's huge shoulder towards the car.

'He's coming in his own car later. Gone over to the builder's yard first,' Geraint said.

'For the roof tiles?' Jack asked. 'Wow, your dad doesn't mess about.'

'I'm sorry,' Phoebe turned to Jack, 'I totally forgot to tell you that I mentioned to him they had some reclaimed ones that matched, and I didn't want them to go before we could buy them.'

'Right...' Jack squinted up at the roof. 'You're sure he knows what to get?'

'Of course,' Phoebe said, not entirely sure at all.

An awkward silence descended on them, until it was broken by Geraint.

'How are the nippers?'

'Good,' Jack replied.

'Charlotte's teething, though,' Phoebe added. 'See these bags?' She pulled at an eye. 'These are what you get for having children.'

Geraint attempted another smile. But it was less assured now, and Phoebe wondered if there was a little sadness to it. She cursed herself for her insensitivity. While Geraint had always seemed like a cheerful, friendly giant, happy with his job and his friends and a pint of real ale with her dad's historical re-enactors on a Sunday, Phoebe knew that what he really wanted was a wife and a family. Still living with his mum and well past thirty-five, he had set his sights on Phoebe until Jack came along. And he seemed to be having a devil of a job locating an alternative Miss Right.

'Do you want to get cracking?' Geraint asked.

'We can if you don't mind,' Phoebe said. 'This clearing out bit is probably the biggest of the jobs we'll have to do ourselves, but it has to be done before we can start anything else.'

'Ripping out is my speciality,' Geraint said. 'Cleared away Mum's kitchen units in an hour last week.'

Jack gave an uneasy smile. 'I don't doubt it.' Phoebe guessed he was recalling the first time he and Geraint had met, when they had become intimately acquainted very quickly and very publicly over a rogue chunk of beef. Jack knew how well suited Geraint was for the job; he just hoped he harboured no homicidal thoughts towards the man who had snatched Phoebe from his pool of prospective wives.

'Who's got the children today? Geraint asked as they ambled towards the house.

'Jack's mum is on babysitting duty today,' Phoebe replied cheerfully, tying a bandana over her hair as they walked. Though she was like a mother tiger where Maria and Charlotte were concerned, today she couldn't help being excited at the prospect of a day without them. Conversations where she didn't have to remind herself not to swear or mention sex were hard to come by, and today, despite the fact that it was going to be tough work and messy, was appealing for that reason alone.

'You need to remember to take it easy,' Jack said, giving Phoebe a stern glance.

Phoebe rolled her eyes. 'You're not still going on about that, are you? I'm pretty sure my caesarean has healed up by now.'

'No lifting, that's all I ask. You can chip and hammer away all you like but you leave the heavy stuff to me.'

'Yes, Mum...' Phoebe said wryly.

Jack pushed open the unlocked front door and allowed Phoebe and Geraint in before following.

'Oooh, it's big, isn't it?' Geraint said with real approval in his voice. 'Lovely high ceilings.'

'Just right for you, then!' Phoebe laughed. 'No chance of you banging your head.'

'What's in here?' Geraint made a move towards a door on his left and yanked on the handle. There was a creaking, tearing, groaning sound, and Geraint stood with his mouth comically open. The door was no longer attached to the frame, but was in his hand.

'Oh...' he said in a voice that seemed impossibly small for such a mountain of a man. 'I am so sorry.' He blushed as he continued to hold the door by the handle, casting around for a place to put it.

Jack stared. And then Phoebe burst into laughter. 'We obviously need some new interior doors.'

Geraint gingerly placed the door against the frame, as if he could somehow hide what he'd done.

'Please, don't worry about it,' Phoebe insisted, still laughing. 'If we let you loose on the rest of the house, we can go for coffee and come back in ten minutes when you're done.'

'Which would be brilliant, actually,' Jack cut in, 'because we're paying two mortgages right now so the quicker we can get this baby stripped and rebuilt, the better.'

Geraint gave them a sheepish smile. 'I'm at your service. Whenever I can help out I will.'

'I know you will,' Phoebe said, 'and we appreciate it more than we can say.'

'So... what do you want me to tackle first?' Geraint asked.

'Well, you've already skilfully tackled that door,' Jack said with a grin. 'But we were thinking of a more general clearing out for today – brushing out, pulling off loose plaster and weeds from the brickwork, birds' nests from the chimney – that sort of thing. We've got roofers booked for tomorrow to start getting the old tiles off and replaced as soon as we can, so that we're not deluged in here if it rains over the next few weeks.'

'Don't forget that some rooms need all the plaster coming off,' Phoebe cut in.

'Oh yes, I suppose so. The plaster probably does need to come off pretty much every room to be honest, but I wasn't going to ask you to do all that today. There's an old kitchen that needs to be ripped out too ready for the new units and the bathroom... well, I don't even know where to start with the bathroom and boiler. Maybe we'll just leave all that to a plumber to worry about.'

'The same goes for rewiring,' Phoebe reminded him.

'Bloody hell, I'd forgotten about the rewiring.' Jack rubbed a hand through his hair. Phoebe recognised his expression and knew that the reality of the task they'd set themselves had finally hit him as he stood in the middle of it, about to begin.

'It'll be fine,' Phoebe said gently. It was strange, because at first she had been dead against the idea of buying this house, but now, as she stood amongst all the dust and damp, she could see amazing potential.

She had fixed the wreck of her life – she and Jack had fixed it together – and an old house was nothing compared to that. Between them, the love they threw at it would see them through, just like it had seen them through everything else.

It was then that a car horn sounded from outside playing *Yankee Doodle Dandy*. Phoebe rushed to the front door.

'Aye, aye,' Jack laughed. 'There's only one car I know that has a horn like that.'

Midnight had only passed her driving test a few months before, but already she was driving like a stunt double from *The Dukes of Hazard*. Phoebe watched her do a handbrake turn and skid to a halt, gravel spitting across the lawn in her wake.

'Bloody hell,' Phoebe breathed. 'I didn't think she could get any sexier and now there's this.'

'Sexy?' Jack asked from behind her. 'I think you mean slightly unhinged like that woman from *Fatal Attraction*. Less sexy and more terrifying if you ask me.'

Midnight climbed out of the passenger side of her bright pink Vauxhall Corsa with a manic grin. Phoebe raced out to meet her.

'Wow… You changed your hair! You look amazing!'

Midnight's trademark purple locks had gone, replaced by a glossy, raven black. She wore a fitted leather jacket, zipped up tight, and jeans that showed every curve of her hips and thighs.

'I thought it was time for a change,' she said carelessly.

She followed Phoebe back to the house.

'Look at you!' Jack called. 'Foxy lady!'

Midnight gave him a saucy wink. 'Thanks, Tiger...'

By this point, Geraint had also arrived to find out what all the fuss was about. As his gaze fell on Midnight striding towards him at the front door, his mouth dropped open.

'Geraint...' Phoebe began, 'this is my good friend, Midnight.'

'How are you doing?' Midnight nodded at him. 'You must be the famous Geraint Phoebe has told me so much about. There can't be two blokes of your size in Millrise.'

Phoebe nudged her in the ribs. 'I never said he was big,' she whispered. She had, but she didn't want Geraint to think that was all she ever told anyone about him. Midnight grinned.

'She never told me you were hot, though,' Midnight added. Geraint simply blinked. And then he looked around as though to check it was really him Midnight was talking to. 'So...' she continued, 'what is it we're actually doing today?'

'Is that all you've brought to wear?' Phoebe asked, giving her friend the once over. 'You look incredible but you're going to get really mucked up because we're cleaning, weeding, smashing off plaster... that sort of thing. I've got some spare overalls at home but…'

'Chill,' Midnight said, 'I've got some old clothes in the boot but there was no way I was wearing them in public.'

Geraint's mouth was still open as Midnight and Phoebe reached the front door where he stood. As Midnight passed him, she tapped it shut with a finger. 'You'll get all sorts flying in there,' she said.

Jack let out a low snigger, but Geraint simply swivelled, his eyes following Midnight as she strode into the house.

As she surveyed the entrance hall, Midnight gave a low whistle. 'This is pretty cool.'

'We think so,' Jack said as he followed her in with Phoebe, 'at least it will be if we ever finish it.'

'We might go grey and mad, but I've no intention of letting this fail now,' Phoebe added with a pointed look at her husband. 'With the amount of money we've sunk into it we don't have a lot of choice.'

'True,' Jack said. 'And once we sell our old one we're faced with either getting this done quickly or living in a caravan on site until we do. I don't fancy doing that for long.'

'Neither would I,' Midnight agreed. She turned to Phoebe. 'Want some help with awesome decorating ideas?'

'Sure,' Phoebe smiled. 'I'd love some.' Midnight had undergone more image changes than Madonna at Wembley Stadium and had bucket-loads of creativity, and Phoebe was looking forward to cherry-picking her best ideas to run past Jack. It would make all the dust and dirt now worthwhile.

There was the sound of another car engine from outside, and the toot of a rather more staid horn. Phoebe rolled her eyes theatrically at Jack. 'We might actually get to start work in a minute.'

'Hello!' Phoebe's dad said a few moments later from the doorway.

Geraint shot him a huge grin. 'At last. We thought you were going to skive off and leave us to do everything.'

'As if I would, lad,' Hugh returned with a grin of his own. He turned to Phoebe. 'Where do I plug the kettle in?' He held up a box which clearly contained a kettle he had bought on the way over. Phoebe laughed and nodded her head at a connecting doorway. 'Trust you, Dad! The kitchen is through there but I warn you, it's not pretty.'

'I'm sure it'll do just fine.' Hugh went off in the direction of the door, pulling the box open as he did. Phoebe mused momentarily on what the state of their tap water might be, but she knew the previous occupant had lived there quite happily on it well into her nineties, and her dad was boiling it too. Still…

Her thoughts were interrupted by Midnight.

'So, an old lady owned this house?'

'Yes, Edna, I think her name was.' Phoebe glanced around, as if she might somehow catch Edna on the stairs looking down at them. Would she have approved of the family who had bought her home, and their plans to change it? 'She spent her whole life here, but she never married so had no immediate family. The relatives who inherited it didn't want to live here when she died, so they decided to sell. I suppose it didn't have the same emotional connection for them.'

'They probably didn't have the bank balance to make it habitable either,' Jack put in.

'Neither did old Edna by the looks of it,' Midnight said.

'Neither do we, when it comes down to a dose of reality,' Phoebe returned.

'No...' Midnight said, 'But you do have lots of people to turn to for help.' She threw a saucy wink at Geraint, who had become so quiet they had almost forgotten he was still there. His expression changed from one of silent awe to an almost violent blush. All he needed was his eyes to pop out accompanied by the sound of a klaxon and his heart beating from his chest, and the image of a lovesick cartoon character would be complete. Midnight turned to Phoebe, seemingly oblivious to the effect she was having on Geraint, but Phoebe knew her better than that. 'Come on, hot stuff, show me around this dump so I can get the creative juices flowing.'

Phoebe turned to Jack but he waved them on. 'Don't mind us. We'll just get on with manly graft down here while you two swan about and talk about curtains.'

'Oi!' Phoebe cried, 'less of that you cheeky pig!' Jack grinned at her and she poked her tongue out in return. 'We'll be getting our hands dirty, just the same as you.'

'Probably dirtier,' Midnight added, looking very deliberately at Geraint again. Phoebe wondered if she'd have to call an ambulance if Midnight didn't stop the barrage of outrageous, but carefully careless, flirting. She was clearly enjoying her power over Geraint, whereas Geraint probably hadn't been this sexually close to a woman since he'd last watched topless darts on a late night cable channel.

'Come on...' Phoebe said, taking her friend by the arm with a knowing smile. Midnight was grinning broadly as they walked through the hallway towards the first set of stairs.

The house was rather a quaint design, which was one of the things that had eventually swayed Phoebe as she and Jack had discussed, and sometimes argued over, buying it. As Phoebe understood it, there had once been two separate terraced cottages on the site that had at some point been knocked through to create one home. So the building now mirrored itself from the middle outwards. A large front entrance that would once have been two front doors led to two a broad set of stairs. There were identical rooms to the left and right of the house, though some now served different functions to those originally intended. The two kitchens at the back had now been knocked into one enormous space, one of the living rooms remained, whilst its partner was now a study. It was all very cute and quirky, and Phoebe already knew that she'd love living here.

'You never said that Geraint was such a Wookie,' Midnight said as they climbed up to the first floor.

'Wookie?'

'Yeah, you know, giant and hairy.'

Phoebe giggled. 'I've thought of him as a lot of things but never as a *Star Wars* character.'

'I wouldn't mind a look at his rocket,' Midnight added.

'What!' Phoebe squeaked. 'You're terrible!'

'Don't tell me you haven't thought about it during an idle half hour. After all, he's got to be hung like a racehorse.'

Phoebe lowered her voice. 'I'll bet he doesn't know what to do with it though.'

'That's easily remedied,' Midnight said carelessly.

Phoebe stopped on the stairs. 'Tell me you're not serious.'

Midnight shrugged. 'He's single, isn't he?'

'Yes, but…'

'And I'm single. It's just two lonely people coming together.'

'Literally?' Phoebe raised her eyebrows. 'I don't think he's into one night stands. He wants marriage, kids… the whole nine yards.'

'Hmmmm, I wouldn't mind his whole nine yards.'

'He'd want more than that.'

'Maybe I would too.'

'You? Settle down? I'd like to see that happen any time this century.'

'Everyone wants a soulmate eventually.'

Phoebe shook her head. 'I just don't see it. You and he are so opposite.' She was thoughtful for a moment. 'You really think he's good looking?'

'Yeah. I think when the novelty of riding his Apollo 11 wears out I could still fancy the pilot.'

'You're full of surprises, that's for sure,' Phoebe muttered as she continued up the stairs.

As they reached the top step, there was a loud crack from down below. It was quickly followed by a shout.

'HUGH!'

Phoebe's smile became a look of grave alarm. Without a word, she and Midnight raced downstairs again and into the kitchen, where Hugh was prone on the floor with Jack and Geraint bent over him.

'What happened?' Phoebe cried.

'I'm alright,' Hugh said, looking dazed nonetheless. 'The plug blew when I switched the kettle on.'

'You were electrocuted!'

'Nothing that dramatic,' he said with a grimace. 'The electrics threw a little tantrum, that's all. I don't know what your old lady used the electricity for, but it wasn't to boil cheap kettles from Argos, that's for sure, otherwise she'd have been dead twenty years earlier.'

Phoebe shared a pained expression with Jack. She guessed he was thinking the same thing as her.

No reliable electricity supply was going to make renovations a lot more difficult and dangerous. So it would change the priority of their work schedule and therefore affect their budget.

Geraint pulled Hugh to his feet and dusted him down.

'Don't fret,' Hugh said. 'We'll have a word after the battle on Sunday and see if any of the lads know a good sparky to come and have a look at what needs doing and give you a decent price.'

Geraint nodded agreement. 'I think John Pink's lad is an electrician, actually.'

Phoebe chewed on her lip as she stared at the offending plug socket. 'Are you sure you're alright, Dad?' she asked, turning to him. He'd suffered a minor heart attack the previous New Year and although he'd recovered well she was pretty sure an electric shock wasn't going to do his delicate ticker much good.

'I'm fine,' he insisted. He glanced around and lowered his voice. 'Just don't tell your mum about this, eh?'

Phoebe nodded. Much as she didn't like the idea, the fact was that her mum's worrying would be twenty times more stressful to his heart than this accident. It was probably for the best.

'Right...' Midnight announced brightly, 'it looks like one of us will have to drive to the nearest Starbucks, then.'

⚜   ⚜   ⚜

The next morning Phoebe couldn't believe the pain. Parts of her body ached that that she never knew *could* ache. Her eyes were sore, her fingers and hands were covered in blisters, and she could still taste plaster dust, despite brushing her teeth three times before bed. But as she stood in front of the old wreck of a house again, she was happy. It was *their* old wreck, and soon it would be their home. Jack snuck up behind and curled his arms around her waist, raining light kisses on her neck. That familiar tingle fizzed up and down her spine.

'Ready for another day of fun?' he whispered.

She turned to him with a wry smile. 'You and I have very different ideas about what constitutes fun.'

'Probably,' he laughed. 'What time did your dad say he was coming over?'

'I'm not so sure he should be coming back after yesterday. He's still got to take it easy and apart from getting electrocuted he also worked far harder than he ought to.'

'I know, but he wouldn't hear of sitting it out, would he? If it makes you feel better, I can have a quiet word with Geraint; between us we'll make sure he doesn't do anything too strenuous.'

'Thanks.' Phoebe reached round to kiss him. She gave him a cheeky smile as another thought occurred to her. 'Speaking of Geraint... what about him and Midnight?'

Jack laughed. 'Geraint may be big and tough looking but he's no match for her.'

'Who is? But I really think she fancies him. He definitely fancies her.'

'Even I could see that a mile off.'

'He'll never do anything about it though.'

'You're too sweet, you know that? You can't fix everyone's lives and you can't make everyone happy. Geraint will find his Miss Right and you shouldn't feel bad that it wasn't you.'

'What you're saying is that I should leave well alone?'

'Yes, no matter how tempted you are to meddle. Besides, Midnight is hardly backwards at coming forwards. If she wants Geraint she won't need any help getting him.' He pulled Phoebe closer. 'Enough of that, you didn't answer my question.'

'Which one?'

'The one about what time your dad was due to arrive.'

'About ten. Why?'

'Because we have an empty house standing here and I don't believe we've christened it yet.'

Phoebe raised her eyebrows. 'The place is filthy! Where, exactly, do you suggest we perform this act?'

Jack grinned. 'I have no idea, but I'm willing to get creative if you are. Just think, you could scream the place down without worrying about disturbing the kids.'

'What about disturbing the neighbourhood?'

'The nearest neighbour is miles away... come on, let's live a little...'

❧ ❧ ❧

Phoebe was feeling distinctly guilty by the time the electrician her dad had texted her about the previous evening arrived on site. Another few minutes and they might have been caught – Jack literally – with their trousers down. She shot a look at Jack, who merely returned it with a broad grin before he strode over to the van and leaned into the open driver's window.

'Martin?' he asked, sticking his hand out in greeting. The man gave an amiable nod before taking Jack's hand in a firm shake.

'At your service.'

Jack moved back to let him step out of the van, the electrician gazing up at the house frontage. 'Hugh says it might be a big job.' Martin gave a low whistle. 'Nice place though.'

'It will be, we hope. Right now we feel like a couple of nutters.'

'I don't blame you. I've been to worse, though.'

'And they've managed to turn things around?'

Martin grinned at him. 'Mostly. Still, I'd be out of business without nutters like you so who am I to complain?' He gave Phoebe a nod. 'How are you, love? Haven't seen you in a while.'

'I don't get down to the battles as often as I used to. You know how it is, kids to look after, bombsite to restore…'

'I know what you mean. So, do you want to show me what needs doing?'

'Jack?' Phoebe asked, 'Could you just show Martin? I need to make a quick phone call and then I'll be right with you.'

'No problem.' Jack led the way while Phoebe pulled out her phone. Her dad was late, and while it was possibly a good thing, it wasn't like him. She hoped he hadn't overdone things the previous day and made himself ill. Though she was sure she'd have received vociferous complaints from her mum if that was the case, she wanted to check just the same.

'Mum...' she began as Martha answered, 'Dad's not here yet. Is everything ok?'

'Yes, fine. He's been trying to get hold of Geraint all morning, that's all.'

'Geraint?'

'He told your father he had a day off today and was happy to come and help out at your place again. Your dad was calling to offer him a lift to save taking two cars but he hasn't been able to get hold of him and he's a bit concerned about it.'

'That's not like Geraint,' Phoebe said.

'That's what your dad said. Anyway, he's had to leave a message on the answer phone and he's on his way now without the big daft lump.'

'Mum!' Phoebe laughed.

'Well, he's got everyone worrying about him and it's probably something and nothing.'

'Won't his mum know where he is?'

'She thinks he's already gone out, says she hasn't seen him at all this morning so assumed he went out first thing.'

'Or he never went home last night,' Phoebe murmured, more to herself than her mum. If Geraint was where Phoebe was beginning to think he was, she had to be impressed. Midnight really did go out and get what she wanted and to hell with the consequences. But the consequences did worry Phoebe. Geraint was a gentle soul, a little wet behind the ears for his age and not very experienced when it came to women. Midnight, on the other hand... Phoebe just hoped Geraint wasn't going to get hurt.

'I can't see that,' Martha said, interrupting her thoughts. 'Will we see you later for tea?'

'Maybe, depends what time we finish here today.'

'I hope so. You've been promising to come over for a week.'

'I'm sorry. We will, I promise. Love you.'

'Love you too.'

Phoebe's mum ended the call. Phoebe tapped the phone against her chin thoughtfully. Perhaps she ought to have a word with Geraint about Midnight. Or a word with Midnight about Geraint. Then again, did she have the right to interfere? And if she did, what could she say to either party that wouldn't sound just a teeny weeny bit insulting or patronising, or both?

'Penny for them?' Jack's voice came from behind her.

'Geraint's gone AWOL,' she said, turning to him.

'Are you worried?'

'Only that it might be something to do with Midnight.'

'And if it is, they're both adults.'

'So you don't think I should have a word?'

'Tell them off for snogging behind the bike shed and show them what a condom is? No I do not! They'll work things out for themselves and they won't thank you for trying to do it for them.'

Phoebe sighed, 'I suppose you're right.' She glanced behind him. 'Where's Martin?'

'I left him doing the sums. It was making me go dizzy, seeing all the zeros he was writing on his pad so I came out to calm down.'

'It's that bad?'

'Hopefully not, but I don't think it's going to be cheap.'

Phoebe nodded. Not the start she had hoped for but it was a job that needed to be tackled, whatever the cost. 'Is the roofer still coming today?'

'He's just called to say the forecast looks clear so he's on his way over.' Jack pulled her close and kissed her. 'Try not to worry about the money.'

'I can't help it. I'm just wondering when we'll have to start selling the family silver.'

'We don't have any silver.'

'What about the family plastic? Or maybe I'll just send you out as a gigolo.'

'That'll be £5.25 towards it, then.'

Phoebe giggled. 'See, I feel better already.'

❧ ❧ ❧

Sometime after midday Geraint arrived. Jack and Phoebe had agreed not to make a fuss about where he had been. They were simply grateful for any help he was willing to offer and didn't want to cause him any embarrassment, in the likely event that he had been somewhere he wanted to keep to himself. Hugh obviously had no such scruples.

'Here he is, the dirty stop-out!' he shouted.

Geraint mumbled an apology and Phoebe shot her dad a look that warned him to drop the subject, which he chose not to notice.

'Where the ruddy hell have you been, lad? You've had us all up hill and down dale looking for you!'

'Ignore him,' Phoebe cut in, 'that's not true at all. You're here now and that's all that matters. I expect you've had a good lie-in, like normal people do when they have a day off.' Geraint gave her a grateful smile. 'Come on,' she added, 'we've got a flask of tea inside, I'll get you a cup before you start.'

'I'm sorry about being late,' Geraint said as he followed her.

'Seriously, please don't apologise. You're here and we're grateful.'

Hugh's voice boomed from behind them. 'Is there any left in that flask for me?'

'Of course, Dad. If not I can always go and get more.'

'Lovely,' Hugh said. 'We'd better get Geraint some first; he looks as if he's been up all night.'

Phoebe tried not to groan and Geraint turned another shade of puce. He put his head down and gave the floor a sheepish grin.

'I'm sure a cuppa and one of Jack's breakfast muffins will perk you right up,' Phoebe said, trying to signal to her father to drop it.

'I'll have one of those,' Hugh said.

'You've already had four!' Phoebe laughed.

'They're only small,' Hugh replied with an expression of deepest offence.

They looked round at the sound of footsteps to see Martin wander into the kitchen. He gave Geraint an amiable nod. 'Alright there?'

'Martin!' Geraint exclaimed, clearly grateful for a distraction to take the heat off him. 'How's things?'

'Can't complain.' Martin turned to Phoebe. 'Do you want the estimate or shall I give it to your fella?'

'I'll take it.'

He handed the sheet of paper over and as Phoebe glanced down at it she couldn't help but catch her breath. Hugh appeared at her side and read over her shoulder. He looked up at the electrician.

'You're sure this is the best you can do for them, lad?'

Martin shrugged. 'I'm cutting it close as it is. Any less and I'll be working for nothing.'

'I'll go and show Jack,' Phoebe said.

Outside, Jack was throwing rubble into a skip. He stopped and wiped a sleeve across his forehead as Phoebe approached.

'You need to see this,' she said.

Jack took the sheet of paper from her.

'Bloody hell. We're going to have to rethink the budget.'

'Decorating will have to wait, that's for sure.'

Jack gave her an unconvincing smile. 'I'm sure we'll manage it all somehow.'

'Hmmm... but are you going to tell Maria that she has to live on beans and stale bread from now on or shall I?'

Jack laughed. 'It might not come to that yet but I'm glad to see that you haven't lost your sense of humour.'

'I'm saving that for three months down the line when I have to pawn all my shoes.'

Phoebe's phone buzzed in her pocket. She pulled it out and unlocked the screen. 'Midnight,' she said, raising her eyebrows as she read the text message. 'Not quite as coy about her night as Geraint is, but I was right, she did take him home. Honestly, that girl.'

'What does she say?'

'She wants to know if I can get his phone number because she forgot to ask when he left her this morning.'

'That's good, isn't it? It means more than a one night stand.'

'And she also says she feels as though she's been riding Nelson's Column all night... eurgh!'

Jack roared with laughter. 'Has she gone to work?'

'I suppose so. I hope she hasn't shared that last revelation with Dixon, I'm not sure his delicate sensibilities could stand it.'

'Or he might be mad with jealousy that nobody has ever compared his John Thomas to Nelson's Column before. I know I am.'

'You don't need to worry; you're small but perfectly formed.'

'OI! Less of the small!'

'Alright, slightly larger than average and perfectly formed,' Phoebe giggled.

'Better.'

'Besides, I imagine everyone is small compared to Geraint.'

'What's that?' They turned to see Geraint wandering over munching one of Jack's muffins.

'I was just saying you're a bit taller than average so you must struggle for shoes,' Phoebe said, trying to look less guilty than she was feeling for gossiping about him. 'Isn't that right, Jack?'

'Yeah, of course. Because you're the size of Nelson's Column.'

Phoebe almost choked trying to contain the peal of laughter that threatened to burst from her. Geraint gave her a worried look.

'Are you alright?'

'Yes,' Phoebe said, trying desperately to compose herself. She was saved from further explanation by the sound of a van coming up the drive.

'Oh,' Jack said with obvious sarcasm, 'how good of the roofers to join us before lunch.'

'Now, don't get narky,' Phoebe warned. 'They may be late but they're cheap and willing to use the tiles dad picked up so I don't want them upset enough to leave us in the lurch.'

'Still, it's a bloody liberty'

'Yes. But let them do our roof and then you can tell them.'

'Ok, you're right. I just hope their roofing is better than their timekeeping. I feel like this house is already getting the better of us.'

⚜   ⚜   ⚜

The next month was a flurry of activity. One day seemed to melt into the next and all Phoebe could recall in years to come was that most of the hours they contained were spent in the new old house covered in plaster dust or paint, apart from the few hours she spent changing nappies and accidentally falling asleep on the sofa with Maria and Charlotte while Jack desperately worked into the night to keep up with his clients and continue to earn their keep. The only quality time she shared with Jack was over a cement mixer or drill. It was desperately hard work, but it should have felt good; they were building a future together with every brick that was laid and every tile that was grouted, a future as solid as the house itself. So why didn't Phoebe feel good?

The truth was that the workload and the task they had set themselves were taking their toll on both Phoebe and Jack's mental reserves. Jack had snapped at Maria, more than once, without even realising he was doing it, and Phoebe had found herself doing the same with her parents whenever they quizzed her about the house. At least a quick sale on Jack's place had now gone through, and they'd bought a suitable caravan (though the prospect of living in that wasn't thrilling) so they could stop paying two mortgages. It was a big plus, but the day they would be able to move into their dream place still seemed so remote. Phoebe tried to be grateful for the opportunity they had been given for a dream place at all – she was well aware how lucky she was and recalled only too well the damp flat she had lived in only a few years before. Neither Phoebe nor Jack would say it to the other, but they both needed a break, and it didn't look as though it would be coming any time soon.

It was on one of these days, when every little task seemed like a mountain to climb, that Midnight turned up to help. She let herself in through the open front door and shouted from the hallway.

'Hurray!' Jack called. 'The cavalry is here! We're upstairs in the first bedroom.'

A few moments later, Midnight appeared at the doorway. 'I really don't need to know about your weird sex life,' she said, cocking an eyebrow at them both. Phoebe was covered in plaster dust, busy mixing a new batch, and Jack was up a set of ladders, applying it to the wall.

'Yeah…' Jack said with a grin as he descended the ladder, 'we're filthy us. Plaster and dirt is a real turn on.'

'Don't tell me you haven't done it in here, though.'

Phoebe shot Jack a knowing smile, although the days when they had seen this place as a glorious sexual playground seemed a million years ago. Now, they really did only work when they were there.

'I'm glad you've turned up,' Jack said to Midnight, I was going to ask you a favour.'

'Really?' Phoebe shot him a look. He hadn't mentioned anything to her.

'Fire away,' Midnight said amiably. A bit too amiably, Phoebe thought. She was beginning to smell a set up.

'Will you take Phoebe for a break?'

And there it was. Midnight's arrival was obviously no accident, and Phoebe had strong suspicions that the two of them had arranged something before today. Had they been discussing her in secret? The idea was weird, and Phoebe wasn't sure she liked it. 'I don't need a break,' she said.

'Yes you do.'

'Then you do too.'

'I'm fine,' Jack said. 'I love getting stuck in but I know it's been harder for you.'

Phoebe folded her arms. 'Patronising much?'

'You know what I mean,' Jack said. 'You look exhausted. I just don't want you to overdo things and make yourself ill.'

Phoebe frowned. 'Stop fussing.'

'I can't help fussing when you look like you need fussing over.'

'You do look like shit,' Midnight agreed carelessly.

'Wow, I had no idea you could be so complimentary,' Phoebe replied in a wry tone.

'I'm not complimenting you. Come for lunch.'

'Midnight…' Phoebe began.

'I know what you're going to say,' her friend cut in, 'you're too busy, can't expect everyone else to work if you're slacking, blah, blah, blah… Nobody else has two kids waking them at night and at stupid o'clock in the morning. And as you won't go home to sleep, come for lunch instead.'

'I don't know…' Phoebe glanced at Jack for support but he just stared pointedly at her. It was obvious she'd get nothing from that quarter. She was about to launch another argument when Midnight anticipated it and cut her off again.

'We'll try that new diner in town.'

'What diner?'

Midnight cocked an eyebrow at her. 'Just goes to show how much you keep up with real life at the moment. It opened last week with a great big fuss.

It's done up like the one from *Back to the Future 2* and has constant eighties music playing. It's an awesome place that just happens to be owned by good friends of mine.'

'Eighties music?' It sounded like it could be fun. Vik used to be crazy about all things eighties and while the idea would once have reduced her to tears, now Phoebe could reflect on the fact with fondness. Happiness with her new life had enabled her to do that. She let out a sigh that signalled defeat.

'Yay! I knew you'd see sense.' Midnight grinned.

'Only an hour, though,' Phoebe warned.

'Right. I'll have to drive you home though first, I'm not rocking up there with you looking like a navvy in drag.'

'You're going to drive her?' Jack asked, suddenly looking concerned. But Midnight had already left the room and headed back to her car. He looked at Phoebe. 'You won't let her –'

'That backfired on you, didn't it?' Phoebe said with a smug grin as the sound of a revving engine cut him off.

'Just don't let her go above seventy on residential streets... and no handbrake turns either.'

'We'll be like Starsky and Hutch and it will serve you right for recruiting her to your sneaky cause.'

'Come on, you need a break.'

'So do you.'

'Not as much as you do. Go and enjoy yourself and I'll be happy knowing that one of us is.'

Phoebe reached up to kiss him. 'Thank you.'

✤   ✤   ✤

Phoebe stood at the entrance and gazed around in awe. 'This place is amazing!'

The diner wasn't as busy as she might have expected, but it was new and Phoebe was certain that once word got round it would be packed every day. It was certainly nice to have an alternative to The Bounty, good as Stav's lunches were. The décor was a faithful reproduction of the eighties themed café in the second Back to the Future film, complete with props such as Marty McFly's hoverboard hanging from the ceiling and Marty Junior's shiny cap gracing the till. A jukebox stood in the corner next to a vintage Atari arcade game, and video screens hung around the room were currently playing Duran Duran.

'It's clever, eh?' Midnight grinned. At that moment, a shout went up from across the restaurant and a well-built man sporting a black and blonde streaked Mohican and ear stretchers greeted Midnight with a huge smile. He bounded over to give her a spine-crushing hug, though she seemed quite happy about a show of affection that Phoebe felt could be construed as actual bodily harm.

'You finally made it!' the man cried. 'We were wondering when we'd see you.' He pulled at a lock of her hair. 'The purple has gone, then...'

'Just till I get bored again. I'm thinking I might go green next time.'

'Daisy will be chuffed to bits you're here. I'll go and shout at her now; she's in the kitchen trying to get her head around the veg order.'

With that, he disappeared behind a heavy swinging door. Moments later, he re-emerged with a petite woman, pony tail high on her head with a pencil slid into it, soft grey eyes and cheeks peppered with freckles. She looked like an overgrown schoolgirl, and only the tight rock t-shirt and jeans stretched over a figure that Betty Boop would be proud of gave away her maturity. Phoebe instantly liked her.

'Midnight!' Daisy pulled her into a kiss on each cheek. 'Where the bloody hell have you been, you cow?'

'Sorry, Dais,' Midnight grinned. 'Been a bit busy.'

'Making your hair look shit?' Daisy surveyed Midnight critically.

'It looks brilliant,' Midnight said carelessly. 'You're just jealous.'

'True,' Daisy said. She turned to the man who had first greeted Midnight. 'I have no idea what Applejack's have charged us for and whether the bill is right. Go and check for me, would you?'

'What makes you think Lars will have a clue if you don't?' Midnight asked.

'He won't, but if he's out of the way I can talk about him,' Daisy laughed.

Lars gave a mock scowl, but then slouched away towards the swinging doors to do as he was asked.

Daisy glanced at Phoebe, and then back at Midnight, clearly looking for an introduction.

'Oh, yeah…' Midnight said, 'this is Phoebe. I work with her at Hendry's.'

'Phoebe?' Daisy asked. 'As in *the* Phoebe? Catwoman on the roof Phoebe?'

Phoebe gave Midnight a weary raise of her eyebrows.

'Yes,' Daisy laughed, 'she really has told almost everyone in Millrise about that.'

'But only after it was already spilled… and not by me either, before you bring all that up again,' Midnight replied with a warning look.

'I wouldn't dream of it,' Phoebe said with an innocent smile.

'And don't go slagging off Applejack's,' Midnight added, turning to Daisy, 'Phoebe is practically related to the guy who owns it.'

Daisy tried to look suitably shamefaced but Phoebe suspected she didn't really care all that much. Phoebe laughed. 'Don't be mean, Midnight. He's my hubby's uncle,' she explained to Daisy, 'but I still think he's as weird as everyone else does. My hubby does, for that matter.'

Daisy smiled. 'Are you both staying for lunch? We've got some pretty cool specials today, if I do say so myself.'

'Midnight hasn't stopped telling me how good your cooking is, so I can't wait to try whatever you bring us,' Phoebe said.

Daisy threw Midnight a delighted look. 'Grab a table and I'll bring you a menu.'

Phoebe followed Midnight to a bright blue Formica table with glittery flecks that glinted in the sunlight from the windows. It was teamed with steel and red vinyl chairs. The whole look could have been a style disaster, but in the context of the café, it really worked.

'Right…' Phoebe began, 'why don't you tell me what we're really doing here?'

'Because Jack said you needed a break.'

'That's not it. When have you ever automatically agreed with something Jack has said? And even if it was, your usual answer would be a bag of chips at the ornamental gardens. So what's up?'

'Nothing…' Midnight picked up a salt cellar, poured a little on the table and started to doodle in it.

'Midnight…' Phoebe said with a frown.

'Oh, alright. It's Geraint.'

Phoebe's eyes widened. 'You've been doing the dance of the beast with two backs, and it seems like you're both having fun. What's the problem?'

'I don't know, I just feel like it's becoming hard work.'

'Why are you still seeing him then?'

'I can't stop. It's weird. I like him.'

'You *like* Geraint? We are talking about the same Geraint, aren't we? And you mean *like* in the same way everyone else means *love*.'

Midnight shrugged. 'I can't stop thinking about him. More specifically I can't stop thinking about that giant redwood between his legs, but it's still pretty weird. It's new, this thinking about someone when they're not there.'

Phoebe was thoughtful for a moment. What was she supposed to make of this? While it had been obvious they were spending time together (more evident from Geraint's furtive and guilty behaviour than from anything Midnight had given away), Phoebe never imagined these kinds of feelings could be blossoming between them. Midnight rarely invited a man back into her bed more than a handful of times – she simply got bored of them – and even though this had been going on under her nose, Phoebe simply didn't see it. Midnight and Geraint made a very odd couple indeed, but could it be that Midnight had finally found someone who could tame her? And in the most unlikely guise of Geraint, who still watched *Songs of Praise* with his mum on a Sunday and wouldn't know a grunge band if he was run over by one. Phoebe would have pointed at a lot of women for potential mates, but never Midnight, not if she had a million years to guess. She shook her head wonderingly.

'What are you going to do?'

'Why do I need to do anything?'

'You're telling me about it, that's why. It's obviously bothering you.'

'It doesn't bother me,' Midnight said. 'Why can't we just keep meeting up for sex?'

'I'm not buying that. You want more, but you don't know how to compute a new desire like that in your own head.'

Midnight grinned. 'See, I knew there was a reason I bothered to talk to you. How come you always make so much sense?'

'Only when I'm sorting other people out. Trying to sort my own life I'm hopeless.'

The discussion was cut short by Daisy returning with their menus. As Midnight chatted with her, Phoebe watched thoughtfully. Midnight deserved a bit of love in her life. On the surface she seemed perfectly content, often scornful of those who had chosen to settle down. But perhaps she was capable of being a little lonely, even if she didn't realise it. But whatever insight Midnight did or didn't have into her own emotional state, Geraint certainly did deserve a happy ending. It was strange, because everyone who spent more than ten minutes in Geraint's company could tell that he was desperate to settle down, and Midnight ought to have been running for her life at the first sniff of it. Sex could be amazing, and it could go a long way towards the longevity of a relationship, but it would only go so far. Surely Midnight and Geraint had passed that point a while ago?

Once they had ordered, Daisy left them again.

'Are you going to tell him how you feel?' Phoebe asked.

'No chance!' Midnight snorted. 'Only you'd be that stupid! The minute I tell him he'll start thinking he can tell me what to do and then it'll all turn to shit.'

'Or... you'll get a really lovely guy and your relationship will move up a gear.'

'How do you know I want it to?'

Phoebe raised her eyebrows as she sucked at the straw in a lush looking glass of strawberry milkshake and for once, Midnight looked as though she was lost for a reply.

❦ ❦ ❦

Two hours later than promised, Midnight returned Phoebe to Jack. The sun was sinking, throwing long shadows across the front lawn, but the afternoon was still warm. It wouldn't be long before a chill crept into the air, the balmy nights of summer already passed, but Phoebe relished the feeling of the sun on her back as she and Midnight wandered across to where Jack was talking to a man she hadn't seen before. They had both been surveying the garden as Midnight's car pulled onto the drive, and they watched now as the two women approached.

'This is Harrison... the landscape gardener I told you about,' Jack said to Phoebe as they drew level.

'Oh, yes!' Phoebe said, shaking Harrison's hand. 'Jack's client!'

'That's me,' Harrison smiled. 'Jack's always looked after me so when he said he'd got this project, I thought I could return the favour.'

'I think your favour might be a little more hard work than any of mine,' Jack laughed. 'All I do is click and push keys.'

'But you do a brilliant job of it.' Harrison turned back to Phoebe, but then his gaze was drawn away, resting very obviously on Midnight as he spoke, as if he couldn't pull it away no matter how hard he tried. 'I'm going to draw up some plans based on what Jack has told me; is there anything you particularly want me to include?'

'We discussed it all so I'm happy that Jack knows what I want.'

Harrison seemed to shake himself at the sound of Phoebe's reply, and he turned to her with a smile, though it seemed as if his eyes longed to be on Midnight again.

Phoebe took a moment to appraise him. He was tall, muscular, dark haired and tanned, mid to late twenties at a guess. He was attractive, there was no doubt. Beneath his thin shirt she could see the outline of a nipple ring, and he wore a full, trendy beard. It looked as if he wasn't a stranger to the odd mosh pit and liked a pint. He was definitely Midnight's type as far as Phoebe could tell. And he was definitely interested. This was classic Midnight territory, and

Phoebe was curious to see how it would play out. Would Midnight be able to resist his interest?

'In that case,' Harrison said, 'I'll do some sketches and let you have some costs.'

'Great,' Phoebe replied.

Harrison turned to Midnight. 'Are you involved in the renovations?'

'Not really,' Midnight replied. 'Unless you count simply being here and adding awesome to the place.

Harrison grinned, and Midnight returned it with her most flirtatious smile. Phoebe would have sworn that Midnight's breast size swelled by ten inches, right there on the spot, if it weren't anatomically impossible. She certainly wasn't thinking about Geraint now. There had been something vaguely unsettling about the notion of Midnight being in love, and it was comforting to see that some things stayed just as Phoebe had always known them.

'Midnight has been brilliant,' Jack cut in. 'She's helped loads with the clearing out and she's got some great ideas for design once we start to decorate.'

'Yeah?' Harrison looked at Midnight hungrily. 'Maybe we can get together some time, see if we can get our designs for inside and out working together.'

Phoebe glanced at Jack, a knowing smile twitching her lips.

'Maybe,' Midnight replied carelessly.

'I'll be off then,' Harrison said. He nodded to Jack and Phoebe. 'I'll be in touch as soon as I have something to show you.'

'No problem,' Jack said. 'And there's no huge rush just yet either so don't worry.'

Harrison turned to Midnight. 'I've got a card in the van... if you follow me down I'll get it for you and you can give me a call when you're ready...'

A card in the van? Phoebe resisted the urge to roll her eyes. He might as well have flicked a condom at Midnight and pulled his trousers down. He might be a good gardener, but he was no good at subtlety.

Jack curled an arm around Phoebe, and they watched Harrison and Midnight walk down to his van together.

'Hmmm... I was going to tell you about this weird conversation I had with Midnight over lunch,' Phoebe said, leaning into him.

'*Was?*'

'I think it was a false alarm. Normal service, as they say, has been resumed.'

There was a peal of laughter from the direction of the van as Midnight flicked her hair and punched Harrison playfully on the arm. Phoebe only hoped that her friend would do the right thing by Geraint.

With a wave in their direction, Phoebe and Jack watched Harrison climb back into his van and pull away, leaving Midnight strolling back to the house.

'Did you get his card?' Phoebe asked.

Midnight held it up.

'And you're going to call him?'

'Maybe. He's got some good ideas.'

Jack gave a grin and turned to go back into the house. 'I'm sure there's some plaster in a bucket drying out up there, so I suppose someone ought to get back to it.'

'I'll be up in a minute,' Phoebe said.

'I'm going anyway,' Midnight said, 'got things to do, so don't leave Jack waiting on my account.'

'What about Geraint?'

'What about him?'

'The thing with Harrison and the card. What are you going to do about Geraint?'

'Nothing.' Midnight frowned. 'I don't know what you're talking about.'

'I'm talking about you getting numbers for other men. Don't break Geraint's heart, he doesn't deserve it.'

'Ok...' Midnight said. 'I won't. Phoebe... can I explain something to you? Just because a hot guy gives me a card with his number on – which is a business card, in case it needed clarifying for you – that doesn't automatically mean I'm going to have sex with him.'

'But you fancy him?'

'Of course I do. Anyone would. Still doesn't mean I'm going to shag him. You see hot guys on the street all the time – do you want to shag them?'

'No, but –'

'Don't insult me then.'

Phoebe felt the blush rise to her cheeks. 'Sorry...' she mumbled.

Midnight glowered at her. But then she broke into a grin. 'I did think about it though.'

❧ ❧ ❧

Faster than she would have liked, winter was approaching, but Phoebe's dream house was still a long way from reality. They did now have a roof, lights that didn't blow up every time someone switched them on and a plumbing system slightly more advanced than a water pump in the yard, but there were still floors to be laid, yet more walls to be plastered, brickwork to be repaired and pointed, and heating pipes to lay so that the upstairs rooms wouldn't be ice cubes in the snowy weather, not to mention the jobs that could wait if they had to, like actual paint on the walls. The caravan they now lived in was parked in the garden of their new house, which was great because it meant they were always on site, but also terrible, because they were always on site, and on days when things had been particularly trying, there was simply no escape from it.

Phoebe was woken gently by Jack on one such evening. She found herself stretched out on the long caravan sofa. The little gas fire in the corner pumped out dry heat and was the only light in the silent room.

'The kids are both in bed,' Jack whispered. 'You should be too by the look of things.'

Phoebe pushed herself up, every joint protesting. She was stiff and sore and very tired. 'What time is it?'

'Just after nine.'

'Hell, I can't be in bed before ten, it does my street cred no good.'

'Don't worry, I won't tell Midnight if you don't.'

'I can't even remember falling asleep.'

'Your head was nearly in your soup at tea. Maria decided to cover you up here when you nodded off, little sweetie, but even though it was well-intentioned I thought I'd better wake you or you won't sleep tonight.'

'I will *definitely* sleep tonight. There is nothing that could keep me awake after the day we've had. I don't know how you have so much energy.'

Jack sat next to her and pulled her close. 'I don't have energy... I have you. It's you and Maria and Charlotte who keep me going. You all keep me focused. I want this to be finished and to be perfect for you all.'

'Now I feel guilty. All I want is for it to be finished.'

'We'll get through this. I know it doesn't seem like it right now, but we will.'

'It really doesn't seem like it,' Phoebe sighed. 'In fact, it feels like the worst decision we've ever made.'

Jack pulled away to look at her. 'You really feel that way?'

'No... of course I don't. Ignore me, it's just the exhaustion talking.'

'Hang in there, Phoebe. We're on the home stretch, I promise. Just stick with me, ok?'

Phoebe fell into his embrace. 'Ok. I'll try but I can't promise I won't get grumpy from time to time.'

'You can be as grumpy as you like, as long as you're with me.'

'I'm with you,' Phoebe said. She just wished she felt as confident as Jack sounded.

❧   ❧   ❧

Phoebe woke to the sound of voices outside. Lots and lots of voices. As their caravan (and, indeed, their house) was not within earshot of their nearest neighbours, Phoebe was confused. The space in the bed next to her was empty. Was Jack involved in some sort of dispute outside? She was just about to leap up and reach for her dressing gown when she heard laughter. So no dispute. It was followed by another laugh rising above the din, and Phoebe would have recognised it anywhere. She got to her knees and leaned across the bed to pull the curtains open a crack.

Outside, there were easily thirty members of her dad's historical battle re-enactment society, gathered around her father, who obviously found something very funny as he was laughing in his own unique and hearty way. Jack was standing next to him, hands dug in his pocket, his hair sticking up as though he hadn't long been awake himself, grinning up at Hugh.

Phoebe scampered off the bed and pulled on some clothes. After tying her hair back and making a quick check on the still sleeping children, she hurried outside.

'Dad!' she called.

Everyone turned at her arrival. She was greeted by a chorus of hellos and good mornings.

'Morning, love!' Hugh shouted back. 'Hope we didn't wake you.'

'Oh, that's alright. What on earth is going on? I hope you're not thinking of using our garden for a battle.'

'Ha ha, we've got slightly bigger fields than this available to us. We've come to help out.'

Phoebe stared at him. 'Help out?' she repeated.

'You know…' he nodded a head at the front of the house. 'With your little problem.'

Phoebe now stared at the others. 'All of you?'

'No, we just fancied a day out,' Hugh said. 'Of course all of us. Why else do you think everyone is here?'

'It's just…'

'Amazing and generous?' Jack finished for her.

'Yes… that…'

'Well, we had a meeting and we figured that for what you need doing, it wouldn't take us more than a day or two. There are a few jobs we can't do, of course, and we'll have to leave those to your tradesmen. But the rest we'll have a crack at. We don't want you and Jack and those kiddies stuck in that caravan come the winter, do we?'

'Oh, Dad!' Phoebe threw herself into his arms. 'I don't know what to say!'

'Steady on; it's not just me here, love!'

'Thank you everyone,' Phoebe said as she looked around at all the familiar faces. They really were an extraordinary bunch of people, who were more like a family than many families Phoebe had met in her time. When one society member needed help, the others were always there for them. As her gaze ran over the little crowd, she realised there was a significant omission from the assembly. Geraint was always where the others were. He had helped with the renovations whenever he could. It wasn't that he owed them anything, or that Phoebe had any right to demand his presence, but she couldn't help thinking it was strange. But at that moment she turned to see Maria calling her from the caravan steps, and realised that asking her dad about it would have to wait.

'I'm coming now, spud,' Jack called as he jogged over to his daughter.

'So... what are we tackling today?' Hugh asked Phoebe. 'We're at your disposal until five, so use us wisely.'

'Now that you're all here I can't remember all the jobs that need doing,' Phoebe laughed. 'I suppose the plastering needs finishing... Jack taught himself how to do it, he's not exactly a pro but –'

'I can plaster!' A tall, gangly man in his sixties raised his hand. 'Did my whole house last year and the wife says it's a lovely finish.'

'Thank you, Bernard,' Phoebe smiled. 'That would be amazing. There's pointing to do too...'

'No problem!' someone else called.

'Kitchen units to be fitted…'

'We'll do that, eh Paul?' another man shouted, and his friend nodded in agreement.

Before long, everyone had volunteered for various tasks. The scene was reminiscent of one of those TV shows where some down-on-their-luck family was treated by a whole host of professionals to a make-over on their falling-down house, and Phoebe was feeling strangely redundant as she realised there wasn't really a lot for her to do. She decided to drive out to a nearby supermarket with the children and buy snacks for everyone to go with the teas and coffees they'd need mid-morning to keep them going. It didn't feel terribly productive, but at least she was doing something.

An hour later she was back and the house was a hive of activity. The air was filled with the sounds of hammering, sawing, laughter and whistling. Someone had a radio blasting out old Motown classics, while some of the men sang along (at least, Phoebe guessed that nobody was actually strangling a cat). Jack was sitting on the caravan steps and he held his arms out for baby Charlotte, who was happily gnawing on a fist. Maria had stopped helping Phoebe carry bags and was now diligently examining a patch of daisies.

'Your dad won't let me near the place to help,' said Jack. He says they've got it all under control and that we're to take a break because we must be worked into the ground.'

'Ah… I think that may be my fault.' Phoebe gave him a sheepish smile. 'Last time I was over there I was moaning a bit about how tired I was. But it was just a general grumble. I didn't mean for all this to happen.'

'He obviously took it very seriously. I have to admit to feeling really guilty about sitting here.'

'Me too. I'll talk to Dad. We have to do something, after all, it is our house.'

'Exactly what I said. Now that you're back, how about I sneak in and get cracking? He'd notice you in there before he noticed me and I think I can stay out of his way until lunch time.'

'Go on,' Phoebe smiled, 'I know you're dying to. Just don't let him catch you!'

※　※　※

It took a whole two hours for Hugh to catch Jack. According to Jack's later report when everyone had gone home, he had clapped his son-in-law on the back and given him a wide grin. 'Alright lad,' he'd said, 'I don't suppose I can really stop you getting stuck in as it's your place.'

Phoebe, meanwhile, had kept herself busy with the children, her mind wandering. While she was glad of the break, she also wanted to be part of the team. Sitting out didn't suit her, and it gave her too much time to think about things that were really none of her business, not to mention unproductive.

Eventually though, as he came down to the caravan to say goodbye at the end of the day, Phoebe plucked up the courage to ask her dad about Geraint. More specifically, his absence. *Plucked up the courage* perhaps wasn't quite the right phrase. It wasn't as if her dad was scary or anything, but for some reason it made her nervous. Perhaps it was because Jack kept telling her that she was best staying out of it – and he was probably right. Perhaps it was also because Midnight herself would disapprove of what she'd see as meddling. But Phoebe could stand it no longer: the question wouldn't leave her head until it got asked. But the problem was, once it had been, it only led to more questions.

'Geraint?' Hugh said, scratching his beard. 'Aye, that's a funny one. I don't know what's got into him. Happen he's having an early mid-life crisis or something; always sneaking off, not answering his phone, not telling folk where he's been. Not that we need to know, of course, but he doesn't usually go about things like this. Missed quite a few meetings now too. There's a big battle next month – council expo – I just hope he's going to turn up for that one; it'd be a shame for him to miss it.'

This was bad. This meant he was already too close to Midnight, didn't it? It wasn't wise for him to forsake the rest of his life and friends for someone as flighty and unpredictable as her. Phoebe resolved to have a quiet word with him when she could. Midnight wouldn't like it if she got to find out, and neither would Jack, but she couldn't rest until she'd at least tried to make Geraint understand what he was getting into or, failing that, had at least persuaded him to hang on to the other important things in his life. It was easy when you were in the first flush of love to forget everything else that had once mattered, but Phoebe couldn't help thinking that Geraint was going to need all those things again once this affair was over.

❧ ❧ ❧

Better even than one weekend of help from the Millrise Historical Battle Re-enactment Society, was that it became two. The majority of them turned out to be quite skilled workers in one area or another, and to Phoebe and Jack's delight (and more than a little guilt) the help returned the following weekend, bringing different people with different skills. The house was barely recognisable by the time they left that Sunday night and for the first time Phoebe could see that the end was almost in sight. They owed a huge debt to her dad and his friends, one that they wouldn't forget in a hurry.

'We'll hardly know what to do with ourselves when all this is over,' Phoebe said over breakfast the following morning.

'Your maternity leave is almost up,' Jack reminded her, 'I think you'll have plenty to keep you busy....

That's if you decide to go back to work…' he added hopefully.

'I haven't changed my mind. I love you and I love the girls, and being here with them has been brilliant. But I also love Hendry's and my job. You understand that, don't you? It's a lot to lose and I've put such a lot of time and energy into building that into something I can be proud of that I can't just let it go.'

'I know. And I respect you for making that decision.' Jack smiled, but Phoebe could still read the disappointment in his expression. He would be the one at home with Charlotte, as he had been with Maria, and he would be doing the school runs too, and playgroups and school award assemblies, as he had done with Maria, and he would be trying to work as well, just like he'd done with Maria. They'd talked about it, and he had agreed that she should go back to work, and she wanted to. That still didn't mean that there wouldn't sometimes be guilt on her part, or that there sometimes wouldn't be resentment on his. But she needed something more than their little family to define her; Jack already had that in the form of his own business, but if Phoebe lost Hendry's, she might well lose herself too. She leaned over to kiss him.

'Thank you.'

'Harrison called me yesterday, by the way.' Jack crammed the last corner of a slice of toast into his mouth.

'The gardener?'

'Yes, he wanted to know how we were getting on, so I told him we were doing great. He says he'll pop over today. I thought, as we're ahead of schedule, it wouldn't be a bad idea to get him started, you know, some of the groundwork while the house still isn't decorated. It will save making a mess when it is. I don't think the budget will allow all the work to be done right now and much will have to wait until next summer, but the worst of it will be out of the way.'

Phoebe took a thoughtful sip of her tea. 'I suppose that makes sense. I wish you'd warned me though.'

'Why?'

'Because Midnight is coming over. I did tell you… we're looking at paint and fabric today. I was hoping you'd watch the kids.'

'He's not going to do any actual work today, just measuring up. I can still have the kids.'

'Right…'

'You don't look very happy.'

'I'm fine… of course I'm fine.'

'He's coming over at ten so is that ok?'

'Yes. I doubt Midnight will be here that early anyway. Let's face it, that would mean her rising from her coffin before nightfall and she might turn to dust.'

'You're so cruel,' Jack laughed.

'She'd agree if she was here. In fact, I think she'd be flattered. I think she secretly wishes she was a vampire.'

❧ ❧ ❧

At ten on the dot the sound of a van on the drive brought Phoebe to the caravan steps. She greeted Harrison as he strode towards her. He looked even more attractive than he had done the first time they'd met, in battered jeans and a fitted t-shirt under a black leather jacket. Not Phoebe's type (although it would be hard for anyone to deny he was good looking) but every inch the rock god. Phoebe would not be surprised to learn that he spent his evenings in sweaty clubs playing guitar on stage with a band.

'Nice day for it...' he gestured towards leaden skies that had promised rain all morning.

'Lovely,' Phoebe agreed. 'Do you have a lot to do?'

'Not today. Has Jack told you the plan?'

'He has...' Jack appeared behind Phoebe with Charlotte in his arms.

'Hey, how's it going?' Harrison smiled. 'This is the little one, is it? She wasn't here last time I came over.'

'Yes, this is Charlotte, my youngest. Maria is still in her pyjamas glued to some awful TV show.'

'She's a cute one, Harrison said amiably.

'She looks angelic now, but you wouldn't want to be around her come bedtime. She could be used as an air raid siren when you try to get her to do something she doesn't want to. It's a good job we've got no neighbours nearby.'

'I'll make sure I'm not here then,' Harrison said. 'I've got another appointment to get to in an hour so I'll get cracking if that's ok.' He pulled a tape measure and notebook from a rucksack slung over one broad shoulder.

'Do you need one of us to come with you?' Phoebe asked.

'I'll go,' Jack said, handing Charlotte to her. 'Midnight might arrive so you should be around for her.'

'Midnight?' Harrison asked, his expression suddenly alive with expectation. 'The girl who's doing your decorating?'

'She's not decorating. Helping to design. God forbid we ask her to decorate,' Jack laughed.

Harrison nodded. 'It would be cool if we could get our heads together, though, before I put any ideas down as permanent plans.'

I bet you'd like to get together with a part of the anatomy a little lower than your head, too, Phoebe thought to herself. She also wondered just how much a garden design could hinge on the interior design. It sounded very like an excuse to get some time alone with Midnight. She supposed she couldn't blame him; after all, as far as he was concerned Midnight was a free agent. And it was nothing to do with Phoebe, either way. But she couldn't help the uneasy feeling that got stuck in her throat at the idea of them getting it on. She wanted to say something, to drop some hint that Midnight was spoken for, but her friend would be furious if it came to light that she had.

'We have plans to go out to some DIY stores today,' Phoebe said. 'I really doubt she'll be free, so it's a waste of time waiting for her. Besides, she won't be over this early. And you have that appointment to get to; I'm sure you don't want to get held up and make yourself late…'

Harrison gave her a sunny smile. 'I'm sure ten minutes either way won't matter. My next clients said they'd be in all day anyway and it didn't really matter what time I turned up.'

Jack stepped forward, clearly sensing that Phoebe was not going to succeed in her quest to keep Harrison from pursuing Midnight. 'Right… so I'll show you around the back garden first, eh? I've got some requests to make about a play area for the kids…'

Phoebe watched them go. Quite why she was so desperate to keep Harrison and Midnight apart, she couldn't say. Perhaps it was residual guilt on her part that she hadn't been the one to make Geraint happy, and because he so desperately deserved it she found herself frustrated beyond reason he hadn't chosen a more reliable woman than Midnight to pin his hopes on. It wasn't as if Midnight couldn't get into trouble with other men all by herself, when Phoebe could do nothing to prevent it, and the end result would be the same. Whatever her reasons, although she did like Harrison, she really hoped that he would be gone by the time Midnight arrived. At least it would be one less rival to worry about.

However, with impeccable timing, just as Harrison and Jack wandered back to the front of the house half an hour later, Midnight's pimped up car skidded onto the gravelled driveway.

'Morning!' she called as she got out.

'Bloody hell!' Jack shouted with a broad grin. 'Has someone set your bed on fire?'

'I can do mornings if I have to,' Midnight returned in a haughty voice that made Phoebe want to burst out laughing it was so out of place.

'Especially when you haven't even been to bed in the first place, eh?' Jack added.

Phoebe looked closer, and she could see what Jack meant. Midnight definitely had the look about her of someone who hadn't slept. Was that last night's make up, smudged around her eyes? Her clothes had that crumpled look of being sat around in for long periods of time and her hair was not quite as sleek as it would have been had it seen a brush that morning. '*Have* you been up all night?' Phoebe asked.

'Stargazing,' Midnight returned nonchalantly.

Phoebe was impressed. These days she rarely made it to 10pm before she was nodding off.

Jack glanced up at the sky. 'Doesn't look as if you'd have seen much in this weather.'

'It wasn't cloudy in Scotland.'

Phoebe's mouth fell open. 'Scotland! When did you manage that? I saw you yesterday morning in Millrise!'

'Last night. Four hours there, four hours back, empty roads – sweet as.'

'You went to Scotland to look at stars?'

'Yeah, why not? It was the clearest sky.'

'On your own?'

Midnight tapped the side of her nose. 'That would be telling.'

Harrison watched the exchange with evident interest, slightly open mouthed. Midnight was just being her usual unpredictable self, but anyone not used to her spontaneous, hedonistic ways would either be in complete awe, or completely appalled. Occasionally the reaction was somewhere in between the two. 'Sounds like a laugh to me,' he said.

Midnight turned to him. 'It was.'

He stepped forward and lowered his voice, almost as if he was sharing a secret with her. 'I thought we might have that get together soon. I'm planning Phoebe and Jack's garden if you want to come over to my place and take a look over the next few days.'

Take a look at what? Phoebe wondered. She doubted their garden plans would get much attention if Harrison had his way.

'I might just do that,' Midnight said, dropping her voice to a teasing lilt too. But the next sentence had Phoebe almost falling over in shock. 'But first I have to check what my boyfriend has planned.'

Phoebe turned to Jack, who looked almost as surprised as she was. Harrison, on the other hand, looked crestfallen and rather embarrassed.

'Right... no problem....' He closed his pad and shoved it into his bag. 'I guess I'll be off then.'

'Didn't you want to measure up the front garden first?' Jack asked.

'Sorry dude, have to be with my next appointment. Can I come back another time?'

Jack gave a mute nod.

With no further attempt at arranging times, comparing diaries or noting of numbers, Harrison slouched back to his van, only a further promise to call Jack later in the week trailing into the morning air as he left.

Phoebe turned to Midnight. 'Boyfriend? You don't mean –'

'Geraint. Who else would it be?' Midnight replied in a bored voice.

'But...'

'But what? You know I've been seeing him.'

'I thought you were just seeing him, as in physically clapping eyes on him from time to time, not *seeing* him in the boyfriend sense.'

'You obviously weren't paying attention then.' Midnight pulled her hair from the collar of her jacket and smoothed a hand over it.

'So you were with Geraint in Scotland last night?'

'Yep.'

'Stargazing? I didn't think that was your sort of thing.'

'Why? Who says you have to be able to predict what is and isn't my thing? Geraint suggested it and it sounded like a laugh.'

'I suppose it must have been,' Phoebe murmured. Life was full of little surprises. And then there was Midnight.

❧ ❧ ❧

Another year was almost at an end. Phoebe had wanted to thank all the people who had made their dream home possible, and what better way than a New Year's housewarming? So, at eight o'clock, Phoebe and Jack were standing at their open front door waiting. The garden was strung with fairy lights and lanterns, Christmas music playing from a borrowed sound system, a huge trestle table standing beneath a canvas roof containing decorations, food and an enormous bowl of steaming, fragrant mulled wine. A few feet away a jazz band made up of former clients of Jack's were setting up to provide music for dancing to later, while Daisy, Midnight's friend from the eighties diner in Millrise, was busy telling her partner that he was putting too much charcoal on the barbeque. The smoke was a smell so entrenched in Phoebe's memories of summer that it was odd to feel cold at the same time as it hit her nose, but it still smelt good and she was getting hungry. She was sure people would like it as a change from mountains of leftover turkey.

'I think we invited too many people,' Jack said quietly from the corner of his mouth as they watched another couple arrive. The driveway was a decent size compared to most, but it had already filled with cars, and new arrivals were now parking along the road-sides leading to the house.

'At least our nearest neighbours aren't too close so the noise won't annoy them.'

'I thought you were going to call and invite them?'

'I did,' Phoebe said. 'But they had relatives coming over so they couldn't make it.'

'Still... it *is* a lot of people,' Jack said.

'Don't worry,' Phoebe replied, though she was doing just that herself. They had invited too many in the assumption that some guests would have prior arrangements, or simply wouldn't want to come. So far, however, pretty much everyone had turned up and the place was heaving.

'Do you think we'll have enough food?'

'Daisy has over-catered, so I think there'll be plenty. People will probably think we're mental for having a barbeque in winter, though. Thank God we've got the heaters and the sky is clear.'

'I think it's a brilliant idea,' Jack said. 'My wife is very clever.'

'Let's see if you still think that when you're clearing up tomorrow morning,' Phoebe said with a wry smile as she left his side to greet the newcomers.

Sue Bunce, HR manager of Hendry's Toy Store, kissed Phoebe lightly on both cheeks. With a warm smile, she introduced her husband, Barry.

'I'm so glad you could come,' Phoebe said.

'The place looks fantastic. Does this mean you're not coming back to work after all? If I lived here I'd never want to leave in the mornings!'

'Sorry to disappoint you but I'll be reporting for duty next week.' Phoebe laughed. 'Why don't you grab yourself a drink? There are nibbles too but don't get too full because the barbeque is heating up as we speak.'

'Sounds lovely.' Sue and Barry made their way over to the refreshments, while Phoebe caught up with Jack who was greeting Martin, the electrician, and his wife. Jack looked as if he was enjoying playing the host almost as much as Phoebe was, although he'd had reservations about the idea at first. Once Phoebe had reminded him that he'd be able to bake for a whole new audience, along with the promise of drunken New Year sex while the kids spent the night with May and Carol (who both hated parties and rather liked the idea of seeing the New Year in together with Jools Holland on the telly and a bottle of Bailey's between them), he was sold.

Next to arrive was Archie, with a girl in tow. Phoebe wondered if anyone had warned her that a large part of the night's entertainment would take place outside, as she was wearing a dress that would have her arrested in some countries, and definitely lead to hyperthermia in a British December. On the other hand, Phoebe reflected, while everyone else would be outside, Archie would probably be under a pile of coats in a bedroom with her inside the hour, so perhaps she'd be warm enough after all.

'Alright bro…' Archie said with a grin.

'Glad you could make it to our little party. I had wondered if it wouldn't be kickin' enough for you,' Jack said with a grin of his own.

'Oh, man! Do not try to be street; it doesn't suit you.'

Phoebe giggled. 'I keep telling him that.' She turned to the girl. 'I'm Phoebe.'

The girl gave a shy and really rather sweet smile. 'Jess…'

'Pleased to meet you, Jess. Help yourself to a drink and a snack.'

'What have you got?' Archie asked.

'Mulled wine, crackers and cheese for everyone else,' Jack said. 'For you there's a can of special brew and some pork scratchings in the kitchen.'

'You know me so well.' Archie grinned as he led his date away. 'See you later.'

'Do you think someone should warn her?' Phoebe said to Jack in a low voice as they watched them go.

'Would it make any difference if they did?'

'Probably not. Poor girl.'

Jack put an arm around her. 'You love him really.'

'Yeah, like I love nappy changing and teething.'

On the heels of Archie's arrival was his dad, who had tagged along with Phoebe's mum and dad and it looked as if they were getting on famously, much to Phoebe's relief. They had obviously met before, but never without careful refereeing by Phoebe or Jack. Some more of the historical battle re-enactment society followed them with partners or simply using the invite as an excuse to go somewhere without partners; and then came Melissa Brassington with a girl, whose hand she furtively clasped as she looked nervously around. She was so painfully shy that Phoebe had not expected her to come but she was glad to be proved wrong. Shortly afterwards Steve, the shop floor manager of Hendry's, arrived with an actual wife, which would no doubt amuse Midnight no end when she finally decided to show up. Janitor Jeff arrived by taxi on his own and, true to form, already legless, a Santa hat that looked suspiciously like the one he wore at Hendry's grotto perched on his head at a drunken angle. Lastly Dixon arrived with a very distinguished looking man in a perfectly tailored suit and immaculately coiffured grey hair – Phoebe thought he looked like newsreader or something equally glamorous – who introduced himself as Rupert. Dixon said he was a very good friend, and left it at that.

It was almost ten by the time Midnight sauntered through the garden gates on Geraint's arm, and the party was in full swing. Phoebe had been dancing – or rather, trying to dance – with Jack when she spotted her arrival.

'Oooh! Midnight and Geraint have come together!' she squealed.

'I'll bet they have,' Jack said, 'which'll be why they're late.'

Phoebe slapped him on the arm. 'Behave your-self. It doesn't matter as long as they're here. Anyway, I think it's lovely.' Without waiting for a reply, she rushed over to meet them and threw her arms around them both in turn. 'I'm so glad you could come!' she cried, her eyes bright and cheeks flushed with a com-bination of booze, dancing, cold and excitement.

'Of course you are,' Midnight grinned. 'What have you been drinking, you're steaming.'

'No I'm not.'

'If you say so…' Midnight looked up at the house – a warm glow from every window, lanterns and fairy lights twinkling amongst the trees of the garden, the band playing while people danced, the warm smell of the barbeque on the air and laughter coming from all quarters. 'It's a pretty amazing party,' she said in a softer voice, and she smiled at Phoebe. 'We wouldn't have missed this; not for the world.'

Phoebe felt a lump rise in her throat. Perhaps it was the drink that was making her sentimental, but was that Midnight actually telling her how much she cared? 'I love you so much!' she squeaked as she threw her arms around her again.

'Steady on… you'll be making my man jealous,' Midnight laughed.

Geraint, who had been silent and grinning throughout the exchange, merely grinned a little more broadly.

'We might as well tell you something else, before we get into trouble for keeping secrets,' Midnight added.

'What?' Phoebe asked breathlessly. 'Are you getting married?'

'Don't be stupid,' Midnight replied, more like her old self. 'But we are moving in together.'

'You are? That's brilliant!' Phoebe beamed.

'Yeah… and you are coming back to the office soon to help Dixon, aren't you?'

'Yes… next week.'

'Good, because I won't be able to.'

'You don't have to go back to the shop floor; I'm sure Dixon will have a word with Adam about it…'

'I won't be able to because we've managed to get me up the duff.'

Phoebe stared at her, and then at Geraint, who simply blushed, though he looked rather pleased with himself all the same. 'You're going to have a baby?' Phoebe said in a small voice.

'Looks like it.'

'And you're ok with it?'

'You did it. How hard can it be?'

'But…'

'Don't worry,' Midnight smiled. 'It was an accident but we're happy about it.'

'You are?'

'Yes. Which is more than can be said for Geraint's mother.'

'You've met her?'

'Earlier tonight. That's why we were late.'

'Mummy Midnight… it has a ring, don't you think?'

'Don't you dare!' Midnight growled.

'You can have my breast pump. And I probably have some stretch mark oil left over somewhere, and support tights... and –'

'Oi!' Midnight cried. 'Stop it!'

Phoebe giggled. 'If you're happy then I think it's amazing. And you'll make fantastic parents.'

'You think?' Midnight asked, for the first time looking less than supremely confident about the whole thing.

'I know so.'

Jack joined them. 'Sorry... got held up by Archie.... Or rather, I had to hold him up while I sat him in a chair to sober up. What have I missed?'

Phoebe giggled, while Midnight and Geraint just grinned.

'Have I missed some massive joke?' Jack asked.

Phoebe twirled around into his arms and pulled him close. 'You know what?'

'What?' Jack asked, smiling down at her.

'Life is perfect.'

The End...

...The real and actual end this time

ABOUT THE AUTHOR

Tilly Tennant was born in Dorset, the eldest of four children, but now lives in Staffordshire with a family of her own. Tilly is married to Mr Tennant (not *that* one, though a girl can dream). After years of dismal and disastrous jobs, including paper plate stacking, shop girl, newspaper promotions and waitressing (she never could carry a bowl of soup without spilling a bit), she decided to indulge her passion for the written word by embarking on a degree in English and creative writing, graduating in 2009. She wrote a novel during her first summer break at university and has not stopped writing since. She also works as a freelance editor, and considers herself very lucky that this enables her to read many wonderful books before the rest of the world gets them.

Contact Details:

Do get in touch via Tilly's Website or find her on Twitter or Facebook

14075224R00328

Printed in Great Britain
by Amazon.co.uk, Ltd.,
Marston Gate.